CONTENTS

BEAUTIFUL SIN SERIES BOOK 1

Beautiful Sin

JENNILYNN WYER

COPYRIGHT

Cover Design: Angela Haddon

Photographer: Wander Aguiar

Cover Model: Cooper A.

Copy Editor: Ellie McLove @ My Brother's Editor

Formatting By: Jennilynn Wyer

Interior image: Shutterstock (royalty-free stock image ID 1389306659)

Reader's Note: Intended for mature audiences due to sexual and mature content. Beautiful Sin is dark reverse harem that contains scenes that may be triggering for sensitive readers (mild torture, violence/abuse, foul language and f-bombs, praise kink, and MF/MFMM scenes).

Connect with the Author

Website: https://www.jennilynnwyer.com

Linktree: https://linktr.ee/jennilynnwyer

Email: jennilynnwyerauthor@gmail.com

Facebook: https://www.facebook.com/JennilynnWyerRomanceAuthor/

Twitter: https://www.twitter.com/JennilynnWyer

Instagram: https://www.instagram.com/jennilynnwyer

TikTok: https://www.tiktok.com/@jennilynnwyer

Threads: https://www.threads.net/@jennilynnwyer

Verve Romance: https://ververomance.com/app/JennilynnWyer

Goodreads: https://www.goodreads.com/author/show/20502667.Jennilynn_Wyer

BookBub: https://www.bookbub.com/authors/jennilynn-wyer

BingeBooks: https://bingebooks.com/author/jennilynn-wyer

Books2Read: https://books2read.com/ap/nAAgBb/Jennilynn-Wyer

Amazon Author Page: https://www.amazon.com/author/jennilynnwyer

Newsletter: https://forms.gle/vYX64JHJVBX7iQvy8

SUBSCRIBE TO MY NEWSLETTER for news on upcoming releases, cover reveals, sneak peeks, author giveaways, and other fun stuff!

JOIN THE J-CREW: A JENNILYNN WYER ROMANCE READER GROUP

Join link https://www.facebook.com/groups/19021259614743 5

SYNOPSIS

I was at the wrong place at the wrong time with the wrong men. Men who are not what they seem. But neither am I.

Scarred, isolated, and practically alone–that was my life before attending Darlington Founders University.

I spent my days in the shadows, fading into the background and hiding the person I was ten years ago. A broken, damaged girl I didn't want to remember.

My life changed when I met *them*. Three men who altered everything. I witnessed something I shouldn't have, and now I'm suddenly the object of their obsession. Tristan Amato, Hendrix Knight, and Constantine Ferreira. Wealthy playboys hellbent on claiming me for their own.

When I'm thrust into their lives and given no choice but to live with them for my protection, I realize there is a lot more to these dangerous, enigmatic men than meets the eye. As the past and the present collide, dark truths are revealed and whispers of a secret society start to surface. I'm forced to face the very things I suppressed all those years ago and question everything I know about who I am, who I can trust… and something much worse…

Am I falling in love with the enemy?

Beautiful Sin *is a full-length new adult romance with dark themes and damaged anti-heroes. It is book one in the Beautiful Sin series and ends in a cliffhanger. Recommended for mature readers. Please check Reader's Note in the front matter of the book for potential TWs.*

Beautiful Sin Series:
#1 Beautiful Sin
#2 Beautiful Sinners
#3 Beautiful Chaos

DEDICATION

To my sweet, supportive husband who never grumbles when I swoon over my fictional book boyfriends. You are my real-life friends-to-lovers trope. Love you to the moon and back.

DEAR READER

Thank you so much for picking up my book baby, Beautiful Sin. It's the first book in my new reverse harem/why choose series. Is this your first RH? Just know that why choose romances mean that the woman is in a relationship (yes, this also includes sex) with multiple men. Trust me, once you read your first RH, you will become addicted.

So, about that sex. It's so hard to determine spice levels because each reader is subjective and has their own scale. For example, one reader may give a book 5 chili peppers, while another says it's a 1.5. I wrote Beautiful Sin in the same vein as I did Savage Princess when it came to building the relationships between the characters. If you're looking for pure porn starting from chapter 1 where all the guys wham-bam the FMC from the get-go, then this book isn't for you.

If you're familiar with my Savage Kingdom Series, then you already know how I love to throw a complicated story at you, one filled with twists and turns. Beautiful Sin isn't as dark as Savage Princess, but I hope I leave you breathless with the cliffhanger, just like I did with Savage. And if you throw your Kindle after reading the last chapter, then Yay!

Please keep in mind that because this is book 1 in a trilogy, I'll introduce plotlines and characters that will develop as the story progresses. I won't just come out and say, "This is this, and that is that." Nope. I want to keep you guessing and asking questions. Things won't be resolved or tied up into neat bows until the end. I may not go super dark in book 1 (depending on your tolerance levels), but it's coming. Trust me.

And if you're wondering, yes, Andie, Keane, Jax, Liam, and Rafael from my Savage Series will show up at some point. Calm down, you Jax fanatics. If you haven't read Savage Princess, Savage Kings, or Savage Kingdom yet, and you don't want any spoilers ruined, now's your chance to run to Kindle Unlimited to download them or grab the audiobook.

So, who's ready to dive into the world of Darlington Founders with Synthia (a.k.a. Syn, pronounced "sin"), Tristan, Constantine, and Hendrix? Oh, whenever you see the name Aoife, it's pronounced "eefa." ;-) And don't forget to look for those Easter eggs I love to put in every one of my books. The journal (About That Night) and the knife (Savage Princess) are two of them.

Shoot! Almost forgot about those triggers. The story contains mild torture, violence/abuse, foul language and f-bombs, a little bit of praise kink, and sexy times that involve more than one partner.

Love and happy reading,

PROLOGUE

Ten Years Ago

I'm not here.

I'm not here.

I'm not here.

I am no one.

The scream that fills my ears is unworldly, like the gates of hell have opened up, letting loose the demons to rip flesh from human bone. My hands grip the sides of my head until it feels like I'm trying to crush in my own skull.

Block out the sounds.

Block out the screams.

But the screams are coming from me. And they won't stop.

"Shut the fuck up!" the man snarls in my face, his spit splashing across my nose and mouth.

A harsh hand grips my long hair and wrenches my head back. I couldn't look anymore as the other man with a jagged red line down the left side of his face defiled my mother in the cruelest of ways.

When my eyes find her again, her body is unnaturally contorted, bent at an odd angle on the living room's red floral Château rug. Her head is turned in my direction, her once beautiful, clover-green irises are black, like a doll's soulless eyes. I think she's dead.

They already killed Papa. They killed him first. And I'm next.

Because the Society demands it. That's what the guy with the constellations drawn on his neck said right before he shot my father in the head.

A strange odor, both acrid and sweet, assaults my nose, but I'm not able to process it over the searing pain of the knife being shoved into my side. The pain comes again and again, each time hurting a little less until there's no pain at all.

A whoosh whispers in my ear as a bright light erupts behind my closed eyelids. Heat scorches all around me, tiny licks of fire dancing across my body like magical forest sprites.

I wonder if I'll become a phoenix once the fire burns me to ash, like the one in the story Papa reads to me at bedtime. I'd like that. I'd like to be able to spread my wings and fly.

I feel like I'm flying now. Higher and higher toward a bright light. It's beautiful. Peaceful. I am the phoenix.

Right before the light surrounds me, I'm pulled back down to earth, my wings clipped and useless. As life courses through my body once again, the pain comes. My torn, damaged vocal cords cry out a sound much like that of a kitten's strangled mewl.

I don't want to come back. I want to be the phoenix and fly into the bright light like Icarus did the sun.

But I can't because the person who saved me won't let me go.

"You're safe now. You're safe. I've got you."

CHAPTER 1

Flinging the employee locker room door open, I yank the shirt and jeans from the hook in my small cubicle and head to the one-stall bathroom in the back. I've only worked at the Bierkeller for three weeks, but I'm quickly coming to hate my Saturday night shifts at the bar. It's the third Saturday in a row where some drunk asshole who can't hold his liquor—literally—has spilled his beer all over me. Hence why, after the second time it happened in as many weeks, I started bringing an extra set of clothes with me to work. The stupid dumbass even managed to get it in my hair. So even with a change of clothes, I'm going to smell like a brewery for the rest of my shift until I can get home to shower.

As soon as I enter the bathroom, I shut and lock the door and quickly strip out of the sodden cotton tee before the motion sensor triggers the overhead strip lights to flicker on. The harsh fluorescent light punches a fist through the once-inky darkness of the small room and slices across my scarred, bra-covered torso.

My reflection mocks me as I stare into the rectangular

mirror secured to the wall above the sink. Every imperfection, every burn and red, raised ridge that mars my pale skin are exposed and illuminated in all their ugly, horrifying glory. Not able to stop myself, I touch the razor-thin lines left by the knife used on me. Those ugly reminders are inconsequential when compared to the melted skin that scores down my left arm and side, the end of the gory patchwork stopping on my upper thigh.

And like with every other time I'm greeted with my mirror image, I ignore the gruesome reminders of the night ten years ago when I lost everything.

Don't look. Don't remember.

Mumbling under my breath, I drape the clean clothes over the closed toilet seat and torque the faucet knob at the sink to turn on the water. The guy who spilled his beer on me was also the same guy who palmed my ass when I walked by his table.

Taking my anger out on the paper towel dispenser, I rip out several sheets and wet them, then do a quick wipe down over my arms, neck, face, and chest. My cornflower blue eyes take stock of the state of my hair.

Fantastic.

I look like a sad, drowned rat. Finger combing through the damp tresses, I remove the elastic band I always wear around my wrist when I work and pile the mass of red, wavy hair into a top bun, not bothering to tame the loose wisps that escape.

It's not like I'm trying to impress anyone. My job is to deliver food to the tables, not look pretty. There's nothing pretty about my appearance. One peek at my scars is enough to send guys running the other way. Or stare with morbid curiosity. I get that a lot from both men and women. To avoid the stares, I used to wear long-sleeved shirts, even in the summer. Not anymore. If people can't handle how I look, then don't fucking look at me.

"Yeah?" I call out when there's a knock at the bathroom door.

"Hey, country girl. Keith said to go ahead and clock out," Shelby says through the pressed wood.

Country girl is the nickname she started calling me when she found out I grew up on a farm in the Shenandoah Valley of Virginia. She's a few years older than I am and a city girl through and through. Tall and gorgeous, with the clearest blue eyes. Paired with her jet-black hair, it creates a stunning contrast that has every man who comes in to the Bierkeller turning his head in interest. Unfortunately for them, Shelby only cares for one man in her life: her three-year-old son, Christian.

I look down at the pink plastic watch on my wrist. "I don't get off for another thirty minutes."

Clocking out now computes to thirty minutes of missed tips and wages. Money I need because my scholarship to the prestigious Darlington Founders University only covers the cost of tuition.

"I'm just the messenger, babe."

Sighing deeply, I hang my head. "Thanks for letting me know. Tell Keith I'll be right out to cash in my tips."

There's a repetition of three taps on the door. "You got it."

Toeing off my black Skechers that somehow missed the beer dousing my clothes got, I quickly slip into the dry, black Randy's Custom Auto tee emblazoned with the name of my favorite Motocross racer, Seamus Knox, before taking off my trousers. I bundle the wet clothes together into a ball and place them in the sink. Reaching for the clean pair of jeans, the soft, worn denim slides easily up my legs. Once I put my sneakers back on, I gather my clothes and hurry out of the bathroom to collect my bag and head out to the main area.

The Bierkeller is actually a very cool place. It was built in 1875, around the same time as the college. The walls are the original red brick, but the bar is the best feature by far. It's handcrafted mahogany with 'flame' panels stained a deep, dark brown. During Prohibition, the underground cellars were converted into a speakeasy. Keith gave me the mini history lesson on my first day.

The cacophonic racket of people talking over one another and the pervasive aroma of burgers sizzling on the kitchen's large griddle hit me as soon as I step out into the hallway—and careen directly into a wall of tall, muscled man standing outside the men's restroom.

Well, shit. Is anything going to go right tonight?

"I am so sorry!" I apologize to the guy's dark-blue dress shirt.

I'm tall at five-foot-nine, so for me to be eye level with his chest puts him a couple of inches over six feet.

Firm hands steady my shoulders when I teeter backward.

"No apology needed."

His voice is as smooth and sophisticated as a whiskey neat. Cultured, with a slight accent. Bostonian, maybe? My gaze trails up the broad chest of a swimmer's body to meet eyes the same color as the simile I used for his voice: a light, golden brown. I've never been struck stupid by a guy before, but *this guy* is hands down the most gorgeous man I've ever seen. Even his imperfections—a slight bend in his nose where it looks like it was broken not once, but twice, and the faint line of an old scar that runs through one dark brown eyebrow, slicing it in half—are intriguingly gorgeous.

He must have just arrived or was sitting in the section at the other end of the bar because I definitely would have noticed him.

When I continue to stare, his mouth spreads slowly in a lopsided, dimpled smile.

"I could say something inappropriate, like the only time I render a woman speechless is when she's choking on my massive co—"

And he just ruined the moment.

I cut him off by abruptly walking away. "You can keep the rest of that to yourself," I throw over my shoulder.

"Not what they usually say," he replies, his amused chuckle following behind me.

It takes me a second to get the double entendre. Why are cute guys such assholes?

From the tailored, expensive look of his clothes to his albeit gorgeous, Gen-Z, manscaped appearance, he must be one of the trust-fund frat babies that goes to Darlington Founders. Which means I'll probably run into him again at some point on campus, or here at work.

Determined to forget the stunning jerk and go home, I scan the main floor for Keith until I spot him behind the bar, pouring a draft. When I approach, he glances up at me, giving my new attire a once-over before he slides the full pint glass of beer down the bar to the customer who ordered it. Without missing a beat, he starts mixing the ingredients for some fruity-looking cocktail.

"Shelby said you wanted me to clock out early?"

He stops for a second in his movements and jerks his chin at a plain white envelope sitting to the side of the register.

"Tips for the night are in there. I'll add a little extra to your next paycheck to help cover the cost of some new clothes."

Wow. That's really… nice of him.

Keith hired me on a part-time basis since, starting Monday, I'll have a full course load during the week. I'm scheduled to work every Wednesday night, as well as the six-to-eleven evening shifts on Fridays and Saturdays. Tomorrow is Sunday, which means I get to do nothing but sleep in and be lazy.

I'd moved to Darlington at the beginning of the month, wanting time to acclimate to my new surroundings and look for a job before the fall semester began. Because of my severe aversion to having people in my personal space, I chose not to live in the dorms with the rest of the freshmen. It took a couple of weeks of scouring online listings for places to rent or lease before I found a cute, little, one-bedroom studio apartment located within walking distance of campus. My adoptive mom, Alana, insisted on paying the monthly rent; hence, the second reason for needing gainful employment, even if it is only part-time. I'm determined to pay her back every penny. It's difficult for me when she gives me money or buys me things. It always has been, even when I was younger. She's done so much for me already. Alana took me in and gave me a home. Paid for my surgeries and skin grafts. She loved me like I was her flesh and blood. I owe her everything.

"Thanks, but you don't have to do that."

His bald head gleams, and his gray peepers twinkle under the bar lights. "Already done, sweetheart. You walking home tonight?"

"That's the plan."

"Got your mace handy?"

Keith has two teenage daughters, which makes sense why he's so overprotective of his female employees.

I pat my bag. "Yep."

I also carry a switchblade. I keep it as a morbid reminder of the night that changed my life forever. But I'm not going to tell him that.

"Always be—"

"—situationally aware. I know. I don't have to walk far. I'll be fine," I assure him.

Stuffing the envelope in my carry bag, I wave good night and head out the back, deciding to cut through the alleyway over to Chesterton Street. Once on Chesterton, it's only a short two-block walk to my apartment.

When I push the door open and step out into the night, a cool breeze caresses my face, rejuvenating me after a long five-hour shift. I inhale deeply, needing to breathe air that isn't infused with cloying perfume, body odor, and beer. Unfortunately, I can still smell it in my hair.

The service door closes with a resounding click when the inside locking mechanism automatically engages. But I don't notice because I can't stop staring at the bloodied body crumpled on the ground in front of me, his face bruised and stained crimson. The man lifts his arm, and I jolt when a muffled pop sounds next to my ear. Tiny shards of brick strike my face, leaving stings of pain in their wake. I touch a tentative finger to my cheek and feel something wet and warm. I think I'm bleeding.

What the fuck? Was that a *bullet*? Shouldn't there have been a loud bang or something if a gun was fired?

My disbelieving shock meets the color of whiskey brown framed by thick lashes on an alluring face that I recognize.

"Get down!"

Wait. That voice with the Bostonian lilt. It's the gorgeous asshole from the bar.

Like being hit by a wrecking ball made from granite, his body crashes into my side, spinning me around and slamming me into the wall of the Bierkeller. Pain explodes in my left shoulder which took the brunt of the impact.

Motherfucker!

But before my brain can even process what's going on, all hell breaks loose.

CHAPTER 2

Sitting in a dark corner of the crowded bar, I tune out the noise bombarding me from all directions. I can already feel the migraine trying to stab its way into my brain.

Hendrix leans over from the chair next to me. "You okay, T?" he asks in that subtle British accent that gets him laid more often than not.

I hate that he sees it. My weakness. If there is one thing my father has beaten into me over the years, it is to never show weakness of any kind. Rulers of an empire must be infallible. As the only male child and heir of Francesco Amato, my fate in this world was decided the day I was born. I was destined to rule, regardless of whether I wanted to or not.

"I'm good. I could use another drink."

Hendrix looks around for our waitress, but she's nowhere in sight. With students arriving for the start of the academic year, the Bierkeller is at capacity.

"On it. Con, heading to the bar. You want anything?"

Con glances up from his phone, his expression stony

and his dark eyes blank. Then again, that's how he always looks. He gives Hendrix an almost indiscernible shake of the head before dropping his attention back to his phone, but it's enough of an answer.

As soon as Hendrix's six-foot-two frame disappears into a sea of people, a flash of red from across the room catches my attention. The pretty redhead caught my eye as soon as we walked into the place. Not many women do, so it intrigues me as to why this one does. I've never seen her before, so she must be new. There's no way in hell I wouldn't have noticed her during the three years that me and the guys have been at Darlington Founders and coming to the Bierkeller on the regular.

When I feel Constantine boring a hole into the side of my skull, I tear my interest away from the girl and meet his coal-black glare with a challenge.

"What?" I snap.

Con gives me a warning with a narrowed scowl, and I'm tempted to tell him to fuck off with his silent reproach. He doesn't need to remind me how important this final year at Darlington is. We can't allow for any distractions, not even for a hot redhead.

My line of sight to where the redhead is currently delivering drinks to a table of four guys is cut off when Hendrix returns quicker than I would've expected with our beer.

"The Stepanoff fucktwins just walked in," he says as he takes his seat, only this time, he swivels his chair around to face the room.

It's an intuitive reflex. Never turn your back on your enemy.

Hendrix may appear to be your quintessential rich, preppy prick with a quick laugh and bright smile, but behind that easy-going façade hides a lethal animal you do not ever want to let out. Then again, I wouldn't be in my right mind either if I survived the horrible shit he was forced to endure. I glance at Con. Each of us carries the scars of our birthright.

Con puts his phone away and follows where Hendrix is looking. I can feel the tension rolling off him, and it has me on edge. There's a long line of bad blood between Aleksander and me that started the day we met. Because I'll inherit my father's role at the head of the Council table when he steps down, Aleksander has been gunning for me. Egotistical fucker wants what's mine.

The twins push their massive bodies through the crowd and head over to the opposite side of the room, where there's an empty table. Taking my beer from Hendrix, I immediately drink half of it, hoping the quick infusion of alcohol will help stave off the headache that is now throbbing like a jackhammer.

I repose back in my seat, wearing a pretense of apathy, even though I feel the exact opposite. Knowing Aleksander and his twin brother Aleksei are here, breathing the same air as me, makes me fucking livid.

My voice oozes the hatred I feel when I say, "Fuck them. We have more important things to worry about this year."

Darlington Founders pretends to be an elite ivy school, educating the best and the brightest. Graduating from Darlington practically guarantees your success in life, which is why it's so hard to get into. If only people really knew the truth of what transpires behind the dark shadows and locked doors.

"We need to just kill them and be done with it,"

Hendrix says and takes a sip of what I know is imported beer.

He refuses to drink anything American, even though he was born in the States and only gets his British heritage from his dad, who he despises.

Con makes a disgruntled grunt, his way of agreeing with Hendrix.

"You know we can't do that."

I glance around the table at my two best friends. My brothers. Once we take our positions on the Council, we'll be able to take control and do things our way, and I'll finally get to kill that smug son of a bitch.

Hendrix rolls his eyes. "You sound like your father."

I'm *nothing* like my father, and I know he's saying it just to piss me off.

"Fuck you."

Hendrix sucks on his middle finger, pulls it out, and uses it to blow me a kiss. Asshole.

Con kicks me under the table, silently telling me to chill the hell out. I glare at him because, one, it was a stupidly girly thing to do, and two, it fucking hurt.

A small commotion across the noisy room draws my attention. Some drunk asshole tries to grope my sexy redhead, then spills his beer all over her when she smacks his hand away.

"Seems like you're not the only one interested in the hot waitress," Hendrix comments and nods at where the twins are sitting.

Aleksander and Aleksei are staring at her with a deadly focus I don't like.

When she walks off toward the back hallway where the restrooms are located, the twins get up from their table and follow her.

Without a second thought, I quickly stand. "Be right back."

"T, she's none of our business," Hendrix warns me, but I don't listen and am already walking away.

When I reach the hallway, it's empty. Canting my head, I listen as I stride down the narrow, brick-walled corridor. When I get near the restrooms, there are faint mumblings of a female voice behind a closed door to my left. I don't hear anything else, so I peek inside the men's and women's restrooms behind me. Nothing.

As soon as I close the men's bathroom door, muffled footfalls echo between the walls.

"Hey, Tristan."

Seeing it's Shelby, another waitress, I feign aloofness by leaning back against the wall and pretending I'm scrolling through my phone. "What's up, Shelbs? How's Chris?"

She's worked here almost the entire time we've been coming. Hendrix tried to hit on her once, but he shut it down quickly after he found out she had a kid. If there's one thing he's allergic to, it's children.

Shelby's smile is warm and bright when she replies, "Growing up too fast and giving me premature gray hair. I'm dreading the teenage years. Happy to be back?"

Loathing having to play the role of a carefree university student but given no other choice, I say, "Hell, no. Graduation can't come soon enough."

College for Hendrix, Con, and me isn't about getting a higher education or clenching that hard-earned degree in our hands at graduation. It's a stupid tradition dating back to when the Council was first formed. Every child from the families that make up the Society has attended Darlington Founders. And god forbid we ever break stuffy, old traditions.

Shelby chuckles and raps on the closed door with her knuckle. "I hear ya. Wish I could stop and chat longer, but boss man wants me to check on the new girl and then get my ass back out onto the floor. I swear this chick has the worst luck. Every shift, she gets beer spilled on her." Raising her voice, she calls out, "Hey, country girl. Keith said to go ahead and clock out."

Country girl?

I go back to pretending to look at my phone while they converse through the door. Of course, I blatantly eavesdrop.

"Catch ya later," Shelby tells me, and I flash her a two-finger wave as she walks off.

A half minute later, the door to the office flies open, and a head of red hair attached to a sinfully curvy body slams into me.

My sexy redhead grips my shirt to steady her balance just as I grasp her shoulders to hold her in place. It's like touching fire, an instant burn that awakens something primal inside me. My cock thickens when her gardenia scent wraps itself around me. Not even the stale stench of beer can mask her floral fragrance.

She lifts her face, her cheeks flushed with embarrassment, and I swear I lose the ability to breathe. I thought she was gorgeous from afar, but that was before I got an up-close look at her. This woman is natural beauty personified. Golden strands streak her crimson locks, her berry-tinted lips are bee-stung, and her eyes—they're an unusual shade of light-blue.

But it's the pink, fibrous scars on her bare left forearm that intrigue me the most. Burn scars that seem to span her entire arm from wrist to elbow and continue up toward her shoulder. I can't tell where they stop because her shirt sleeve covers her upper arm.

Instead of detracting from her beauty, the horrific remnants of whatever happened to her only amplify her allure and pique my interest in this woman even more.

"I am so sorry!"

Fuck, even her voice is sexy. Husky with a hint of a Southern twang.

"No apology needed."

Her stunning eyes dip and roam my chest before taking their time to raise back up to meet my heated gaze. A slow smile spreads across my face when she raptly stares at me. I know when a woman is interested, and right now, she is fucking the hell out of me with her eyes. The urge to push her up against the wall and take her like an animal is powerful, but I tighten the leash on that beast and put him back in his cage.

Smirking like the asshole I am, I tell her, "I could say something inappropriate, like the only time I render a woman speechless is when she's choking on my massive co—"

As I speak, her nose crinkles with displeasure. Out of all the things I could say to her, I choose the one thing that makes me sound like the biggest jackass in the world, just so I can see her reaction.

With a cutting look, she storms away before I can finish.

"You can keep the rest of that to yourself."

"Not what they usually say," I reply, my light chuckle following her as she disappears down the hallway.

With a smile still on my face, I type out a quick text to Con.

Me: Did they come back to their table?

Constantine: No.

My smile falls.

Then where did they go? I don't need this shit, but curiosity has me walking toward the back exit service door at the end of the hall that leads to an alleyway behind the building. When I push the exit open, I'm surprised an alarm isn't triggered. Humid air that stinks of rotting garbage shoves up my nose as soon as I step outside into the dark of night. It's a perfect euphemism for this place. On the outside, Darlington appears to be your prototypical small college town wrapped in a bow of breathtaking Gothic architecture and quaint tree-lined streets. Not many people notice the cracks in the town's polished veneer. The dark crevices that hide the shadows that lurk like ghosts, always present. The townsfolk walk around clueless to the seedy underbelly that surrounds them, controls them, manipulates every aspect of their lives like a puppeteer pulling the strings of his marionette.

Looking down the alley, I find nothing but shadows and rats feasting on the garbage leaking out of the metal trash receptacles. It's not until one of the shadows moves that I realize I made a huge fucking mistake.

I catch the glint of a gun's suppressor reflecting the faint light above the door as it swings up in an arc, slicing the air right in front of my face. Adrenaline and muscle memory kick into play, and I grab the man's wrist, twisting it counterclockwise until his grip loosens, and he drops the weapon. I twist his wrist until the satisfying *snap* of bone breaking has me grinning demonically.

Not wasting time, I use my leverage on his arm to flip

him over my knee and slam him down onto the wet, dank pavement. Dropping down to straddle his chest, my fist connects with his square face. Once, twice, three times. I don't feel any pain when my knuckles crack wide open with each hit. I never do. Learning how to block out pain was a lesson I learned early in life. A lesson my father taught well.

Digging a knee into the man's sternum, I grab his collar in a chokehold. His right eye is already swollen shut, and he's barely moving; the only sign of life is his chest expanding and falling with each labored breath.

"Who are you?" I demand to know. "Where's Aleksander?"

I don't recognize this asshole, but him trying to shoot me shortly after the twins got up and vanished can't be a coincidence. If this is how Aleksander wants to play things this year, so fucking be it.

"Fuck you," the man garbles as blood fills his mouth from the gaping split lip I gave him.

Sweat drips down my face and back, making my shirt stick uncomfortably to my skin.

"Nah, man. That's a pleasure you'll be getting once Con shoves your gun up your ass and fucks you with it before pulling the trigger. So I suggest you answer my questions before he gets here."

I know the guys will come looking for me soon if they already aren't by now.

The stupid prick tries to spit at me but the bloody blob dribbles down his chin instead. Spotting a broken shard of glass from a smashed beer bottle, I reach out and grab it. Covering his mouth with one hand to silence his scream, I plunge the jagged, sharp tip into his neck near his carotid artery. Just one inch deeper and to the right, and he'll bleed out all over the alley.

"Last time. Where are Aleksander and Aleksei?" I apply more pressure, cutting a little farther into the soft flesh.

His deep-set brown eyes flare with panic. The man is ugly as sin. Pock-marked, pale face that he tries to half hide with a scraggly brown beard. Long, greasy hair and thick eyebrows. He's thin, not muscled like I would expect from a would-be assassin. The twins must be desperate if this is the best that they can hire to take me out.

"I don't know any Aleksander. I was sent... for the girl."

"What girl?"

His jaw clamps shut, and he limply shakes his head from side to side.

"What girl?" I ask one more time.

When he refuses to tell me, I'm done playing. I'll let Con work his magic and get my answers.

Standing up, I kick him twice in the stomach and once in the head to knock him out. I'm pissed that my night has turned into this. My headache is now a tap-dancing elephant inside my skull which just ramps up my irritation at this entire shit show.

I know there aren't any security cameras in the alley, which sucks, because there's nothing for Con to hack into to do a facial recognition. Guess we'll have to do it the old-fashioned way.

Wiping the blood from my hand on my trousers, I reach around to take my phone from my back pocket.

As I approach the Bierkeller, there's a loud noise when the service door suddenly opens. I move into a defensive stance, ready to take down whoever comes through, but just as I do, a bullet whizzes past my ear, missing me by scant millimeters and lodging into the brick of the building next to my sexy redhead.

Wide, shocked eyes meet mine as she touches her cheek to find small trickles of blood starting to ooze from tiny cuts caused by flying pieces of mortar, and I react without thought.

"Get down!"

Crashing into her, we smash in a heap against the side of the building.

Hendrix's shouts echo down the alleyway as feet pound the trash-littered asphalt. He and Con must have left the bar from the front entrance and looped around.

In my peripheral, I see a blur run past me as the guy takes off down the alley.

"*Ohmygodohmygod.*"

She struggles to twist around, and I lean back just enough to look at the woman pinned between me and the wall. I can feel the rapid thumps of her heart and the fast twitch of her muscles as fear floods her bloodstream. It's a fight or flight reaction, another thing I learned to control by the time I was six.

Cupping her face, I gently force her to look at me. The blue of her irises blot black when her pupils expand, her breaths become stilted pants, and she stares up at me with a glassy gaze. Shit. She's going into shock.

"Hey, Red. I need you to breathe with me, yeah? Slowly, in and out."

With huge, unblinking eyes on an ashen face leached of color, she shakily nods and takes a stuttering inhalation. Her face between my hands is slicked with cold sweat, the pallor of her lips a grayish blue.

"In and out," I repeat and breathe with her.

When the morbid tincture starts to fade from her plush lips, I push damp wisps of her hair away from her face and let my thumbs brush up the apples of her cheeks.

"Not my idea of what we'd be doing when I got you underneath me, but I'm not complaining."

Her dusky blues squint at me, and a rush of irritation burns her cheeks.

Smiling, I touch our foreheads together. "That's much better. Keep breathing."

I'll spout off every sexist, crude thing I can think of if it puts color back in her complexion.

A breathless Hendrix comes up next to me. When he sees who I'm caging against the wall, a blond eyebrow quirks in interest.

"Who the hell was that guy?"

"No fucking clue."

"He had a gun," Red says in a barely audible whisper and peeks over my shoulder at Constantine.

I crowd her in and block her view so she doesn't see what he's doing. Tampering with a crime scene is a no-no, but we can't leave any evidence of what happened behind. The shell casing, the bullet lodged in the brick of the building, the blood on the ground. Once Con gets done, there will be no trace left that anything happened.

"The twins?" I ask Hendrix.

Hendrix scrapes a hand through his perfectly coiffed hair and blows out a breath. "Couldn't be them. They came back to their table a few minutes ago. That's when we left to come find you."

Disagreeing with Hendrix, I argue, "The guy said he didn't know who Aleksander was, but I'm not buying it. I wouldn't put it past those cocksuckers to try something like this."

Red makes a frantic sound in her throat, fists my shirt and tugs. "Boston," she whispers.

I briefly glance down at her, wondering what the hell Boston means.

Hendrix cuffs my shoulder. "Not to state the obvious, but we need to get the hell out of here. Should we call Malin?"

"Fuck no."

Malin is my father's right-hand man. His fixer. And if there's one thing I absolutely don't want, it's for my father to get wind of this.

"We handle things ourselves."

"What about her?"

Red yanks on my shirt again, harder this time. "Boston."

Why does she keep saying that? But before I can ask her, her eyes roll to the back of her head.

I barely catch her when her legs give way, and she drops like a stone. Hendrix slaps her across the face a few times. Nothing. No response.

"Well, that's fucking fantastic."

"Red." I shake her to wake her up.

The motion causes her hair to fall out of its bun and cascade down to the ground in a waterfall of curls. That's when I see the bright red bloom spreading down the sleeve of her shirt like a fucked-up Rorschach.

"Get the car." When neither Con nor Hendrix move, I shout, "Now!"

CHAPTER 3

A low groan wakes me, and I try to blink my eyelids open, but they're cemented shut and refuse to budge. The sound comes again, weak and barely audible, but I hear it… and realize the pitiful noise is coming from me.

"Aw, fuck."

"T, she's waking up," I think someone says. I'm not sure.

My head hurts, I'm bent in the most uncomfortable position, and every muscle in my body aches to the point where I can barely move. Even swallowing is painful, made more difficult by the burning in my throat, like I gargled a thousand serrated-edged glass needles.

"Almost there. Two minutes." Boston's voice.

My thoughts are chaotic, slurred and fuzzy, as flashes of reality viciously assault me like shutter clicks from a camera.

Click.

Spilled beer. The hot guy with a Yankee accent. The alley. A gunshot with no sound. The sizzle of the bullet as it enters my shoulder. Constellations in the starry night sky. Knife. Blood. Smoke. Fire.

No, that's not right.

Click.

The torturous precision of the blade slices me open, again and again. The agonizing, searing pain that is unending. The pungent smell of gasoline mixed with charred flesh.

I am the phoenix.

Click.

I jolt awake with a strangled gasp and suck in a harsh breath when my shoulder explodes in a fireball of pain that travels down my arm to my fingers.

"I wouldn't move around too much if I were you," a masculine British accent warns me.

What?

"Fuck! Jesus fucking Christ!" I scream when the rough pads of his fingers dig around the flesh of my shoulder, the searing hot pain almost too much to bear.

I'm lying face down on something flat, my arms pinned at my sides. Panic sets in, and I thrash around, trying to kick at the man excavating my shoulder. My foot connects with something solid.

"Fucking hell, Red, stop," the guy I know only as Boston growls near my ear. "Hendrix, will you kindly help me hold her down before she takes my balls off?"

"I'm a little busy at the moment," the man, Hendrix, snaps.

I try to raise my head enough to see what Hendrix is doing. There's a third man standing menacingly behind me—the scary one from the alley with eyes as dark as an eclipse. He grabs my ankles with bruising force and pins them down.

"Get off me!"

I'm able to slip a foot from his steely grip and slam my heel into his abdomen. Huge mistake. I think I broke my damn foot.

A hint of spearmint mixed with beer tickles my nose when Boston squats in front of me and grabs my face, forcing me to look directly into his whiskey-colored eyes.

"Red, if you don't stop, I'm going to have to knock you out, and I really don't want to do that."

Panting to the point of almost hyperventilating, what he says, his threat, breaks through the fog of panic clouding my brain.

Tears fill my eyes, and I despise them. I despise feeling helpless and weak.

The caramel of Boston's irises softens, as does his touch. "You've got a nasty graze on your shoulder. Hendrix needs to stitch it up."

I pant through the pain and can only get out one word. "Hospital."

Boston turns his head and shares an unspoken conversation with Hendrix, then looks back at me.

"Sorry, gorgeous. No hospitals."

"Now, be a good girl and hold still," the British-accented voice that I now know belongs to Hendrix says.

Fuck you is on the tip of my tongue. He's not the one who got thrown at a building, shot at, and is currently being held down and tortured by three inept assholes who think they can play doctor.

This can't be sanitary. I could get tetanus or an infection.

"Hospital!" I shout my damn head off when I feel

Hendrix dig into my shoulder.

"We're trying to help you, you daft bint."

I shake and buck and do everything in my power to escape their hold.

Hendrix flattens a hand on my shoulder, pressing down, and I tense. "Guess we're doing things the hard way."

He holds up a needle with what looks like dental floss threaded through the eyelet.

"Don't you dare—"

"This is going to hurt like a motherfucker."

"No! Stop! Don't you fucking—"

CHAPTER 4

"You're out of your goddamned mind!"

I'm getting angrier the longer Tristan stands there with his arms crossed over his chest and that annoyingly stubborn expression on his face I want to punch.

"She stays."

The look I give his bullshit response would cower a lesser man and make him piss his pants. Instead, Tristan just double-downs by adjusting his stance and planting his feet, like he'll stand there all fucking day and argue with me, knowing he'll get his way regardless.

Stupid asshole.

We should be focusing our attention on finding out who to go after for tonight's little contretemps, not babysitting some chick I couldn't care less about.

Tristan thinks the guy was working for the Stepanoffs. I'm not so sure.

Needing some distance from my best friend before I kill his obstinate ass, I pace to the other side of the room where Con slumps back in the silk-upholstered Louis XVI armchair, looking uninterested as usual and playing on his phone.

I pick up the gold-plated stapler from the matching mahogany desk. It's gaudy and overtly pretentious, just like everything else in this room and in this house. The regality of wealth and grandeur perfectly personifies the masks we wear. No one ever sees us for the spawns of Satan we really are. All they see are the dollar signs and the privilege attached to our last names.

"When you said get the car, I didn't realize you were going to kidnap her and lock her in the room upstairs. She needs to be dealt with—"

"No!" Tristan bellows, cutting me off.

"—before she opens her mouth to the wrong person."

"I said no."

I look down at Con's dark head of hair. "Help me out here."

He ignores me.

"Hendrix, she got hurt because of me. I owe her."

Talk about being in the wrong place at the wrong time. I kind of feel sorry for her, then I immediately get over it.

"You and your goddamn white hat complex."

Tristan's eyes narrow at me in warning. "You saw what happened to her."

I tip my face up to the ceiling and let out a low groan of frustration. I should have known that's where his mind would go as soon as I removed her shirt so I could suture where the bullet grazed her, and we all got an eyeful of the torture that ran the entire left side of her body from her shoulder to her thigh. A macabre mural of cruel destruction that was oddly beautiful in a twisted way.

Unfortunately for her, she's going to be left with another scar. There was only so much I could do on the fly without proper medical equipment or supplies. I'm not God. Or perhaps I am, according to the blonde I fucked the other night.

Gentling my tone a fraction, I remind him, "What happened to your sister is not your fault. Helping this girl won't buy you the absolution you seek or lessen the guilt you feel. If the Council finds out about her, that she was there in the alley and witnessed what went down, you know what they'll do." To slide my point home, I add, "You know what your father will do."

He rubs his hands down his face and heaves a sigh full of weariness. Tristan carries the weight of the world on his shoulders. Always has. It's who he was born to be. A divine emperor amid the plebians of the world. Tristan is heir to his father's throne of wealth and power, and Francesco Amato will do anything to protect his family's legacy.

"They won't find out."

My bark of laughter cracks like the tip of a whip. There are only so many secrets the three of us can veil under a subterfuge of false illusion. Adding an unknown redhead to the mix will bring nothing but a shit-ton of trouble we don't need.

"You're delusional."

I'm tired of arguing, my clothes reek of that woman's blood, and all I want is a hot shower, followed by a gin and tonic.

"He wanted her. I need to find out why."

Con finally looks up, interested in Tristan's vague comment.

I grit my teeth, beyond annoyed now.

"Okay, I'll bite. Who wants her, and honestly why should we care?"

Tristan eats up the distance between us and stands in front of me, his demeanor severe. I grow concerned when I see that his right pupil is blown while the left is a pinprick; a precursor to the debilitating migraine that's imminent. If he doesn't take his medication soon, he'll be incapacitated for twenty-four hours or longer.

"You need your meds."

"I'll survive," Tristan snaps.

Taking matters into my own hands, I tell him, "Sit your ass down."

My tone says not to argue, but just to make sure, I push him down into the chair next to Con.

With a disgruntled huff, Tristan reposes back into the armchair and closes his eyes. He hates appearing vulnerable in front of anyone, especially us.

"The guy said he was there for the girl."

I drop to my haunches in front of him, my hands gripping the arms of the chair to make sure he doesn't try to get up.

"And how do you know he was referring specifically to the redhead?"

Tristan had been tracking her the entire time we were in the Bierkeller. I don't blame him. She's hot as fuck. But I prefer blondes.

His eyes open, and he tips his chin down. He looks so much like his father at that moment, but I know if I told him that, he would beat my ass. I already used up my free pass earlier at the bar with my previous quip.

Tristan hates Francesco Amato, much like I hate my father and Con hates his. Then again, abused, degraded, tortured animals have a predilection for turning rabid and biting off the hand that feeds them.

"I don't know, but until I'm sure—" He winces and grips the sides of his head, massaging his temples.

"Stay put. I'll be right back." I point at Con to let him know he's on babysitting duty. "He moves from the chair, knock his ass out."

Tristan holds up his middle finger, but I know he'll behave while I go fetch his prescription.

As soon as I exit the room, I navigate the darkened hallways by memory. Since the day we started Darlington as freshmen, the three of us have lived in this old Victorian just off campus. I have to admit, I'll be sorry to leave this place when we graduate.

My footfalls are quiet as I cross the sickle-leaf Persian carpet that sits atop the antique distressed wood floor of the foyer. I head for the stairs that will take me up to the bedrooms. Tristan keeps his prescription bottle in the drawer of his nightstand.

Reaching the bottom step, I freeze in place when there's a flicker of motion, a tiny slip of a silhouette, to my right at the top of the stairs. The moonlight casts its dim glow through the upper, stained-glass windows, barely providing enough ambient light for me to make out any details, but it's enough for me to see the red highlights in her hair.

Tristan's redhead.

CHAPTER 5

The man Boston called Hendrix stares at me from the bottom of the stairs, and like the cliché, I'm a deer caught in headlights, frozen in place. With each step he climbs and with each inch of distance he erases between us, my brain screams at me to run, but my body won't obey.

Fractals of moonlight shine through the stained-glass window above the front door, creating colorful patterns of yellow, orange, and red that dance across his body. Hendrix is exceptionally good-looking for a kidnapping psychopath. Classic chiseled jawline, straight nose, perfectly arched brows, and the most sensuous lips I have ever seen on a man. His stupidly handsome face is perfect, unlike Boston whose good looks are enhanced by his slightly crooked nose and eyebrow scar.

However, it's Hendrix's eyes that draw me in. Even in the darkness, I can make out their unique color: a deep, navy blue with a light turquoise ring around the irises. His beauty is deceptive and hides the monster I know

now lurks beneath the surface. Only bad guys abduct innocent women.

For some unknown reason, something my adoptive mother, Alana, once said to me springs to mind as I watch him come closer. An old Biblical verse. *"Beware the devil that disguises itself as an angel of light."*

He stops at the top step, and the air seems to crackle with an ominous current, much like the electric charge of ozone you feel during a violent thunderstorm after a lightning strike. Mute and somewhat captivated, all I can do is blink a few times before I'm able to find my voice.

"Where am I?"

His blond head cants to the side, his perusal of me oddly intimate, and it puts me on edge. He takes the last step, and my legs finally decide to move. I quickly back up a couple of feet, not because I'm scared, which is odd. I should be. Every instinct is warning me that this man is dangerous.

"Where's Boston?"

Even though Boston is part of the fucked-up mess from tonight, he's the only anchor to reality I have at the moment. Illogical logic, but it's what I'm going with.

"Massachusetts."

His deadpan reply takes me by surprise. It'd be funny if I wasn't terrified out of my damn mind.

Hendrix tilts his head the other way, his ocean eyes scanning me from head to toe. His leisurely inspection is both predatory and fascinated. As he invades my personal space, I'm helpless to stop him when he reaches an elegant finger toward my face. I instinctively flinch when that finger lifts a lock of my hair. He stolidly observes how it slips over the center knuckle before he grabs the end between his middle finger and thumb, and my heart thrashes about inside my chest like a trapped bird.

"Since you seem to want to play a round-robin of twenty questions, I've got a few." He tugs sharply on the strand of hair, and the sting of pain makes me gasp. "Like how you were able to get out of a locked room."

He releases my hair, and I retreat another step.

"I didn't." I don't know what he's talking about.

Hendrix follows me, matching me step for step until my back plasters itself to the wall behind me, causing my shoulder to throb with renewed pain, but I ignore it.

"Or where you found that shirt."

I glance down at what I'm wearing only to see my pink-painted toes, my bare legs, and the hem of a long-sleeved men's button-down dress shirt brushing the tops of my knees. Where the hell are my clothes?

"I… I don't know."

The backs of his fingers caress the fabric of the shirt between my breasts, and I smack his hand away, cursing the goose bumps that explode across my skin at his touch.

"You don't know?" he mocks in that British inflection I'm quickly coming to despise.

Whatever trepidation I had been feeling quickly morphs into irritation. "*I. Don't. Know.*"

I honestly don't remember putting on the shirt or where I found it.

"How do you know Aleksander and Aleksei Stepanoff?"

My forehead crinkles with confusion. "I don't know who they are."

"You seem to not know a lot of things. Let's see if we

can jog your memory."

Producing a rectangular piece of plastic from his back trouser pocket, he flicks my nose with it, then turns it at an angle so I can't see what it is.

"Synthia Carmichael, no middle name, age twenty from Dilliwyll, Virginia." He scowls in displeasure. "What the fuck kind of name is Dilliwyll?"

My mouth gapes open before I can shut it. He has my driver's license. He knows my name and where I live. *Shitshitshit.* Then a thought hits. If he's holding my license, he must have gotten it from my bag. *My bag.* Where I keep pepper spray and my switchblade.

"Whatever you're thinking of doing, firefly, don't. I can promise you'll regret it."

Alana always warned me not to say the first thing that popped into my head. It's a bad habit, one I haven't been able to break.

"I already do, asshole."

Apparently, that was the worst and possibly the stupidest thing I could say.

The scream that almost breaks free is abruptly cut off when Hendrix's free hand whips out and circles my throat, fingers digging into the pliable flesh until barely a whisper of air can enter my lungs. As his hand tightens its crushing grip, his stunningly gorgeous face draws nearer, the blue of his eyes blotted out and completely black with suppressed rage.

Struggling, tears leak from my eyes, and black dots dance around the periphery of my consciousness. It's funny the bizarre things you think about when you brace yourself for death. See it coming for you. Know that it's imminent as its dark form creeps up on you.

Hendrix pulls me forward with a hard jerk, then

slams me back against the wall. “Stupid cunt. You’re only alive because of Tristan. If it were up to me, I’d have slit your throat while you were unconscious.”

“Please,” I whisper, not knowing whether I’m begging for my life or asking him for a quick death. I’d take either one, honestly. “I am no one.”

And as morbid and ungrateful as it sounds, other than Alana, it’s not like I have anyone left in this world who would care if I’m gone. I grew up isolated and sequestered because of my scars. To my peers in high school, I was a monster. An outcast. The freakish oddity who everyone looked at with either pity or ridicule.

“What did you just say?”

The agonizing constriction abruptly releases, and oxygen scours in a painful burst down my windpipe, filling my lungs. Jagged coughs erupt up my burning throat, doubling me over with the force of them.

“I said…” I wheeze in a breath. “Fuck… you.”

His rough hand grabs the wrist of my uninjured arm, and he drags me down the hallway.

“I don’t have time for this shit.”

I try to pull free, but it’s no use.

“Well, neither do I. Let me go.”

“Can’t do that, so shut the fuck up and be quiet.”

My bare feet slide along the polished wood floor as he walks inside another bedroom, one-hands a nightstand drawer open and pulls out a prescription bottle of pills.

Oh, hell no. I’ve heard the horror stories about women being drugged and raped. I’d rather be dead than let that happen.

Struggling in earnest to break his hold, I frenetically look around for anything I can use as a weapon and see nothing other than a lamp that is out of reach.

The room is cloaked in darkness, and I can't make out details. I doubt there would be any way to escape except out the second-story window.

Finding nothing resourceful, I resort to childishly kicking at his shins. "If you think I'm going to take those willingly and let you rape me, you—"

He gives me a constipated look and pockets the bottle, then manhandles me out of the room.

"Jesus, you're dramatic. And they're not for you. Besides, you're not my type."

I shouldn't be bothered by what he said. He wants to kill me. Tried to do just that when he choked me. I detest this man. I don't want his interest. What I want is to push him down the stairs and get the hell out of wherever I am. Call the police. Get a real doctor to look at my shoulder.

But dammit, his snide rejection does hurt. Just another reminder that no one will ever see past the hideous trauma that covers my body. That no man will ever find me beautiful or desirable because on the outside, I'm ugly and grotesque.

My will to fight him suddenly depletes, and I go limp as he stumbles me down the stairs and shoves me inside another dark room. Do they not have lights?

"Don't ask," he quietly says to someone.

My foot gets caught on the corner of what feels like a rug, but I'm caught before I faceplant. The sudden stop in momentum jars my shoulder, and I bite my tongue to hold in the anguished cry that wants to come out.

When I look up, I'm met with the black, soulless eyes of the scary guy. Shit. I didn't think things could get worse.

"Watch her," Hendrix tells him.

What's with the whispering?

Scary guy says nothing. In fact, I haven't heard him say a single word. At all. Not in the alley, and not when I kicked him while Hendrix stitched up my shoulder.

Pale light drifts in through the open shutter blinds of the window, but it's enough for me to make out Hendrix as he walks over to the chair Boston is asleep in. At least, that's what it looks like.

Hendrix kneels in front of him. The prescription bottle rattles when he twists the cap off and shakes out two pills.

"T, open up and swallow."

When Boston cracks his mouth a fraction, Hendrix manually feeds him the pills. Relief that whatever is in the bottle wasn't going to be forced on me turns to worry when Hendrix has to pat Boston's face a few times to get him to swallow the medication.

"What's wrong with him?"

"None of your goddamn business."

I ignore Hendrix's hissed rebuke and pull out of scary guy's grasp. He doesn't stop me when I carefully approach where Boston is sitting. I spent most of my teenage years in and out of hospitals. I know more medical stuff than a trained registered nurse. It's why I decided to become a doctor. Darlington Founders has one of the best pre-med programs in the country. I may not be able to heal myself, but hopefully, I can help others.

"Is he sick?"

Boston moans as if in pain. "Get her out… don't want her to see," he slurs.

"Back the fuck off," Hendrix warns.

"I'm pre-med. I can help," I stupidly say.

I really am out of my ever-loving mind. I should be trying to figure out how to escape, not help them.

There's a clap from behind, and Hendrix and I look over to our right at the sound. Scary guy slashes his hands through the air. His fingers contort into a flurry of shapes. Sign language. He's using ASL. Is that why he hasn't spoken? Because he can't? Or do they converse in sign language so that no one will be able to understand what they're saying to one another? Like a secret code.

Along with the Spanish classes I was required to take at school for the foreign language credit needed to graduate, I also took American Sign Language through free online classes. There was this elderly woman, Linda, at our local grocery store who was deaf. She worked the check-out line and bagged groceries. Linda always snuck me a pack of chewing gum every time Alana and I went to the store. She was one of only a handful of people who had ever shown me any kindness.

Scary guy makes the letter d with his index finger pointed up and taps his nose. *Stop being a dick*, he signs.

Hendrix's warm breath feathers across my ear when he leans in and threatens, "If you hurt him in any way, I will happily lock you in the trunk of my car and drive it into a river."

God, I want to punch him in the face—*so* badly. Out of the three of them, Boston is the only one I don't want to murder at the moment.

"*I won't*." Bastard. "What did you give him?"

"His meds."

I want to roll my eyes, but I don't because I'm not twelve. "What is the medication for?"

"Migraines."

That explains the talking in hushed voices and the dark room. A lot of migraine patients are sensitive to noises and lights.

"Hey, Boston," I say. He doesn't even crack an eye open.

"Don't see," he says weakly.

I have no clue what that means.

"Did he take a sedative?"

"No," Hendrix snaps.

He must be on something. Drugs, most likely, and not the legal kind Hendrix gave him.

When I reach for Boston's hand, Hendrix snags my forearm. Scary guy claps again, but I don't look over this time to see what he signs. Whatever he says to Hendrix makes him let go of my arm.

"Could you back off and give me some room?" I ask.

"No."

I swear to almighty Christ, if he says *no* one more time, I really am going to punch him in the face.

I shift from a squat to kneel on my knees like Hendrix, trying my best to ignore the ass beside me, and take Boston's hand. Wide palm, long fingers, and a smattering of calluses that shows he uses his hands for manual labor. *Like taking on bad guys with guns in alleys.*

"Why do you call him Boston?"

I jump at Hendrix's voice because it's right there, in my ear. He's too close.

"His accent."

Hendrix watches as I press the Hegu pressure point between the base of the thumb and index finger of Boston's hand. His fingers curl in, and for a second, it looks like he's trying to hold my hand.

"His name is Tristan."

Tristan. Like the Celtic legend of Tristan and Iseult, a Cornish prince who falls in love with an Irish princess. Two star-crossed lovers doomed to a tragic fate. Their story predates Shakespeare's *Romeo and Juliet* by four centuries.

"What's his name?" I ask, angling my head a fraction in the direction of where scary guy is standing.

Tristan sighs, and the hand I'm holding goes lax.

"Constantine. What are you doing?"

"A type of acupressure. There are certain places on the hand and ear that help lessen pain and have shown to mitigate the severity of headaches. And before you ask in your snotty British way how I know this, I just do."

I know a lot of random stuff. After Alana adopted me, I had a lot of free time on my own recovering from surgeries. When I was able to go to school, I had zero friends, so found things to entertain myself with. I filled most of those lonely hours reading. Didn't matter what it was. However, the acupressure stuff I picked up from Alana. She gets ocular migraines.

Hendrix scoffs. "I was born in the States, not the UK."

"Then what's with the posh accent? Rich prick syndrome?"

Constantine makes a noise that sounds suspiciously like a chuckle.

"It was expected of me," Hendrix cryptically replies.

I physically hip-bump him out of my way and scoot between Tristan's legs. It looks way more sexual than it feels, and if I wasn't the kidnap victim in this scenario, I'd probably be blushing like a schoolgirl. The most intimate I've ever been with a member of the opposite sex has been never. No boy at my high school wanted to date the girl with the ugly scars.

Speaking of scars, lifting my left arm takes effort, but I push through the pain so I can massage Tristan's ears just above the opening to the ear canal where the Daith point is located. Some people get a Daith piercing in their ear to help preclude headaches. Alana has one.

As I tenderly press down with my thumbs, Tristan's eyes blink open, and I'm close enough to see small flecks of blue swirling in the golden brown of his irises.

"Red."

"How are you feeling? And please refrain from saying anything assholery."

My gaze drops to his mouth when it curves into a half smile. Damn, he's gorgeous.

"Better. Why are you wearing my shirt?"

His shirt? I completely forgot that I was wearing nothing but my underwear and a men's dress shirt I have no recollection of putting on.

One second, I'm staring slack-jawed at Tristan's face trying to come up with an excuse, and the next, I'm hefted off the floor with Hendrix's arms circled tightly around my waist.

"Hey! What the hell?" My legs flail uselessly, causing the shirt to ride up, and I go stock-still.

"You may want to skip the questions. She'll just reply with *'I don't know.'*"

Tristan sits up but otherwise doesn't try to save me from his jackass of a friend.

"Hen, what are you doing?"

"Put me down!"

"Since you won't let me kill her, there are other ways to ensure her silence."

CHAPTER 6

Scenery blurs by in the darkness as I stare out the passenger window of the car Hendrix forced me into and is driving me to who the hell knows where. He told Tristan he wasn't going to kill me, but I don't believe him. He already tried to choke me.

Funny how so much can happen in such a short amount of time. When I woke up yesterday morning, my only concern was that I still needed to buy that textbook for my calculus class.

Shivers race up my bare legs, and I try my best to keep warm by tucking my knees under the men's shirt. I'm cold and tired and just want whatever is going to happen to me to be over with.

I thought Darlington Founders was going to be a fresh start at a new life. I would meet new people who would look past my tarnished outer shell. I would try new things and enjoy new experiences. Well, I got my wish, except this new experience could go fuck itself. That goes for the man sitting in the driver's seat, too.

My fingernail nervously taps the inside door handle.

Maybe if I could get the car door open, I could fling myself out and hopefully roll into a ditch because the thought of getting road rash isn't appealing.

"How's your shoulder?"

It fucking hurts. Thanks for asking, I want to say but keep my mouth shut.

It's been a blessed half hour of not being subjected to the sound of Hendrix's voice.

"Why do you care?" I ask through chattering teeth.

"I don't."

The car slows, and Hendrix makes a right onto a dirt road that isn't a road. More like a rutted path made by a tractor. I grab the overhead handle when the car suddenly jerks to a stop. He opens the driver's side door and gets out.

Adrenaline floods my blood, erasing the fatigue. Now is my chance. I frantically pull on the door handle and… nothing happens. So I try again. And again.

I scream at the stupid car and take my frustrations out by bending my legs and kicking the crap out of the dashboard. The glove compartment pops open and bangs against my foot.

Knuckles tap on the glass.

"Get out of the car."

"No."

He's not the only one who can use that word. And if he plans to bury me out in the woods, he's going to have to work for it. I may not care about dying, but I won't go easily either.

"Jesus fucking Christ," I hear him mutter through the closed window.

I'm shocked when the door flies open. Why wouldn't it open for me?

"Stubborn pain in my ass," he says and reaches for me, but I don't budge when he yanks because of the seat belt. "Get out of the fucking car, firefly."

It's the second time he's called me that. Tristan calls me Red. Even though I asked what their names were, no one bothered to find out mine. The only reason Hendrix knows is because he stole my driver's license. *It's because you don't matter.*

When I shake my head no, he sighs and leans across me to undo the clasp. I decide what the hell and try to leap out of the car as soon as the seat belt comes undone, hoping for a fast getaway. Instead, I go tumbling head over ass out of the car.

Stars dance behind my eyes when my shoulder hits the hard ground, the pain so intense I almost black out. My view of the ground turns to one of the night sky when Hendrix rolls me over onto my back with a push from his dark brown leather loafer.

His tall frame bends over me, blocking out the breathtaking view of the Milky Way. Then again, the view of his face is breathtaking in its own way.

A symphony of crickets plays a sad song, their music accompanied by the high-pitched chirps of frogs. The sound is nice. Peaceful. And is another stark reminder that I have no idea where I am. I'm not from this area and don't know where things are. A gas station. A house. A fast food place. Help could be miles away or right down the road.

"You going to stop being a difficult bitch?"

I scowl up at him.

"Call me a bitch again and you'll be singing soprano when I kick you in the balls." I blow my mess of tangled hair out of my face and push myself up onto my good elbow. "Just kill me already, so I don't have to hear your stupid voice anymore."

He laughs, and it startles me.

"You may be gorgeous, but you're more trouble than you're worth."

I suck in an unintended breath at the backward compliment. *Gorgeous.* Not something I'm used to hearing, and a complete lie coming out of his mouth.

His denim-blue gaze runs up my legs, lingering a moment at the apex of my thighs where the shirt has pulled up, then continues until it stops on my face.

His eyebrow quirks up when he catches me staring at him.

"Your Jekyll and Hyde persona is giving me whiplash."

He goes from asshole to almost sweet too fast for me to keep up.

With as much grace as a deer on ice, I awkwardly stand up and tug the bottom hem of the shirt down as far as it will go.

Night dew clinging to the long grass has soaked into my underwear and shirt, while the visible humidity hazes the air and dampens my skin, making the tepid August night feel frigid. I glance around as much as I can and see nothing but grass, trees, and darkness. I know if I try to run now, he'll catch me.

"I think you popped the stitches. There's blood on the back of your shirt."

A familiar static charge tingles along my neck when he brushes my matted hair off my back to get a better look at my shoulder, and I hate my reaction to his touch. I hate him.

"Falling out of a stationary vehicle will do that."

His fingers are whisper-light as they pull the collar to the side, and with the first two buttons unfastened, the expensive silk fabric slips down my shoulder.

"I'll fix the stitches and redress it."

His words are like a cold bucket of water dumped over my head. I wish he'd make up his damn mind. Does he plan to kill me or not?

Going with the latter, I tell him, "Stop touching me and leave me alone."

His hand glides along the outside of my hip, and I squeeze my thighs together when a certain throb begins to build between my legs. *Get a grip, Syn.*

"I like touching you."

His hand moves lower, and I close my eyes, valiantly trying to regain my composure. I'm ashamed of myself for how my body is betraying me. Because God help me, I like it, too.

"Stop it," I warn him when his hand comes around and splays across my stomach, anchoring me in place.

He presses his nose to my hair. "I can smell your arousal."

Refusing to admit the truth of that, I ask, "Why did you bring me out here?"

"You're a puzzle, firefly. One I'm going to enjoy solving."

I lose the ability to breathe when he dips a hand under the shirt and slowly slides it up. Sensations I have never felt before slash me like a whip.

"Not interested. And stop calling me firefly. My name is Syn."

Moving our bodies together, he bulldozes me around to the trunk of the car.

"What are you doing?"

His smile curves against my ear. "I hope you know how to swim."

He's not seriously going through with his threat to lock me in the trunk of his car and drive it into a river.

"This isn't funny, Hendrix."

Crushing me to him with one arm so I can't escape, he pops the trunk.

"In you go."

I panic and struggle with all my might when he shoves me forward.

Wake up.

Something dark stirs inside me. It swirls and bleeds into my psyche. Everything around me goes deathly silent, and then I hear it whisper...

Aoife.

CHAPTER 7

The door to the bedroom snicks open, and light from the outside hallway spills inside the room. Even though it's early morning, the blackout curtains draping the window block out the offending sun, and it takes a second for my eyes to acclimate.

Tristan quietly walks over to the bed, hands shoved deep inside his pockets. Keeping his voice low, he asks, "How is she?"

I peel my eyes away from the woman lying in the bed and give him a small shake of the head to let him know there has been no change. Not even a muscle twitch. She hasn't moved or made a sound. I feel like I've been watching over a corpse for the last three hours.

Still feeling okay? I sign.

"Surprisingly, yeah."

Whatever voodoo the girl did to him, worked.

Tristan started getting migraines when he was thirteen. It's worrying how much they fuck him up, and even worse that he knows they're coming, and there's nothing he can do to stop them.

"Hen fucked up." He scrubs a hand up his face and through his hair, making the strands stick up.

Tristan was pissed when Hendrix came back, carrying an unconscious redhead in his arms.

I have no idea what the hell he was thinking. Was he wanting to scare her? Play with her? Whatever his intention, it backfired.

Hendrix may be crazy, but he's smart. What he did was not only reckless, it was also asinine and pointless. Things I never associate with him. Out of the three of us, Hendrix is the most meticulous. He thinks everything through a dozen times before he acts. But he didn't tonight. Which circles me back around to *her*. The redhead is the outlier. A Pandora's box.

I pass my phone to Tristan when he comes around the foot of the bed where I'm sitting quietly in the corner armchair. I've been doing a little digging on Miss Carmichael. I haven't found much on her other than what Darlington Founders has in her student file and application. The university is an ivy league college, one of the best and most prestigious with a selective admittance policy, so it was interesting to find out she's here on scholarship.

I also did a quick run on her social security number but didn't pull up anything useful. She has no social media presence online. No posted images or photographs I can find.

Tristan hands me back my phone.

"I left Hen in the living room."

Which is his roundabout way to tell me he's called a meeting and to get my ass up.

A small groan comes from the woman, and the hand that's resting near her face on the pillow convulses as her eyes rapidly flick back and forth under her closed eyelids. I'd love to burrow inside her head and see what she's dreaming. Her nightmares.

Dreams are a person's unconscious reflection of their desires, fantasies, and fears. To someone like me, each one is a weakness that can be exploited. Fears can bend people to your will. Make them beg and agree to do anything you want. Desires are more varied. Desires like love can break even the strongest person. For many, it's when I threaten a loved one, a child, a lover. If a person's desire is wealth, I can funnel a few thousand into their bank account to get what I want. If it's revenge, I give them the tools and resources to take it. Everyone thinks there's a line in the sand they will never cross, but they always do once I figure out the right motivation.

I surreptitiously watch as Tristan lifts a crimson lock of hair covering the woman's face and moves it behind her ear. The caring gesture is uncharacteristic of him. He's fixated on this girl, and I don't like it.

The chair creaks when I stand up, my legs stiff after sitting in one position for too long. I follow Tristan out of the room. The wood boards of the stairs moan as we descend. The bones of the house may be old, but the upgrades aren't. I re-did all the electrical and added fiber optic cables for faster internet speed when we first moved in. Hendrix remodeled the kitchen, his domain since he likes to cook. Tristan took care of everything else. Anything that our fathers had added when they lived here was immediately torn down and tossed with the trash. If we had to reside in this stuffy shithole for four years while at Darlington, we sure as hell weren't going to be surrounded with reminders of the bastards that helped procreate us.

"We have a problem," Hendrix says as soon as we enter the living room.

Tristan leans a shoulder on the doorframe, arms crossed over his chest. "You fucking think?"

I make sure not to stand in the middle of their impending blow-up and drop down at the other end of the sectional where I can pretend to ignore them. I may look uninterested and not give a shit, but my ears are always tuned in, and my senses are always vigilant.

"If you'd have let me talk earlier instead of telling me to shut the fuck up, I wouldn't be saying what I'm about to say now."

I get a whiff of Hendrix's stench from five feet away.

You stink.

He aims his hard blue glare at me. "If you just said I smelled, I haven't showered yet. And stop interrupting."

Hendrix can't read me as well as Tristan. And it's not like I can't talk. I can. It's just difficult. The damage to my vocal cords is severe and left scar tissue that makes it hard for me to produce sounds.

He looks back at Tristan. "Something's off with Syn."

Tristan holds up a finger and walks over to the minibar we installed two years ago. He grabs a chilled beer and pops the cap off.

"Am I supposed to know what that means?"

"Syn. That's her name."

"Whose?"

"The girl upstairs who you've developed a sudden obsession with."

Tristan carefully places the beer bottle on the bar top. "Watch it. And her name is Synthia."

"I get it. I do. Syn is gorgeous. And those blue eyes look so much like—"

Tristan hurls the bottle across the room. It explodes into a frothy geyser when it shatters on impact. "Shut the fuck up! Don't you dare say her name!"

We have suffered so much loss. Had so much taken from us. Our heart. Our humanity. What was left of our souls.

Hendrix tries to mollify Tristan's defensiveness with a rare show of empathy. He gestures toward the ceiling. "You can't save her. She's already broken. Whatever happened to her can't be undone."

"I know that," Tristan snaps.

"She's also not what she appears to be."

That gets my attention.

What do you mean?

Hendrix pushes back into the sofa cushions. "She was shot at. We technically kidnapped her. She hardly reacted at all when I choked her—"

"You did *what*?" Tristan bellows and lunges for Hendrix.

I'm out of my seat in an instant, putting myself directly between the two of them. Hendrix cartwheels over the back of the couch, letting the piece of furniture act as a barrier against an enraged Tristan.

"She's not afraid of us. Doesn't that seem off to you? The last guy I looked sideways at shit himself, but this girl doesn't flinch."

"I told you not to lay a fucking finger on her!"

Tristan can't hear over his anger what Hendrix is saying. But I do.

I let go of him. *Hear him out.*

"T, she almost took me down. Shocked the fuck out of me."

Regaining some of his composure, Tristan backs up a

step and smooths down his rumpled shirt.

"Explain."

"I knew I fucked up as soon as the words left my mouth. I just wanted to scare her to make sure she would never talk about what happened in the alley. But it's like a switch flipped, and she became a different person. She can fight. Like really fight."

"I don't see any bruises." Tristan looks over Hendrix with skepticism.

Hendrix scoffs. "Please, fucker."

I snap to get his attention. *How good was she?*

"Good. When I got my opportunity, I knocked her out and brought her back here."

We were trained killers by the time we turned twelve years old. If what Hendrix says is true, that she held her own against him in a fight…

Who is this girl?

An ominous ringtone plays from Tristan's pocket. The theme song for Darth Vader from *Star Wars*. Tristan's father.

The mood in the room sobers as he puts the phone up to his ear. His face gives nothing away as he listens intently. The call lasts less than thirty seconds.

"What did he want?" Hendrix asks, coming around the couch to stand beside me.

Tristan pockets his phone. His mouth thins into a grim line. "I've been summoned."

Fuck. That's not good.

Do you think he knows?

His shoulders tighten slightly, the only tell that he's worried.

"I guess we're about to find out."

CHAPTER 8

Because I enjoy making the old man wait, I opted to drive instead of using the helicopter service we have on standby at the private airfield located just outside of Darlington. It takes almost an hour to cross the state line into Massachusetts, then another half hour before I arrive at the Amato country estate; one of the dozens of homes my family owns around the world.

However, none of them were ever home for me. My home growing up was the exclusive boarding school in Geneva every male child of the Council is forced to attend. Con, Hen, and I were never given roots except for the ones binding us by blood and death to the Society and to each other.

Watching the world through the window of my dormitory at school, I envied the other students. The ones who would walk around campus with smiles on their faces and not a care in the world. What would it feel like to be that carefree? To be happy?

I was happy once. Sometimes, it's hard for me to remember that feeling. Happiness, contentment. Those long-ago memories fade a little more as each day passes. Each day without her. Each day I'm forced into a role I never wanted. To see the blood of the souls I took too early that never completely washes from my hands.

The two-story iron spires of the gate that stand sentinel at the entrance of the private drive that leads up to the house comes into view. I slow the Maserati down to a crawl as I approach the imposing structure and send a quick text to Con.

Me: Just arrived.

His response is immediate. Then again, Con is always on his phone, blocking out the world that exists around him.

Con: She hasn't woken up yet.

Not surprising. Hendrix doesn't fuck around.

After I left the house, it took a good ten minutes for my anger to die down before the implications of what he said about Syn sunk in. What's the adage about an enigma wrapped in a mystery rolled into one hot as hell woman?

And could her nickname be more perfect? Fuck me. All that fiery hair on a tight, curvaceous body built for dirty fucking and made for sin. That luscious Cupid's bow mouth that would feel like heaven wrapped around my cock. Hendrix thinks I want to save her. He couldn't be more wrong.

I should tread carefully. We don't know anything about her. Unfortunately, my dick doesn't give a shit. It's been a long fucking time since any woman has caught my interest. A woman I choose who isn't forced on me by my manipulative mother who cares more about pedigree than compatibility.

Me: Is she breathing?

Con: Yeah.

Me: Then she's good. Going silent. Will text when I'm on the road.

Con: I don't like this.

The unprompted phone call from my father has us on edge. The timing too coincidental.

Con: If I don't hear from you in two hours, I'm coming to get your ass.

Me: Give me four.

Con and Hen will always have my back. They would sacrifice their lives for me, as I would for them. Our bonds of brotherhood run deep; our unbreakable tethers forged in the pits of hell.

As I approach the gate, I roll my window down.

"Good morning, Mr. Amato," the guard says as he walks out of the stone gatehouse.

The small structure looks like something from Medieval times, but it's steel-reinforced with bullet-proof glass windows.

I don't recognize him. Then again, it's been years since I was last here. My father usually does his business out of the New York office.

The guard does a cursory inspection of the vehicle, but otherwise doesn't delay me too long.

"I've already notified the house of your arrival. Have a nice day, sir."

He looks older than me by two decades, and yet, he's required to address me respectfully as sir. I'm sure he knows the consequences if he doesn't.

Rolling up the window, I don't dignify him with a response. The last time I spoke to an employee, someone of a lower standing than me, my father took a cane to my back. *Amato men are kings*, he said as the polished wood cracked against my flesh, splitting it open, again and again. I still carry those painful lessons, along with all the others that riddle my body. Con and Hendrix cover theirs with ink. I don't. The gory patchwork of abuse I endured at my father's hands are the only tattoos that will ever mark my skin other than the one on my chest.

As soon as the gate clambers open, I drive through at a snail's pace, hoping to prolong every second before I face Francesco Amato. The white limestone overlay of the Châteauesque mansion comes into view as the smooth asphalt turns into the pale paver brick of the circle drive that wraps around the three-tiered fountain in front of the house. There are new hedgerows of Mom's favorite redvein enkianthus whose leaves will change from green to reddish-copper once fall arrives. My sister used to love the drooping clusters of bell flowers that bloomed every summer. A lone redvein grows in the backyard of the house in Darlington, one I planted three years ago. Every year on her birthday, I sit next to that damn shrub and beg her to forgive me for not being a better brother. For not protecting her like I promised.

Pulling around the circle drive, I clock six armed guards—two on the roof, three patrolling the front grounds, and one standing beside the veranda steps. I know there are more walking the perimeter wall. All of them necessary. To the general public, the Amatos control one of the biggest international shipping companies in the world. Our wealth and influence create enemies in those who want what we have. However, what we are out of the public eye creates enemies as well, even within our exclusive and secretive society.

A hundred or so years ago, several wealthy New England families came together and created the Society. Think Illuminati, and that's basically what it is. Influential families who wanted to shape the world around them and reap the benefits. It all comes down to power and greed.

The Stepanoffs have been trying to gain a seat at the Council. And for once, I'm thankful for those old, stuffy traditions because only founding families are allowed those seats. Gabriel Ferreira, Con's father, has been pushing for the rules to change. Over my dead damn body will I allow the Stepanoffs and their twin devil spawns to ever sit at the Council.

"Mr. Amato."

I'm greeted once again by another guard when I get out of the car. He stands at attention, and I half expect him to salute me. Dad and his fucking god complex.

The right side of the massive double front doors opens as soon as I walk up the portico steps. The inside of the house is like entering a museum that smells sickly sweet of lemon-scented furniture polish.

I disregard the greetings from the servants and the offers of something to drink. I just want this over with as quickly as possible so I can get back to Darlington and a certain redheaded conundrum currently sleeping in my bed.

I know to wait in the foyer until I'm summoned, so I pass the time looking around. Little has changed from what I can remember. Same oil paintings of Italian landscapes and old patriarchs of the Amato family that are long dead hang on the walls. The Steinway grand piano I was forced to learn how to play as a child sits as an ornamental centerpiece under the foyer's large rotunda. Beneath my feet and inlaid into the marble floor is the Amato family crest. Coiled vipers adorn the shield. Fitting. The twenty-four-carat gold embossing sparkles in a kaleidoscope of colors coming from the overhead Swarovski crystal chandelier.

I look up when the *click-clacking* of high heels announces my mother's arrival.

"Your father is in the study."

No hello. No welcoming hug. No smile. Her resting bitch face is permanently etched onto her skull, courtesy of the plastic surgery and Botox injections she gets on the regular.

"Hello, Helena. You look well."

I stopped calling her mother when I was three.

She preens at the compliment while fluffing her newly dyed ash-blonde hair. It's different than the dark brown she usually has it colored.

Helena is still beautiful at fifty if you prefer the look of a plastic blow-up doll. Most of her youthfulness she bought. Nose job, multiple face lifts, breast implants, collagen lip injections, liposuction. I usually know when she has caught Dad having another affair because her next plastic surgery of choice soon follows.

"Thank you. It's a Robuschi," she replies about the green silk wrap dress she's wearing.

Like I care who the designer is.

Her hazel eyes consider what I'm wearing with disgust. I left the house in what I already had on—jeans, a T-shirt, and my leather jacket I put on when I grabbed my car keys.

"Do you know what he wants? Classes start tomorrow, and I have shit to do."

Her forehead remains wrinkle-free when she scowls at me.

"I only know that he wants to speak with you in private."

Shit. Not good. I run through all the excuses I came up with during the drive here.

Helena fiddles with the diamonds around her neck, and I brace for whatever is about to come out of her mouth.

"When you're done with your father, come out to the courtyard for brunch. Katalina will be arriving around eleven."

And there it fucking is.

Once she found out I was coming, I'm sure she didn't waste a second before she called Katalina.

Helena has been trying to set me up with her for over a year. I'm not stupid. I know the reason behind it, and it has everything to do with her father, Mathis Laurent. My father has been trying and failing to secure a foothold in Eastern Asia. Me marrying Laurent's daughter would solve that particular problem.

"I already have plans."

"Cancel them."

"Can't," I reply and walk off before she can make her retort. She usually goes straight to threatening.

Feeling the eyes of security cameras on me, I keep my pace steady, and my gaze focused straight ahead. However, when I enter through the French doors of the study, I stop when I see Malin standing next to my father.

Malin is my father's lapdog. Rabid and under the heel of its master. And one ugly motherfucker. The fact that he's here means something big has come up. Something that may require a bullet to the head. Maybe mine.

Luckily, I brought my own gun to even the odds. A Sig Sauer sits snuggled in its holster hidden underneath my leather jacket.

With a flick of his thick fingers, Dad motions me over.

I take the only available chair, readjusting my sitting position so I can easily reach my weapon. "I'm here. Why the sudden urgency?"

My father sits like a king on his throne behind his executive desk. It pisses me off every time I look at him because it's like looking at my future reflection in a mirror.

"Levine is restructuring and handing over the reins to his daughter," he states, getting straight to the point.

It takes a second to process because my first reaction is profound relief. If he knew about Syn or Hen's fuck up or what happened in the alley, he would have led with that with a backhand to my face.

Declan Levine is one of the biggest black-market arms dealers in the country. He and my father have been in *business* together for a while. Declan transports his guns and other weapons using our cargo ships. In return, my father gets certain perks from the Irish mafia. It's a win-win.

Without saying a word, Dad nods at Malin, who immediately goes over to the wet bar and pours two whiskey neats.

My eyebrows jack up. "I didn't know he had a daughter."

"Neither did I until last night. You went to school with her."

If I did, we were ships in the night because I never met anyone at the boarding school with the last name

Levine.

"What's her name?"

Malin offers Dad his drink first, then places mine in front of me on a coaster on the desk. I take the crystal in hand but don't drink from it.

Dad sips his and murmurs his approval. "Alexandria McCarthy."

Rifling through all the names of the girls who I remember at the boarding school, the only Alexandria I can conjure was this blonde chick who everyone steered clear of. She'd rip your balls off and feed them to you if you looked at her funny. Alexandria hung out with that smart techie girl, Tessa.

"Yeah, I'm vaguely familiar with Alexandria. Never talked to her."

Levine has a daughter. So what? I don't understand why I had to drive all the way to Massachusetts for him to tell me that.

My father eyes me over the lip of his glass, takes another sip, and says slowly as if he's explaining things to a dimwitted child, "That mess in New York earlier this year wasn't because of Rossi. It was Levine. Rossi is dead. Keane Agosti has taken the mantle with Jaxson West as his second, and guess who Levine's new son-in-law is?"

Fucking hell. Mob wars get very messy. They're something we steer clear of getting involved in, unless absolutely necessary.

"What do you need me to do?" I ask, but I'm pretty sure I already know.

The control of the major southern shipping ports now belongs to Keane Agosti. Dad would want to set up a meeting, feel him out.

Dad lifts his massive six-three frame to stand. "With Rossi out of the picture, I think it's time we set up a meeting with Mister Agosti."

Fucking bingo.

He slides the velvet-lined cigar box he keeps on his desk toward him and opens the ornate wood top. Selecting one and snipping off the tip, he lights a match and rolls the foot in the flame. The tobacco glows a dark red as he holds it up, turning it this way and that.

"Use your school connection. Whatever it takes. I want a deal to use those ports."

"I'll get right on it."

He puffs on the end of the cigar a few times. Circles of fragrant smoke billow out of his mouth as he looks down at me. "Good."

"Is that all?" I ask.

I'm past ready to get the hell out. The less time I spend in the presence of my father, the better.

"One more thing," he says, watching me with cold, brown eyes. "Did you think I wouldn't find out?"

My father's deep gravelly timbre turns my blood to ice.

On the inside, I'm losing it, but on the outside, my face goes blank, and I sit up straighter. I cannot show any fear in front of this man.

"I'm handling it."

"No, what you did was fuck up as usual. I had Malin go clean up your mess."

Which means, Malin found the guy and killed him.

"Who was he?" I ask.

"Some drugged-out loser," Malin replies.

Dad taps the loose ash of his cigar. "Who's the girl?"

Shitshitshit.

Thinking quickly, I use some of the info Con found in Syn's registrar's file. "Another student. A freshman. Hendrix's current fucktoy. She's nobody."

There's hardly a day that Hendrix isn't balls deep inside a woman, so I use his playboy reputation to take my father's interest off Syn and cross my fingers that it works.

He makes a guttural humming noise of acceptance.

I only get a second to breathe a sigh of relief before my father says, "You do not keep secrets from me. Now, I have to teach you a lesson. Hand on the desk."

Fuck you!

My muscles twitch with the need to fight back. Shoot the bastard between the eyes. But I do neither. Instead, I place my hand, palm down, on the desk as he commanded. I don't flinch. I don't move. I shut down and detach. Go someplace else. Somewhere safe. Away from him, this room.

I am no one.

My mind conjures vibrant red hair and blue eyes. My beautifully broken Syn.

"Amatos are kings," my father says, his voice now distant and far away.

There's a hiss and a sizzle as he brings the foot of the cigar down onto the back of my hand.

CHAPTER 9

Awareness worms its way through the dense, heavy fog of sleep. Someone's watching me.

I also smell coffee.

My eyes blink open.

Scary guy.

He's sitting in a chair in the corner of the room, the glow from his phone creating odd shadows on his face. It reminds me of my first Halloween with Alana. I was in the hospital after receiving a mesh graft on my hip and had just finished my immobilization period—which is exactly how it sounds. Immobilization is used to promote new blood vessel growth from the tissue below to the grafted skin.

Since I wasn't able to go out and enjoy any Halloween activity, Alana and I had our own Halloween fun. We binged on candy, watched scary movies, and when I was ready for bed, she read me Edgar Allan Poe's "The Tell-Tale Heart" while holding a flashlight under her chin to make her face appear ghostly.

If Constantine is here, it means I'm back at their house. I didn't manage to escape. But what happened?

Did I hit my head? Or did I have another episode?

I thought I was better. My episodes of losing time had become almost nonexistent. The last event I had was two years ago. At first, Alana thought I was sleepwalking. But you can't sleepwalk if you're not asleep first. One doctor diagnosed me with PTSD. It made sense. Whatever had happened to me when I was younger—the chemical burns, the burns from where the fire touched my left side, the stab wounds—would absolutely have been traumatizing.

I gasp when Constantine's dark eyes lift from his screen and lock with mine. His eyes are like twin black holes, empty voids of nothingness whose gravitational pull draws you in. You want to look away but can't.

Our stare-off ends when the rich roasted aroma of freshly brewed coffee snares my attention once again.

The black silk sheet falls to my lap when I sit up, and I snatch at it, cinching it at my chest. Luckily, I'm still wearing the long men's shirt. Unfortunately, it reeks. Dirt and sweat. I'd give anything for a shower.

Grabbing my thick, unruly hair with my left hand, I gather the mass and throw it over my head to get it out of my eyes.

"What time is it?"

Dear god, my voice sounds like the rumble of a chainsaw.

Constantine turns his phone around. The digital display says it's ten o'clock. With the room dark, I don't know whether it's ten a.m. or p.m. Constantine answers that question by reaching out and pulling open one side of the curtains. A flood of sunlight pours into the room, blinding me. By the time my eyes stop stinging, he is by the bedside, holding out two oblong pills in his open palm.

"Is this where I have to choose? Take the blue pill and I'll wake up in my own bed. Take the red one and you'll show me how deep the rabbit hole goes?"

His lip twitches with a peek of a smile. He got my *Matrix* reference, and damn, even the hint of a grin transforms his face into devastatingly breathtaking. With everything that happened, I hadn't paid much attention to him. Really noticed him. But I do now.

His jet-black, wavy hair is shorn close to the sides but longer at top. The color so richly black that it shines like pure onyx in the sunlight coming in through the window. I had thought his eyes were black as well, but they're not. They're dark brown. His skin carries the caramel color of a perpetual tan, as if he spends every day outdoors. The golden skin of his arms is covered in tattoos down to both wrists. Beautiful, intricate designs of climbing vines with delicate flowers colored a deep, blood-red. Interwoven in the vines are words written in script in a language I don't understand.

He lightly bounces his hand, drawing my attention back to it and away from his arms. Recognizing the two pills he's holding as ibuprofen, I pop each one in my mouth. A dumb thing to do, but for some insane, illogical reason, I trust him. A coffee cup gets thrust in front of my face, and I take that as well.

Thank you, I sign, flattening my hand and bringing my fingertips to my chin then gesturing outward in an arc. And I regret it immediately when Constantine's eyes flicker with recognition.

It wasn't on purpose. I had every intention of pretending ignorance around them. If they didn't know I could understand their conversations whenever

Constantine signed to Tristan or Hendrix, I could've used that to my advantage.

You know A-S-L? He signs each letter.

"Yes." I don't pontificate further because my need for caffeine comes first. I'm tired, but otherwise woke up feeling better than I have in a long time. My shoulder twinges but otherwise isn't bothering me.

Testing the temperature of the coffee, I take a tentative sip. It's not sweetened, but beggars can't be choosy, or however that saying goes.

It wasn't in your transcript.

Lovely. Hendrix stole my driver's license, and Constantine hacked into my student record.

I shrug a shoulder with as much nonchalance as I can muster and take in my surroundings. The bedroom is large and clean. The bed I'm in has to be a California king. The four posters at each corner are thick like tree trunks and have circular metal rings hanging off them, like doorknockers. Weird. A dresser, a mirror, and an armchair in the corner are the only other pieces of furniture in the room. It's simple and understated, yet still masculine.

I don't know if this is the same room as the one I allegedly escaped from—according to Hendrix—because I don't remember. Which means I've blacked out twice in only a few hours' time. Alana will have a cow if she finds out. She'll also flip her shit if she finds out about any of this. How is this my life? I grew up mostly solitary in a rural county of Virginia, population nothing. My life was boring and predictable.

Clearly, not anymore.

Are you afraid?

Out of my ever-loving mind, but I reply with, "Should

I be?"

I figured, if they were going to do anything to me, they would've done so already. Hendrix had plenty of opportunities. Constantine could've held a pillow to my face while I was out, but he brought me coffee and pain medication. Tristan saved me in the alley. So I guess, the question I should be asking is, what do they want? I have nothing to offer other than the promise of my eternal silence about what happened in the alley.

Constantine continues to observe me from his place at the side of the bed. That's what it feels like. Like I'm some exotic and fascinating animal you see in a cage at the zoo for the first time.

"Am I a prisoner?"

Moronic to ask, but I need a clear definition of exactly what the hell is going on.

No.

"So I can go?" It's worth a try.

That half-tip curvature of his mouth happens again, and I almost aspirate the coffee instead of swallowing it when I see twin dimples appear. I'd hate to see a full smile. I may not survive it.

No.

Avoiding spilling hot coffee all over myself, I set the mug on the nightstand.

"You say that I'm not a prisoner, but then you say I can't go. I hate to break it to you, but that literally makes me a prisoner."

Where did you learn how to fight?

I blink at him. Big owl eyes. I've never laid a hand on anyone in my entire life, not even when they deserved it.

"What are you talking about?"

"Oh, good. The crazy chick is awake."

Hendrix comes strolling in looking cocky and gorgeous in nothing but low-hanging black sweatpants. Holy shit, he's cut. And covered in ink. His entire chest and arms. Gruesome images of skulls and death and blood. Being subjected to both his bare chest and tattoos, the combination is almost painful to take in all at once.

I avert my gaze back to Constantine. A single black eyebrow arches.

"Wow, morning does not agree with you."

I hold up my middle finger, then ask Constantine, *Did he come out of the womb already a jackass or does he just behave like one?*

Pretty much on both counts, he responds.

I smile at Constantine in shared camaraderie before it drops. *He's not your friend*, my conscience reminds me.

Mumbling under his breath, Hendrix makes himself comfortable on the bed beside me.

"Of course, you know how to do the freaky finger stuff. There are a lot of things you seem to know how to do, firefly."

"Syn," I correct him, knowing it'll go in one ear and out the other.

He's holding a large plate of scrambled eggs and what I hope is bacon. I would give up my firstborn for some bacon right now. I haven't eaten anything since yesterday, and I'm starving.

Hendrix puts the large platter of food across my thighs and wraps an arm around my shoulders.

"Do you mind?" I sneer.

"Not at all." He hands me a fork, offers one to Constantine, then leans over and sniffs me.

"You—"

I point the prongs of my fork at his nose. "Hush. You cooked this?" The food smells and looks fantastic. What the hell. I dig right in.

Hendrix's grin is a mile wide. "Yep. Hope you like dill, Synthia Carmichael from Dilliwyll."

I do. Alana taught me how to cook. We live on a small farm. Doesn't mean we're farmers, but we do have a vegetable and herb garden. We shop the grocery store mostly to buy meat and junk food.

"You're an ass." My hunger overrides my irritation that Hendrix is once again encroaching in my personal space and is too close. I moan as soon as I shovel a forkful of food into my mouth. "Oh my god. This is delicious."

Both men stare intently at me as I eat, and a blush heats my face when Hendrix not-so-discreetly adjusts himself.

"Have you heard from T yet?" he asks Constantine.

Constantine frowns at his phone, and I grow concerned.

"Is Boston… I mean, Tristan okay?"

Tristan was barely functional when Hendrix forced me out of the house and into his car. I shouldn't care, but unfortunately, I do. I'll blame it on temporary Stockholm Syndrome.

A door slams from downstairs, rattling the entire house.

"Speak of the devil."

Something is wrong. I feel it. Pushing the plate from my lap, I scramble off the bed before either of them can stop me—and come to a jarring halt when Tristan suddenly materializes in the doorway.

My heart irrationally leaps at the sight of him, then plummets to the floor when he tells me, "You're moving in."

CHAPTER 10

"I most certainly am not!"

"For once I agree with her."

I send Hendrix fuck-you eyes.

"He knows about last night. About her."

"How the fuck did he find out?" Hendrix yells.

"Who?" I demand to know.

"I don't goddamn know how."

I grab Tristan's arm. His muscles are bunched so tightly, they're barely constrained by the fabric of his shirt.

"Who knows about me?"

Hendrix rolls off the side of the bed. "If he knows what happened last night, it means we have eyes watching us. The fucktwins?"

"I didn't even consider that. They were at the Bierkeller. Would make sense."

I'm so confused about what they're talking about, so I circle back around to the one thing I do understand.

"I am *not* moving in."

Tristan's fierce gaze pins me in place. "Yeah, you are. Not up for discussion."

This can't be happening. It can't. Emotions well up in a torrent, strong and fast. Tears that I seldom shed gather in my eyes and threaten to spill over.

"I just want to go home," I choke out on a whisper.

I want Alana. I want to have never met any of them. I just want my life to go back to the way it was before. Boring and predictable.

"Red—"

"Don't touch me." I smack Tristan's hand away when he reaches for me.

I can't deal with any of this. With them. It's too much. The ugly, prickly sensation of a panic attack makes itself known. The constriction in my chest, the rapid heartbeat, the way my skin feels too tight on my body like it's about to split open like a butterfly's exoskeleton when it molts.

I'm too overwhelmed. I need to get out. I need some space and some air. With Tristan blocking the doorway and the other two seeming to take up the rest of the room, I dash into the adjoining bathroom where I promptly slam and lock the door. My back slides down the wood until my butt hits the cold tile floor, and I can do nothing but cup my ears to block out the loud argument that erupts outside the bathroom.

I'm not here.

"Red, unlock the door."

My head thumps against the wood when Tristan pounds a heavy fist to it.

Distress turns to rage. "My fucking name is Synthia Carmichael!" I scream.

Ignoring the continued pounding and doorknob rattling, I bolt up from the floor and tear off the filthy men's shirt I'm wearing. I can't take the smell any longer. I need to be clean. To wash away the sweat and grime that covers me like sticky tar.

Buttons fly every which way and clink against the sink, the floor, the wall. I hurl the offending shirt across the bathroom, but it snags on the towel bar and hangs there limply, mocking me.

I make the mistake of looking over at the mirror, and at first, I don't recognize that it's me. Wild blue eyes. Tangled, frizzy hair. The scars that stand out like a fucked-up Picasso under the unforgiving recessed lights. I'm a horror show. A gory patchwork of piecemeal flesh on one side. Not able to stand the sight any longer, I turn, but something stops me. Almost as if my reflection reaches out and grabs hold of me. At the angle I'm twisted, I can see my shoulder in the mirror. Curiosity gets the better of me. With shaky fingers, I peel away the medical tape securing the gauze and brace myself for the worst. The area is red, but the stitches are clean, no signs of infection. It hasn't bothered me much, so must not have been as bad as I'd first thought.

"Syn, please open the door. We need to talk."

"Just bust the door down and drag her drama queen ass out," Hendrix says.

I really do absolutely loathe that man.

Rifling through the contents of the vanity drawer, all I find are a box of condoms and two bottles of lube. Gross. I open the cabinet under the sink and locate what I'm looking for. A first aid kit.

"Syn, open the goddamn door." More banging.

Doing the best that I can to redress my shoulder, I cover it completely with tape, hoping that'll keep the area dry enough in the shower. I'll put another square of clean gauze on it when I get out. I have tunnel vision at this point, my only concern is lather, rinse, repeat.

There's a panel next to the massive glass-enclosed tile shower. I press every button until water pours out from an overhead panel like the deluge of a thunderstorm. There is no door to open, so I immediately step inside and am surprised that the water is already hot. It feels wonderful on my skin and helps dispel some of the stone-cold chill that has taken up residence in my bones. The white noise of the water fills my ears, and I shut my eyes, letting my mind drift and take me away. Somewhere beautiful. Safe.

"Icarus soon forgot his father Daedalus's warning about flying too close to the sun. Icarus's joy at being able to fly like a bird made him blind to the dangers his father warned him about. But you won't forget what I told you, will you?"

"No, Papa. I won't forget."

"Syn."

I jump at the sound of his voice, my feet almost slipping out from under me. I can barely make out Tristan's dark head of hair through the dense fog of steam. Why am I not surprised he's in here? He probably ripped the door off its hinges.

His silhouette blurs as it comes closer, and my pulse quickens with anticipation as fear and anger become something else, evidenced by the arousal I feel slicking between my thighs and the hardening of my nipples. A Pavlovian response, one I'm helpless to stop. It's twisted and depraved, and I'm ashamed of my body's reaction. What's wrong with me?

"You shouldn't get your shoulder wet."

Coming out of whatever haze I'm experiencing, it registers that I'm completely naked.

"Get out!" Covering my breasts with my arms, I

fling myself back and away from the glass partition, smacking against the hard shower wall. "Shit! Fuck!" I yelp when my shoulder protests.

"I'm coming in."

"No!" I don't want him to see me like this. Exposed. Damaged. Ugly. "Just give me one damn second."

I slide sideways to hide on the other side of the waterfall coming from the ceiling. The shower is pure luxury, and I wish I was in a better mindset to enjoy it.

"You have five minutes," he warns.

Spurred into motion, I take a bottle labeled shampoo from the inset shelf. The soap lathers into a rich foam, and I quick-scrub every inch of my body. I use more to wash my hair. Mint, lemon, and a lighter hint of cedar. It smells like him, which means *I'll* smell like him. Great. That's all I need.

"One minute," he says.

Overbearing, pushy jackhole.

Rinsing my hair as best as I can, I blurt, "Done."

His shadow moves and the waterfall raining down on me suddenly shuts off. I wring out my hair and look around for a towel. *Fuck.* I hadn't thought that far ahead. No towel. No clean clothes.

"Could you hand me a towel, please?"

Before I even finish asking, an arm pokes through the opening, and I snatch the white bath towel from his hand and secure it around my torso. Tight. Very tight.

"Clothes?"

"Time's up, Red."

"Clothes," I demand again. He doesn't say anything.

Dammit all to hell.

The steam is dissipating rapidly, and he'll soon be able to see me fully through the shower glass. I have no choice. With my head held high, I walk out.

Tristan leans back against the bathroom vanity—ankles crossed and arms outstretched behind him, hands gripping the counter. He really is wonderful to look at. Not because he's gorgeous. There's just something about him. The magnitude of his presence. The power he emanates. He's the type of man who walks into a room and draws your attention like a magnet. You can't help but stare.

Tristan's perusal slowly travels up my body. "Your name suits you."

I expected revulsion. But what I see is heat. Lust. Desire. For *me*.

My breath catches when he pushes off the counter and trails a finger down my arm. No man, other than my doctors, has ever touched my scars. Has ever wanted to. The nerve endings are dead where the flames burned me, so I don't feel it, but in a way I do. Phantom tingles. My mind conjures them, and god, it feels wonderful to be touched like this. Intimate instead of clinical. Goose bumps erupt by the thousands that have nothing to do with the cooler air hitting my wet skin.

"I hope one day you'll tell me what happened."

My eyelids flutter close when his finger brushes along the edge of the towel where it's knotted above my breast.

"I don't remember what happened to me." Only flickers and flashes that come to me in my nightmares. I open my eyes. "Tristan, what's going on? What do you want from me?"

I miss his touch as soon as he drops his hand to his side. He turns me slightly and removes the soaking gauze from my shoulder and tosses it into the small trash bin beside the toilet. Our eyes meet in the mirror.

"Do you know who I am?"

That's a specifically odd question. My savior. My captor.

"Tristan?" I say as a question, not sure what he's getting at.

The first aid kit is open next to the sink, and he takes the items he needs to redress my wound.

"My last name is Amato. Are you familiar with that name?"

Darlington is the go-to ivy league university for America's wealthiest families to send their children, Tristan clearly being one of them. I about lost my mind when I received the acceptance letter from DF, then literally passed the hell out when the offer of a scholarship arrived a week after. For an orphaned nobody like me who comes from a rural upbringing, getting into Darlington was as unlikely as Charlie finding the golden ticket to go to Willy Wonka's Chocolate Factory. I would've been the stupidest person on the planet if I turned down their offer.

"Should I be?"

As sheltered as I grew up, the only famous people I know are movie celebrities and influencers I see on TikTok.

He brings his thumb up to smooth across his bottom lip, a thinking man's gesture. "How about the Ferreiras or Knights?"

My scholarship is from the Knight Foundation. When the corner of the towel begins to slip, I re-tuck it.

"Look, Tristan. Most of my life I don't even remember, and the other part was spent living in and out of hospitals after Alana adopted me. Since Hendrix stole my driver's license, you probably already know as much about me as I do. I'm not a threat to you or Hendrix or Constantine. I'm a nobody. So, please, *please*, let me leave—"

"I can't do that."

"—I swear on my life, I won't say a word to anybody."

Firm hands grip my waist and heft me onto the vanity countertop, making the two ends of the towel split wide open at my thighs, something Tristan takes advantage of by stepping between them.

My back arches as he leans in close. "What you're not understanding, Syn, is that my father is a dangerous man."

"So are you," I say breathlessly.

He smiles like it's a compliment.

"I am. But I would never hurt you. My father, on the other hand..." He trails off when he looks at my neck. "I'm sorry Hendrix did that."

I saw the faint purple marks around my neck when I looked in the mirror.

"It doesn't hurt."

"He'll never lay a hand on you again. You have my word."

"Why do you care what happens to me?"

He steps closer, and my core clenches with need when I feel the ridge of his hardness pressing into me. Wanting the thing you're most terrified of is extremely disconcerting and further proves that I really am crazy.

"I don't know why," he replies almost regretfully. "But you're now on my father's radar. You're not safe on your own. I can only protect you if you're here with me and the guys."

"No. *No!*" I shove at him, but he doesn't budge. "This

isn't fair! I never asked for any of this. I don't even know you! I have classes. I have a life. A mother who loves and cares for me."

If I thought it would help, I'd list my pet rooster, my book collection, how hard I fought to live after each surgery, even though all I wanted to do was die because of the endless pain of recovery. Anything to humanize me, make me more sympathetic. Isn't that what hostages are told to do? The crazy kidnapper is less likely to harm you if you make a personal connection with them. *You watch too much Netflix.*

"You don't have a choice, Red. Until my father no longer sees you as a potential threat, you'll do exactly what I say."

Feeling more helpless than ever, I hiss, "*I hate you.*"

He grips my chin, pushing it up with his thumb, his face so close. So devastatingly handsome.

"I'd rather you hate me than become one of my father's playthings. He'll break you."

I shudder at the implied threat. "You can't break what's already broken," I tell him.

"Trust me, you don't want to take that chance. Not with him."

His left hand balls into a fist, and that's when I notice the angry, red circle. Something that wasn't there last night. Oh, god. His skin has been burned.

Aoife.

I shut out the whispers and take his hand, cradling it between mine as gently as possible, needing to give him whatever comfort I can.

"What happened?"

He peels my fingers off, one by one, clearly not wanting my sympathy.

"My father happened."

His father did this? I wasn't Alana's biological child, but she cared for me deeply. There wasn't a day that went by where I didn't feel loved. My heart hurts for Tristan. Is horrified that a parent would do this to their own child. He said his father was dangerous. That *he* was dangerous. What have I gotten myself involved in?

He takes a step away from me. Then another, and another.

I slide the first aid kit closer and look for burn cream. "Let me put something on it. It looks bad."

"Clean clothes are on the bed. Come downstairs when you're dressed," he says and walks out of the bathroom, leaving me with a myriad of disturbing thoughts.

CHAPTER 11

I pace the kitchen floor, back and forth, back and forth, grabbing ingredients to make cinnamon scones. It was one of the first things my governess taught me how to make. She was a nice woman. Young, sweet, and pretty. My father held my small hand as he guided the knife across her throat. A lesson not to get attached to any woman. I was six.

"You see that burn?"

Constantine looks up from his phone at his place at the counter island. He nods.

I was born to wreak havoc and bring chaos. To bring war. One day, my father, Francesco Amato, Gabriel Ferreira, and I are going to find ourselves alone in a room together. I'll be the only one walking out alive.

Slicing a lemon in half, I squeeze the juices into a cup of milk to make homemade buttermilk, then cut a stick of butter into tiny cubes that I'll place in the freezer to harden. Grabbing one large egg from the carton, I crack it in a small bowl and whisk it briskly with a fork.

Tristan has got blinders on when it comes to Syn and

is letting his dick do all the thinking. There's something going on with her, and after last night, I'm going to enjoy finding out what it is. I guess T's idea of her living with us isn't a bad one after all. The rush I feel, it's heady. I love devising ways to break new toys. Shatter them completely, then put them back together.

Mixing the cinnamon with the other dry ingredients, I set the bowl aside, turn on the top oven to preheat, and wash my hands. The milk and butter need to chill for at least ten minutes before I can add them.

I prop my elbows on the countertop and ask Constantine, "I know you've been digging into her. Find anything?"

Not much. I got her medical records from Duke.

"I thought she was from Dickweed."

He gives me a droll look. *Her surgeries were done at Duke. Two-hour drive from Dilliwyll.*

He has to spell the town name out. Such a stupid fucking thing to name a town.

Whatever happened to her was bad.

He offers me his phone, and as much as I want to say I'm not interested, I am. Constantine deals in death. My specialty is torture.

"Damn," I say as I read.

The full workup they did before her first skin graft showed evidence of past childhood abuse. Scar tissue from old fractures and broken bones in multiple sites. Three healed areas on her side near her kidney and lower rib cage they concluded were made with a knife. The severe chemical burns to her left arm and torso. The arson burns on her upper thigh and side. I scroll through more records. She was later diagnosed with trauma-induced dissociative amnesia and PTSD.

Things are beginning to make sense now. Why her favorite phrase is *"I don't know."* It also explains why she attacked me, and why her reactions to things seem off. People dissociate when triggered. Stress, pain, a traumatic memory. I've seen it happen with a few of the people I've tortured.

"What about the mother, the one who adopted her?"

Con signs slowly so I can keep up.

Alana Carmichael. Syn's adoption records are sealed. I'll work on it, but I can't do much more than that. Maybe me looking into Syn last night was how Francesco found out.

"Not likely."

"She'll be down in a minute," Tristan announces as he walks into the kitchen. He heads straight for the fridge. "What the fuck is this?" He holds up the glass of fermented milk.

"That is for the scones I'm making."

I take it from him and add it and the egg to the mixing bowl. I forgot to put the butter in the freezer, so I dump the mushy diced cubes in as well and fold everything together.

You were supposed to text me when you left, Con angrily signs. At least, that's what I think he says.

"I don't need you to babysit me. I can handle my father," Tristan replies.

Sometimes I wonder about that. Hypothetically speaking, if it came down to it, would Tristan be able to put a bullet between his father's eyes? Con and I would have no fucking problem doing it to ours. Callous to say, but there is no love lost between us and our dear old daddies.

I knead the dough and flatten it into a circle on a non-stick baking sheet. Using a butterknife, I cut the circle like a pizza to create triangles and pop the pan into the oven.

"Want to fill us in before Little Red Riding Hood walks in?"

"Would it kill you to be nice to her?"

"Yes."

Tristan pops a K-cup into the Keurig. "There's some business stuff Dad wants me to deal with."

"You know damn well that's not what I was asking about."

He pours a bottle of water into the receptacle and hits the button to start the coffeemaker.

"There isn't much else to say than what I already said upstairs. Somehow, he found out about what happened in the alley and sent Malin."

Malin is a weaselly little cocksucking bastard who lives with his head shoved up Francesco's ass.

Con reaches over the counter island to stop me from picking up the butterknife, but he's not fast enough. I fling it across the room and enjoy the satisfying thud it makes when it embeds into the drywall. What I'd really like to do is stab it through Malin's ugly face.

"Who are the fucktwins?"

Syn stands under the door arch, looking innocently sexy with her wet scarlet hair cascading down over her shoulders. The striped men's boxers she has on are rolled low at her waist. She's tied the plain white tee in a side knot. It hangs loose over her tinier frame but is thin enough for me to make out her hourglass shape and dusky nipples. God damn. I may have to change my opinion about only preferring blondes, because I would absolutely fuck the hell out of her if given the chance.

"The twins are none of your business," I reply because

I can't help myself. Something about her makes me want to be an asshole. See how far I can push her.

"Wasn't talking to you."

Yeah, I want to fuck her.

Tristan doesn't give her a second glance. "Sit down."

Trouble in paradise already?

I'm shocked as shit when she does what he says without any snarky backtalk. She takes the barstool next to Constantine, who immediately hides his phone by flipping it over to lie face down on the counter.

You hungry? he asks her.

He's as bad as Tristan with the coddling.

She picks at her cuticles, glances at me, then away. "I ate the rest of the cold eggs and bacon upstairs."

The Keurig hisses and splutters as it finishes its brew cycle, and she eyes the coffee with envy. Tristan makes a discontented grunt and slides the steaming mug over to her.

"Thank you." Holding it between her hands, her lips pucker and blow to cool it off, and my mind conjures all the illicit, probably illegal things I could do with that mouth.

"Here's the deal," Tristan says, resting a hip to the counter. "You saw something last night that you shouldn't have."

"That's a huge under—"

"Shut. Up."

Her mouth snaps closed at his harsh reproach, her pretty blue eyes wounded.

"You're not from our world, Red, so I get that you don't understand the danger you're now in. But you are. Last night, the guy in the alley said he was there for the girl. I think he was talking about you."

"That's ridiculous."

"The fucktwins are two big, sadistic Russian motherfuckers who were at the Bierkeller last night. They were watching you."

"I'm a waitress, and Saturday nights are busy. They were probably trying to get my attention so they could order or get their check."

Tristan talks right over her. "You've piqued my father's interest, something you never want to do. I had to come up with an excuse for why you were with us. I told him you were with Hendrix."

I'm a little offended at the horror on her face.

"I am *not* with Hendrix."

"Until this thing blows over, yes you are."

Her jaw drops. "No. Absolutely not."

And I absolutely agree. Jabbing a thumb her way, I state, "What she said."

"Hendrix has a reputation, one my father won't question."

Jesus fucking Christ.

The timer beeps, and I shove my hands into oven mitts and take out the scones. Slamming the hot pan on the counter island, I rip the mitts off.

"You want me to treat her like one of my dolls?"

His expression is murderous and proves my point.

"That's what I thought."

Syn's head whips around so fast her wet hair flies out in a pinwheel, smacking Con in the face. For once, he hasn't been deep in his phone. His rapt attention has been on the volley of conversation between Tristan, Syn, and me.

"Your dolls?"

I have certain predilections when it comes to sex. The

women I fuck know what my expectations are upfront. Depraved things that Little Miss Innocent Farm Girl from Dilliwyll, Virginia, wouldn't be able to handle.

"Women I fuck, firefly." I tear off a paper towel and wrap it around one of the freshly baked scones, take a huge bite, and smirk like the entitled bastard I am.

She makes a disgusted noise, then says to Tristan, "I have classes."

"So do we," he replies, snatching a scone and dunking it into his coffee.

Fucking nasty.

"I already promised you I wouldn't say anything. And one thing I never break is my word."

"Duly noted. Still don't care."

She picks up a scone and throws it at his head. He catches it one-handed and puts it back on the plate.

Changing tactics, she argues, "Do you know how rare it is for someone like me to get accepted into a college like Darlington Founders? It's like seeing a unicorn in real life. It doesn't happen. And I'm not going to let you screw things up for me and jeopardize my scholarship."

Tristan jerks his chin at me. "Seeing as your scholarship is funded by the Knight Family Foundation, we can ensure you won't lose it—*if* you do what we say."

Not deterred, Syn rolls over that threat like he never spoke it.

"My mother is going to want to know why I'm not living in my apartment. My boss, Keith, will get concerned when I don't show up for work. They'll ask questions, something you seem to be allergic to."

I seal my mouth shut mid-chew to hold in my chuckle. The girl has balls. So fucking feisty. Watching them argue is making me hard.

"Didn't say you had to stop working or go to class. You just have to move in here where we can keep an eye on you," Tristan tells her.

The barstool Syn's sitting on angrily scrapes across the floor. She grabs the countertop and leans in, all business.

"For the last time, I am not moving in here."

He puts down his coffee and mimics her stance.

"Wanna bet? Remember what I told you upstairs about my family? It wouldn't just be my father. It would be theirs, too. Wealthy, powerful men with connections who can do whatever the fuck they want because there are no repercussions or consequences. Men who wouldn't think twice about going after you or your mother or anyone else you care about. So, I guess the question you should ask yourself is: how much is Alana's life worth to you?"

CHAPTER 12

Pulling into a parking space in front of my apartment building, Constantine cuts off the engine but I don't make a move to get out. When I do, it'll mean I've accepted my fate, and I'm not ready to do that yet. It's inevitable, though. Tristan hit me where he knew it would hurt the most. Alana. I would do anything to keep her safe.

The sunset is behind us, shining in through the back windshield, making the interior of the car glow with a fiery orange hue. Unlike Hendrix's fancy Mercedes, Constantine drives an old-school muscle car, all black, similar to the dark-green Ford GT from that movie *Bullitt*. It suits him.

He sits mutely in the driver's seat, staring straight ahead. Constantine pretends to be apathetic, but that doesn't mean he's not present or aware. Tristan may be the bold, authoritative one of the group, Hendrix the cocky, threatening one, but I think Constantine is the most dangerous. The quiet ones usually are—at least, according to all the books I've read.

I don't know what it is about him. Whatever it is, I feel safe in his presence, which is a very strange, crazy thing to think. What's even crazier is that I'm sitting in this car about to go up to my apartment and pack my things so I can move into a house with three men I don't know.

Unclipping my seat belt, I grab the door handle. The first thing I'm going to do when we get inside my apartment is change into my own clothes and drag a brush through my knotted hair. I'll need to remember to pack conditioner to take with me. Toothbrush and lotion, too. And my bookbag and textbooks.

A young couple walks out of the apartment directly in front of us. The girl talks animatedly as the guy is completely glued to his phone. Constantine watches them with a steely focus as they head toward a red pickup truck. Like they're a threat. How sad to feel like you always have to view the world that way. I guess that's one gift my screwed-up memory gave me. If I remembered what happened to me, I might've become just as jaded. Hated and felt distrustful of everyone.

I pull the door handle to get out of the car. *Run. Open the door and run.* I do the complete opposite.

"Are you coming up with me?"

Constantine looks over, face blank, and nods. The coldness of his gaze unsettles me, and I can't look into it for long. My eyes drop a fraction and land on his mouth. Full, alluring lips that would be perfect if not for how both corners turn down slightly. I would give anything at that moment to make him smile.

We get out of the car, and Constantine follows me as we climb the stairs to my second-floor unit. I take each step at a snail's pace, prolonging the inevitable as much as possible.

"Wait." I stop on the top step and turn around, gripping the handrail.

Even though he's standing on the second step below mine, he's taller than I am by a couple of inches. Brooding and breathtaking.

"What's your favorite color?"

His jet-black brows scrunch together, and I'm tempted to reach out and rub those frown lines away with my thumb.

"I know it's stupid, but humor me," I say.

If I'm going to be forced to live with them, I'd like to know something about them, other than the bad, scary stuff.

Yellow.

I admit, I'm surprised. I thought for sure he would say black or dark gray. Yellow is a happy color. It's the color of sunshine, smiley faces, sunflowers, dandelions, and buttercups. It's also a color of caution and cowardice.

"Mine is green. Like a four-leaf clover."

With that dumb response I can't unsay, I give him my back and take that final step. As soon as we get to my door, I reach into my pocket to fish out a set of keys that isn't there, and curse.

"Hendrix has my keys."

He also has my license, wallet, phone, and everything else.

Constantine's arm reaches around me, a silver key dangling from a rooster keychain held in his hand. Alana gave it to me before I left. A little trinket to remind me of home and my pet rooster, Cocky Bastard.

He slips the key into the door lock and turns it.

"Home sweet home," I tell him, crossing the threshold when he pushes the door wide open with ease.

Home for a short, sad two weeks, but I love my tiny one-bedroom studio. Alana helped me buy the furniture. We found the cute daisy-print sofa and matching armchair at a garage sale. Some things we ordered online for convenience, like dishware, cooking stuff, and bathroom essentials. The full-size four-poster bed I draped with gauzy linen to create a canopy is a spare Alana had in one of the guest rooms back home. Management recently upgraded all the appliances to stainless steel and installed new laminate wood flooring. A large window takes up most of the living room wall and gives amazing views of the sunrise every morning.

"How long am I going to have to live at the house?"

I don't know.

Okay, not very helpful.

"I have to pay rent by the first of every month."

It'll be taken care of.

I force my mouth closed when it falls open. I'm about to argue but think better of it. They can damn well pay my rent for putting me through all this shit.

"Do you want anything to drink?" I offer, pulling out an already chilled bottle of water from the refrigerator.

Constantine walks the short distance from the door to the bedroom and pokes his head inside, then does the same to the bathroom and to the storage closet that holds the washer-dryer combo. I don't know what he expects to find. I don't have much.

No, thank you. Nice place. You play the guitar?

He must have seen my acoustic on its stand next to

the bed.

"Yeah. Kept the boredom from getting too bad when I was stuck in the hospital."

Bring it.

"Do you play?"

He makes a nondescript hum, which I take as a yes.

The thought of Constantine with a guitar strapped over his chest, long fingers plucking the strings... I eye him over the water bottle as I drink from it. There's so much I don't know about any of them.

His last name must be Ferreira if Tristan's is Amato, and Hendrix's is Knight. Ferreira is a Portuguese surname, another tidbit of useless knowledge I picked up along the way. I can see the lineage in his dark coloring and golden skin.

I guzzle water to help cool my suddenly parched throat and toss the empty bottle into the trash.

"Make yourself at home. I'm going to get cleaned up first, then I'll pack."

Before I make it two feet, Constantine puts himself in my way, blocking my path.

I have to crick my neck to look up at him. "I'm not going to try anything. Besides, where would I go? We're two stories up."

He shakes his head and lifts my right hand, slapping my phone into it. All I can do is gape at it. He gave me my phone. A phone I could easily use to dial nine-one-one. Why does his show of trust feel monumentally significant?

"Thank you. Is it okay if I call my mom?"

Yes.

As soon as he signs it with a simple bob of his fist, I'm swiping to unlock the screen. And immediately feel terrible. Alana has tried to call me five times since last night when I was supposed to be home from work. There are also a dozen text messages. Shit. She must be worried out of her mind.

"Call home," I tell my phone's voice command. It barely rings on the other end before Alana picks up.

"Why haven't you answered your phone? Where have you been?"

I pull the device away from my ear and put it on speaker as I walk to my bedroom. I need to come up with something convincing and fast.

Putting the phone on the bed, I head straight for the tiny closet and grab my rolling suitcase.

"I'm so sorry. My phone died at work, then things got crazy when I got back to the apartment. Some residents complained about seeing mice, so management is going to get exterminators to inspect all the apartments. I don't want to be here for that, so I'm going to stay at a friend's place for a few days. Shelby, that girl I work with."

I hate lying to the one person who has loved and cared for me. I can only hope what I said sounds plausible.

I grab some clothes, underwear, and socks from the dresser and toss them into the case, keeping some stuff out for me to change into. I kick my tennis shoes, sandals, and a pair of flip-flops into a pile that I'll throw in a trash bag to take with me.

"That's nice of her. Isn't she the one with a small child?"

"That's her. I'm packing some stuff and will head out soon. Hold on."

Taking the phone and a change of clothes with me

into the bathroom, I shut the door but don't lock it. I learned my lesson earlier with Tristan; however, I don't think Constantine would barge in like he did. With the phone propped against the wall mirror, I gather all my personal supplies and makeup and dump them into the brand-new, empty waste basket to carry with me.

"You can't worry me like that, Synthia. If your phone dies, use someone else's. I was about to call the police to your apartment!" she shouts. Alana has never yelled at me, and it just makes me feel that much more guilty.

"I know. I'm sorry. I promise it won't happen again. Things just got crazy last night, and I crashed once I was able to go to bed."

How did I become such a good fibber? I'm just thankful she doesn't insist on a video chat. She'd take one look at my face and know I was lying through my damn teeth.

Since I don't need another shower, I splash some water over my face and pat it dry with a hand towel.

"Are you excited about classes tomorrow?"

I send a silent thank you that she's letting it drop and moving on to safer subjects that I won't have to lie about.

"I am. Does that make me too nerdy?"

I remove the clothes Tristan gave me to wear and fold them neatly, so I can return them to him.

"You're not a nerd, sweetie. You're intelligent. How was work?"

"Got beer spilled on me." See? I can tell the truth.

"Again? Are you sure you don't want to find somewhere else to work?"

I wrestle with the black yoga pants, tugging them up my legs. When I try to lift my left arm to put on my favorite Seamus Knox graphic tee, my shoulder decides to act up.

"Keith is an awesome boss, and the tips are great. It's just the customers that sometimes suck."

Giving up on the shirt, I drag a round hairbrush through the mess that's sitting on my head. Selecting a few elastic hairbands from my vanity drawer, I use one to put my hair up in a ponytail and the others go around my wrist.

"I was thinking it'd be nice to spend New Year's in Asheville this year. We could rent someplace near Biltmore. Drive along the Blue Ridge. What do you think?"

When I can't get the damn shirt on, I open the bathroom door. Constantine is sitting on the edge of my bed, my guitar in his lap, his fingers lightly strumming a melody that's vaguely familiar.

"I'd like that."

Constantine's awareness shifts from the guitar to me standing in the doorway. It makes my pulse go wild for some unknown reason. Those dark eyes of his swirl with such visceral emotion, it crashes into me from across the room and knocks the breath right out of my lungs.

"Hey, Mom. Shelby just arrived to pick me up. Can I call you in the morning before class?"

"You know I'll be up."

"Miss you. Love you."

The first time I said I loved her two years ago, she bawled her eyes out. Said it was the most wonderful gift anyone had ever given her. Since that day, I've made it a point to say it often. If anyone deserves to hear those two words, it's her.

"And I love you. Go be amazing. And remember to charge your phone."

"I will." My smile falters when I end the call because Constantine keeps staring. "What?"

I cover my left arm with my hand, feeling self-conscious about my scars. It's then I realize that I don't have a shirt on, only a white cotton bra.

My feet refuse to move when Constantine sets the guitar aside and stands up. He walks over, slow and deliberate, and my pulse quickens for a whole other reason. This man with no voice says so much without saying anything at all.

"I was coming out to find a new shirt. This one was too difficult to get on with my shoulder." I hold up my graphic tee to show him.

My body comes alive when his hand brushes down my cheek, a tender caress that quickens my blood and floods my senses. I shouldn't be attracted to him or to Tristan, but god help me, I am, and that scares the shit out of me.

"Beautiful."

It comes out broken, guttural, jagged. But I heard it.

Holy shit. He just talked. How is that possible?

Completely flustered, I babble, "I thought you couldn't... how can you..." Clearly, I've completely lost the ability to form coherent sentences.

His other hand comes up, and I wait on bated breath as his fingers explore my face, my lips, my brow. My heart hurls itself against my ribcage when his face dips, inching closer and closer, like he's about to kiss me. With a lazy seduction, he traces a line down the strap of my bra, stopping just above the swell of my breast. His touch is intimate. Possessive. Like I'm his. I grab hold of his forearms to keep upright since my legs feel like they might give out. I stand as still as possible, chest rising and falling with effort. I want him to kiss me. I suddenly want it more than anything.

But it never comes.

The soft cotton slips from my fingers and into his hand when he pulls on it. He taps my arm for me to hold it out. Taking his time, he maneuvers the shirt up one arm and over my head. He stops to check my shoulder, making sure the medical tape is still secure, then taps my other arm for me to push through the remaining armhole.

Profound disappointment wraps around me when Constantine signs, *We should go. I will leave you alone to finish packing.*

He picks up my guitar by the neck and leaves the room as I helplessly stand there more confused than ever.

Constantine spoke. He said I was beautiful.

What the hell just happened?

CHAPTER 13

I've been sending out feelers all evening trying to arrange a meeting with Keane Agosti and hitting a virtual brick wall every time. A guy I know who does some under-the-table shit for Declan Levine said Agosti and Alexandria have gone off grid. As in, left the country, and until they return, there's not much I can do. My father won't be happy about it. He wants access to those southern ports and shipping channels as soon as possible.

Angry footsteps sound just outside the living room right before Syn bursts in.

"We need to talk."

"About?" I swallow down the rest of the Wild Turkey I'd been nursing for over an hour.

She snags the empty glass from my hand and sets it on the coffee table.

"I still have lots of questions, and I deserve some honest answers."

Syn glances behind her when Constantine saunters

in, carrying a guitar of all things.

"Any problems?" I ask. I half expected him to carry her in here kicking and screaming.

No. Which bedroom?

I highly doubt Syn would be agreeable if I said I wanted her in mine.

"The one next to mine."

Which would also be the one next to his, since the empty bedroom is sandwiched between the two. It's the furthest available bedroom from Hendrix. With how he and Syn have been at each other's throats—more on his part—I think it would be best to keep them as far away from each other as possible.

I snatch Syn's wrist and yank her down to my lap. She immediately tries to clamber off, but I hold her in place by the hips.

"What are you doing?"

"You said you wanted to talk, so talk. Like your shirt."

Her perky breasts are practically suffocating me as she wiggles to get free. I'm a man who has fucked his fist in the past month more than I care to admit, so having her tits at eye level is way too tempting. I'm not a fucking saint.

Her finger presses under my chin, tilting my face up, until I'm looking into her soft blue eyes.

"You're almost as bad as the drunk frat guys who grope me at work."

That sobers me up instantly and erases any buzz I had going from the cheap whiskey.

"Men who take what they want from a woman aren't men."

"That's probably the most progressive, least sexist thing you've said to me."

Her ponytail hangs over one shoulder, and I play with the ends of it. "You caught me on an off moment."

When she doesn't make another attempt to get off my lap, I settle back into the couch cushions but keep my hand where it is on her waist.

"What really happened with that man in the alley?"

Seeing an opportunity, I tug on her ponytail and love the small gasp she makes.

"You want answers? Quid pro quo, Red."

Her eyes narrow while she nibbles on her bottom lip as she thinks about it. Her face is so expressive, so real. A natural beauty. For a redhead, she doesn't have many freckles. I count six small ones that sprinkle across her nose.

"Okay," she finally says.

There's a lot I can't tell her. Stuff about the Society and the Council. The things I've done in the name of both.

"You want to know what really happened in the alley? Simple answer: I have no fucking clue."

Syn makes a disappointed sigh. "I knew you weren't going to be honest with me."

Needing to feel her, I slide a hand up her shirt and splay it across the dip of her lower back.

"It's the truth. After running into you in the hall, I went out the back exit into the alley and he was there, waiting. He had a gun. We fought, and I thought I knocked him out."

"You failed." A small grin crinkles her lips.

She's teasing me. It's progress.

My thumb makes small circles over her soft skin. "It's rare but it happens."

"Are men with guns a regular occurrence for you?"

"Eh."

Her eyes round with surprise. "*Eh?* That's it?"

"Hmm."

She leans back, and my hand presses into her spine so she doesn't tumble off my lap onto the floor.

"Who *are* you?"

"Nuh-uh, gorgeous. Quid pro quo, remember? Besides, that question has already been asked and answered. You know my name, and who my family is. Why pre-med?"

"I want to help people like me."

Wanting to dig deeper, I ask, "Like you?"

She looks down at my chest and fiddles with one of the buttons on my shirt. "People who are damaged."

"Is that what you think you are?"

Because that is not what I see when I look at her. I see a gorgeous woman who snared my attention and has kept it. A woman I'm already half-obsessed with, and I don't know why. She's also a woman who is under my protection. I couldn't save my sister, but I will make sure nothing bad happens to Syn. She reminds me of Dierdre. Innocent and beautiful. A combination that is rare in my world.

"It's my turn to ask a question," she says.

"Go for it."

"May I please get up?"

The blush that has crept across her face probably has a lot to do with how hard my dick is right now, something that can't be helped while she's straddling my lap. But it's her show of deference by asking my permission that further stokes my desire. Syn has proven she can hold her own. Her lack of fear is alluring. But a strong woman who can also be submissive is my goddamn kryptonite.

Reluctantly, I let her go, and she slides off my lap to sit next to me on the couch, tucking her long legs under her and getting comfortable.

"Where are you from?" she asks.

"That's another question."

"Humor me."

I shift so I can rest my arm along the back of the couch. I start playing with her hair again because I can't stop touching her.

"Born in Boston."

Her pretty face lights up. "I knew it!"

A lightbulb of insight goes off. "Is that why you kept saying Boston?"

"I didn't know your name. I could only go by the accent."

I playfully grin at her. "I'm not the one with an accent, *country girl.*"

She groans and rolls her eyes. "I'm going to kill Shelby the next time I see her."

I twist a strand of her hair around my finger. "I like your Southern accent. Say *'y'all.'*"

Her nose wrinkles when I butcher it. "Pass. How old are you?"

Even though it's my turn to ask a question, I reply, "Twenty-three. So is Con. Con and I were born a week apart in July. Hen is twenty-two. His birthday is in October. You're twenty, right? Did you take a gap year or something?"

She pulls her ponytail out of my hand and drapes it over her other shoulder.

"I got held back a grade in school because I was in the hospital. To answer your first question, that's what

Alana tells me."

What an odd thing to say. "You don't know how old you are?"

She lays her head against my arm. "I don't remember a lot of my life. And what I do remember comes in flashes in my nightmares. At least, I think they're memories." She touches her scarred arm. "Why would Constantine ask me where I learned to fight?"

"Hen said you freaked out last night and turned into a murder bot. Not many people can take him on. Have you taken self-defense lessons?" I watch her face closely for any sign of dishonesty.

"No."

"Any type of martial arts?"

A self-deprecating laugh accompanies her fervent "Hell no."

"The way Hendrix told it, you about kicked his ass. He had to knock you out."

"That asshole punched me?"

Seeing as she has no bruises on her face, Hendrix didn't hit her.

I stroke her shoulder. "There are other ways to incapacitate someone that doesn't involve fists."

"I don't remember a lot of what happened last night."

I mostly believe her, but I'm still skeptical. There is so much more to learn about Synthia Carmichael.

"Does that happen a lot? You not remembering stuff?"

"It hasn't happened in a while." Her fingers flex, but I hold tight. Lowering her voice, like she's ashamed to admit it, she confesses, "But recently, yeah. It scares me."

I bring our hands to my lips and kiss her fingers. I'm

not a gentle man. I don't do tenderness. But I want to with her.

"I promise I won't let anything happen to you."

She slips her hand free. "You can't make promises like that. Bad stuff happens. Look at me."

Our eyes meet. In hers, I see so much pain.

"I am looking at you, Red, and I very much like what I see."

Constantine comes back and sets a small plate on the coffee table in front of Syn.

Turkey sandwich. Eat.

She selects one of the perfectly cut triangles from the plate and picks at it. "So, how is this going to work? I have classes and a job. And if you try to interfere with either, I'm going to choke you with this sandwich."

I share a glance with Constantine, but as usual, I can't get a read on what he's thinking.

"One of us will walk you to each class and meet you afterward. We will also drive you to and from work. You do not go anywhere with anyone unless it's me, Con, or Hen."

She pulls a piece of turkey from between the bread, folds it, and pops it into her mouth. "Is all that really necessary?"

Both Constantine and I say yes at the same time. I stare at him in astonishment. When the fuck did he start talking again? I haven't heard him utter one word since we were kids.

I sign, *What the fuck?*

Syn kicks me in the shin with her flip-flop. "Can't you just tell your father or whoever that I'm not a threat?"

Both my and Con's phones go off.

"It's not just him that you have to worry about."

I check the alert that came in. The cameras we installed outside the house are motion-triggered, and an alert is automatically sent to our phones. Hendrix had left right after Con took Syn back to her apartment. Looks like he brought home someone to play with tonight.

Syn stops mid-chew when the front door slams shut.

"It's just Hendrix," I tell her when she looks like she's about to bolt.

A feminine titter hits my ears just as he strolls past, his arm around a familiar blonde. Noticing us, he backs up, dragging the girl with him and making her stumble in her sky-high heels.

"Look who I found at Kappa Cunt."

Hendrix never brings women to the house, and I'm not looking forward to being subjected to the noises of him fucking all night.

"That's not how you say the sorority's name."

The platinum blonde's name is Serena. She's been after Hendrix since sophomore year. He knows this and uses it. The shit he's gotten her to do just for the chance to ride his dick is embarrassing.

He slings her in front of him, then reaches around and cups her breasts through the skintight red dress she's barely wearing. Serena moans like it's the best thing in the world to be groped in front of a room full of people. I bet her father, the venerable Senator Worthington, would be shocked to see the videos we have of his precious daughter. Serena is a very naughty girl with a predilection for three-ways and anything she can snort up her nose.

"Don't really care." He wipes something from her top lip, then shoves his fingers inside her mouth. She obediently sucks them clean. "Not going to give you my cum anymore if you can't swallow it all. Going to have to punish you."

Serena's grin is pure sex. "I look forward to it."

In my periphery, I see Syn frown. She's farm-girl pure, so I'm sure stuff like this is probably scandalous to her innocent eyes.

"Good night, firefly." He winks at Syn and lifts Serena up, dumping her over his shoulder.

"Who's that girl?" Serena giggles as Hendrix carries her out of the living room.

"She's nobody," we hear him answer.

Syn puts down her half-eaten sandwich and touches her arm. I've noticed her do that a few times now.

"I am *not* going to pretend to be that Lothario's flavor of the week. Why can't Constantine be my fake boyfriend?"

Con smiles at her, and she smiles back. Suddenly, I feel like the odd one out, and I don't care for it. Looks like I'm not the only one who is enamored with the gorgeous redhead.

"I already told my father you were Hen's."

"And I just vomited inside my mouth."

Women do some crazy-ass stuff to get Hendrix's attention. He only has to crook his finger, and they drop to their knees, eager to do whatever he tells them to. And I know it's a petty thing to think because Hendrix is one of my best friends, but I like that Syn despises him.

"Sorry you don't like it, but you don't have a choice."

Syn slides the band from her ponytail, gathers her hair on top of her head in a messy bun, and uses the band to secure it in place.

Challenge sparks in her light-blue eyes. "That's where

you're mistaken, Boston. Everyone has a choice. I could choose to tell you to go fuck yourself. I could get up and walk out the front door. I could choose not to believe a word out of your mouth and go back to my nice, cozy apartment."

Anger spikes because that ain't fucking happening. Getting up from the couch, I brace my hands on either side of her head and lean in close, needing her to hear me loud and fucking clear.

"You're so wrong, Red. You lost those choices the moment you stepped out into the alley. You're ours now."

CHAPTER 14

Aoife. Wake up.

My eyes fly open but only darkness greets me. *Fuck.* I'd love to have one night where the goddamn nightmares didn't come.

Scraping my sweat-slicked hair off my face, I stare up at the ceiling, imagining it's the night sky. One star. Two stars. Three. Four. I trace the imaginary constellation I see in my dreams with a finger, connecting the same pattern of shimmering dots that don't exist in real life.

Back at the farm in Dilliwyll, I'd lie in the grass, searching the night sky for answers to my dreams' secrets. Away from the lights of the bigger cities, the view of the heavens was unobstructed and fascinating. It helped remind me that not all things born of fire are ugly.

My legs get tangled in the sheet when I roll onto my stomach to reach over the side of the bed where my phone is lying on the floor. I double tap the screen to wake it up. Three-sixteen a.m.

"Why?" I whine into my pillow.

I'm exhausted but fully awake, two things that do not go together. Peanut butter and jelly. Yes. Chocolate and peanut butter. Absolutely. Hobbling around all day like an extra from *The Walking Dead*, no. Luckily, I have two hours between calculus and biology lecture where I can find a nice shady place out in the quad and snooze for an hour.

Gingerly sitting up, I tap the base of the ball lamp next to me and see the bottle of water and ibuprofen someone left on the nightstand. *Constantine.* The man confounds me. They all do.

Deciding I might as well get up, I shake out two pills and use the water to swallow them down. The floorboards groan when I get out of bed. As soon as my bare feet land on the floor rug, I curl my toes into the hand-tufted shag. The room is actually quite nice. Quiet and comfortable. And if I were being completely honest, much nicer than my little apartment. King bed with a memory foam mattress that feels like a cloud, a secretary desk, and one of those antique-looking wardrobes. The thing I love the most about the room is the inset bench seat at the window that's piled with overstuffed throw pillows. I rearrange them to one side and sit down, using them as a back support.

I left the curtains open when I turned in because I could see the almost full moon from the bed. It's no longer in the same position, having moved along its path from east to west, the same as the sun. The days when the sun and the moon can be seen together in the bright blue sky are my favorite. I equate the moon to be a woman and the sun a man. Two playful lovers. The man gives chase, and every so often, the woman will let him catch her.

A warm draft seeps in through the cracks of the window, and I tuck my knees to my chest. The room isn't as stuffy as it was when Tristan showed it to me, but I know if I try to open the window to allow fresh air to come in, the alarm will go off. Tristan gave me a very brief rundown of the house, pointed out a few of the security cameras, and promised that the bathrooms didn't have any. He never said anything about the bedrooms. Once I was left alone, I searched the room just in case and didn't find anything.

Loneliness hits me hard as I stare out the window into the dark of night. It's an all too familiar feeling. Even though I didn't have any close friends back home, I was never lonely. I had Alana. Darlington is different. I'm on my own for the first time, navigating a new life.

For the millionth time since Tristan boldly asserted that I was moving in, I question my sanity. There's an internal compass inside every person, the one that guides you and keeps you on the path that you were meant to travel. Your true north. Clearly, my compass is broken. Tristan says I have no choice, but he's wrong. I do have a choice. My broken compass led me to them for a reason.

Not wanting to dwell on that, my brain decides it needs caffeine. Tristan said I had the run of the house and could raid the pantry any time if I was hungry. The only thing he didn't share was the code to disarm the alarm, so until one of them gets up, I can't sit outside on the back patio and wait for the sun to rise.

Before I leave the room to go in search of the coffeemaker downstairs in the kitchen, I tie my hair up and slip on my leggings over the boy shorts I wore to sleep. I debate whether to keep on my tank top or change into a long-sleeved sleep shirt to cover my arms. The guys have already seen my scars, so there's no point in hiding them around them anymore.

I haven't figured out yet how I should feel about that. I'm used to gawking stares and disgust, but I haven't gotten that from them at all.

As quietly as I can, I open the bedroom door, which turns out not to be so quiet because the door hinges creak. Loudly. But not loud enough that I don't hear the muffled noises coming from Hendrix's room down the hallway. Sex noises.

I take a few steps closer, drawn to the cries of pleasure being made by the woman Hendrix brought home. The beautiful blonde. A small part of me wants to be her. To know the sexual touch of a man. His hands and mouth kissing me on my mouth, my breasts, my pussy. To feel his weight on top of me, his warm skin pressed to mine, and the flex of his muscles as he moves inside me with slow, deliberate thrusts.

"Give it five minutes, and he'll be fucking her again."

"Jesus!"

Tristan's voice from out of the blue scares the shit out of me. I spin around and smack his chest.

"Don't do that!"

With his shoulder leaning against the doorframe, he grins at me, not remorseful in the least.

"You're the one creeping outside my room."

"I am not," I protest, even though I'm standing right in front of his bedroom door.

He scratches his chest, and I can't help but stare. He's got a tantalizing dusting of dark hair that arrows down from his pectorals and disappears under the low-hanging waistband of his sweatpants. Unlike Hendrix who is covered in tattoos, Tristan only has one. On the left side, right above where his real heart would beat is the swirled shape of a black heart with a lotus flower growing inside it. The design is delicate, not what I would picture a man like him would have inked on his skin.

His grin widens. "Couldn't sleep?"

"Nightmares."

Why the hell did I just say that?

His smile vanishes. "Want to talk about it?"

I had accused Hendrix of having a Jekyll and Hyde complex. I think Tristan does, too. He goes from bossy and demanding to sweet and concerned, or from cocky to boyishly charming.

"Not really." The woman's moans start up again. "I can guess why you're awake."

"I never got to sleep. Serena's been howling like a cat in heat for the last five hours."

I hold in my giggle. She kind of does sound like that.

"I was going to make some coffee. Want to join me? Maybe sit out on the patio and wait for the sun to rise?" I ask, wanting the company to help dispel the sudden loneliness that I'd been feeling.

He takes a loose wisp of my hair and loops it behind my ear.

"Let me grab a shirt. Mosquitoes can be a bitch at this hour."

As soon as he turns his back to me, I cover my mouth to mute the horrified gasp. Ugly lines criss-cross over each other. Some are pinkish in color, some are white and faded. His back is covered with them. Did his father give him those? My hand goes to my side where I carry similar lines of carnage. Ones I was told were caused by a knife. Tristan's don't look like mine—his are longer and wider—but I still feel a certain kinship with him because of them. We are both survivors.

Constantine comes out of his room, looking surly and half asleep, wearing nothing but a tight pair of black Calvins. For the second time this morning, I'm subjected to something that shocks me, but it's not in horror. Complete opposite.

His entire body from his neck to his ankles is covered in ink. I've never seen anything like it. He must have a very high tolerance for pain to sit for the hundreds of hours that must've taken for all of that to be done.

He lifts his hand *hi* when he sees me. And damn it all to hell, why does he have to look so gorgeous in the wee hours of the morning? I'm living in a house with three insanely hot men. It's just not fair. Thank god, it's only temporary. As much as I'd appreciate the daily eye candy, I like having my own space away from other people. It's one of the reasons why I chose to live in an off-campus apartment and not the dorms.

I gesture awkwardly toward Hendrix's room. "Seems like everyone's awake… the noise, and… yeah."

I feel my face heat and know I must be blushing. Not a good look for someone with red hair.

Sorry about that.

"It's fine. I honestly didn't hear it until I came out."

Wondering what's taking Tristan so long, I peek inside his room. It's the same room I woke up in yesterday morning. The bathroom door is closed and light spills out from the gap at the bottom.

My need for coffee and to get away from Serena's shouts of "fuck me harder" have me not wanting to loiter in the hallway any longer.

"Can you show me how to set the coffeemaker going?"

The thing looked expensive and hi-tech and probably requires a degree in engineering to operate.

Constantine nods, and I follow him down the stairs. And yes, I stare at his ass the entire way down.

When we walk into the kitchen, the lights automatically turn on. The first thing I see is my old laptop computer covered in rooster stickers sitting on the counter island where I left it last night after Constantine helped me connect to their Wi-Fi.

"I can do that," I offer when he goes straight for the Keurig.

Sit.

I don't argue and slide a stool out. With him facing away, I study the swirls of color and images covering his back. A weeping angel with blood coming out of her eyes spans from shoulder to shoulder. I'm sitting in front of every woman's fantasy—a sexy, tatted-up man in the kitchen, barely clothed and only in his underwear—and I don't know how to act. I've never been in this situation before. *Just don't stare at his dick when he turns around.*

Looking elsewhere, I notice two left-over scones sitting in a plate covered in plastic wrap. Thankful for something else to focus my attention on, I peel the plastic back and take a bite out of one.

The stool is bar height, tall enough that my feet don't touch the floor. Getting comfortable, I tap the space bar to wake my laptop up. There's a message notification from Alana. When I open our chat, a GIF of a rooster pouring a pot of coffee and saying "Cock-a-doodle-doo mothercluckers" greets me good morning. I burst out laughing.

Alana: Happy official first day of college! I am so very proud of you!

Constantine looks over his shoulder, and those dark eyes fluster the hell out of me.

"Sorry."

He slides a coffee mug my way across the counter island.

"Do you happen to have any of those yellow packets of sweetener?" I ask. I'll take it black if I have to. Just not with milk. Ever.

He offers me a small sugar dish with a tiny spoon sticking out of it.

"I'll just drink it plain. Thanks."

I like your laugh.

Out of all the things he could have said, I'm not prepared for him to say that. I'm also emboldened by it. And curious. There's this tug I feel whenever I'm around him—like we're both opposite poles of a magnet and I'm naturally drawn to him by an invisible force.

"I like your eyes."

...and shutting up now. I pretend that the hot coffee isn't burning the fuck out of my mouth as I sip it to stop myself from saying anything else.

What time do we need to leave?

The clock on my laptop says that it's almost four. The guys are seniors to my lowly freshman, which means we don't have any classes in common. I think it's completely pointless that Tristan insists I have one of them take and pick me up. How dangerous can his father be?

I think I've seen enough of the trauma on his body to know the answer to that question. I want to talk to

Tristan about it, but I know I'm going to need to broach the subject very carefully. I doubt he'd appreciate a virtual stranger sticking her nose into his personal business.

"My calc class is at eight, but I have to stop by the student store and pick up the textbook for it first."

The coffee sloshes over the lip of the mug when Tristan startles me. He rests his chin on my shoulder, and the tease of spearmint hits my nose. It must be his toothpaste.

"What is it with you and roosters?"

I shut my laptop closed to stop his prying, nosy eyes.

"I like them."

I found Cocky Bastard wandering around the farm one day. He was a tiny, fluffy, brown and pale-yellow chick that must have wandered off from another nearby farm. It didn't matter. I found him, therefore, he was mine.

"You really are a country girl."

I tense when he slides an arm around my middle. I don't like people touching my left side.

"Stop."

Constantine had been wiping up the coffee spill with a paper towel and frowns at my sharp rebuke.

"Not you," I tell him, and push Tristan's hand off me. "Please don't touch me there."

"Red—"

A very disheveled Serena stumbles into the kitchen dressed in only a black see-through lace bra and matching panties. She looks a mess. Streaks of mascara score down her cheeks and around her eyes, making her look like a possessed raccoon. I thought she was beautiful when I first saw her, but now without her mask of perfect makeup, not so much. She's too thin, almost boney, and her face is gaunt and sunken in. I'm a nurturer by nature, and I'm half tempted to fix her a sandwich.

"Oh, thank god." She makes a grab for my coffee, but Constantine moves it out of her reach.

"There's a Starbucks right down the street," Tristan informs her.

She wedges herself between me and Tristan like I'm not even there. The problem with being invisible is that someone notices something is missing. They just don't care enough to find out what it is.

Serena leans back against the counter, which only shoves her ample bosom in my direction. Constantine and Tristan don't seem nonplussed that her tits and ass are hanging out all over the place. I'm envious, in a way. I wish I had that much confidence. A bra and panties are no different than a bikini, something you will never find me wearing for obvious reasons.

"Heard you were going to the gala with Katalina."

Tristan has a girlfriend? My gaze darts to him but he's scowling at Serena.

Reaching behind her, she pinches off the corner of the scone I'd been eating. And I just lost my appetite. God only knows what she and Hendrix did upstairs, and I highly doubt she washed her hands before coming down.

"Fuck, no. Who told you that?"

"Little birdie."

I try my best to be stealthy and slip off my stool for a hasty getaway, but Tristan moves and blocks me. Serena finally notices I exist when Tristan plasters himself to my back. I see the second her dissecting appraisal decides I'm not her competition. That I'm beneath her. A nobody. It's something I witnessed a lot in high school. I didn't like it then, and I don't like it now.

"She yours?" she asks Tristan.

The feminist side of me takes affront at her insinuation that I belong to any man. Women are not chattel.

"God, no," I reply.

"Yes," he says.

Well, that's just great. First, I'm supposed to be 'with Hendrix'—or so he wants his father to think—and now, Tristan told Serena I was also with him. Might as well let Constantine join in on the fun.

"I'm with him," I tell her, batting my eyelashes at Constantine.

His mouth quirks to one side.

"Both of them. Got it."

"Got what?" I naïvely ask.

She wiggles a perfectly French-manicured finger between Constantine and Tristan.

"Tristan and Hendrix like to share, so I just assumed..."

She trails off, but the picture she paints is vivid. Tristan and Hendrix like to share women. Have they shared her? I'm instantly revolted by the thought.

Tristan pulls me back when she leans in. "Did you need anything, Serena? Like an Uber?"

She waves him off. "Hendrix will take me."

"Then go get him."

"In a minute. I'm talking to... what's your name?"

"Syn," I helpfully supply.

She zeros in on my scars and pokes at them with a fingernail. "Hendrix said you were fucked up with some hideous shit like Freddy Krueger, but damn, girl, that's just nasty."

Hendrix said? He talked about me to *her*? God only knows what he really said. All those ugly insecurities try to rush forward but I battle them back.

I thought I had left all this behind me in Virginia, but it seems that college is going to be the same old mean girl bullshit from high school. Well, fuck her, and fuck Hendrix.

Tristan jumps to my defense. "Stop being such a catty bitch and apologize."

She doesn't.

"I need to call Mom and get ready. It was nice to meet you," I tell Serena, which is a huge ass lie, but Alana always says to kill them with kindness.

I pick up my laptop and hightail it out of the kitchen and up the stairs. Hendrix's bedroom door is wide open, and the asshole himself is standing there, pulling a black hoodie over his head.

"What's the hurry, firefly?"

I'm pissed and hurt, and it bleeds out into what I say to him. There is no killing it with kindness. Fuck that.

"Next time you want to make fun of me to your girlfriend, come say it to my face, you entitled prick."

"What the fuck are you—"

But I'm done.

The sunrise I had been looking forward to seeing can go to hell. They all can go to hell.

Even though it's juvenile, I take a small amount of pleasure in slamming the bedroom door shut.

CHAPTER 15

Fucking Serena.

I don't know what the hell she said to Syn, but I just got my ass handed to me.

Serena's pussy isn't worth her damn drama. I knew bringing her here was a bad idea, but I did it anyway. And I blame the enigmatic redhead with the innocent blue eyes and Tristan's idiotic plan to appease his father's suspicions for my bad decision.

Grabbing the red dress and matching shoes from the floor, I slow as I pass by Syn's bedroom door. I shouldn't care about her hurt feelings or the pain I saw in her baby blues, and the guilt I'm feeling over both only ticks me off. Syn has gotten under my skin and messed with my head, and I don't like it.

Leaving well enough alone, I go downstairs only to be met with loud arguing from the kitchen. It's too goddamn early for this shit.

Serena sees me as soon as I walk in. She looks completely ravaged, and not in a good way—sexed-up hair, smeared makeup, pallid skin stretched over a stick-thin body. Bad mistakes always appear worse after the fact when clarity comes crashing in.

I just spent hours fucking her—her ass, her pussy, her mouth—searching for that unobtainable high that no woman has been able to give me. Meaningless orgasms that fill an emotional void and only serve to temporarily remind me that I have the capability to feel… *something.*

"Hey, baby. I was just—"

I toss Serena's stuff on the floor at her feet.

"Get the fuck out."

"Thank fucking god," Tristan mumbles.

"But—"

"Now."

She hesitates, debating whether to push back, then bends over to pick up her dress. I steal whoever's coffee off the counter and drink it cold.

Serena may think it's okay to mouth off to Tristan, but she knows not to do it with me. Without a word, she wrestles to put on her tight dress, then slips her feet into her high heels.

"One more thing," I tell her when she starts to leave. "Don't you ever open your mouth to that girl again. Syn is off limits."

Serena makes the mistake of turning around. "But you said she was nobody."

Before Tristan can get to her, I have her by the throat and slammed up against the wall. Her blood-red fingernails break skin as she frantically claws at my hand, but I'm desensitized to the pain. I feed off her fear and panic, growing feral by them. The way small, red capillaries fork across the whites of her eyes like miniature streaks of lightning as I cut off her oxygen. Her erratic, shallow pants as she tries to draw in air. The way her pupils dilate and eclipse the brown of her irises.

"What she is, Serena, is none of your concern. Understand?"

She nods shakily.

"Hen, enough," Tristan says, and I reluctantly let go.

She slumps against the wall, hand to her neck. Fresh tears run tracks through her mascara.

"You know where the door is," I tell her and go into the butler's pantry.

I know Con will have already disengaged the alarm from his phone. I hear the front door close when I reappear with a box of cereal. Of course, Tristan starts right in.

"What the fuck is wrong with you?"

I take out a bowl from the cabinet and a spoon from the utensil drawer and ask my own question.

"What exactly did she say to Syn?"

"Only what you told her."

Con hands me the milk from the fridge. I pour some into the bowl and hand it back.

"I didn't tell her shit."

He knows I don't lie. Not to him or to Con. It's a promise we made to each other when we were kids. Our lives are filled with enough subterfuge.

Tristan pushes my bowl away right as I'm about to dig in.

"You want her. Admit it."

He doesn't have to say which *her* he's talking about. I won't lie to him, but I also don't have to answer him.

"I want an easy fuck. Goodie two-shoes upstairs isn't it."

The words taste bitter on my tongue. A devil like me shouldn't touch an angel like her.

"It's okay to move on." He cuffs my shoulder, and I shrug it off.

Appetite gone, I throw the spoon in the sink.

"Maybe for you."

I can't go there with him now. I can't allow those old memories to surface and pull me under. I'd fucking drown.

"Don't forget you're picking Syn up after class this morning," he reminds me as I walk out.

I give him the British two-fingered salute that looks like a backward peace sign. It's the equivalent of an American middle finger.

I take the stairs three at a time, wanting to grab a shower to wash off Serena's smell from my skin before I head to the gym.

Like a moth drawn to a wildfire, my footsteps backtrack, and I find myself standing outside Syn's room. Wanting her. And hating her for it.

I press my palm flat to the door.

Can you feel me, little firefly? Can you feel the devil standing right outside your door?

CHAPTER 16

I debate whether to call Alana, knowing she'd be up —needing to see a friendly face, wanting her comfort— then decide not to. I can't keep running to her all the time. I need to learn how to stand on my own and deal with my own shit. Alana is my emotional safety net. I know she'll be there to catch me when I fall. But the point of falling is to learn how to get back up.

I am the phoenix.

When the thought comes, I quickly rummage through my carry bag and pull out my journal and pen, desperate to put the thought to paper. Journaling was something I started doing years ago in hopes that it would help me make sense of the nightmares; the ones that came in my sleep, and the ones that haunted me when I was awake.

I have several journals filled with my ramblings and drawings of things my mind conjures. Stuff that doesn't make sense. Crazy stuff. I just wish I knew what it all meant.

Pulling the tie to the soft leather casing, I turn to

the next blank page and start drawing the shape of a phoenix rising from a pyre, its wings outstretched. Within the clutches of its sharp talons is... something. I can never get a clear image of what it is. The flashes I have are so fleeting. My subconscious gives me just a bare glimpse before it steals them back.

Above the phoenix at the top of the page, I write *eefa*. It's what I heard right before I woke up this morning. Is it an acronym or a place? I go to the beginning of the journal. Drawings of fire, phoenixes, and constellations blur past like the flickering images of an animation flipbook. Something catches my attention. Sketches I don't remember drawing. Amorphous black blobs that look like smoke in the shapes of shadowy silhouettes. On the same page, I wrote, "*They all will die.*" What the hell? When did I make this?

Opening my laptop, I do an online search for *eefa*. A whole bunch of stuff relating to energy efficiency turns up. Not helpful. I look up the meaning for shadow people in imagery and get references to useless paranormal shit. Then my fingers type "Tristan Amato" in the search box.

And down the rabbit hole I go.

It takes a little searching because he's not the only Tristan Amato, but I eventually find something. There are several articles about his father and the shipping business he runs, some photographs at various events, mostly for charity. I examine an image taken at some fancy function in Boston last year. Tristan in a tuxedo is orgasm-inducing. He's standing next to a man who must be his father. Other than the obvious age difference, they are mirror images of one another. I stare at the older man—the grim line of his unsmiling mouth and the hardness of his eyes. Does no one notice the monster that lurks within?

I go through a few more search results. For someone from a wealthy and powerful family, Tristan has very little online presence, which is odd. Today, everything is about social media. It's why I mostly stay away from it. What Serena said was a common occurrence for me. I don't need that mean crap from faceless people who want to spout hateful commentary online because they get to hide behind a wall of anonymity. Hard pass. But curiosity gets the better of me, and I open my IG app on my phone.

Searching for Tristan's name, nothing pops up. I look for Constantine. Nothing. But when I type in Hendrix's name, it's a whole other story. Tens of thousands of followers. I get lost scrolling through his posts. Images of him and all the other beautiful people living a carefree, beautiful life. But it's a façade. I've seen glimpses of the darkness they live in. I've seen the evidence of the abuse Tristan has suffered at the hands of his father etched into his back.

"I'd rather you hate me than become one of my father's playthings. He'll break you."

There's a light knocking on my bedroom door right before it opens. I shut my laptop and slide it under my pillow and do the same with my phone and journal.

"I'm not in the mood," I tell Tristan, but of course, he waltzes right on in. At least he knocked this time.

"She's gone."

I pick at my cuticles. "Okay."

His footfalls are muted as he walks across the rug. "I find it interesting that Hendrix has never brought a woman here before. He likes to keep his personal life private. The psychological meaning behind why a guy pulls a girl's pigtails has merit in this case."

I move from the bed to the window bench and grab a pillow to hold in my lap. I can see his ghostly outline in the window glass, and it reminds me of the shadow drawing in my journal.

"Is there a point you're trying to make?"

Tristan takes something out of his pocket and places it on my nightstand.

"There's this rare orchid in Australia, *Rhizanthella*. Its flowers are pink and quite lovely, but unless you know where to look, you don't see them."

Intrigued, I ask, "Why?"

He kneels behind me, and our gazes meet in the window glass.

"Because they grow completely underground. You have to dig just below the surface to find one."

His hand reaches around and grips my neck. It's nothing like the way Hendrix grabbed me. Tristan's thumb tenderly caresses under my chin as he gradually tips my face until I'm gazing at myself in our dual reflection.

"Do you see the orchid, Syn?"

The pressure around my neck tightens when I swallow. It's not painful. The opposite. The slight constriction is unexpectedly… pleasurable.

"I don't understand," I rasp.

The heat of his breath on my neck incites my senses even more.

"Tell me what you see?"

His eyes shimmer off the clear glass and bore into mine. I try to avert my gaze, but his hand holds fast and refuses to let me look away.

Ugly. Damaged. Unworthy. Freakish. That's what I see when I look at myself.

"Chaos," I answer.

His lips tease my outer ear. Such a simple thing that sends my nerve endings off kilter.

"Beautiful chaos. Every damaged, broken piece of you is beautiful."

What he says makes it almost impossible to breathe. So many emotions well up inside me. Constantine said I was beautiful. Now Tristan. I want to believe them. Am desperate to, but… my hand curls around the rough flesh of my left arm.

Tristan shifts so that I can see him fully in the window through eyes blurred with unshed tears.

"Do you trust me?"

My mouth opens to say no, but something stops me. I'm terrified to trust anyone. Alana is the only person I've truly let in. I'm scared that if I let Tristen see me, the *real* me, he'll be disappointed. Or worse, he'll look at me with pity.

"I can't," I admit truthfully.

"You can, Red. I'll show you every day that you can." His hand moves down the length of my neck, but his eyes never leave mine in the reflection. "Downstairs, you told me not to touch your left side."

Careful of my bandage, his lips brush across the top of my shoulder. Filaments of desire slowly unfurl like the petals of a flower after they're kissed by the first rays of the sun. My eyes close, and I shudder out a breath when his lips trail back up my neck to my ear.

"I will never take from you without your permission." His nose buries in my hair at my temple, and he breathes in deeply. "You can trust me, Syn. Tell me to stop, and I will."

I'm overwhelmed by him. Seduced by his promises. So, when his hands begin to move down my arms, I'm powerless to speak that one word.

Because I don't want him to stop.

He positions me so that he takes my weight, my back flush with his chest.

"Lean into me and close your eyes."

My head nestles into the crook of his shoulder as my body turns to putty under his exploring fingers.

He starts at my hands, tracing the outside of each finger.

"How does that feel?" he asks.

It's strange, but oddly familiar, like a phantom memory.

"It tickles a little. What cologne do you wear?"

The long-sleeved button-up I was wearing yesterday carried his scent. With my eyes closed, my other senses take over.

"L'Homme."

"I like it."

He slips his hands under mine, threading our fingers together. With my eyes shut, I can feel how much larger his hands are to mine, and I marvel at the juxtaposition.

"I'm moving to your wrists."

Tristan waits a second, allowing me time to say no, and when I don't, his fingers curl around each wrist, his thumbs creating soothing circles that feel like brushstrokes on a painter's canvas.

"More?"

"Please."

"Your skin is so soft. Can you feel me?" he asks when he gets to the uneven, discolored part of my left arm.

The explosion of sensations that erupt everywhere he touches is indescribable. God, yes, I can feel him. I shouldn't be able to, but I do. Every cell thrums and pulses with new life. An awakening. The tears that refused to fall before, cascade down my cheeks. To be touched like this, to have someone *want* to touch me—

I bring the hand his father hurt to my lips and hold it there. I want to show him that his scars are beautiful, too.

"Thank you," I rasp, choking up.

His arms come fully around me, holding me.

"You're welcome."

My mind and my body wage a war with my conscience, wanting things I know I shouldn't.

I open my eyes just in time to see the sky lighten with the sunrise outside the window... and the reflection of Constantine as he soundlessly closes my bedroom door.

CHAPTER 17

I stand motionless in the center of campus among the old brick buildings and Neo-Georgian river houses and take in every detail of the magnificence that is Darlington Founders University. Even though I'd moved to Darlington two weeks earlier, it hadn't hit me until that very second. I'm really here. It's thrilling and heart-wrenching and scary and exciting. And I think I may have to throw up.

"I'm going to be a doctor," I say out loud to no one with all the awe I'm feeling.

I reach for Constantine's hand, needing an anchor to keep me grounded. Today is the first day of the brighter future I planned for myself. A stepping stone to medical school and then, hopefully one day, my own private practice. Or maybe Doctors Without Borders. It's something I've thought about more than once. The possibilities of what I want to accomplish with my life are endless.

When Constantine squeezes my hand, I look up at him with a watery smile. I must be hormonal because

I've teared up at least four times in the past two days. I don't cry. Ever. Tears don't make things better. All they do is give me a headache.

The campus is already buzzing with early morning activity as students rush around. You can pick out the freshman from the other classes just by their facial expressions. Some look overwhelmed and lost, some amazed and giddy. But the one thing that stands out like a sore thumb is me, based on the furtive glances I keep getting from passersby.

I'm the odd one out from most of the people here who come from well-off families. Look at the way I'm dressed. A lot of the girls walking around are wearing cute skirts, summer dresses, or halters that expose their toned midriffs. Because I wanted as much coverage as possible and not caring that it would be eighty degrees by afternoon, I wore my powder blue long-sleeved slub-knit shirt with the thumb holes at the bottom of the sleeves and yoga leggings. I gathered my hair into a high ponytail since I didn't want to waste any time this morning blowing it dry. Compared to everyone else, I'm an ugly weed among a garden of roses.

My stomach reminds me that I only had half a bite of a cinnamon scone for breakfast and a long-ass day ahead of me. I need sustenance and an IV of coffee if I'm going to survive three classes.

"I'm hungry. Feed me."

Constantine's eyebrow arches in that sexy way only a few men can pull off without it looking comical.

He's been more quiet than usual since we left the house. I tried starting a conversation with him several times in the car on the way over, but the drive only took three minutes. We could have walked from their house to campus in the same amount of time.

"Breakfast burrito. Hash browns. Pancakes. Something with bacon. I'd even go for a protein smoothie," I say when he doesn't sign a response.

I can't read his mind, and I don't know if his silence is because of what he thought he saw when he walked in on Tristan and me. Something I haven't been able to stop thinking about since it happened.

Placing my hands on Constantine's broad shoulders, I raise up on tiptoe until our eyes meet. I cross my eyes and make a funny face and get nothing.

"How about you *hepeat* it."

"*Hepeat*?"

I feel immense joy when I hear him speak again. A flurry of butterflies comes to life inside my stomach, their thousands of wings flapping like crazy and creating havoc.

"Say something else."

The other eyebrow arches.

"Nuh-uh. You started it. I heard you, and you can't unsay it," I tell him.

I'm about to switch to emotional blackmail to get him to say something, *anything*, when he asks, "What does *hepeat* mean?"

The question comes out gravelly and halting, but it's the most wonderful thing I've ever heard.

When my feet begin to cramp from being on tiptoe for too long, I lower and loop my arm through his to keep my balance.

"*Hepeat* is when a woman says something and is ignored, but when a man says the exact same thing, everyone listens."

He smiles—a real honest-to-goodness smile—and I'm

struck stupid. Constantine Ferreira is the sun poking through the clouds after a summer thunderstorm. Bright, blinding, and spectacular.

As quickly as it formed, his smile disappears and is replaced with displeasure. Not at me but at something behind me. Pinpricks of unease skitter up my arms, and I turn to see what he's looking at. There's a trio of girls congregated around two men on the other side of the quad. I remember seeing them at the Bierkeller on Saturday. They were sitting at the back corner table of the bar. Big guys, blond hair, hard faces, looked like carbon copies of each other.

One of them is staring right at us. The twin with the buzzed haircut. Constantine's entire demeanor goes rigid with tension. It's his reaction that triggers the recollection of what Tristan said about the fucktwins. How dangerous they are.

"Is that them?" I ask.

"Yes."

One word said with such cold hostility, it makes me shiver. The Constantine I was just joking with is gone. Someone else has taken his place. It's another reminder that I really don't know him or Tristan or Hendrix at all.

"Come on."

It takes a couple of tugs on his hand for Constantine to start following. He swiftly takes out his phone and starts texting someone, and I decide to leave him alone and not ask questions. By the time I stop by the student union and pick up a sausage and egg biscuit to go, I only have five minutes to get to my calculus class. I guess I'll pick up my textbook afterward. The professor will be going over the syllabus today anyway, so I shouldn't need it.

When we get to Barnaby Hall where my first class is held, Constantine stops us at the bottom steps and takes my bag off his shoulder. He'd been carrying it so I wouldn't have to.

I want to ask him if he's okay. I want to ask him more about the fucktwins. Instead, I ask, "Do I meet you out here after?"

He shakes his head no.

Hendrix will meet you.

Joy. Not looking forward to that. This entire situation of being carted to and from places is ridiculous. I'm on a crowded college campus, it's daytime, and I'll be surrounded by people. But Tristan is adamant.

Constantine jerks his chin to tell me to go. I hate that we're back to nonverbal communication, but I know how difficult it is for him to talk. The fact that he even wants to try to talk to me means the world. I get a part of him that not many others do.

Wanting to leave him with something good to help dispel the bad mood that seeing the twins put him in, I peck a quick kiss to his stubbled cheek.

"Thank you for walking me to class."

Settling my bag on my good shoulder, I dash up the stairs into Barnaby Hall and head to the auditorium. Throngs of other students mill about in the hallway, talking and laughing. The energy is insane, and I soak it in. My high school in Dilliwyll had two hundred students total. The auditorium I walk into looks like it holds more than that. I'm amazed to see so many people already seated—for a calculus class.

"Excuse me," someone says, and I sidestep out of the way so I'm not blocking the aisle.

Needing to share my excitement, I snap a quick photo

of the room with my phone and send it to Alana.

Me: I'm officially here!!!

As more people come in, I park myself in the aisle seat of the last row. It'll make it easier to leave when class gets out. Dropping my bag to the floor, I take out a spiral notebook and pencil to take notes and store my phone in the front zipper pocket.

"Do you mind if I sit there?"

I glance up at the girl who spoke and am met with a cheery smile and bright brown eyes behind green-rimmed glasses. If Kerry Washington had a younger sister, it would be this girl.

"Not at all."

I angle my knees so she can slide past me. The auditorium seats are similar to an airplane's with their folding tables attached to the right armrest.

"I think you dropped this. It's pretty. What flower is it?"

She hands me the pink and white pressed flower that Tristan left on my nightstand. I found it when I got out of the shower.

"Oh, my gosh, thank you so much."

I take it from her and rummage around in my bag for my journal. I turn to the page where I keep my pressed five-leaf clover and slip the *Rhizanthella* next to it.

"My friend said it was an orchid that grows completely underground."

"Really? That's cool." She points to the clover. "Did you know that finding one of those is one in a million?"

I tightly cinch the tie around my journal to make sure Tristen's flower doesn't fall out again and put it back in my bag.

"Nerd after my own heart," I reply, and her smile

widens.

"I'm Raquelle. Lowly freshman pleb and LA native."

From her designer messenger bag, she takes out one of those two-in-one laptops that can also be used as a tablet. She smells like vanilla, and all it does is make my stomach mad that I haven't yet eaten the breakfast biscuit I bought.

"Syn. Also a freshman."

"Which dorm do you live in? I got stuck in Danby."

How to answer that? I decide not to use the same lie I told Alana about sleeping over at Shelby's. Maybe a partial truth?

"I, um… I'm staying with some friends until I can go back to my apartment."

Luckily, I'm saved from further questions when a side door opens and in walks who must be the professor and two other people who look my age.

"Everyone, please find a seat and put your phones on silent."

Cacophony ensues when two-thirds of the room take out their phones.

"Where's your phone?" Raquelle whispers.

"In my bag."

"Get it out."

"Why?" I ask, even though I'm doing just that.

"So I can give you my number." I unlock my screen, and she takes over, entering her contact details. She sends herself a text. "Now I have yours, too."

CHAPTER 18

As soon as the professor dismisses us, Raquelle and I are out of our seats.

"I hate to bail, but I've got twenty minutes to get to my class."

We're at the head of the mass exodus and are the first to push through the heavy entrance doors that lead to outside.

"Which class?" I ask, shielding my eyes from the intense sun.

The humidity jacked up since this morning and with the clothes I'm wearing, I'm already starting to sweat. Lovely. I search for Hendrix but don't see him. I'll give him five more minutes and then I'm out of here.

"Art History. You?"

"I have biology at eleven. I was hoping to get a short nap in."

We stop at a hedgerow of yaupon bushes next to the stairs, and I take out my phone. Constantine added each of their numbers and set up a group chat but there's nothing from any of them.

"Late night?" She unclips a glass water bottle filled with lemon slices from her bag.

"More like wee hours of the early morning."

Raquelle shifts her bag and unscrews the top to her water. "Want to walk with me?"

"I'm supposed to wait here for a friend."

She leans in for a hug, taking me by surprise. I'm not used to spontaneous shows of affection from people.

"Seeing as I'm going to be sitting next to you for the semester, consider us friends, too. Text you later," she says and skips off.

While I wait, I unwrap my sausage biscuit and devour it in three bites, then I spend the next four minutes people-watching. The main campus is centered around a large grassy quad with buildings lining the perimeter. A lot of students are already taking advantage of the beautiful day and warm weather. A half dozen sweaty, shirtless guys fling a frisbee back and forth. A few sunbathers lie on blankets in the grass, while others sit under the shade of the maple and sweet gum trees and work on their laptops.

When Hendrix doesn't materialize, I wait another five minutes, getting more irritated as each second passes. Such an asshole. If Tristan thinks I'm going to stand around every day for one of them to show up, he can kiss my ass. And I'm damn well not going to text them about it. It should be the other way around. If Hendrix is going to be late, it's just common courtesy to let the other person know.

That sudden, prickly feeling you get when you feel eyes on you hits me, causing the hairs on my neck to stand.

Screw this.

Clutching the strap to my bag, I take the sidewalk that cuts through the middle of the quad toward the large fountain. A statue of the university founder, Matthew Darlington, sits atop a rearing horse, as jets of water geyser up in a circle around him. Why are all the historic statues either men on horses or men with one hand tucked inside their shirts?

Spotting the Ionic columns of the library, I head that way. I can find a nice quiet corner behind the stacks and enjoy the air conditioning until my next class.

The guy behind the reception desk looks up when I walk in, then goes back to the book he was reading. The much cooler air inside the library washes over my face and feels wonderful. I may have to rethink my clothing choices tomorrow if it's going to be another hot day, but I don't know what else I could wear other than changing my leggings for shorts. I'm just not ready to expose all my flaws to new strangers, so for the time being, the long sleeves stay. When fall weather hits, it won't make a difference.

When I get to the elevator, I check the signage to see which floor the history books are located, figuring no one would be there at this time of day. Pressing the button to summon the elevator, I count the numbers down as they display on the digital panel until it reaches my floor. As soon as the doors slide open, I step inside. So does someone else.

And that's when I know that the eyes on me were real.

The doors shut, sealing me inside. With him. Shit.

"Floor?" one of the fucktwins politely asks, no hint of the Russian accent I was expecting.

I hide my bag behind me and edge away until I'm plastered against the elevator wall, so I can quietly unzip the front pouch where I stored my phone.

"Five, please."

I mentally call Hendrix every foul thing I can think of because now would be a good time for me to have my pepper spray and knife handy. He hasn't given either back to me.

"You're the first girl I've ever seen Constantine with. I wonder what makes you so special."

Within the confines of the small space, his deep voice booms and makes me flinch. Where's my goddamn phone?

"I'm sorry. Have we met?"

Thank god my voice stays steady because my heart is racing. He must hear it. I sure as hell can.

"Aleksander Stepanoff. I'm an… acquaintance of your boyfriend."

Not 'friend of your boyfriend' or 'I know your boyfriend,' but an acquaintance. What an odd thing to say.

I also don't correct him about Constantine being my boyfriend. My only concern at the moment is getting off this ride and away from him.

Light-gray eyes watch me with amused interest. Aleksander is a very big guy. Bigger than Constantine, which is saying something. The small elevator feels claustrophobic with him in it.

He holds out his hand, and I assume he's offering it for me to shake, but he reaches around me and slips my bag from behind me.

"Give that back," I say with more courage than I feel.

How the fuck long does it take to go up five floors?

He zips up the pocket and transfers my bag to his other hand. Like Hendrix and Constantine,

Aleksander's arms are covered in tattoos all the way down to his fingertips. But what draws my gaze are the letters written across the upper knuckles of each finger that spell out ANGEL and DEVIL.

The elevator jars to a stop, and the doors open.

"After you," he says, holding his arm out to prevent the doors from closing.

So many things come to mind for me to say. Excuses I can make so I can get the hell out of there. *I'm meeting a friend. My boyfriend is picking me up. I'm here for a study group, which means there will be a group of people around.*

"Forgive me for not being one of the girls you see in the movies that stupidly follows the serial killer to their demise. I don't know you, which means I'm not getting off this elevator with you."

He smiles, and a dimple appears on his left cheek. It helps soften his rugged face.

"If I wanted to hurt you, I would have done so already."

His cold tone of voice tells me he's not kidding.

"Answer is still no. Give me back my bag."

I'm shocked as shit when he hands it over and steps off the elevator. I hit the button for the first floor and mash the 'close doors' button—which *never* works fast enough on any elevator—and heave a sigh of relief when the doors start to come together.

"See you around, Synthia," Aleksander says.

His cocky smile vanishes when the doors finally close.

How in the hell does he know my name?

"Dammit!"

My hands shake as I try to get to my phone.

Come on… come on. Constantine's contact is the first I

see.

Me: I just met Aleksander Stepanoff. And not by choice. He followed me into the library.

The elevator gets to the ground floor, and I haul ass out of the library. As soon as I'm outside and feel the warm sun on my face, I'm able to calm down. *I'm not alone. There are people.*

Constantine: Where's Hendrix?

I speed walk to the busier part of the quad where the six guys are still throwing frisbee. Ducking behind a tree, I lean back against it and catch my breath.

Me: He never showed up.

Constantine: Where RU?

Me: Main quad.

Constantine: Stay there. Don't move.

I peek around the trunk, half expecting Aleksander to pop up again like a bogeyman. When I don't see him or feel that icky sensation like I had before, my heart slows to a more normal beat.

"Where the fuck were you?"

Hendrix appears out of nowhere, lines of anger creasing his pretty face.

"Will everyone stop scaring me?"

My shout turns a few heads and garners the attention of the group of frisbee guys. Hendrix glares them down, and unbelievably it works. They slink back to their game.

He crowds me against the tree and gets into my face. "You were supposed to wait outside for me."

I've had enough of men thinking they can intimidate me today.

"I *did*. I waited for ten minutes," I reply through gritted teeth, incensed by his arrogance. "You know what? I don't need to explain anything to you."

Constantine said to stay put, but he didn't say which part of the quad, and right now, I don't want to be anywhere near Hendrix. Which is why I walk away. I'm too angry.

"Syn, stop."

Not a chance.

"You're off babysitting duty. I texted Constantine."

The fountain and statue come into view.

"Will you bloody fucking stop?"

It's like time fast forwards. One second, I'm walking. The next second, I have my hand around his throat, much like the chokehold he gave me the other night. His mouth is moving but there's no sound other than the ringing in my ears.

"Red. Let him go."

Tristan's voice penetrates through the high-pitched noise. When did he get here? I back away from Hendrix, only to bump into Constantine.

"What's going on?"

But I know. I lost time again.

"Somebody's got a temper. Kind of like the other night when you—"

Hendrix doesn't see Tristan rear his fist back.

"You had one fucking job to do. Meet her after class."

Hendrix rubs his jaw. "Hit me again and we're going to have problems."

"You're my goddamn problem."

"And I'm not her fucking keeper."

The two of them face off, a battle of wills being played out in public for everyone to see.

"Eyes are watching," Constantine says.

All heads turn to the right. There's a girl pointing her

phone in our direction. Tristan moves to the other side of Hendrix and blocks the girl's view of me.

"You're talking now?"

Constantine acts like he didn't hear Hendrix. He cradles my face between his hands.

Are you okay? he silently mouths, but I'm able to read his lips.

Tristan pulls me away from Constantine. "Tell me exactly what Aleksander said to you."

A sullen Hendrix crosses his arms over his chest. "Aleksander talked to you?"

Can't they give me a damn second to think? I sit down on the retaining wall of the fountain. Spray being blown by the wind sprinkles down on me in a fine mist.

Tristan's profile blots the sun when he moves to stand in front of me. "Red, I need to know exactly what he said."

Behind the rage is deep worry. It's the worry I hear that coaxes me to answer him.

"He saw me with Constantine before class. When Hendrix didn't show, I went to the library. Aleksander got on the elevator with me. Introduced himself. Mentioned Constantine. Said he could hurt me anytime he wanted, or something to that effect. He knew my name."

I know I'm babbling and probably not making much sense.

"Fuck, firefly."

"Don't," I snap at Hendrix. I don't want to hear it or the nickname he calls me.

Tristan squats to my level. "Did Aleksander touch you?"

"No."

"Can I touch you?"

Years in the future, when I look back on today, I'm pretty sure his question is what I'm going to remember. Not the first-day jitters, or meeting Raquelle, or what Serena said. Not even coming face to face with Aleksander Stepanoff for the first time. They all pale in comparison to Tristan asking my permission to touch me.

"A hug would be nice."

His handsome face breaks out in a smile brighter than the giant yellow ball floating in the clear blue sky above.

"You got it, Red."

He wraps his arms around me, and I sink forward into his embrace, giving myself a few seconds of comfort before I pull away. Tristan brushes his hand down the length of my ponytail.

"I'll handle it. Con is going to stay with you for the rest of the day."

I swallow my protest when Hendrix says, "I can watch her."

Oh, hell no.

Tristan's eyes cut to Hendrix. "Con stays with her. You're coming with me."

CHAPTER 19

The bell tower on the other side of campus takes about twenty minutes to get to by foot.

Me: How is she?

Con sends an image. It's at an odd angle, but I can clearly make out Syn's mess of red hair and her head resting on Con's thigh. I save the picture to my private cloud storage.

Con: Popped her earbuds in and curled up next to me under a tree in the quad. Passed out as soon as she closed her eyes. Napping.

I've noticed how comfortable Syn acts around Con. I've also noticed how he acts around her. Con ignores the world and everyone in it. But for some unexplainable reason, he responds to Syn. He fucking talked. He hasn't spoken a word to either Hen or me since we were twelve.

Me: I think it's time to do a deep dive.

Con: It'll take time. Can't go through regular channels.

Me: Do what you can.

Once we reach the building that houses the tower, I pocket my phone.

My father, and now Aleksander, have taken an interest in Syn. And as reluctant as I am to admit it, Hendrix was right about something being off with her. I witnessed what she did in the quad, that 'flip' Hendrix had mentioned.

The small lobby is empty when I pull the doors open and walk inside. Past Society members at Darlington Founders used the bell tower for meetings… and other things. The second and third floors were refurbished into apartments, and it's where the fucktwins live while here. I don't know which floor is Aleksander's, but it doesn't matter. Either twin will do.

The doors to the elevator are already open and waiting. He knows we're here.

Stepping inside with Hendrix right beside me, I mash the button for the third floor and wait for the doors to close. I can smell him—the heavy, spicy amber scent of the cologne Aleksander likes to wear lingers in the small confines of the elevator box. It's nauseating.

Hendrix grunts. "Are you going to be a bitch and ignore me for the rest of the day?"

Pretty much. I'd been doing a great job of it for the last quarter hour.

I can see Hen's surly reflection in the polished stainless-steel walls. If I say anything right now, it'll be with my fist when I lay his ass out. He's lucky I held back in the quad and pulled my punch.

All he had to do was meet Syn after class. One simple, easy thing. Aleksander would have never been able to get near her if Hendrix did what he was supposed to fucking do. I promised her that she would be safe with us. Aleksander approaching her so soon after the incident in the alleyway only solidifies my suspicions that she really is the woman the guy was targeting that night. But why?

The lift slows and bounces to a stop.

"How are we playing this?"

Regardless of our fight, Hendrix will have my back. Always.

I don't answer because the doors slide open.

Sitting on a couch like a king in his castle, Aleksander smiles and lifts a tumbler of amber liquid to his lips, taking a sip.

"Tristan."

"Aleksander," I reply, carefully approaching him.

That all too familiar darkness that lives inside me slithers its poison into my bloodstream. It whispers the sweet words of revenge in my ear. How easy it would be to strangle the life out of him until his gray eyes clouded over with the black of death.

"Would you care for a drink?" he offers, looking uninterested and unaffected, but the tension radiating off him says otherwise.

He can cut the hospitality bullshit.

I take a seat in the leather armchair across from him, and Hen purposefully stands behind me, protecting my back.

We're not stupid. Aleksei is around somewhere. The twins never go anywhere without the other. It's fucking creepy.

Setting his glass down on the coffee table, Aleksander flicks his gaze to Hendrix. "Knight."

In typical Hendrix fashion, I catch the middle finger in my periphery that he gives to Aleksander. All that does is make the cocky fucker smile. He and his brother are the only two people I know who aren't afraid of Hen. Probably because they're as crazy as he is.

Another lesson my father taught me well: never let others see your emotions. Emotions are a vulnerability. A weapon that can be used against you.

"You wanted my attention, you got it."

"Funny that, but we'll get to your redhead in a minute."

This motherfucker.

He juts his square jaw at Hendrix. "Heard Serena isn't too happy with you."

It's no secret Aleksander has been fucking Serena the past year. I think she does it hoping to get a rise out of Hendrix.

I feel Hen subtly shift behind me.

"She was very happy this morning when I was dick deep in her ass."

Aleksander's smirk falls, and a scowl forms along his forehead. He sits forward, elbows propped on his knees and hands clasped together.

"Help me out because I'm a little confused."

And I'm already bored with this conversation. "Isn't that normal for you?"

He picks his glass back up, but his fingertips are white with how hard he's gripping it.

"Katalina will be displeased to find out that you're slumming it with a waitress—"

I talk over him. "I don't give a shit what Katalina thinks."

"—here on a scholarship granted by his family," he finishes, taking another swallow of whiskey while nodding at Hendrix. "Miss Carmichael must be something extraordinary to have you and Constantine sniffing after her. She's not Society."

Aleksander seems to know as much about Syn as we do, which is jack shit. But the fact that he's been looking into her is not good. Which makes me question even more what went down at the Bierkeller the other night.

"You and your brother seemed very interested in her the other night."

He counters with, "Interesting that she's now living in your house when she just leased an apartment."

The air grows thick with animosity. His is a veiled threat. One I need to defuse quickly. If he thinks Syn means anything to me, no telling what he'll do.

"Seems Serena's been running her mouth about shit she knows nothing about. The girl isn't mine or Con's. She's Hendrix's."

I about choke on the words when I say them.

Because fuck that. Syn is *mine.*

The stiff leather of the couch squeaks when Aleksander repositions and reposes back into the cushions, a look of incredulity on his face. "She doesn't mind you fucking other women in front of her?"

"She doesn't watch. Not her style," Hendrix flippantly answers.

Aleksander's eyes brighten. "Sounds like she's fair game then."

Hen's hand comes down on my shoulder to hold me in place, so I don't lunge over the coffee table and beat the shit out of him.

"Are you really that desperate for *all* my sloppy seconds?"

Aleksander slams the glass down on the table. "Fuck you, Knight."

I'm fed up with the posturing and want to get out of there.

"Was there a point you wanted to make at the library or do you just like stalking innocent women?"

"Miss Carmichael is far from innocent if she's his."

That's it. Time to go.

"We're done," I tell him.

Standing, I catch Aleksei watching from the kitchen and eating a sandwich. The thing about Aleksei is that he's the more dangerous of the two brothers. Quiet and unpredictable. And very protective of his twin.

Aleksander lifts his bulky six-foot frame and stands as well. "Things between us are just getting started, Tristan. You have no idea what's coming for you."

What-*the fuck*-ever. I'm not going to pander to his inane threats. I acknowledge Aleksei with a chin lift as Hendrix and I get back on the elevator.

"Gun, right side holster," I murmur under my breath.

"See it."

The ride to the ground floor is done in silence. We're vulnerable inside this damn thing, so as soon as fresh air greets me when we step outside into the sunshine, I breathe it in. It doesn't help. Needing an outlet for the anger eating me, I round on Hendrix and shove him back against the building.

"What happened inside just now is your fault."

Those blue eyes fire with defiance. Hendrix can be a stubborn ass when he feels cornered.

"If that's what you want to tell yourself." He grips the wrist of my arm that's holding him in place and twists, and I unwillingly let go. "You know he says that shit to get a reaction. The guy lives to fuck with you."

I start walking. We have class in twenty.

The entire university experience is a stupid pretense. An unnecessary education because we'll inherit our families' legacies. We don't need degrees to run the business. We have more money than we know what to do with. But god forbid if we each don't graduate with an MBA from this pretentious, overpriced university. It was the same with the boarding school in Switzerland. The Society and its fucking rules that everyone must adhere to.

"We cannot allow the Stepanoffs to get a seat on the Council."

Hendrix's long strides catch up with me. "They won't, no matter how hard Con's father tries to sell it. They've burned too many bridges and made too many enemies. No other member will back them. So, stop worrying."

As long as Aleksander's breathing, I won't be able to let my guard down.

And from his parting remark, he's up to something.

Days like today are hard ones to push through. There's never any peace. No real happiness. I didn't ask for this life. I don't want it. I'm the circumstance of my birth. The Amato heir. The future king to a kingdom I plan to burn to the ground the second I get the chance. Wealth and power mean nothing to me.

I watch other students as they pass. They look so normal. Happy. I envy them. What would it be like to be them? To not regret every morning I wake up, knowing the future that awaits me. There is no happy ever after for men like me, Hendrix, and Constantine.

Just as we get to the west end of the quad, I slow my gait when I see Con and Syn. The serene scene before me takes my goddamn breath away. She's fast asleep on his lap, and he's looking down at her, stroking her hair. A tortured killer with a black soul and a beautiful, damaged angel with a mysterious dark past.

I sidestep closer to Hendrix and lower my voice.

"Take a good, hard look. Regardless of how much you want to deny you want her, and regardless of whatever past she survived that we don't fully know about yet, you protect her, so he gets to experience that for a little while longer. Don't take that away from him."

Hendrix huffs, then nods. "Fine. I won't be late again to pick her up after class."

Con raises his head at that moment, and I tap my watch to remind him to wake her before her eleven o'clock class.

"Come on. Higher education awaits. Then we're hitting the gym. I need to pound the shit out of the bag for a while."

CHAPTER 20

"I met a girl in calculus class. Seems nice," I tell Alana as I change.

There's a distinct smell to the outdoors that clings to my clothes. It's like a musty, sour smell. Alana used to complain about how many loads of laundry she'd have to do because every time I went outside, I'd have to put on a fresh set of clothes as soon as I came back in. The doctor who diagnosed my PTSD said I displayed obsessive-compulsive traits. I disagree. I already look gross. I don't need to smell gross as well.

Not knowing where to put my dirty clothes because I don't have a hamper, I fold them and leave them on the bathroom vanity. I'll need to ask Tristan if they have a washing machine. They may just send everything to a service or the dry cleaners. Two things I can't afford. I can always stop by my apartment and use the tiny washer-dryer tower it came with. The sink or shower would do as well. Alana and I had to hand wash our clothes for a week one time after a big ice storm took down the power lines.

"That's wonderful. What's her name?"

I grab my phone off the bathroom counter and head over to the window bench. The sun is about to set.

"Raquelle. We exchanged numbers. See? I'm being proactive and meeting new people."

"I wasn't worried you would."

I laugh and settle back against the pillows. "Yes, you were."

Alana never pushed me to be more social at home, but I knew my aversion to people and preference to be alone bothered her. I think she thought she failed me in some way because I didn't get the same experiences as my peers. I was in and out of the hospital a lot. I didn't date or go to parties or have friends.

I wonder what she would think of me now living with three men who are virtual strangers.

"Did you meet anyone else?"

A tiny bat swoops down in front of the window chasing its evening meal, and I get distracted as I watch its erratic pattern. Something moves in the backyard, and at first, I think it might be a deer. I sit up straighter when I see it's Tristan. He's sitting in the backyard next to a lone bush covered in red bell-shaped flowers, arms circled around his knees that are tucked to his chest, staring off into the distance like he's worlds away in his thoughts right now.

Being as vague as possible because I don't want her to know about the guys yet, I reply, "I met a few other people. Enough about my boring day, what did you do?"

The less questions she asks, the less guilty I'll feel about lying to her.

"Typical day. Nothing exciting. Miss having you around."

I hate that she's there by herself. It would be nice if she could meet someone. Go out on a date. Something. Alana is as closed-off as I am.

A delicious smell wafts into my bedroom from downstairs.

"I'm going to grab dinner and then get some work done."

The professors already piled a ton of reading on us for the week. I thought first days were supposed to be going over the syllabus for the semester.

"Okay, sweetheart. Check in with me at some point tomorrow. Love you."

"Love you, too."

With one last glance at a contemplative Tristan, I hook my phone up to charge and head down the stairs to the kitchen.

My hungry stomach twists into unfamiliar knots when I see Hendrix cutting vegetables at the counter island. A quick glance around shows no sign of Constantine. As soon as he brought me back to the house after my last class, he disappeared.

Soft guitar music starts playing from somewhere, and Hendrix hums the melody as he juliennes a carrot. I recognize the song and find myself mentally humming right along with him.

I take a hesitant step into the kitchen, not sure if I should offer to help or turn around and leave.

"Can I do anything?"

Hendrix's blue eyes lift and pin me in place. "No."

Not deterred, I ramble, "I love to cook. Did it all the time back home. I make a mean country fried steak and homemade buttermilk biscuits with brown gravy and caramelized onions."

He reaches for a yellow onion and slams it down on the cutting board. Using a large butcher's knife, he dices the onion into small cubes.

"I don't need your help."

Okay, then. I rub my suddenly nervous hands over the fronts of my thighs and look around.

"I could set the table or get drinks prepared."

He turns around and throws the carrots and onion into an already-heated frying pan and gives things a toss. Oil sizzles and pops but the aroma is unmistakable. He's making a stir fry. My hunger turns ravenous. I haven't had stir fry in forever.

"I *don't* need *your* help," he repeats with emphasis.

His brusque manner pisses me off. "Why do you always have to be such an asshole?"

He keeps his broad back to me and adds some tamari sauce to the pan.

Giving up on trying to be nice, I walk inside the pantry to grab a snack. No matter how good what he's making smells, I won't give him the satisfaction of eating it.

Most of the stuff on the shelves is gourmet crap, but after a quick inspection, I spot a box of saltines and a jar of peanut butter. That should tide me over until morning.

Just as I reach up on tiptoe to get the crackers, Hendrix's large, warm body presses to my back, and every muscle locks when he leans into me and grabs a can of water chestnuts from the top shelf. I hate how he makes my heart flutter or how my breath catches when I feel his lips on my hair.

"Back off."

"Make me, firefly."

Hendrix doesn't move. Neither do I. Time suspends and is in direct opposition to how fast my pulse thrums.

One forever second ticks by. Then another. And another.

It's like my entire being becomes an exposed live wire. A small shudder shakes me when his head dips and he runs his nose along the curve of my neck to my ear. Explosions detonate along the skin he touches, and I purse my lips together to hold back my moan.

"Syn."

Just a whisper in that low accented voice, and arousal gathers between my legs. I'm overwhelmed and intoxicated, barely able to string two coherent thoughts together. I've lived my entire life without knowing desire, but somehow these three men bring it out of me so effortlessly. And I despise myself for the weakness.

The pressure on my back eases, and with my next panted breath, he's gone.

Holy shit. I lean my forehead to a shelf and try to calm down. Hendrix Knight confuses the hell out of me.

Snatching the crackers and peanut butter, I haul ass out of the kitchen, not daring to look in Hendrix's direction as I scurry past and rush out the back door to the patio. I need some air. And apparently a lobotomy.

Barefoot, I walk down the steps and across the cut grass to where Tristan is still sitting and staring at nothing. Behind him, fire red and pink clouds scorch the horizon as the sun makes its final goodbye to the day.

There's something so lonely and lost about him out here by himself, and I feel an immediate kinship with him because I know that feeling all too well. Just because I prefer to be alone doesn't mean I like it.

Without announcing my presence, I quietly take a seat beside him and put the food to the side so I can stretch out my legs and lean back on my hands. The sun warms my shoulders and helps me relax. The guitar music I heard in the kitchen plays softly from Constantine's open second-story window. I close my eyes and sink into the lyrical notes.

"If you could travel anywhere in the world, where would it be?"

I crack an eye open and peek over at Tristan's profile. All that gorgeous thick hair, tawny eyes, and twin dimples that pop when he smiles.

"Can I pick more than one place?"

He grins and that left dimple makes an appearance.

"That would be cheating."

I give his question serious thought. One day, I'd love to travel the world.

"Home."

"Dilliwyll?"

I giggle at his confused grimace of disgust. It really is a horrible name.

"Don't judge. It's a very lovely place. The farm I grew up on was a kid's paradise. So many things to explore. My favorite spots were the creek that ran along the south property line and the barn. But I wasn't talking about Dilliwyll. Home is family. Love. Acceptance. As long as I have those things, anywhere I go would be wonderful because I'd get to share it with the people that mean the most to me."

Tristan circles a thumb over his temple, indicating a possible headache may be coming. Scooting behind him, I slide forward so he's sitting between my legs. His hands grip the outside of my thighs, and I dismiss the clench in my core.

"What about you? Where would you like to go?" I ask, squeezing the back of his neck.

It's like an instant tension release, and he goes lax. Tristan is a big guy, but I'm able to support his weight easily when he slumps back into me.

"My sister loved Australia. We had plans to go back after I graduated. Do a walkabout. But going without her now seems wrong somehow."

Australia, like where the pressed flower is from that he gave me that I haven't thanked him for. I have a feeling that he wouldn't want me to, which is why I haven't said anything.

I didn't know he had a sister, but the way he speaks about her tells me she's no longer with us. My heart aches for him.

"Can I ask you a question?"

He twists around and looks up at me. "Depends on the question. It's a definite yes if you want to massage lower."

My eye roll is intentional.

"Do you always have to ruin a moment with a jerk response—Don't," I quickly say when I see his eyes alight with humor, and I realize my verbal faux pas.

"I didn't know we were having a moment."

He flips fully over, taking me by surprise, and I collapse backward onto the soft ground with Tristan braced above me. Without thinking, I flatten my palms to his chest. I can feel the solid thump of his heartbeat beneath my fingertips. My gaze gravitates to his mouth. He's not smiling anymore.

"Are you involved in organized crime? Like the son of a don or something?"

He bursts out laughing, and the sight is wondrous.

"Was that the question you wanted to ask?"

I nod, feeling foolish, but it was the only thing I could come up with to explain everything that has happened. I'm trying to make sense of things that are way outside my realm of comprehension. Guns. Violence. His abusive father. Aleksander. Why Tristan thinks my life may be in danger from the latter two.

"No, Red. Just because my family is Italian—"

Shit. Not what I meant.

"I swear that's not what I was implying. It's just..."

Flustered, I turn my head and look at the red bell flowers hanging down in clusters on the nearby bush, but he takes my face and forces me to look at him.

"Who *are* you?" I whisper, afraid to find out the real answer.

I want him to lie to me. Make up a story. Anything to maintain the illusion.

"Who are *you*, Synthia Carmichael?" he counters.

"I am no one."

The effect those words have on Tristan is the same as Hendrix when I say it. He takes my throat and leans in. But unlike with Hendrix that night at the top of the stairs, Tristan's touch is enticingly provocative, not punishing. Seems I like both.

"Don't ever say that again."

He moves his hand from my throat to my mouth and pulls at my bottom lip, then shoves his finger inside. Some innate instinct takes over, and I suck, stroking my tongue up his thumb. Black eclipses his irises, hiding the golden brown.

His voice is husky when he warns, "Careful, Red. I won't ask for your permission. I'll just take what I fucking want."

I'm barraged with lurid promises of what it would be like to be taken by a man like him. Hendrix in the pantry had stoked those embers, but Tristan is the gasoline that will ignite those sparks into a wildfire.

And I would burn once again.

Which is why I push him off me and scramble to my feet, then run back inside the house and up the stairs to my room.

I'm good at running away. I've been doing it my entire life.

"Don't look, baby. Close your eyes and don't look. It'll be okay."

Papa's dead stare blindly watches as blood oozes out of the hole in his head.

Mama's lies turn into cries of pain and pleas of mercy to spare me as the man with the scar rapes her.

I'm not here.

I'm not here.

I'm not here.

I am no one.

The scream that fills my ears is unworldly, like the gates of hell have opened up, letting loose the demons to rip flesh from human bone. My hands grip the sides of my head until it feels like I'm trying to crush in my own skull.

Block out the sounds.

Block out the screams.

But the screams are coming from me. And they won't stop.

Abruptly waking in a panic and not knowing why, I

blindly throw off the covers and sit up in bed. I hate the fucking nightmares. I hate not being able to remember. I hate feeling scared of every unknown shadow.

With shaking hands, I push the hair from my face and glower at the clock when I see that it's two in the morning. Grabbing my pillow, I pad silently to the bedroom door and open it. The house is dark, and thankfully, no noises are coming from the room down the hall. It takes three steps to get to Constantine's door.

I hesitate for a second before turning the doorknob and slipping inside. I can feel him, his presence, his cologne, and it instantly soothes me. I'm safe here. With him.

My eyes have adjusted enough so that I can see the outline of his bed. The covers rustle as he turns onto his side, those coal-black eyes glowing in the darkness, following me as I come closer.

"Syn?"

The sound of his voice lures me like a Siren's song. I stop at the side of his bed and clutch the pillow to my chest.

He doesn't make me ask. He seems to know why I'm there. What I need. He shifts and lifts the bedspread, and I crawl under the covers with him.

Constantine's arm reaches over me and pulls me to him when I curl into a ball around my pillow. He fits his body to mine, my back to his front. He tucks his head to my shoulder and places a soft kiss on the side of my neck.

Safe. Warm. Protected. He'll keep the nightmares away.

"Sleep," he says.

And I do.

CHAPTER 21

Syn flinches and whimpers in her sleep, tortured by whatever demons haunt her dreams. I caress her soft hair with my lips, and she settles with a relieved sigh. She always smells so good. Like fucking sunshine and flower petals.

With her arms bare and uncovered by her tank top, I use the moonlight coming in from the window to study her scars. She often hides them, thinks they're ugly, but I find them beautiful. Syn fascinates me like most damaged things do.

I trace a finger over the uneven skin of her triceps, and she sighs again. The sound stirs something in me. Something feral and needy. For her.

We know nothing about this girl, yet I want her. So do Tristan and Hendrix. Syn is a complication we don't need. She seems to invite chaos and trouble—just look at what's happened the past couple of days. But for some inexplicable reason, I don't fucking care.

I shouldn't touch something so pure, but I can't stop myself as I slide the backs of my knuckles over her shoulder. Syn's quiet moan spurs on my hunger. Snuggled to my side, she looks small and fragile. I break fragile things. Hurt them. It's what I was born to do. Pain is my sustenance. Receiving it and giving it. I crave it in a way that is unhealthy, but it's the only thing that makes me feel alive.

Until Syn.

And that makes her dangerous.

Three men wanting the same woman. It doesn't matter that we're best friends and brothers in every way that matters. Things will not end well if we keep going down this path. But I'll still walk it and damn the consequences.

I glide my hand down to her hip, and she makes a hungry whimper in her sleep. Goose flesh erupts over her stomach where her top has drawn up to expose her midriff. When she doesn't rouse, I move my hand lower to her navel to find a small round diamond stud protruding at the top. Syn has a piercing, and I find that sexy as fuck.

She mumbles something and places her hand on top of mine. Our fingers thread, and it's the most thrilling thing I've ever felt. She isn't afraid of me. She doesn't look at me and see the devil I was forced to become. She accepts me for what I am and makes me feel things I haven't felt in a long fucking time. Emotions that are painful and barbed. They slice you open, leaving behind a gaping wound, deep and jagged, that never truly heals. The organ in my chest was ripped out of me when I was twelve, so I'm surprised there's anything left, but I feel it beating now.

"Con."

It's barely audible, but in the stillness of the room, I

hear it clearly.

She's never called me that. It's always Constantine.

I go stock-still when Syn slides our joined hands down her abdomen and between her legs to her cunt. The heat of her is potent, and it takes every ounce of willpower not to slip my hand inside her sleep shorts and sink deep inside her.

"Syn."

She doesn't respond. Her breaths are even, and her eyes dart behind her lids. She's still fast asleep and dreaming.

She urges our hands down and relaxes her thighs, opening them wider. Her neck arches, and her head pushes into my shoulder.

"*Please*."

A better man would wake her up.

I'm not him.

She keeps her hand in mine when I delve underneath the elastic of the tiny shorts she wore to sleep in.

I wait a beat. Nothing.

With too much damn temptation right at my fingertips, I ease a finger between her folds to find her soaked.

My cock throbs with the need to pound into her. To experience the euphoria I know I'd feel fucking her. How gorgeous she'd look with my cum coating her luminous skin. The way she'd gaze up at me with those pale-blue eyes, all that Titian hair spread out on my pillow. The sounds she'd make.

Slowly, I ease a finger in, and her breath catches. Jesus fuck, she's tight. So goddamn good. Her hips pulse forward, pushing my finger deeper. I feel the barrier. That thin membrane that tells me she's untouched.

Innocent. And fuck me if that doesn't turn me on even more.

She moans so prettily when I add another finger and shallowly slide them in and out, fucking her. I don't go deeper because I don't want to hurt her.

"More."

I find her clit and flick it with my thumb. Her moan hitches, and it's the sweetest music. I watch her face. She runs her teeth over her bottom lip, and there's a pink blush that brightens her cheeks. How in the hell can she still be asleep? Whatever dream she's lost in must be a fucking good one for her not to wake up with my hand shoved up her pussy. If she did, it wouldn't matter. I'm past that point of control. I need to see her come. Know what she looks like when she does.

I take my time building her to climax because I can't get enough of her whispered moans or how soft her pussy is. She rides my hand, chasing her release, and when it comes, when her internal walls clamp down and her body bows and she says my damn name, it's the most exquisite fucking sight.

With a breathy exhale, her muscles relax, and she sinks back into the pillow with a smile gracing her face, never once coming fully awake.

I regretfully remove my fingers from the heaven they found and bring them to my lips, painting them with her essence and tasting her for the first time. She smells and tastes like the sweetest sin I'll ever commit, one I know I'll make again.

I'm so hard right now, and I know I won't be able to go back to sleep until I take care of things. My dick curses me because it doesn't want my hand. It wants her.

Not tonight, I tell him and slip out of bed. I walk

over to the other side and look down at her. Taking a length of her hair, I rub the soft, curled ends between my fingers.

"Beautiful Syn."

Just as I turn to head to the adjoining bathroom to take the coldest shower known to man, I hear her mumble, "*Gheobhaidh mo chroí do chroí.*"

CHAPTER 22

Bright, blinding sunlight—well, it would be blinding if my eyes were open—creeps over my face and works better than any alarm clock or Cocky Bastard when he would crow right under my window at five in the morning.

Deliciously warm and feeling more well rested than I can remember, I wake knowing three things: I'm in Constantine's bed. I'm spooned against a shirtless Constantine. And my hand is shoved down my sleep shorts. *Oh, dear god.*

Feeling absolutely mortified that I would touch myself in my sleep with Constantine *right freaking there*, I carefully extricate my hand from my underwear and tell my pounding heart to stop making so much noise.

There's no clock in his room that I can see, so I don't know what time it is. All I know is that I need to get the hell out of his bed as quietly as possible, which may be impossible to do without waking him because his arm is draped over my chest, pinning me in place.

I allow a few seconds to enjoy being held in this man's

arms. I don't like being touched in general, but for some reason that I will not overthink, I like being touched by him. Too much.

Okay. I can do this. Just go snail-ass slow. I wiggle to shift to my back and make the mistake of turning my head. Constantine's eyes are open, and he's staring at me.

Fuck me.

Feeling like someone cranked a furnace centered right in the middle of my chest, heat flushes my body with a blush so hard, I'm probably the color of a ripe tomato.

"Hi."

His lips curve.

"What time is it?"

I startle when he shifts to his side and props his weight on his elbow, looking down at me. He runs a thumb over the rapidly beating pulse point in my neck, then brushes it over the arch of my eyebrow. His eyes haltingly move over my face, lingering on one area before moving to the next. I don't know exactly what's going on, but I'm literally melting into the mattress the longer he looks at me. Like I'm precious. Like I mean something. Constantine looks at me like I imagine a man would when he desires a woman. It's probably the same way I'm gazing up at him.

I must be out of my damn mind, developing feelings for men who I know nothing about. Men who are clearly dangerous and live in a reality far from the simple rural life I grew up in. I don't belong in their world. I shouldn't even be here, no matter what Tristan says. So, why am I not running?

After what seems like forever, Constantine's broken,

raspy voice replies, "Eight."

At least I didn't oversleep. My first class on Tuesdays is at ten.

Not knowing how to react in this situation, because I've never been in this situation, I dumbly say, "Thank you… for last night. For, um…" I close my eyes and breathe in, which is a mistake because the subtle sandalwood of his skin invades my lungs. The air smells like him. The sheets smell like him. *I* smell like him after a night held in his arms. "For letting me sleep in here."

Without my consent, my hand cups his cheek, enjoying the way his short stubble abrades my palm.

The door to the bedroom crashes open and scares the shit out of me.

"Con. Get the fuck up. I can't find Syn—"

Tristan cuts off mid-sentence when his gaze fixes on me, and a perplexed expression crosses his face. I thought I was embarrassed before, but that's nothing compared to the pure panic I feel now. That feeling ratchets up when I notice Hendrix standing behind him. His mouth is pinched, his face shuttered, but his cobalt blue eyes bore into me with something akin to jealousy. Tristan, on the other hand, leans a casual shoulder to the doorframe, crosses his arms over his chest, and the smug smirk he loves to wear stretches his full lips.

"I'm a little insulted I didn't get an invite to the slumber party."

I shrink against Constantine and try to hide under the covers, but he won't let me. Grasping my waist, he turns me so I'm fully facing Tristan and tucks his head in the crook of my shoulder.

Hendrix wordlessly walks off, and I hear the stomp of

his footsteps as he goes down the stairs.

Feeling I need to explain since Constantine isn't doing it, I rush out, "I couldn't sleep. Nightmares. So, I came in here, and... yeah."

The smirk falls, and Tristan walks over to the bed. Constantine's grip tightens around my waist and feels almost territorial.

"Want some breakfast?"

Tristan brushes a hand down my hair, not acting at all awkward that I'm in bed with his best friend.

"Coffee?" I ask hopefully.

Caffeine always comes before food in the morning, no matter how hungry I am.

"Go get dressed and come downstairs. I've got a class at nine, but I'll pick you up after your chem lab."

My mood dampens at the reminder that I can't go anywhere without one of them tagging along. Gilded cages, no matter how appealing, are still cages.

I nod my reply. It takes effort to free myself out from under Constantine. I keep my gaze lowered to the floor because I can't look at either of them as I scurry off the bed and back to my room. Once inside, I run to the bathroom and shut the door.

Facing my reflection in the mirror, I take in my appearance. The blue of my eyes seems brighter. My complexion healthier. There's a plumpness and glow to my cheeks, as if I'm fighting a smile. I almost look—happy.

"Oh, Syn, you are in so much trouble."

Not wanting to wash Constantine's scent from my body, I skip a shower and scrub my face, brush my teeth, and swipe on some deodorant. I haven't fully unpacked yet, so I grab some clean clothes from my suitcase. When I take out a long-sleeved shirt, I pause and immediately discard it in exchange for one of my favorite Seamus Knox tees and a pair of frayed jean shorts.

Looking around for my backpack when I don't see it on the floor next to the nightstand where I swear I put it, I unplug my phone and check my messages. There's one from Alana saying good morning and one from Raquelle asking if I want to meet up for lunch.

Time to put myself out there.

Me: Would love to. I have a bio lab at 12:30, then nothing until 3.

I find my bag when I trip over the strap as I round the corner of the bed. Dropping down to sit cross-legged on the rug, I check to make sure I have everything I need for the day and groan when I remember the readings I was supposed to do last night but never did. Not a great way to start the academic year.

My phone chimes with an incoming text.

Raquelle: 1 at the SU café ok?

SU? Oh, student union.

Me: See you there.

I take out my journal and set it down next to me when I find an elastic band in the front zipper pocket. I use it to secure my hair in a bun. The weather is too hot and muggy to leave it down. Pen in hand, I open my journal to the next blank page and... nothing. I don't know what to write because whatever fleeting remnants of the nightmare I had are completely gone, and I sure as shit am not going to write about the dream I do remember. It was intense and felt so real, and I'm blushing just thinking about it. Not because of the dream itself but because Constantine and Tristan were both in it. With me. Doing stuff that definitely does not belong in this journal. I'm so going to hell.

I turn to the front cover page and touch the pressed five-leaf clover, then the flower Tristan gave me. Something I read a while back pops into my mind, and I flip back to the empty page and write: *"Hope is being able to see that there is light despite all of the darkness."* It's a quote from Desmond Tutu. I quick-sketch a heart cracked in four places and outline the letters that spell H-O-P-E in each of the four broken pieces.

Storing everything back in its place, I slip on my flip-flops and head downstairs, letting my nose lead the way to the heavenly aroma of roasted coffee beans and frying bacon.

Hendrix is bent over the counter island shoveling cereal into his mouth. He doesn't look up when I walk over.

"Where's everybody?" I ask when I don't see Constantine or Tristan anywhere.

Hendrix slides a plate my way with a bacon and egg croissant on it, turns and grabs a freshly brewed cup of coffee from the Keurig and places it in front of me, then goes back to eating. I take a seat on one of the stools.

"Thanks," I gratefully tell him and take a sip of coffee, not caring that it practically burns the tip of my tongue off.

When I bite into the breakfast sandwich, I can't help the pleased hum I make. Hendrix's spoon arrests in front of his mouth.

"This is probably the best croissant I've ever tasted. Did you make this?"

I've noticed Hendrix likes to cook. He's always in here making or baking something from scratch.

He makes a nondescript noise in his throat that I assume is a yes and places his empty bowl in the sink.

I take another bite. "This is so good." Covering my mouth with my hand, I ask, "Why aren't you eating one?"

There's a baking pan with four other pastries still on it. If I had a choice between dry cereal and a buttery, flaky croissant, the choice is obvious.

He removes a plastic-wrapped one from the fridge and drops it on the counter island.

"What's this?"

"Turkey and cheese."

Why does he make trying to talk to him feel like my nails are being pulled with pliers?

"I can see that."

"It's your lunch. We leave in thirty." He walks out.

He made me breakfast and lunch? I know for a fact that homemade croissants take at least thirteen hours total prep and bake time. That's the main reason why I never tried to make them at home.

"Hendrix, wait."

I jump off the stool and go after him.

"Will you please wait a minute?" I implore, trying to catch up as his long strides take the stairs two at a time.

I lose sight of him when he disappears inside his room. A light turns on in the closet, and I hover at the threshold like an idiot because I'm scared to cross over. Entering his bedroom, seeing his most private area, is something I'm not sure I'm ready for.

Fuck it.

I take a giant step forward—and frown. There's nothing in here other than a perfectly made bed that looks like it's never been slept in. No dresser or armoire.

No television or desk. A small, framed pencil sketch of a cliffside view overlooking the ocean sits on the windowsill. There's a pallet made of blankets on the floor near the window and one pillow. Does he sleep on it instead of the bed?

Hendrix's room is almost barren. The curtains are drawn, leaving everything cloaked in darkness. And yet, the space fits the man who sleeps in it.

I pivot on my heels when Hendrix walks out of the closet, pulling a shirt over his head. But not before I get a good eyeful of his gorgeously inked chest. I've never been a fan of tattooed men, but I guess it depends on the man. He and Constantine are completely covered in them, and each time I see even a peek of ink showing on their skin, my fingertips vibrate with the need to touch and explore every design on their bodies.

Hendrix slows to a standstill in front of me, and my hands fidget, my fingers tapping out piano keys in a flurried rhythm on the fronts of my shorts.

"Somebody's a nosy bitch."

My head jerks back with surprise when he calls me a bitch. Can nothing nice come out of this jackass's mouth?

Anger shakes me to the core because I've had enough. Of him. Of the way he speaks to me. Of the way he treats me.

I slap him across the face.

"Don't you *ever* call me a bitch again. I don't give a shit if you don't like me, but you will *never* call me that again."

Our chests heave with pent-up fury, neither one of us backing down. He towers over me, all muscle and lethality and so goddamn handsome, it just pisses me off more.

"You and that sassy fucking mouth," he growls.

"Fuck you."

I shriek when I'm suddenly lifted. All the air gusts out of my lungs when I'm slammed against the wall, making the stitches in my shoulder protest and pull at my skin.

Then Hendrix kisses me.

Brutally. Savagely. Like he has something to prove and is willing to destroy me to do it. And god help me, he does.

All it takes is one kiss, and I fly apart in a million glittery pieces.

He fucks my mouth with his tongue, invading and conquering with deep, penetrating thrusts, stealing my common sense. I need to stop this. Knee him in the balls for forcing himself on me without my permission. Hit him again for taking something that isn't his to take. I've never been kissed before, and now I'm ruined because I know I'll never be kissed like this again. Damn him for that, and damn me for wanting more.

My legs wrap around his lean waist, and my hands sink into his thick blond hair, as I fight for control, wanting to punish him for the pleasure I'm feeling. The want and the need and the desperation.

He brings a hand to my throat, and I moan into his mouth. His fingers tighten in the way that I'm quickly becoming addicted to. There is definitely something very wrong with me.

Pushing my chin up with his thumb, he nips my bottom lip hard with his teeth, and the metallic taste of blood coats my tongue.

"I can smell him on you, firefly."

He's talking about Constantine, and a thrill races through me at his envious tone.

Hendrix holds me in place and lowers his head. My gasp of pain fills the room when he bites me just above my breast through my shirt.

"You may smell like him, but you'll be wearing my mark."

He lets go of me and abruptly backs away, and unless I want to plummet ass-first to the ground, I have no choice but to drop my legs from around him and plant my feet to the floor.

Hendrix leaves me standing there, staring after him in a daze. A confused mess of disgust and lust. I touch a shaking finger to my mouth, and it comes away sanguine with blood.

"Time to go, Syn," I hear him call as he goes back downstairs.

I slip into his bathroom. Lifting my shirt, I inspect the teeth-shaped bruise on my chest in the mirror. *Jesus Christ.* In a last act of defiance, I use the blood oozing from my lip to write "I hate you" across the mirror.

Staring at my reflection, I firm my resolve and construct a barbed-wire fence around my heart. Hendrix Knight will never kiss me again.

CHAPTER 23

The walk across campus to the building where my lab is being held is done in strained silence and stresses me the hell out. By the time I run up the steps to get away from a brooding Hendrix, I'm in a shit mood that gets worse with the uncomfortable stares being thrown at me when they see my arm. It's my own fault for wearing a short-sleeved T-shirt.

"What?" I snap at a guy I pass whose face is pinched in disgust.

His averted gaze is instantaneous.

And then, the whispers start. The ones that aren't whispers at all but can be heard as loudly as a sneeze in church. It's fucking high school all over again.

Finding an empty station in the back corner, I drop my bag and take a seat on the metal stool. Various lab equipment is set up under the fume hood, and I pick up a glass stir rod to play with as I wait for the professor to show up.

A guy walks over, and all I can think is, *here we go*.

"Hey."

Tilting my head, I wait for the intrusive questions to come. In the mood Hendrix put me in, I'm feeling a little stabby, and the glass rod in my hand will do nicely.

The corner of the guy's mouth quirks in a half smile. He sets his stuff down at the station next to me and starts pulling papers out of his large backpack. He's cute in a Clark Kent kind of way with his black hair, black wire-frame glasses that show off pretty hazel eyes that are more green than brown.

When he doesn't say anything else, I begin to relax. Who I assume is the professor walks in and the chatter in the room diminishes.

"Here."

Something gets pushed across the floor and stops at the leg of my stool. I look down and see a pair of worn cross-trainers and a balled-up pair of white socks.

"Professor Carlyle will kick you out of class if he sees that you're wearing sandals."

Goddammit, Hendrix. I curse him and that mind-blowing kiss for scrambling every brain cell in my head. I left the house forgetting to switch my flip-flops for sneakers. I also forgot to put on a pair of long pants. It's lab safety protocol, and I knew not to show up without wearing them.

A pair of balled-up sweatpants gets placed in my lap.

"They're clean. Just got them out of the dryer this morning."

Is this guy for real?

"Thank you so much." I quickly slip on the sweats over my shorts and put on the socks and shoes, which are way too big.

"No problem."

He slides a stapled stack of copy paper over to me

as the professor walks around the room. The guy's warning comes true when the professor throws a fit at one girl for wearing heels and a mini skirt, then promptly tosses her ass out of class.

When he gets to my row, he looks me over, then greets the guy beside me.

"Evan."

"Professor Carlyle."

When he walks away, Evan leans over and says, "I'm Evan."

"I got that," I reply and grin. When he waits expectantly for me to say more, I relent and introduce myself. "I'm Synthia."

He holds out his fist for me to bump, and I tap it with my knuckles.

"Nice to meet you, Synthia."

"You've had him before?" I ask, looking over the papers he put in front of me. It's the syllabus for the semester.

"I'm his TA."

As soon as he says it, Professor Carlyle calls Evan up to the front.

"Can I help?" I offer as Evan wipes down the lab stations and collects the safety goggles that were left out. We're the only two left in the room.

"Thanks. I've got it."

I leave the stuff he let me borrow on the stool and pick up my bag. The pain in my shoulder has dulled but I'll get Constantine to check it later to make sure I haven't popped a stitch. As soon as I think it, he appears at the doorway to the room as if I conjured him out of thin air. A ridiculously huge smile spreads across my face at the sight of him looking all surly and gruff and gorgeous.

"See you next week," I tell Evan, who doesn't look up from what he's doing.

"See ya, Synthia," he replies.

As soon as I'm in front of Constantine, he touches the corner of my mouth where Hendrix broke the skin. I didn't think anyone would notice, but Constantine seems to notice everything.

"What happened?"

Just hearing his voice, and the anger from the drama with Hendrix from this morning finally dissipates.

"It's nothing."

I take out my phone and send Raquelle a courtesy text that I'm on my way. "Where did you go this morning?"

With his attention hyper-focused on Evan, he slides the strap of my bag off my shoulder and loops it onto his.

I had stuff to do, he signs.

He gives Evan what I would call a dirty lour, then trails his hand down my arm to my hand and threads his fingers with mine. My heart trips over itself at the unexpected show of affection, but I don't pull away. Because I like it. A lot.

The hall outside the lab room is packed wall to wall with people moving in opposite directions like cars on an expressway. Constantine and I get a few curious glances from both girls and guys that I try my best to ignore. I hate that my life is this. Will always be this because of the way I look. No one is perfect. Everyone has flaws. Mine are just more visible, but they shouldn't define who I am to someone.

As soon as sunlight hits us when we walk outside, I tip my face up and soak it in.

"I'm supposed to meet a girl from my calc class at one. Can you join us?"

He signals no, and my effervescent mood fizzles.

"Can't stick around. Told Tristan I'd get you after class. Wanted to see you," he says hoarsely.

This freaking guy. I bring our joined hands to my lips and brush my mouth across his fingers. Thin white lines crisscross his tanned skin that remind me of the whip marks on Tristan's back. What type of horrors did they have to endure? We may live worlds apart, but we share similar trauma. Tristan laughed when I asked if they were involved in the mafia. I knew it was an absurd thing to say even before I uttered it. But I'm neither stupid nor ignorant. I can choose to bury my head in figurative sand and pretend not to notice the ugliness that surrounds these three men, or I can accept the fate that has been unceremoniously shoved at me and take that giant leap into the unknown—I look up at Constantine—and today I feel like jumping.

"Walk with me?" I ask.

He deeply inhales like he's pleased that I asked.

The SU is nearby, but I decide to take the long way to get there and circumvent the main quad by walking around it.

"Where are you from?"

Constantine's eyes dart around, tagging everyone and everything around us. I tug on his hand.

"Born in New York."

I notice he says born in, not from.

"Where'd you grow up?"

His face tightens and makes me want to backtrack

my question, but I wait him out.

"Boarding school in Switzerland."

It's clearly something he doesn't want to talk about. I don't ask him anything else and enjoy the rest of the five minutes it takes us to get to the student union. Right now, I just want to be a regular girl with a great guy, holding hands like it's the most natural thing to do.

Crossing the main walkway, I see Raquelle waiting outside the SU, scrolling on her phone. Today, she's dressed in the cutest pair of pale pink suspender overalls that are streaked with paint smears of various colors. She looks up and waves when she sees me, then arches a querying eyebrow when she gets an eyeful of Constantine.

Shaking out of her stupefaction, she smiles. "Hey! I'm so glad we could meet up."

She comes to hug me, and I step back, bumping into Constantine. I don't mean to do it. It's just a natural aversion I have to people getting too close. I let go of his hand and force myself to meet her embrace.

"Me, too," I reply, self-consciously hugging her back.

She gives my arm a very brief look, then hooks her hand at my elbow. Standing next to her, I feel like a weed growing beside a hot house orchid. Raquelle is gorgeous, and I'm… well, I'm me.

"Hi, I'm Raquelle," she offers Constantine, and the manners Alana instilled in me kick in.

"Shit. Sorry. This is Constantine." I gesture to Raquelle. "And this is Raquelle."

I am the lamest person on the planet.

"Boyfriend?" she says quietly near my ear.

I cough out, "What?"

With a fixed smile full of teeth, she side-whispers like

a ventriloquist, not moving her mouth. “Are you two together?”

I know Constantine heard her from the smirk he’s giving me. My face goes up in tattletale flames. A curse of being fair-skinned.

“Friends?” I say it as a question, my gaze firmly fixed on Constantine, beseeching him to help me out. He doesn’t. His smirk only gets bigger.

Laughing, she asks, “Do you not know?”

“Friends,” I say more firmly, hoping it sounds convincing.

Constantine kisses the top of my head, then signs, *See you tonight. I’ll text Tristan and tell him to pick you up here. What time?*

“In an hour,” I reply, taking back my bag when he holds it out to me.

Raquelle pokes me in the side as we watch him walk away but I barely feel it because of the substantial nerve damage there.

“Girl, you two are *not* just friends.”

I voice my inner thoughts without meaning to. “I don’t know what we are.”

“He definitely does by the way he was looking at you. The semester just started. Where in the heck did you meet that sexy thing?”

If she only knew the truth.

“At work.” Not a lie. “I’m a waitress at the Bierkeller.”

She pulls me inside the air-conditioned building and leads me to the open café located at the back. The place has an odd smell. A mix of something sweet like cake when it comes right out of the oven and that ozone odor copier machines give off when they’re printing.

“I’ve heard people talking about that place. I’ll

definitely need to drop by now. When do you work?"

"Wednesday, Friday, and Saturday evenings."

There's a short line at the café's counter that we join.

"How has your second day been?" Raquelle asks.

"Just a lab so far and one more class to go. Tuesday-Thursdays are my short days. You?"

She adjusts her glasses. "Been painting most of the morning. I have two classes later this afternoon."

We step up to the counter when it's our turn. The cupcakes behind the glass partition are too tempting, so when the barista asks what I want, I order an iced coffee and two cupcakes, so Raquelle can have one if she wants. If not, I'll save it for after dinner.

"Want to sit outside?" She points to the left with her coffee.

Taking my drink and small pastry box, I follow her out a side door to where a cluster of small tables and chairs are set out, a few people already seated at a couple of them. At each table, bright blue umbrellas with the university's crest emblazoned across them provide shade from the midday sun.

A cool breeze blows, helping to dispel some of the summer heat. One more month before the official start of fall, and I can't wait. Autumn on the farm was one of my favorite seasons. I loved the kaleidoscope of color as the leaves changed on the trees. In the fall, the stars at night glow brighter since they're not being obscured by the haze of summer humidity.

Opening the pastry box, I offer her first pick.

"You are too sweet. Pun intended," she comments, taking the chocolate one. "I'll have to run an extra mile to burn these calories, but it'll be so worth it."

I peel back the wrapping on the vanilla one with

sprinkles.

"Tell me a little bit about yourself," she says.

Sitting back, I kiss the frosting, coating my lips in icing lipstick, then lick them clean. It's one of a million weird things I like to do. Instead of the sugary buttercream, all I taste is Hendrix's kiss.

Using the fingers of my left hand, I tick off the main points of my life. "Lived on a farm. I'm adopted. My life is boring. I'm shy. I'm here on scholarship."

She mimics me and says, "I'm from Los Angeles, but I already told you that. Only child who got stuck with her father in the divorce settlement because my mother didn't want to give up her modeling career. I'm an aspiring artist, canvas not music," she clarifies. "I fell in love with my stepbrother. My—"

I stop her. "Hold on, hold on. Back that up. You and your stepbrother?"

Her grin turns Cheshire and a little bit naughty. "Oh yeah. Want to see a picture?"

I nod emphatically. When she slides over her phone, I gape at the shirtless hot guy and his six pack. He's got his arm around her and is smiling down at her like she is the sun in his universe. I want that. I want to be that person to someone.

"What's his name?" I ask, giving her back her phone.

With a tiny, contented sigh, she says, "Drake. He's coming for homecoming week, so you'll get to meet him."

A flash of blond hair in a blue shirt snags my gaze. At first, I think it's Hendrix. My stomach plummets like a stone made of lead when gray eyes fix on me. Not Aleksander's, but his twin's. I remember seeing him in the quad with his brother. Different hairstyles. This guy's head is shaved, not shorn short.

And he's watching me.

With shrill alarms clanging like church bells in my head, I try to focus on what Raquelle is saying.

"...a party on Friday night if you're interested."

"I work until eleven."

Licking icing off her thumb, she twists around to see who I keep slicing glances to.

"You know him?"

"No."

Something ugly snakes up my spine when he walks over, pulls a chair from another table, then sits down in the space between Raquelle and me.

He leans an elbow to the table and considers me for a second. "Syn, right?"

His question is harmless, but I get a feeling that this brother is more dangerous than his twin.

With a practiced resting bitch face, I meet his intimidating stare. "Fuck. Off."

Raquelle's eyes flare wide at my tone, then she frowns at him, immediately taking my side even though she doesn't know what the hell is going on.

"You heard her."

Like she doesn't exist, he says to me, "Thought you were Hendrix's woman, but you and Con seem to be quite handsy with each other."

The play on words is threateningly intentional. How long has he been watching me?

I toss my uneaten cupcake in the box and leave my iced coffee, not wanting them anymore. I curl my fingers through the top loop of my bag.

"You ready to go?" I ask Raquelle.

"Absolutely."

She stands up, but when I try to, he snatches my wrist.

Aoife.

I shove down the voice in my head and hurl my irritation at the man whose touch makes my skin crawl.

"Let go."

He makes no disguise of raking his gaze over my scarred arm, and a furrow develops on his forehead.

"Tristan was about to throw down with my brother over you yesterday when he stormed into his apartment. Hendrix, not so much."

Again with the barbed insult like the one I received from Serena. It pricks just as much knowing Hendrix is the cause. But that's not what I'm stuck on. Tristan and Hendrix went to see Aleksander and didn't say anything. A head's up would have been nice, so I could have avoided being ambushed now.

Raquelle whips out her phone and holds it up. "I'm recording you, asshole. She said let go. If you don't want your face to be plastered all over social media with the hashtags 'rapist in training' and 'can't take no for an answer,' I suggest you get your ass up and walk away."

Without removing the punishing grip he has on me, he slowly stands, engulfing me in his shadow. The twins are huge, their shoulders twice the width of mine.

The gray of his eyes is frigid, chilling me to the bone.

"Get your fucking hands off her." He's ripped away from me by an enraged Tristan.

Tristan slides in front of me, tucking me protectively behind him. Everyone at the other tables turns their heads in synchronicity in our direction. Raquelle keeps recording.

With a grin as cold as his eyes, the twin backs away

with a chuckle. "See you around, Synthia."

It's the exact same thing Aleksander said to me.

"No, you won't."

"Holy shit," Raquelle blusters when he's gone, then, "Hi," when Tristan scowls at her.

He spins around and takes my shoulders, holding me at arm's length. "You okay?"

I have two scary twins stalking me, one of them I can't remember the name of. No, I'm not fucking okay.

CHAPTER 24

Keeping my face downturned, I blend in with the chaos surrounding me as fire alarms pierce the air with their eardrum-shattering shrieks. I join the melee of confusion and follow the stream of panicked office workers out of the building and into the bright sunlight.

The distraction of setting off the fire alarm is an old one, but still a good one and will give Con enough time to do... whatever... to Derek Langstrom's office computer.

People shuffle around, most of them disgruntled at the inconvenience, some asking questions about which floor the fire is on and some complaining that it's a false alarm. They'd be partially correct. I did set a small fire in the fifth floor's custodian closet where the cleaning supplies and whatnot are kept. There are no cameras in that part of the building. Even if there were, Con would have already taken care of it. Wiped the server or messed with the video feed.

Someone shoves by me, bumping my shoulder, and I shove them back, making them trip and bounce off the woman in front of them. He looks around, bewildered, trying to figure out who did it. Idiot.

The wail of fire engines can be heard in the distance, giving Con about three minutes to get the hell out of there. It takes only two.

With casual nonchalance, I start walking down the sidewalk once he exits the double front glass doors.

"All good?"

Con grunts, about as happy as I am at the moment.

This espionage shit is a fucking waste of our time, but the Council ordered us to slip a little something incriminating onto Langstrom's hard drive that the FBI would find once an anonymous tip was called in. All because Langstrom asked the wrong questions to the wrong person. Pity we weren't sent to kill him. I have a shitload of pent-up frustration that needs an outlet. And since I can't fuck the redhead who's the cause of that frustration, maybe pounding on Con for a few rounds in the ring once we get back will help.

All I can think about is that fucking kiss and Syn's soft lips. And I want more. The way she reacted. How she responded to me. The sounds she made.

Con clearly has laid claim to her. It was glaringly obvious after finding her in his bed this morning. He couldn't have been more obvious about it if he'd whipped out his dick and pissed a circle around her. Same with Tristan. He's infatuated with her. And then there's me. I don't know what the hell I feel, and it's driving me to distraction.

I send a text to my father, letting him know we're done and heading back to Darlington, but not in those exact words. My text is a bunch of gibberish in code. Can't be too careful. I'll get rid of the burner phone as soon as possible. Too many people walking around downtown Boston for me to chance tossing it in a street gutter.

Boston is a beautiful city, a mix of old and new. It never loses its appeal, no matter how many times I've visited.

Spotting one of a million beer gardens the historic city has, I head in its direction, knowing Con will follow.

We order two pints of whatever IPA they have on tap and find an unoccupied picnic table out back. The day is too nice to waste sitting inside.

I sip my beer and look around, enjoying the few precious seconds of peace I get to experience before I open my mouth and ask the one thing I shouldn't.

"Did you fuck her?"

I shouldn't care, but it's been eating me alive since this morning.

Con sets his pint glass down—the froth at the top spilling over the lip and sliding down the side—and gives me a scathing look. I give one back.

"What? You can talk to her but not to me or T? What the fuck, Con?"

That right there stings worse than anything. Like Tristan, Con is my brother. My family and best friend. I'd die for them. Almost did a couple of times. Con hasn't spoken a word since *that day*. Then Syn shows up, and he can't seem to keep his fucking mouth shut.

"No."

"No? To which one? Talking or fucking her."

He gives an exaggerated huff and signs, *Not your business*, huffs again, then says in a gravelly timbre that sounds like jagged shards of glass, "She had nightmares. Came to my room."

I'm baffled that I'm more jealous about that than the thought of him fucking her. Then again, she hates my guts. *Not this morning when I had my tongue shoved down her throat, and her sexy moans filled my ears.*

"Find out anything else about her?"

His posture stiffens, and he grabs his drink.

I know Tristan told him to. Syn is shrouded in secrets, and secrets are nothing but trouble we don't need, especially with Aleksander and Aleksei lurking. My hand tightens around the glass at the memory of Aleksander asking if Syn was fair game. Hell to the fuck no is he ever touching her.

"Still looking," Con eventually replies.

I check my watch for the time. It'll take us a little under two hours to get back to Darlington, which means we'll miss our next lecture. Tristan and Con hate being forced to forgo four years of uni. I don't mind it. I've enjoyed the reprieve, one that will soon be over come May when we graduate and be forced to join our fathers in the Council. It's all ceremonial nonsense that means not a damn thing. We won't get a vote or a say. That will only happen once our fathers step down and transfer power over to us. Or we take it by force.

"Sperm donor wants to see me this weekend," I tell him, swallowing down half of my IPA.

He called me right after I dropped Syn off this morning.

The less I see my father, the better. Luckily, most of his time is spent in London at the corporate offices, but he'll be flying to New York on Friday for a meeting.

I don't add that Syn is also coming because Francesco Amato has a big fucking mouth. Dear old dad has never deigned to lower himself to meet any of the women I've supposedly screwed, but he's demanding I bring Syn for some reason. And I don't like it.

Con's scowly face gets even scowlier. *What about?*

Con doesn't mouth the words he signs, so I have to watch his hands carefully.

"Who the fuck knows?"

Before I say anything to him or Tristan, I want to talk to Syn first and get her to agree to the trip. If she's on board, they'll fall in line and there won't be a fight. Okay, there will be a fight. I'm looking forward to sparring with my little firefly because I know the first words out of her mouth will be "fuck off" and "hell no." Gets me hard to hear her back talk with all that attitude.

Heard some chatter. Internet.

A juvenile snort of laughter escapes because the sign for chatter looks like a hungry squirrel eating a dick.

Stepanoff, he finger-spells the letters. *Whispers.*

Reading between the lines, I ask, "Your dad involved?"

That ever-present scowl turns murderous. We all despise our fathers, but Con more so.

Con has been trying to get a finger on the pulse over his father's push for the Stepanoffs to get a seat on the Council. There's no rhyme or reason for it.

Don't know.

That is the damn truth in a nutshell.

There's a lot we don't fucking know.

After a couple of hours at the gym, it's nearing seven by the time Con and I return to the house. Everything is quiet, and I assume Tristan and Syn aren't back yet, but then I catch the flicker of light from the television bouncing off the walls in the living room.

Con goes upstairs to take a shower. We're both covered in dried sweat and a little bit of blood from the cathartic beating we dished out in the ring at the gym. No gloves. My knuckles are raw and scabbed over, I have a split lip and bruised cheek, same as Con. It was something we both needed. The beasts inside us are calmer. For now.

"Hey."

Tristan looks up from his laptop. "How'd it go?"

"No problems."

"Good," he says distractedly.

"Where's Syn?" I ask when I don't see any sign of her.

He closes the laptop and rubs his hands over his face. He looks tired.

"Upstairs in her room."

He beckons me over, but I don't take a seat. I want a shower and some food.

"Aleksei made an appearance. Was there at the SU after Con dropped her off."

Those doppelgänger motherfuckers.

That brief calm I'd been enjoying disappears faster than a raindrop on a hot sidewalk.

"You didn't text Con or me about it."

"The two of you were in Boston and couldn't do anything even if you wanted to," he says to preempt the vulgarity I'm about to spew all over him for being a twat. "There was a girl with her. Didn't recognize her, so not Society. We'll need to vet her and make sure she has no connections with the Romanoffs."

Done with all the day's bullshit, I reply, "Con can do it. I'm taking a shower."

Loping upstairs, my muscles twitch the closer I get to her room, but I force myself to keep walking. With my bedroom door wide open, I strip out of my still-damp clothes that reek with perspiration and toss them on the floor. Walking into the bathroom, I flick on the light. A grin spreads slowly when I see the message Syn wrote on the mirror.

I run a finger through the letter H written in her blood and savor it on my tongue, and my dick stiffens, demanding relief. I give in to the temptation immediately.

Bracing one hand on the vanity counter, I take my cock and tightly squeeze with bruising force. Pain is my pleasure and appeases both the sadist and masochist in me.

I jerk my dick with rough strokes, teasing the ball piercing at the tip and imagining Syn on her knees, covered in blood, those soft fucking lips surrounding me, my cock choking her until she gags, tears streaming down her lovely face.

I lock eyes with the mirror, the "I Hate You" adding to the intense pleasure coursing through my body. The tempo of my hand is punishing, chasing that momentary high I know won't last.

There's a small gasp to my left but I don't look away from the mirror. I can see Syn in the reflection, there in the doorway, her gaze riveted to what I'm doing. She doesn't back away, nor does she say anything to announce her presence. She just stands there, face and chest flushed and eyes glassy with arousal.

The cerulean power of her gaze scorches me like a brand, pushing my hand to stroke faster. Harder.

"Syn," I moan, and her breathy moan echoes mine.

When I hear her lips spill my name in a whisper of benediction, I can't hold back any longer. With a drawn-out grunt of release, I come hard, the euphoria too penetrating, too good. It's like nothing I've ever felt before. That emotion I've been desperately chasing by fucking as many women as possible. A bliss I thought I'd never be able to achieve. So goddamn fucking good.

I watch, mesmerized, as tiny trails of my cum coat the vanity and some drips along the mirror, mixing with her blood.

Just as quietly as she arrived, Syn disappears from view.

CHAPTER 25

Raquelle: Proof of life.

Me: What?

Cloistered in my room, I'd been catching up on my assigned readings when her text came in—and maybe being a little bit of a coward because I could tell Tristan was still furious. He hasn't spoken a word since he picked me up after my last class. So, I left him alone and came upstairs. Nothing good would come of me saying anything. We'd only wind up arguing, and I was tired of arguing with him about Aleksander and Aleksei. I now remember his name. Tristan yelled it enough when he lambasted me at the SU after Aleksei left.

Aleks and Aleks. At least their parents had a sense of humor.

Raquelle: Take a picture of yourself right now and send it to me to show proof of life.

Humoring her, I do what she says, then get even more confused when she sends me a GIF of a pink elephant in a tutu.

Me: I don't even know what that means.

Raquelle: It's the elephant in the room. The one we're not avoiding because you're going to tell me why you have two boyfriends and a stalker.

I choke on my own spit—which is disgusting—when I read that because… because… I refuse to go there, even though my brain has no problem conjuring dreams about the three guys who live in this house. Last night's was pornographic.

Me: I DO NOT have two boyfriends!

Raquelle: Then that leaves the stalker.

Me: No stalker.

My fingers type the semi-lie because stalker is singular, whereas I seem to have two. Plural. My good conscience is all about the details in the context.

Raquelle: I know we just met, but if you need anything, even if it's just to talk, my door is always open.

I smile because I've never had a friend like that before. Only Alana. *Shit. Alana.* I forgot to call her. I'll catch her before bedtime.

Me: Thanks. And ditto. Talk tomorrow?

Raquelle: Yep. See you in class.

I hear noise downstairs and the thud of footsteps, then the shower turns on in Constantine's room. I get my answer about Hendrix also being home when I hear his muted British accent talking to Tristan.

I try my best to concentrate on the biology reading I need to do in order to submit my required GRQ, guided reading question, by midnight tonight. It's pretty easy stuff I had ad nauseum in my AP Biology class in high school, but I find I have to keep re-reading the same paragraph because I'm distracted by a second set of footsteps coming up the stairs. I know it's Hendrix by the way the hairs on my arms raise. It's like living lightning. An electric spark that ignites as soon as he's near. The bite mark he left pulses with life, and I cover it with my hand.

Like so many other times in the past several days, his footfalls slow at my door before continuing on down the hall. I don't realize I'm holding my breath until my lungs start to burn with the need for oxygen. Shifting the heavy textbook off my lap, I don't think about what I'm doing when I slip off the bed and leave the room.

His bedroom door is open, as is the bathroom. He'd accused me of being a nosy bitch this morning when I invaded his personal domain. My stomach quivers at the recollection of what happened after. The way he lifted me like I weighed nothing. The decadence of his mouth. That kiss that decimated me in the best and worst way possible.

"Oh, shit."

The message I wrote on his bathroom mirror. The bathroom he's in right now.

I rush to the doorway, an explanation on the tip of my tongue, but I come up short with my heart lurching into my throat.

Hendrix is naked. All six feet, two inches of glorious, inked skin and defined muscles on display.

And he's pleasuring himself.

I'm hypnotized where I stand, not able to look away. I should. I shouldn't be watching like I have a right. Like he's mine to watch like this. But the pleasure and the agony etched on his handsome face in the mirror has me paralyzed.

With deft, quick strokes, he pumps his cock. I'm utterly fascinated. The only male member I've ever seen was in books and that one time I accidentally went into the boy's restroom at school and walked in on Farrel Macoby taking a piss in the wall urinal.

Hendrix's cock is tattooed just like his body. To have that done must have hurt. There's a glint of stainless steel that catches the light. The tip of his cock is pierced. My hand slides across my stomach to my navel piercing, then journeys down to the juncture between my thighs before I swiftly drop my hand, horrified at what I was about to do.

"Syn," Hendrix moans, jerking himself faster as he stares at me in the mirror, and I feel the sound vibrate directly in my clit.

Heat crawls up my legs and torso as my breaths turn to shallow pants.

"Hendrix," I rasp, needing to say his name as I watch his orgasm rip through him, the sight of it one of the most erotic things I've ever witnessed.

As silently as I arrived, I retreat the same way, not paying attention in my rush back to my room, and plow directly into Constantine.

Humiliation tears me open like the jaws of life when he angles around my side and closes Hendrix's door just as his shower turns on.

My neck cricks back when I look up into his unemotive face.

"I wasn't... I didn't mean to..." Fuck.

Shut up, Syn. He knows. Constantine always knows.

He presses an unexpected, tender kiss to my forehead and takes my hand, giving me no choice but to stumble after him to his bedroom.

With the clean, masculine scent of the soap he uses still hanging like honeysuckle in the air, the thrum of arousal that accosted me while watching Hendrix deepens when I see his unmade bed. The bed I woke up in this morning.

I don't know what the hell is going on with me, but I need to stop. I can't be thinking things like that. Especially not for these men. Whatever sexual awakening I seem to be having, I need to ignore it and lock it down. There's someone out there for me, waiting. Someone who will love me, damaged and all. Someone who will look at me like I am the center of their universe. Tristan, Constantine, and most definitely Hendrix, are not that man, no matter how much my body yearns to be touched, kissed, and taken by them. It's a path I can't follow and come out unscathed when the journey ends.

"The gate to destruction is wide, and the road that leads there is easy to follow."

I'm not a religious person. Not after everything I've been through. There is no grand design for my life because fuck that. If there is, whoever is in charge is cruel. Murdered parents my fractured mind refuses to remember. The knife wounds and burns. The pain I endured and still endure every single day. The nightmares. The loneliness. The shit happening now. What did I ever do to deserve any of it?

Constantine lifts his acoustic guitar from its stand and pulls me out of his room.

I don't know what he has planned but joy brightens my heavy mood.

"Can I get mine?"

He nods and waits for me to retrieve my Epiphone acoustic. It's the first Christmas present Alana gave me. The thinner mahogany neck is easier for my hands to grip, and the bassy, bluesy sound it creates is like none other. But my inexpensive, little gem is nothing compared to Constantine's Taylor guitar, its koa top and tonewood body stained a gorgeous deep cherry brown.

He leads and I follow as we head downstairs, through the kitchen, and out to the back patio.

We missed the sunset by mere minutes, and it'll get fully dark soon. He presses a button on a small wall panel next to the door, and the back patio lights up with variously placed lights.

There's a nip, a crispness, to the air that hadn't been there in months. A signal that fall is on its way. Tiny goose bumps pop one by one along my arms, and a delightful frisson races up them from fingers to shoulder.

My eyes are drawn to the red-flowered bush and the man sitting next to it. Tristan looks over from his place on the grass where I found him the other evening. I give him a shy smile, not expecting to have an audience to hear me play.

Constantine offers me a seat in one of the thick cushioned chairs, but I decline and sit down on the patio paver stones where I'm more comfortable and can prop my guitar on my thighs easily. He sits across from me, our knees touching and a boyish grin crinkling his cheeks.

"Do you have a particular song you want to play?" I ask.

I'm a play-by-ear person, self-taught. I only need to hear a piece of music to play it back perfectly. Something to do with astute aural memory.

He shrugs and gestures for me to start. Plucking the strings to test the sound since I don't have my pick, I giggle when Constantine mimics me. Playfully, I strum the first measures of Bob Dylan's "Like a Rolling Stone." Constantine echoes the notes.

"We are not doing a rock version of *Deliverance*."

For the first time since I met him, Constantine laughs. A real laugh that stops my heart with the wonder of it.

Leaning forward, I swipe my thumb across the corner of his mouth. "You have the best laugh. Don't ever take that away from me. Promise me."

His expression grows serious. "I promise."

I close my eyes and inhale deeply.

Tristan comes over and sits behind me, fitting me between his legs and resting his hands at my hips.

Propping his chin on my shoulder, he says, "We should throw some steaks on the grill and eat outside tonight."

It's a perfect evening for it.

My cheek presses to his when I turn my head. "I could go for a steak."

While Constantine fiddles with the tuning pegs, Tristan tells me in the barest of whispers, "I haven't heard him laugh since we were kids. Thank you."

A happy warmth glows from the inside out at his praise. Alana, my teachers at school, and the doctors who oversaw my surgeries and various recoveries were the only people who ever praised me. I never knew how much I needed to hear it from a man. It's arcane and primitive, and as an independent woman with her own mind, I should be appalled by the notion of preening with delight from any man's compliments. But I love hearing him and Constantine tell me I'm beautiful. That what I do matters and makes them happy. Even Hendrix and the annoying nickname he calls me makes my tummy flutter with delight.

"Ready?" I ask Constantine and strum a G major chord.

He repeats it. I follow with a C major. We go back and forth like that for a minute, creating music by alternating who plays. I break out in peals of laughter as we play various versions of "Twinkle, Twinkle, Little Star" on dueling guitars.

"Do you know any Bruce Springsteen songs?" Tristan asks.

His thumbs are driving me crazy as he lazily runs them back and forth in the crease at the juncture of my hips and upper thighs. I'm turned on and am finding it impossible not to squirm.

I slip my hands under his and bring them up to the guitar.

"Keep your hands on top of mine and follow my lead," I tell him.

Scenes from the movie *Ghost* play through my mind where Patrick Swayze sits behind Demi Moore at the clay wheel.

We clumsily get through a few measures of "Born to Run" before the back door opens and shuts. Hendrix walks outside, his hair still wet and curling slightly at the ends. I can't look at him without remembering what I witnessed. I can already feel my face go up in flames, so I concentrate on positioning my and Tristan's fingers on the strings and frets. Luckily, Hendrix doesn't say anything, just takes his place in our huddle.

Somehow, us together like this feels right, regardless of my reservations.

I enjoy it for what it is. Temporary. A precious

memory I'll look back on one day. Nothing good ever lasts.

When the horrific dreams chase me into consciousness in the middle of the night, I hug my pillow and slip out of bed. Constantine's door is already open, like he knew I would come. As soon as I appear in his doorway, he lifts the covers, and I climb in, curling myself around him. He holds me tight, my head pillowed on the soft hair of his chest and one leg draped over his muscular thighs.

My eyelids are already drooping when the mattress dips and another arm circles around me. Tristan lies down, fitting himself to my back until I'm snuggled and warm between the two of them. Lips brush my hair, and he buries his nose in the dip of my neck where it meets my shoulder.

"Go back to sleep, baby," he says.

And I do.

CHAPTER 26

I'm woken from a deep sleep by a hand caressing my arm, feather-light.

"Time to wake up," Tristan says against my shoulder, then scrapes his teeth over the tendon.

When I unglue my heavy eyelids, the first thing I see is Constantine's gorgeous face. The dark scruff that covers his jaw creases with his soft smile.

My spine goes taut when I feel something hard pressed intimately to my butt. I vaguely recall coming into Constantine's room last night and Tristan joining us.

The curtains are pulled open, the sky a dewy bluish-gray, which means it's around six in the morning.

Tristan's hand moves from my arm to the gauze taped to my shoulder.

"I can feel you overreacting," he says, pulling back one side of the medical tape.

I'm in bed with two men whose morning erections are poking me. Of course I'm overreacting.

Tristan removes the gauze entirely, and cold air

tickles the area where the bullet grazed.

The bullet.

How all of this started.

When I try to slide my leg off Constantine, he grips under the bend of my knee and pulls me back.

"Stay."

"What?" I ask Tristan, missing the entirety of what he said.

He huffs and starts over. "You need to let this air. The stitches look good. Hen can remove them this weekend."

I recall Serena's comment about how Tristan and Hendrix like to share women. Instead of being appalled at the thought, I'm more intrigued than anything. The mechanisms of how it would work. How it would feel.

Tristan goes back to slowly stroking my arm.

"I work tonight," I say to fill the silence. It gives my brain something else to think about other than how much I like being here in bed with them.

Tristan didn't ask my permission to touch me like he usually does. Then again, he really doesn't need to. Not with me.

"We'll be there."

We, meaning all of them.

"I swear to fucking Christ," a British accent rumbles right before Hendrix sits down at the foot of the bed.

I'm tempted to kick him off.

"Breakfast is ready." Hendrix grabs the ankle of my free foot stuck under the covers, reading my intention. "Who's with the brat this morning?"

Seriously?

I sleepily glare at Hendrix.

"Same as Monday," Tristan replies, sweeping my

tangled hair off my neck before pressing a kiss there. He smacks my butt as he climbs off the bed.

Hendrix eyes the spot Tristan vacated.

"Don't even think about it."

Damn those dimples when a roguish smile creases his cheeks.

"Wouldn't dream of it, firefly. Not unless you begged."

Constantine fulfills my wish and shoves Hendrix off the end of the bed with his foot.

"Dipshit," we hear from the floor, and I turn my face to Constantine's chest and giggle.

Hendrix's messy blond head pops up, and he rests his elbows on the low footboard, propping his chin on his hands like a mischievous child who's trying to act innocent. There is not one innocent bone in his body.

"If I promise to behave, can I talk to Syn alone for a sec?"

A flurry of trepidation pounces on me. If he thinks we're going to discuss what happened yesterday evening...

Constantine doesn't move a muscle.

"Swear I won't intentionally do or say anything to piss her off," Hendrix says.

That leaves unintentionally, which is pretty much a guarantee.

Constantine signs something I don't catch, but Hendrix nods his agreement. No matter how badly I want to claw my fingers into Constantine's arm to stop him from leaving, I don't. I do, however, get a very happy eyeful of Constantine in the black boxer briefs he likes to wear to sleep in. One day I'm going to take my time and study every detail of the tattoos painted on his body. I want to know the stories behind each one.

Constantine grabs his sweats off the corner chair and yanks them on, then takes his phone from the nightstand.

"Coffee?"

"Yes, please," I reply. He doesn't ask Hendrix.

Once Constantine leaves, Hendrix gets off the floor and comes around to the side of the bed where he sees the wadded-up gauze and tape Tristan removed from my shoulder.

"Let me take a look."

Sitting up, I untwist the bra and tank top straps and readjust them to lie flat over my shoulder.

"Tristan said it looked fine."

"I'd like to see for myself."

"I'm good."

A muscle in Hendrix's jaw ticks.

I lean back against the headboard and clutch my pillow to my chest. It smells like me, Constantine, and Tristan.

"I need you to come to New York with me on Friday. We'll be staying the weekend."

"Why?" I wheeze.

"My father is flying in from London, and he insists you come."

Hendrix looks uncomfortable, which makes me uncomfortable.

"But *why*?" I repeat.

And how does his father know about me? Unless... Tristan's father. This is not good.

His shoulders fall, his demeanor completely deflating like a sad balloon that's lost its helium. The man standing before me now is not the arrogant Hendrix I'm used to seeing.

"I don't have an answer for that," he admits and sits down next to me on the bed.

Enigmatic blue eyes flicker over my face. He takes a pen left out on the nightstand and holds it between his teeth. He gathers my hair in his hands and lifts it, then twirls the strands in a corkscrew. Using the pen like a chopstick, he spears the ball of my hair and rotates, then shoves the pen through, locking the loose bun at the back of my head.

It's such a sweet gesture, one I don't know how to process coming from him.

I search his face, needing to understand this complicated man who creates such tumultuous feelings inside me. Hate and want intermix, a complex combination.

Lowering the pillow, I take Hendrix's hand and flip it over, exposing the small green clover on the back of his wrist that I just noticed. He slips his hand out of my grasp.

"Will you come? Please?"

Color me shocked as shit. He knows the word please and can use it in a sentence.

"I have to work Friday and Saturday."

"I'll talk to Keith."

I'm not going to ask how he knows my boss. The guys seem to know everyone in Darlington.

"I can't miss work. I need the money."

"Your rent has been taken care of."

I'm pretty sure every excuse I'll throw at him, he'll have a response for.

My eyebrows knit and pull together as I think.

"How important is this to you?"

Reaching over my legs, he braces his arm on

the mattress and leans in. My imbecilic heart beats erratically.

"Very."

Dammit. I'm going to cave. He sees it, and a victorious grin appears.

But I have one more question.

"Are you and your father close?"

"No."

Should have expected that. All of their fathers seem to be grade-A assholes.

"The Amatos are shipping. What does your family do?"

"Investment banking."

I'm making mental notes of everything and will record them in my journal later, so I don't forget. After falling down that proverbial rabbit hole into social media when I searched their names, I haven't done any more digging.

"What about Constantine's family?"

Those blue eyes flash with exasperation. "You'll need to ask him."

Learning anything about these men is like pulling teeth. They're so damn secretive.

"I'll go on one condition."

Hendrix looks suspicious. "I'm listening."

Maneuvering out from under his arm, I practically roll off the side of the bed and land on my feet. What I'm about to ask him is something I thought about a lot since Aleksander cornered me in the elevator. Yesterday's run-in with Aleksei just solidified it.

"You teach me how to fight."

I'd ask Constantine but the thought of throwing a punch at him or hurting him in any way doesn't sit right. Hendrix, I would have no problem hitting. Tristan would flat out say no.

Hendrix timbers like a tree onto the bed and rolls over onto his stomach.

"Hate to break it to you, firefly, but you already know how to fight."

So they keep saying. But that's something I'll deal with at a later time.

"Those are my terms," I tell him, strolling out of the room with my head held high. "And I want back the knife you stole from me, asshole."

CHAPTER 27

It's almost a sense of déjà vu as I watch Syn over the lip of my beer as she carries a tray to a table of guys. When one of them snatches the back of her pants as she hands him his drink, Con almost rips my shirt in two as he yanks me back down to my seat when I try to get up to go murder the prick.

Syn deftly sidesteps and moves out of the guy's reach while placing everyone else's orders in front of them.

"She can take care of herself. Let her do her fucking job," Hendrix says, but I know he feels the same way from the deadly way he's locked on their table.

"He touches her again, he's going to lose a fucking hand."

The Bierkeller isn't as busy on Wednesday nights like it is on the Fridays and Saturdays when everyone comes to wind down after a long week. I glance up at the large television screen playing a college football game between the Carolina Wildcats and the Duke Blue Devils. After a minute of trying to focus on the game, I give up.

"Find out who that fucker is," I tell Con, who immediately snaps a picture of the guy with his phone.

With the low lights and his profile turned away from me, I can't get a clear picture of who he is.

"Can I get you anything else, boys? Another beer?" Shelby says, appearing at our table with the stacked burgers we ordered.

Syn refused to let us sit in her section. Whatever Hendrix said to her this morning pissed her off. I wish he'd just accept that he wants her and stop fighting it. He's been a surly ass all week long, even more so than usual.

Hen doesn't even give Shelby a second glance, something he always does.

"Thanks, Shelbs. We're good for now."

She retrieves our empty glasses from the table and sashays back to the bar.

I throw a fry at Hendrix. "What's up with you?"

He forces his gaze from Syn. "Your dad's a dick."

Tell me something I don't already know. I flex my hand, stretching the scab left from his cigar. It's been peeling and irritating the hell out of me.

Like Hendrix, Con's gaze is following Syn as she goes back and forth from the bar to the tables.

"Care to fill me in on what Dad has done now?" I ask, taking a bite of my burger.

Juices soak into the bun, and the smoked tarragon used to sauté the mushrooms hits my palette. Almost as good as what Hendrix makes.

"Syn's coming with me to New York this weekend," he says, hurling it out there out of the blue.

"The fuck she is," I immediately reply.

Con sits back and folds his arms over his chest, clearly

displeased.

Hendrix dips a fry into a side dish of white vinegar, which is absolutely fucking disgusting.

"Dad's flying into town. I don't have a choice. Besides, Syn already agreed."

So that's what the private conversation was about with Syn this morning. Sneaky son of a bitch. And if Hen says he doesn't have a choice, it means Patrick Knight wants her there. Goddammit, Dad.

"Con and I are coming with you."

"Don't need you to babysit," Hendrix snaps.

Don't give a shit if he doesn't like it.

"We're coming with you."

Hendrix thumps a fist on the table, making the silverware rattle.

"Are you saying that I can't keep her safe or is it because she'll be with me—*alone*?"

Screw his insinuation. But, yeah, that's exactly what I'm saying.

"We're coming," Con states matter-of-factly, and Hendrix's mouth pulls into a tight line, but he doesn't say anything more.

I'm still not used to hearing Con talk, but fuck if every time he does doesn't make me happy. I've missed my friend. Con has been a shell of himself for so long. A man who's here in body, not soul. We all died that day when *she* did.

I find Syn among the chaos around the bar as she waits for Keith to finish pulling a beer at the tap. It feels good to want something again. Not because my Dad or the Society demands it, but because it's what *I* want.

Changing subjects because the former is officially closed for further discussion, I inform them, "I finally got that meeting scheduled with Keane Agosti. It's in two weeks. I'll need to fly to Texas for a couple of days."

Dad wasn't happy about the timetable but fuck him. Keane is out of the country until then, so there isn't much I can do about it.

Hendrix submerges a few fries in the vinegar and leaves them there to soak into the potato, and my stomach heaves.

"Take one of us to have your back, just in case."

The just in case is because of Keane's right-hand man, Jaxson West. The Grim Reaper. Not someone you ever want to meet in a dark alley at night, or anywhere else. The stories I've heard about him would give the devil nightmares.

Syn's red hair pulled in a high ponytail snags my focus once more when she returns to the table of jackasses. I catch the same guy palm Syn's ass when she places the leather receipt holder containing the bill in front of him. He's about to find out in the most painful of ways that you don't touch what's mine.

As soon as she walks off and disappears down the hallway that leads to the restrooms and back office, I'm out of my seat before Con can stop me.

When I get to the guy's chair, he looks up, all bright-eyed and cocky grin. I recognize him. He's Society. Sophomore. Branson, I think his name is. Youngest son of Benedict Falco, head of Falco Oil. Old money but low on the totem pole in our organization.

Face falling slack in surprise, he stutters, "Mr. Amato."

Branson dips his head in deference and respect. I want to grab a fistful of his blond hair and smash his face into the wood table but that would cause a scene.

I eye each of his friends, one by one. They're too busy drinking and yelling at the football game playing on the big screen. They aren't Society, so I need to be subtle. I don't want to draw attention to the punishment I'm about to inflict.

Laying one hand on the back of his chair and the other on top of his hand resting on the table, I cant my hips and bend at the waist.

"That girl you keep touching like you have a right—" I twist his pinky until the pleasing snap of bone breaking can be felt. Branson recoils with a sudden jerk when the pain hits but doesn't make a sound. He knows better. "She's mine. Are we clear?"

His head bobs with his understanding, sweat breaking out along his hairline when I apply pressure to his already swelling finger before removing my hand from on top of his.

"Drinks are on me," I tell him and slap his back.

"Thank you, Mr. Amato." He slips his right hand onto his lap under the table. He won't be able to grip a pen correctly for a few weeks.

With that settled, I go in search of Red.

And that's when I see him.

The guy from the alley. His back is to me as he slips out of view, but I know it's him. I don't know how I know, I just do. What the fuck? Dad said Malin took care of him.

My adrenaline is already high, and it spikes even higher when his hunched form disappears down the hallway.

Toward Syn.

CHAPTER 28

Using my employee key to get into the back office, I close the door with an irritated slam. Why do guys have to act like such asshats? I'd take getting beer spilled on me over being molested by grabby hands.

Knowing I need to get back out onto the floor, I allow myself two minutes to calm down. After washing my hands and splashing some cold water over my face, I feel almost normal again. *Only an hour to go before my shift ends*, I remind myself.

It's been a long day, and I'm ready to go home with the guys.

Home.

Funny how that thought slides out of my brain with ease. Staying at their house is temporary. I know this. It's not permanent, and neither are they. Something I need to drill into my subconscious with a repeating mantra.

I made them sit in Shelby's section because I knew they'd be distracting. And I was right. Even from across the room, I felt the burden of their stares as I delivered orders to tables—and I honestly kind of liked the attention a little too much.

"Don't get used to it," I tell my reflection and sigh.

What was it Hendrix said to Tristan the other morning about me being one of his toys? In a figurative way, I guess I am. A broken toy they're intrigued by but will get bored with eventually. Then they'll move on to the next toy. A newer, more sparkly one. Someone like Serena.

Having thoroughly depressed myself, I rip a couple of paper towels out of the dispenser and dab my face dry, then re-do my ponytail—and almost scream my damn head off when a man appears behind me in the bathroom mirror.

I spin around and punch Tristan as hard as I can in the chest. He doesn't even flinch.

"Stop doing that!"

Within the confines of the small bathroom, my shout comes out ten times louder.

His movements are a bit manic as he searches the bathroom. He grabs me and does the same anxious perusal of my person. I hold in the scathing names I want to call him for scaring me for a third time in as many days because I see the worry in his eyes.

"Tristan, what's wrong?"

He cups my face between desperate hands. "Did anyone come in here?"

Frown lines form. "No. Why?"

"I swore I saw…" I think he mumbles but I'm not sure because within the next breath, he's crushing me in his arms like he has no plans of ever letting go.

Not understanding what's going on, I try to soothe him the best I can and wrap my arms around his waist, laying my cheek flush against his chest.

"Tristan, what?" I whisper, afraid to speak too loudly.

His fingers play with my ponytail, something I've noticed he likes doing. My frown grows when I feel how chaotic his heartbeat is.

"Is it the twins? Your dad?"

I start to panic because he's internally freaking out. Tristan isn't afraid of anything.

"Shh. Just let me hold you for a second."

I don't know what else to do other than to say, "Okay."

It only takes a minute for his pulse to return to normal but his hold around me stays strong. The heat emanating off his body feels so good, and I close my eyes, letting my mind drift. I think we both needed this hug. Held in his arms, my crappy night isn't so crappy.

"Keith is going to wonder where I got to."

"Keith can wait a damn minute."

My hands move up and down his back in a gentle motion, fingertips kneading the tense muscles around his shoulder blades. Tristan seems to carry the weight of the world. A modern-day Atlas.

"Are you going to tell me what's going on?"

A puff of air exhales into my hair.

"Tristan," I prod, leaning back in his arms.

So many secrets hide in his whiskey eyes.

That full mouth tips up. A smile that doesn't fully form.

"Nothing, Red. I promise."

I don't believe him.

Shelby and I lean against the bar, enjoying the

lull right before Keith announces last call. Ten more minutes before my shift ends.

"You keep staring at him like that, and you're going to burn a hole through his head."

Tristan and Hendrix bailed a little while ago, leaving Constantine to be my delegated bodyguard. After the weird encounter with Tristan in the back office, I've felt… off.

I reach behind me and pick up the iced tea Keith made for me. The condensation drips from the bottom of the glass and plops cold droplets on my trousers.

Chewing on the straw, I reply, "I'm not staring."

Which is a baldfaced lie.

Shelby taps one pink manicured nail on the bar top. "The last time I looked at a man the way you're looking at Constantine Ferreira, I got knocked up with Christian."

I slap a hand over my mouth before I spew iced tea everywhere. Shelby cracks up at my expense.

"You are too easy to fluster, country girl," she says, patting my back.

I groan at the nickname.

"How is Christian?" I ask, crunching on ice to help cool me down because it suddenly feels like the heat has been cranked up.

Shelby excitedly takes out her phone from the front pocket of her server's waist apron.

"He fingerpainted for the first time today."

She stays home during the day with Christian, so he doesn't have to go to preschool. Too goddamn expensive. Her words. Her mother watches him in the evening while she works. She hasn't said anything about Christian's dad, and because it's none of my business, I've never asked.

"Here." She shows me a picture she took of him with paint-smeared hands proudly held high. He's covered in a rainbow of colors from head to toe, the biggest smile lighting his cherubic face. He's the spitting image of Shelby from the jet-black hair to the bright blue eyes.

"Your kid is the most adorable thing I've ever seen."

She beams at me. "He's my little monster. Love him to pieces. Best thing to ever happen to me."

The adoring way she says it brings a pang of grief. Did my mom love me like that? Was my childhood filled with playful fingerpaints? I want to remember so fucking badly.

Keith comes through the swinging doors that lead to the kitchen. "Last call, folks!" he hollers to an almost empty bar.

Instead of ordering one more, the three groups, one an older couple, get up and start corralling toward the front exit door with goodbyes and waves to us as they go.

Flinging the towel from his shoulder, Keith wipes down the bar. He and the kitchen staff will clean up and close.

"That going to be a regular thing?" he asks, waving the towel at Constantine, whose head is bowed as he does something on his phone.

"Maybe?" It's not like I can tell him the truth about why three guys now follow me around everywhere I go.

Keith levels me with a steely gaze. It's a look that I imagine most fathers have in their arsenal.

"Probably?"

"That means the same thing." He chuckles. "Cash out the tips and clock out. You have class tomorrow. Shelby, go home and snuggle with your little boy."

She's already untying her waist apron. "Don't have to tell me twice."

I quickly count out the money while Keith works. He whistles to some old Eagles song playing at low volume, and I find myself humming along as I divide my bill stack by half and add it to Shelby's pile. Keith knows that I give Shelby part of my tip money and never says anything. She needs it more than I do.

"You don't have to do that," I tell Constantine when he lifts and flips over the chairs to set on top of the tables so Keith can mop the floors.

I hate that Constantine was forced to sit around for five hours while I worked. It's so stupid and needless, and something I'm going to have to push Tristan about. There's no need for it. I'm completely safe here. It's not like his father or Aleksander would come in and start anything in a bar full of people and off-duty police officers who Keith hires to work as bouncers on the weekend.

"Tammi will cover your Friday and Saturday shifts."

I blink up at Keith. "Huh?"

"Have fun in the Big Apple."

I completely forgot to ask him for Saturday off, which means one of the guys did.

He turns off the wide screen with the remote he keeps behind the bar and heads to the kitchen with a bucket full of dirty glasses for the dishwasher.

Something else Tristan and I will be discussing is doing things behind my back without talking to me first.

Constantine finishes and walks to the middle of the room. The space seems that much bigger with the chairs off the floor, but also smaller with him in it.

"I'll go grab my stuff."

He curls a finger at me, and for some reason, my stomach explodes in wild flutters.

"It'll only take a second."

He does another come-hither bend of the finger that has those flutters swooping. He points down at the floor directly in front of him, his way of saying 'come here.'

With uncertain steps, I'm reeled in until the toes of our shoes touch. In the span of a microsecond, the mood shifts and everything around me falls away until he is the only thing I see.

Constantine takes my hand and places it directly over his chest where his heart beats a steady rhythm that matches the slow song coming out of the speakers.

"Can I have this dance?"

I don't know why tears suddenly gather behind my eyes or why I imagine two children dancing in the rain on a white sand beach. Neither makes sense.

"You want to dance with me?"

He nods.

"*Here?*"

He pulls his bottom lip with his teeth and nods again.

How is this the same man I met a week ago? The guy with the lifeless eyes who scared the shit out of me with one look.

I'm inundated with emotions. Drown in them. His simple request to dance with him terrifies me, and I can't quite decipher the reason for it.

With one hand holding mine to his chest, he cradles the other at the small of my back and pulls me closer. Every cell in my body pulses to life when he dips his head. I want his mouth on mine. I want to know what it feels like to be kissed by Constantine.

Hendrix's kiss may have ruined me, but I'm certain that one kiss from Constantine will shatter me to my foundation.

I need to stop this. It's not right to want three men, one of them I hate more often than not. I don't really know them, and they don't know me—*I* don't even know me. Things between us are not normal.

I furl his shirt in my hand. "Hendrix kissed me," comes out of my mouth.

It's official. I'm out of my damn mind.

Constantine's fingers press into my spine, and I'm not expecting him to reply, "Good."

Good? Nothing good can come from this. It has disaster written all over it.

Constantine keeps me firmly pressed against him. We're in a heated stare-off, his lips so close to mine that I can taste the hops of the beer he drank.

"You can't run from this, Syn," he says in that gravelly tone that makes my pussy throb with unfulfilled need.

I jump like a startled cat when Keith loudly announces from the kitchen, "I'm locking up."

"Just need to grab my stuff!" I call back. With sweaty palms and erratic palpitations, I tell Constantine, "I'm not running."

But my actions speak otherwise as I dash off to the back office to collect my things.

CHAPTER 29

"Mind telling me what we're doing here?" I ask Tristan when he parks in front of Syn's apartment.

Other than tell me to come with him, he hasn't said much since we left the Bierkeller. Something is bothering him, and I fucking hate when he goes all quiet.

The engine idles as he folds his hands over the steering wheel and leans forward to look through the front windshield. Light from a nearby lamppost washes his face an eerie yellow.

"I thought I saw the guy from the alley tonight."

Immediately alert, I turn in the car seat. "Where?"

Tristan is the only one of us who got a good look at him. By the time Con and I arrived, the fucker was already sprinting down the other end of the alley.

"The bar. His beard was gone, but I swear it was him."

Tristan is never wrong. He has good recall for faces and details, and if he says he saw the guy, I don't doubt it for a second.

Feeling his paranoia, I open the glove compartment box and remove the false backing to get the compact Smith and Wesson he keeps there.

"Thought your dad said he took care of him."

Tristan sits back in his seat and runs his hands through his hair, making it stick up at odd angles.

"He said Malin did."

Same difference. Malin is Francesco's pit bull. The one sent to do the dirty work so Francesco keeps his hands clean.

"You think he's fucking with us?"

Tristan's huff belays his suspicions. "I think something is going on. Something we're not seeing."

Already knowing what he wants to do, I ask anyway. "We searching her place?"

His head swivels my way. "I need to know."

Syn seems to be on everyone's radar, and we need to know why. That girl carries around too many unknowns, and I think her past is the key. She claims she can't remember it, but what if she's lying? Is she a Trojan horse our fathers placed in our path? I'll put a bullet in her head if we find out she's been playing us.

I cross the distance between us with my arm and grab the back of his neck. "Yeah, brother, we do."

He and Con are already invested in our little redhead. Worse, she's fucked with my head, niggled her way inside, until I don't know what to think.

Pulling the handle, I get out of the car, making sure to tuck the gun in my back waistband and pull my shirt down to hide it. Tristan scans the parking lot, and once he's satisfied that no one is lurking, we climb the stairs to Syn's apartment. Someone's television blares from one of the adjacent apartments, the volume loud enough to carry outside so I can tell it's an old episode of *CSI: Miami* from the distinctive intro music.

The building is one of the newer ones constructed in Darlington. A little on the cheaper side since it caters to the university crowd and students who don't want to live in the dorms.

"Key?" I ask when we get to her door. If not, I can pick the lock.

"Grabbed it from her bag in the back office."

Tristan produces a single key from his pocket and inserts it, only to find that the door gives way. Our eyes briefly meet right before I'm pulling out my gun. Con wouldn't have forgotten to lock up when he brought Syn to get her stuff.

Tristan slowly inches the door open wider for me to see inside. The interior is dark and quiet, but that doesn't mean shit.

"Stay here," I whisper and step inside.

Tristan can absolutely hold his own, but I'm the one with the weapon.

I stop just past the threshold and cock my head to listen. A noise, a rustle, anything that would alert me to someone else in here. My pulse stays steady and even, my gun ready, as I walk farther into the room. Something bumps my foot and clatters across the floor. If there is someone in here, I just rang the fucking bell to give myself away.

I reach out to feel along the wall until my fingers touch an outlet cover, then a switch. Recessed lights immediately turn on overhead.

"What the hell?" Tristan says from the open doorway.

Syn's place is completely trashed. Shit scattered all over the place, furniture upturned, cushions and throw pillows shredded with their white stuffing hanging out.

Tristan comes inside and shuts the door. We can't take the chance of a noisy neighbor walking by and thinking it was us who did this.

"Let me clear the place."

Syn's apartment is a small studio with an open square floor plan. No hallway, just a living room, kitchen, bedroom, and attached bathroom, all interconnected in one big space. The only demarcation between the rooms is one door. Syn's bedroom.

Turning on the light attached to a five-blade ceiling fan, I find her room in the same state as the rest of her place—destroyed in a chaotic mess.

I check any hiding places and make sure the window latch is still locked.

"Jesus fucking Christ," Tristan says when he joins me.

"Random burglary?" I ask. But we both know it's not.

"I'd say Aleksander or Aleksei, but I honestly don't fucking know."

The drawers to her dresser are pulled out and rifled through. I do my own search. Delicate lace thongs in different colors. Not what I expected. I grab the black pair and shove them inside my back jeans pocket. Tristan notices with interest, so I throw him a pair.

"She really doesn't have that much," he comments, poking at various discarded items of clothing. He picks up a small framed photograph of a rooster, the only thing that hasn't been broken or tossed.

"What is it with her and roosters?"

"She grew up isolated on a farm with no friends." At least that's the story she told us.

"Be wary of those who come to you in sheep's clothing, for inwardly they are ravenous wolves."

We meticulously go through the rest of the apartment and find not a damn thing. Nothing that would give us any insight into her or why someone would break in.

Opening the fridge, it's empty except for a bottle of water, which I take.

Tristan turns a slow circle, taking in the living room one last time. "I'll get Con to come and clean this mess up. Say nothing to Syn about it."

A few droplets of water spill down my chin as I guzzle the entire contents of the bottle, then toss it into the trash bin I find next to the small kitchen island.

"I think it's time we call in a favor from a certain blonde."

Con hasn't had any luck finding info on Syn, but Tessa Goodwyn sure as hell can. She went to the same boarding school as us. Scary smart. Computer genius. Can hack into anything, including secured government databases. She used to sell her specialized skills to anyone who could afford it. Heard she's at MIT, which is a stone's throw away from Darlington Founders.

"Unfortunately, I think you're right," Tristan replies.

CHAPTER 30

The one thing I hate about working at a bar is the stench I come home with. Grease and beer are as bad as the funky outdoor smell I detest. As soon as Constantine and I get back to the house, I'm in the shower. I didn't see Tristan or Hendrix when we came in and am curious where they got off to so late in the evening. Just another secret to add to the million that shroud them like a thick fog.

Walking out of the bathroom with a towel wrapped around my chest, I grab the button-up dress shirt I stole from Constantine's room and slip the sleeves up my arms. As I fasten each button, the silky material brushes my sensitive nipples, tightening them into aching points. I leave the top two undone, so the shirt hangs crookedly off one shoulder, then tie the bottom tails in a knot at my navel. I opt for no underwear and dress in a loose pair of sweats, ones that are Tristan's that I haven't been able to return. I have to roll them at the waist, so they fit snugly along my hip bones and won't fall off. Because I'm too tired to take the time to blow dry it, I braid my wet hair in a fishtail side braid that drapes over my neck.

Lifting my bag from the chair where I left it, I get settled on the window bench to do an hour of coursework before bed. Unfortunately, my mind won't stop thinking about what happened with Constantine or about what he said when I told him Hendrix kissed me.

"Good."

The way Hendrix kissed me was definitely good. More than good. The fact that Constantine liked that he did is... perplexing and something I've been obsessing over since we left the Bierkeller.

Staring out the window, the all too familiar loneliness creeps in. I wish I had someone to talk to about it. A friend who could help me figure out these bizarre feelings I keep having. Alana would listen and not judge, but she's my mom and it would be weird. Maybe Raquelle?

Foregoing calculus problems in lieu of writing in my journal, I pull it out of my bag and flip through it, looking at each picture I've drawn and the words that accompany them. The story of my past is locked in this journal, written in coded ramblings and pencil sketches of vague nightmares that continue to elude me.

I place the journal in front of me and start from the beginning where I keep the pressed clover and Tristan's flower tucked into the crease of the page where it meets the spine. When I come across "They all will die," a shudder races over me, but also a sense of purpose. A thrill of... god, I don't know how to describe it, but it scares me.

I turn to the next page and find something that

doesn't belong there.

There's a small triangle of paper with uneven edges. It was torn from the corner of the journal page. I don't remember doing that. Doesn't mean that I didn't.

When I flip it over, the handwriting isn't mine. It's messy with elongated lines, like someone wrote it in a hurry.

He knows. Trust no one.

What does that even mean? The only connection I can make to the cryptic message is with Tristan's father. Maybe Aleksander and Aleksei. Why tell me something I already know?

But the answer I really want right now is how did someone find my journal? A stranger went through my private thoughts. Touched my things. It feels violating on so many levels. The things in this journal are *mine*. *My* secrets and fears. *My* fucking life I'm trying to piece together.

Knowing exactly where he'll be, I lock sights on Tristan sitting on the grass in the dark backyard. He came into the office of the Bierkeller tonight where I leave my bag while I work. An office that's locked at all times, but somehow, he was able to enter.

I think it's time I demand some real answers. No more willful ignorance.

Constantine looks up when I walk past his bedroom, no doubt waiting for me since I've made it a habit of sleeping in his bed every night.

Hendrix walks out of the kitchen and stops at the bottom of the stairs when he sees me coming.

"Don't say one fucking word to me," I inform him, but that doesn't stop him from blocking my way.

"What stick crawled up your ass?"

With as much attitude as the displeasure I'm feeling, I reply, "Where did you and Tristan go tonight?"

All his cocky pseudo-British arrogance vanishes and is replaced with a blank stare.

"Why do you want to know?"

I don't like the way he says that. It's filled with mistrust, and I have done nothing to warrant it. I've played by their rules and have done what they've said. And for what? My life is suddenly a crazy mess because of them.

I slap a hand flat to his chest and push. When that doesn't get him out of my way, I duck under his arm, but he grabs me in a crushing grip that will leave bruises.

"Watch it, firefly."

I let my gaze fall to his hand, then rake my tempestuous eyes up to his face.

"You don't get to touch me. *Ever*. Not unless you beg."

I enjoy throwing his own words back at him. Apparently, so does he. A malicious grin worthy of the devil curves his mouth.

Constantine bounds down the stairs.

"Let her go. Now."

From his menacing expression to his intimidating stance, the threat of what he'll do if Hendrix doesn't listen is clear as day.

I don't wait. I jerk my arm away from him and leave both of them to head outside. The midnight sky is overcast with a thick blanket of clouds. It smells like rain. I hope it's a thunderstorm. I love watching the fury of nature as lightning forks across the sky in a zigzag. The reverberating boom of thunder as it shakes the windows. Alana and I would sit outside whenever there was a nighttime storm. We'd howl up at the sky just as the thunder rolled over us, and we would dance under the pounding deluge, getting mud caked all over our feet and legs. Those are some of the best memories I keep and cherish. New ones that I go back to again and again when I get sad. I miss Alana. I miss home. I miss the tranquility of the farm and the boring life I used to live.

"Can we talk?"

Tristan doesn't look over when I approach. "Now's not a good time, Red."

He picks off a bell flower from a twig he must have snapped off the bush. I had thought the tattoo on his chest was that of a lotus. Looking at the small flower now, I realize that I was wrong.

I sit down in front of him so he has no choice but to look me in the eye.

"There never seems to be a good time."

A few mosquitoes buzz around me that I swat away, and I'm thankful I'm wearing a long-sleeved shirt and sweatpants.

"Whose shirt is that?"

"Constantine's."

He slides a finger under the opening at my shoulder, and my nipples respond instantaneously, making me wish I wore a bra.

"I'll give you one of mine to wear."

I don't give him the satisfaction of the eye roll that possessive reply deserves.

"I like wearing this one. I'm wearing your sweatpants."

A pleased grin stretches wide. "Good."

When his finger moves to my collarbone, I become profoundly crestfallen when he doesn't do anything more.

"You didn't ask if you could touch me."

He licks his lips and pushes his thumb into my jugular notch. "I think we're past that point, don't you?"

I turn my head slowly from side to side, denying the truth of it.

"Why did you come find me tonight in the back office?"

He picks at a blade of grass. "No reason."

"You acted like you were freaked out."

His snort is dismissive and ticks me off.

I unfold the small piece of paper I'd been holding and thrust it at him. "Did you put this in my bag? Did you go through my things?"

Taking the scribbled note, he reads it, then crushes it in a fist before I can take it back.

"Where'd you get this?"

I try to snatch at the paper, but he holds his hand out of my reach.

"Like I said, it was in my bag which I keep in Keith's office when I work. So I'm asking you, did you put it there?"

"Why the fuck would I do that?"

"You tell me."

Our matching scowls last for an entire sixty seconds. I know this because I count them.

I hold my palm out. "If it's not from you, then kindly give it back."

He doesn't. Surprise, surprise.

"When exactly did you find it?"

"Jesus, Tristan. I'm not answering any more of your questions until you start answering some of mine."

I despise the vacant look he's wearing. It's so similar

to Constantine's. Block out the world and pretend it doesn't exist.

I decide to throw down a challenge.

"If you won't answer me about the note, then tell me something real. Not the playboy bullshit remarks or the sexual innuendos. I want you to tell me a truth that not many people know. I need something because all this cloak and dagger crap is driving me insane."

He glances away, and I can already see him shutting down behind a brick wall of apathy, but I won't let him.

"No more secrets, Tristan. You're the one who brought me into your world. If you want me to stay, I need answers."

I swipe away a few curled pieces of hair that stick to my cheek and wait. Tension ratchets between us the longer the silence goes on. The disappointment that hits me when he doesn't say anything after long minutes is crushing.

"How did you get into the back office tonight?"

"The door was open."

"Don't lie to me!"

He takes my braid like a rein and uses it to pull me forward. "You want to talk about lies? You're full of them, Synthia Carmichael—small-town girl with no past that she claims she can't remember."

"Because I fucking can't!" I yell, pulling my braid free.

His finger hooks in the open V of my shirt, keeping me in place.

"You want something real, Red? A truth that no one else knows?" He invades my personal space, putting his lips to my ear. "I don't fucking believe you."

I'm officially done. With them, this house, with all of it. I'll take my chances with his father and the twins.

The only reason they're interested in me is because the guys are. Remove myself from that particular equation, and hopefully things will go back to the way they were before.

"Where are you going?" he asks when I push off the ground to stand.

"Back to my apartment."

I'm across the yard and reach the back patio when Tristan says from behind me, "Take another step and you'll regret it."

I suspend in place at his warning. Fight or flight endorphins flood my blood at the perceived threat. I didn't hear him follow me.

I carefully pivot and almost run at the sight of him. Dark. Dangerous. Deadly. This isn't the playful Tristan I'm used to, or the caring one who left me a beautiful pressed flower on my nightstand. The man in front of me now is something else entirely.

The first drops of rain pelt down from above, one by one in an uneven rhythm, and soak into my clothes, bringing a chill with them. In contrast, a thin veil of steam rises from Tristan where the cool rain meets his heated skin.

Mist clings to my lashes, blurring my vision. Even in my red haze of anger, Tristan is so devastatingly handsome, it hurts to look at him. Or perhaps I'm the one hurting because I've come to care for him.

"You're not leaving, Syn."

The rain beats down more heavily, plastering my hair to my head. Bright flashes of lightning pulsate the sky with white light which is soon followed by a long procession of thunder.

"Then give me a reason to stay!"

I barely have enough time to brace before he moves. Arms band around me, and my feet come off the ground.

"I'm your goddamn reason," he practically snarls as he kicks the back door open and carries me inside the house.

There's an instant chill from the air conditioning, and any protestation I would have made comes out in a whoosh of breath when my back unceremoniously meets the hard surface of the kitchen counter island. Rainwater from my clothes pools beneath me on the slick granite.

Tristan forces his way between my legs at the same time that he grabs my hips and yanks me toward him. I wrap my legs around his waist and lock my feet, so I don't slide right off the edge. I'm spread on the counter like a sacrifice at the altar. Hard meets soft when his thick erection pushes into my core through our clothing, and I go up in flames from that simple contact. I try to get closer, seeking more of the promise of pleasure he could give me.

Tristan slides a hand down my left leg from knee to hip and braces his other hand next to my head, then leans over me until all I can see is him.

His hand leaves my hip and runs up my chest, bunching the sopping silk as it goes. Fire and ice is the best way to describe the juxtaposition of his warm hand on my stomach. He tugs on my navel piercing, and my abdominal muscles quiver with excitement.

"Tell me to stop. Tell me you don't want this."

His savage gaze holds me hostage, his ownership of me commanding and unrelenting.

I try to speak, I swear I do, but I can't. I don't know

what I want anymore. I just know that I want this. I want him.

I accused Hendrix of having a Jekyll and Hyde complex. I guess I do, too. These men have me so screwed up in the head, questioning my morals of what is right and wrong and normal, I don't know up from down.

Tristan doesn't see me as broken. He doesn't see those flaws I carry that are reminders of the horrors inflicted upon me by some tragedy my mind refuses to remember. I'm so damn tired of existing in those nightmares, only to wake up feeling lost and alone and empty.

I want to live in this fantasy with him. I deserve the chance to experience what it would be like to have a man desire me, his hands roaming over my body, eager and possessive.

Tristan takes my silence as the consent I intended. His golden brown eyes smolder to a deeper hue of umber.

"The things I want to do to you, Red."

Say no. He'll stop if you say no. He promised he would.

"Do them," I hear myself say.

A startled gasp escapes when his lips descend and kiss a path from my stomach to my breastbone where my shirt gapes open, welcoming him to feast as he pleases. He tortures me with slowness, sucking and licking my tender skin until I can't lie still and writhe underneath him.

I cinch his hair in my hand and guide his mouth the rest of the way up my body so I can claim his lips. I'm the one initiating and taking what I want. And what I want is for Tristan Amato to kiss me.

"I put my mouth on you, Syn, and you're mine."

I heed the warning and willingly step over that precipice with zero regrets.

"I want your mouth on me."

The first touch of his lips is pure bliss, but the way he kisses me is nothing but debauched. He takes and takes with sinful swipes of his tongue until the sounds coming from me are pornographic.

"Has anyone touched you here before?" he hushes against my lips.

I jolt when his hand tickles down my stomach to between my legs.

"N… no." I can't tell whether my teeth are chattering from the cold of being in wet clothes or from how scared I am that I'll disappoint him in some way. I'm not Serena. I've never had sex or even kissed a guy before Hendrix.

"No?" He slips one finger under the rolled waistband of the sweatpants, teasing a fingertip across my stomach—back and forth, back and forth.

"I mean, yes. I… have. Touched myself, I mean."

I'd be mortified as shit confessing that but I'm too delirious from what he's doing to care.

Tristan places the barest of kisses at the corner of my mouth. "Fuck, woman. The thought of you touching yourself. Fucking your sweet pussy with your fingers. The moans you'd make."

The things he says incite a hunger inside me. I'm at the point of begging him to make me come, and he's hardly done anything.

He kisses the shell of my ear and bites the lobe between his teeth, then licks away the sting.

"Please, Tristan." My hips buck off the counter island,

demanding that his hand move lower.

He chuckles. It's a breathy, sexy sound that only heightens every incredible thing I'm feeling.

His hand slides farther down under the sweatpants but stops at my mons to play with the soft pubic hair there.

"No panties?"

My cheeks flush, and he smiles, one as devilish as the smile Hendrix gave me at the bottom of the stairs.

"Sweet Syn. How I'm going to enjoy ruining you."

I don't care what he does as long as he doesn't stop.

If I had the ability of rational thought, I'd be shocked at myself for what I'm allowing Tristan to do. Instead, I widen my legs.

"Be a good girl and put your hands above your head."

I obey. The kitchen island isn't very wide, and I'm able to grip the counter ledge on the other side. My spine bends in the new position, and Tristan doesn't hesitate to take advantage. One side of my shirt falls open to expose my bare breast, and my nipple puckers into a taut bud. But that isn't what Tristan pays attention to.

He sees the scars.

Tears clog my throat, and I close my eyes to will them away. This is where he'll walk away in disgust, and I can't watch him when he does.

"You're beautiful," he says, tenderly kissing the uneven skin where the doctors performed the first of many grafts.

Squeezing my eyes tight, I let the tears come.

"Open your eyes for me, baby."

As soon as I do, a moan rips from me when he plunges a finger inside my pussy. I wasn't prepared for it, which makes the stretch that much more intense.

Tristan watches my face closely. "Do you feel that?" he asks, wiggling his finger and rubbing some magical place that has me seeing literal stars.

"Oh, fuck."

He swipes his tongue up my breast and strokes the same spot along my internal walls again. I white-knuckle the countertop.

"Tristan."

"That's your G spot."

His mouth closes over my nipple and sucks, and a whole-body shudder shakes me.

"And this is your clit." The tip of his thumb circles the tiny bundle of nerves.

I want to tell him I know what a clit is, but I don't get the opportunity because he adds a second finger and begins to shallowly fuck me with them.

Higher and higher I climb to where he takes me. He's in control of my orgasm and uses that power to drive me out of my ever-loving mind.

"Please, please, please," I chant when he edges me to the peak, only to pull me back.

"You'll come when I tell you to."

That shouldn't sound as hot as it does but damn if it doesn't.

As Tristan's hand works me back up again, he nuzzles my chest, placing open-mouthed kisses along the side of each breast.

Then he stops.

"What the hell is this?"

I don't understand what he's asking until I peer down my chest to where the shirt reveals the bite mark Hendrix left.

I rush to sit up and get hit with a bout of dizziness.

"Answer me, Syn."

Embarrassed beyond belief, we play tug-of-war as I try to cover myself to no avail. Buttons pop off one by one as he rends the shirt right down the middle. The lips that were just kissing me turn down in a severe frown when he traces the purplish-red bruise.

I look away to stare out the window. A jagged bolt of lightning streaks down from cloud to ground in the distance.

"I'm not asking you again. Who did this?"

"I did."

CHAPTER 31

My heart stops when Hendrix walks into the kitchen, then electroshocks back to life when I see Constantine standing in the doorway, his gaze riveted to me.

"You're" —Hendrix smiles at me when he finishes with— "wet."

His innuendo tells me what I was afraid of. He saw everything.

Drops of water from Tristan's hair splash and sizzle on my skin when he twists around to look at Hendrix.

"I told you not to fucking touch her again."

Casual as can be, Hendrix saunters over to the fridge and takes out a beer.

"She didn't say no," he replies, twisting the cap off the bottle and flicking it into the sink.

This is not happening.

I'm sitting on the counter island with Tristan standing between my legs, suffering from the worst case of lady blue balls because he wouldn't let me come, and trying my best to cover myself—without any buttons because Tristan made sure to tear off every single one. I'm left holding the shirt together at my breasts. The cold that envelops me is caused by humiliation and not the still-damp clothes that encase my skin.

"You let him touch you?"

I can't tell if Tristan is angry or not, so I err on the side of caution.

Head bowed, I mumble, "Not exactly. It just happened."

I implore Constantine with mental telepathy to help me. Do something. I want to tuck tail and run to my room so I can hide and never come out.

"Fucking hell, Hen. You broke the skin," Tristan chastises, trying to force another peek by pulling the shirt to the side but I have a death grip on it.

"She had Con's smell all over her. Why aren't you barking at him?"

If Hendrix was any closer, I'd smack the crap out of him. What I do or don't do with Constantine isn't his business.

"Because he didn't fucking bite her!"

I wiggle in place, hoping Tristan gets the message that I want to get down. "Could you move, please?"

The three of them can laugh and joke and talk about me when I'm no longer in the room. I'll never be able to look them in the eye again. I can only imagine the nasty things Hendrix will enjoy telling Serena the next time he fucks her. How I was so desperate for a man that I jumped from guy to guy, hoping to get any scrap of attention they would give me.

"Did you like it?"

Shocked that he'd ask, my head jerks up and I balk at Constantine.

He walks over and plants himself next to Tristan. One long, inked finger feathers down my cheek, then continues on its way across my sternum to Hendrix's mark.

"Did you like it when he did that to you?"

I'd be crazy to say yes.

"I'm sorry."

I don't know which I'm apologizing for: yes, I did like it, or that I didn't stop Hendrix from doing it. It would kill me if I hurt Constantine. I'm attracted to Hendrix for fuck knows what reason, but I genuinely care for and like Constantine. He's my safe place, and I'd like to also think he's becoming a friend. Hendrix may make my heart beat wilder, but Constantine makes it beat stronger. And Tristan... he may be a little bit of both.

"Never apologize. Not to me."

His voice cracks at the end, not used to speaking more than a few words at a time.

The entire time Constantine has been talking, Tristan has been playing with my hair. Even braided, it must look like a frizzy mess after getting wet in the rain. I haven't heard any more thunder.

I swallow down the shame I feel. "I'm not a slut. I don't—"

Constantine shuts me up by saying, "No one in this room would ever think that."

I shake my head to knock some sense into me. "I should leave. This is getting too complicated. I don't belong here."

"Yes, you do," Tristan argues, hemming me in.

Constantine takes off his shirt and slips it over my head. The cotton is warmed from his body heat. I'm able to slip my arms out of the button-up and push them through the armholes of the T-shirt without flashing my tits. If only I could do the same with the sweatpants.

"Thank you."

His bare chest is distracting, and I try not to stare.

Constantine takes my ruined shirt, which is really his, and tosses it into the trash.

Hendrix gets out four mugs from an upper cabinet. "Since we seem to be having a kumbaya moment in the kitchen, who wants coffee?"

If they're going to pretend everything is fine, then I will, too.

"Hot chocolate?" I ask. "I can make it." I remember seeing a canister of powdered cocoa in the pantry.

This time when I indicate I want to get down, Tristan lets me.

Hendrix already has a small pot out when I come back with the cocoa, a can of sweetened condensed milk, and a bag of marshmallows I also find. For guys, they really do have a nicely stocked kitchen. Isn't the stereotype of male food preferences either takeout or frozen pizza?

"Can opener?"

Tristan and Constantine pull out barstools and sit down, content to watch.

Hendrix takes out a manual one from a drawer and opens the can for me. I eyeball how much cocoa to pour and add the condensed milk. Hendrix spoons in some sugar and turns on the gas hob, taking over to stir the mixture on low heat.

"Grab me the vanilla extract," he says, gesturing to a thin cabinet next to the fume hood. "And take off your pants."

My arm stops midway when reaching to get the vanilla. "Why?"

"You're dripping all over my fucking floor."

I peer down at my feet and don't see anything. And even though Constantine's shirt hangs to my knees, the sweatpants stay on since I'm not wearing any underwear.

"I'm good."

"Prude."

"Asshat."

Tristan stops our immature verbal volley. "Can we talk about the note?"

"No."

"What note?" Hendrix asks.

"The one Red incorrectly assumes is from me." Tristan offers the piece of paper to Constantine.

Where did you get this? he signs.

His throat must be hurting after talking so much.

"I found it in my bag after we got home."

I don't say journal because they'll insist I show it to them.

Hendrix turns the burner off and adds a splash of vanilla to the heated mixture. The smell of chocolate and vanilla has me almost drooling.

"Is somebody going to tell me what it says?"

"I'm not doing this again with you," I tell Tristan and reach over the counter island to snatch the note from Constantine. "You had your chance to be straight with me, and you blew it."

"I told you I didn't write it, and you didn't believe me," he angrily retorts.

"I do believe you." Now.

When Aleksander was in the elevator with me, he took my bag as I was trying to get to my phone. It would have been easy for him to drop the note inside the front pocket where I keep my journal. Just another mindfuck from the twins who seem hellbent on messing with me because they want a reaction from Tristan.

Hendrix pours a mug of hot chocolate and offers it to me. When I try to take it, he pulls it back.

"What did the note say?"

"I'm sure Tristan will be more than happy to fill you in."

I'm not telling them anything again until they start reciprocating.

I grab the ladle Hendrix was using and make my own cup of hot chocolate. Instead of opening the bag of marshmallows, I take the entire thing. I need some sugar therapy and plan to eat half the bag in my room.

"You're ruining my life."

"Red—"

My chest constricts until I can barely breathe. "I never asked for any of this."

Pressure builds and builds as the pounding in my head grows louder and louder. It's like someone is banging a fist against a door, wanting to be let out.

Pound. Pound. Pound.

"Neither did we," Tristan stoically states, but it sounds like he's talking about something more than me.

CHAPTER 32

I wait until I hear Syn's bedroom door close upstairs before addressing Con.

"Hen and I went to her place. Someone broke in and trashed it." I hadn't had a chance to tell him since we returned to the house.

Con doesn't react, which is typical.

"She's demanding to know stuff we can't tell her. Said she would leave."

That gets a reaction. A swift one.

"No."

I wholeheartedly agree. I'll tie her sweet ass to my bed if she tries. I fucking meant what I said when I told her that she was mine.

Hendrix offers me the hot chocolate he and Syn made. I've never had any before. Growing up, I missed out on many of the simple pleasures a kid gets to enjoy. Then again, I was never allowed to be a kid.

"This is really good," I say after taking a sip.

Hendrix pulls out a bottle of bourbon. "This will make it even better."

I hold out my mug.

"You can't hurt her like that. She's not one of your toys to play with until you break her."

Hen makes a scoff of annoyance as he takes a swig of bourbon straight from the bottle. "That girl is made of titanium. I doubt there is much that can break her."

Syn is indeed strong, but everyone has a breaking point. Mine happened ten years ago.

"You fucking her?" he asks.

Con signs, *He asked me the same thing.*

"Do you care?"

"No."

Yes, he does. He's so fucking jealous, it stinks the air.

"For someone who says he isn't interested, you act the opposite," Con says and coughs.

He's strained his voice too much tonight.

Take it easy. No more talking, I sign.

"If you aren't screwing her, what the hell did Con and I interrupt?"

I smirk. "An argument that I was winning."

Once we're done here, I'm going to crawl into her bed and finish what we started, only this time, she'll be coming on my mouth, not my hand.

Did you find anything at her apartment? Do you know who did it? Con asks.

"We didn't find a damn thing. Hopefully, you can. You're on clean-up duty."

He'll want to do it anyway so he can go through her place himself. If there's any clue to find, he'll find it.

The bourbon does its job and mellows me out a little.

"There's something else you should know. I saw the guy from the alley tonight at the Bierkeller. He followed Syn. I think he's the one who left her the note."

How he got in and out of the back office without me noticing is bothering me. We should have crossed paths in the hallway. Unless… I never checked the room when I barged in. I went straight for Syn. There are a few places in Keith's office he could have hidden out of sight.

Con gets quiet. Too quiet. That's never a good sign. He may not say much or show his emotions but that doesn't mean I can't hear him. Right now, the chaotic energy emanating from him is loud as fuck.

Hendrix hears it, too. "We'll find him. And when we do, you get first dibs on torturing the bastard."

I do not envy the man or the slow, painful death that awaits him. Hendrix and Con have the reputations they do in our world for a reason. They were raised to serve a purpose as weapons the Society uses to do their dirty work. I was born to rule, whereas they were born to destroy.

"We need to figure out if Dad is behind the sudden resurrection of an alleged dead man and why."

"Or Malin lied," Hen interjects.

Either could be plausible. I wouldn't put it past my father to keep the man alive as blackmail material against me in the future. A way to keep me in line. He loves collecting skeletons that people try to hide. It's how he's remained at the head of the Council. He has dirt on everybody. It doesn't explain the note, though. Why warn her by telling her something she already knows?

"I'm also calling in a favor to Tessa Goodwyn to find out what she can about Syn."

"No!" Con erupts off the stool. It topples over sideways and crashes to the floor. "I said I was handling it. No outsiders."

His voice is so raw, it sounds demonic.

"Tessa isn't Society. She'll easily be able to get the information we want without any blowback."

"I said no." Con takes a threatening stance like he's about to strangle the life out of me but checks himself at the last second. "We keep Syn to ourselves."

"Con," I call when he storms out.

The front door slams and my phone goes off when the outside security cameras' motion sensors kick in. Idiot left without a shirt on.

"He's more obsessed with her than you are." Hen chugs the rest of the bourbon.

"She's good for him."

I want Syn. In my bed and in my life. But I don't only want her for me. I want her for us. I think she's the missing piece we need to replace the one we lost. In a short expanse of time, Syn has brought Con back to us, made my life feel not so lonely, and has broken through Hendrix's defenses, whether he wants to admit it or not. He and Syn fight and act like they hate each other but it's all foreplay.

Hendrix curses under his breath. "*She* is a disaster waiting to happen. We know fuck-all about her, and the shit that has happened this week only confirms my suspicions that we're being played. You can't let your dick make bad decisions. Not when we're so close to getting what we want. And I'll be damned if I let some girl from Dilliwyll fuck it all up. She's not worth it."

He barely gets the last part out, but what he said hits me with the cold, hard truth, and I fucking hate it because I know he's right. However, he's also wrong. There's something in my gut, not my dick, that's telling me to keep Syn close. That we'll regret it if we don't.

"I'll get in touch with Tessa. Don't say a word to Con."

Hendrix patronizingly slaps me on the back on the way out. "I don't want to be you when he finds out."

Turning off the lights, I walk into the living room and wearily collapse onto the couch. Using the arm rest as a pillow and kicking my feet up at the other end, I shut my eyes and will myself to relax. Using a sensory trick my sister Dierdre taught me when I was a kid, I imagine I'm walking on the beach. Sight. Sound. Smell. Taste. Touch. I see the white, frothy caps of the breakers as they curl and collapse onto the beach. I hear the sounds of the sand crinkle and pop as the wave retreats back into the ocean. I smell the slightly fishy odor in the air left by the spray. I taste the salt. And I feel my sister's hand in mine as we walk barefoot in the sand. Our trip to Nantucket Island is the last good memory I have of her.

Fuck, how I miss her. Every damn day. Dierdre was ten years older than me. A happy accident, my mother once said. Not many sixteen-year-old girls would think there was anything happy about getting knocked up at that age by a twenty-year-old man who should've kept his dick in his pants. I'd say Dad did the honorable thing by marrying her, but what he really did was trap my mother in a faithless marriage and a life she despises. There's no love. No happiness. No joy. No comfort. It turned my mother into someone I despise. I hate her weakness for him. I hate her for never leaving him and taking us with her. She condemned her children to hell by staying. And it cost my sister her life. I will never forgive my mother for that.

"Hey."

I roll my head to the side. Syn is standing a few feet away, a pillow tucked to her chest. She unbraided her hair, and it falls in a wavy red waterfall over her shoulders and chest. She looks so fucking young and innocent.

"I, um..." She looks around, then down at the pillow. "Do you know where Constantine is?"

"He went out."

Even in the dark, I can see the disconsolate look on her pretty face.

"Oh."

She turns to leave.

"Can't sleep?"

"Yeah. My mind is too wired, it's hard to settle down."

I sit up. "Come here."

She goes to Con's room every night. It's the only thing that seems to help her get some rest. I joined them last night because I can't seem to stay away from her. I held her in my arms and watched her sleep all fucking night long. It was the sweetest torture.

It takes her longer than I'd like to make the decision to stay. When she does eventually walk over, I squeeze as far back into the cushions as I can and wait for her to lie down with me and get comfortable. When the pillow she brought gets in the way, she tosses it to the floor and uses my arm to support her head. Our faces are close, our noses almost bumping.

"It's a tight fit."

The more she squirms, the more my cock hardens, and hearing her say that doesn't help.

"Yes, you are," I reply, wanting to sink my fingers inside her pussy again.

She's still wearing Con's shirt, but her legs are bare. So easy to just slip underneath and—

She smacks my hand when it starts to wander. "I'm

still mad."

"I can make you feel better."

She kills the mood when she bursts into giggles.

"You really suck at one-liners."

Affronted, I tickle her in retaliation and almost get my balls crushed.

"Tristan, stop," she shrieks, thrashing about.

"Be still, woman." I cross my leg over hers to pin them down.

She turns her face to look up at me. Bright blue eyes, huge smile, a light scattering of freckles that adorn the bridge of her nose. So goddamn breathtaking.

"I'm sorry about tonight. About what I said. I didn't mean it."

I kiss the tip of her nose.

"You did, but it's okay. What you said is the truth."

"I hate all the secrets. It's hard for me to trust you."

"I know. Unfortunately, there are things I won't be able to tell you. But you *can* trust me, Syn."

I brush her hair back from her face. The red color looks like blood spilling over my arm.

Wanting to give her something, I say, "I'm the heir to the Amato shipping empire. Something I was born into, not something I ever wanted. My father is a sadistic asshole who cheats on my mother and treats his children like pawns on a chessboard. My sister—"

Syn stops me by placing her fingers to my lips. "I don't need to know anymore right now."

I pull her hand away. "You had asked me to tell you something real. You and me, Syn, that's what's real."

She rests her head on my chest and draws pictures over my heart with her finger.

"My something real is that I want to remember what

happened to me, but I can't. Even when I dream, I wake up to only vague snippets of things. Fire, stars, a phoenix. None of them make sense."

I listen intently to what she is saying, trying to hear the lie in any of it and finding none.

"Have you ever tried to find your biological parents?"

She pauses in her drawing. "They're dead."

"How do you know?"

Her brow scrunches. "It's what I was told."

"By who?"

"Whom."

I pinch her thigh. "Smartass."

She retaliates and bites my pectoral.

"Alana told me they died in the fire trying to save me."

How did Alana find out what happened? A social worker? The adoption agency? I have so many questions, but I don't want to push with too much, too fast. Baby steps.

"I asked Hendrix to teach me how to fight," she says, switching subjects.

He hasn't said anything. I'm curious to see it. What she can do and if Hendrix's suspicions are correct. I also think it'll be good for her to know. Every woman should have the skills to defend herself against the assholes of the world.

"You did?"

Noticing she's not wearing a bra, I palm her breast because I'm a bastard. I enjoy how her nipple hardens and beads underneath the shirt.

"Tristan," she admonishes, her chest quickening with each shallow breath, but she lies still and lets me play.

I swipe my thumb across the tight nub, loving the

small moan she makes. She's so damn responsive to my touch.

"I can teach you."

Those words are a dangerous double-edged sword. There are so many things I could teach her, show her, do to her. Bring sweet, innocent Syn over to the dark side of pleasure.

I replace my hand with my mouth and gently suck her tit through the cotton, and her back arches off the cushions.

"It's hard to think when you're doing that."

I smile against her breast. "Do you want me to stop?"

My teeth scrape her nipple.

"No... *oh, god...* I mean, yes."

Keeping my promise to stop if she ever gave the word, I pull back but don't get far because she lifts her head and kisses me. Her sweet tongue licks along the seam of my mouth, then dips in to taste me. Syn may be innocent, but the way she kisses is far from it.

I tangle my hands in her hair to control the kiss. One day soon, I'll have her in my bed and all this gorgeous hair tumbling down around me while I fuck her from below as she rides me.

"Baby, unless you want me to defile you on this sofa, we need to stop."

She hides her face in my shoulder. "Sorry."

Fuck me. This girl.

It takes a massive strength of will not to slither down her body, open her legs, and feast until she's screaming my fucking name.

"Not that I'm upset about you asking him, but why not me or Con?"

"I wouldn't be able to hit you or Constantine.

Hendrix, I'd have no problem punching. Or kneeing in the balls."

Can't wait to rub that in Hendrix's face.

She yawns and stretches her legs out, putting them parallel to mine. I don't expect her to stay awake for much longer.

"I lose time," she sleepily says.

Surprised that she'd tell me, I ask, "Do you black out?"

I saw what she did to Hendrix in the quad when she grabbed him by the throat then acted like she had no clue she did it when Con and I arrived. It took me a full minute of saying her name before she snapped out of whatever trance she was in. I know shit like that can happen with soldiers who suffer from PTSD. They get triggered and lash out, not aware of their actions.

Another yawn. "Wouldn't I have to be unconscious if I blacked out?"

I concede to that logic.

"When's the last time you saw a doctor?"

Her eyes droop, growing heavier by the second. "I'm tired of doctors. All they do is poke and prod and hurt me and make guesses but give me no real answers."

I'm prepared to burn down the world if anyone tries to hurt her again.

"My shoulder doesn't hurt anymore."

She's rambling, trying to stay awake. It's cute.

"Hendrix did a good job of stitching you up. I don't expect that you'll have much of a scar when it fully heals."

"Good."

I rest my forehead to hers. She keeps trying to force her eyes open when they flutter close.

"Stop fighting it. Go to sleep. Only sweet dreams

tonight."

With a soft sigh, she mumbles, "M'kay."

I don't know how much time passes before Hendrix comes downstairs. I hold my finger to my lips so he knows not to wake her.

"Con still gone?"

Syn twitches but settles, curling into me.

"Yeah."

He'll take his time going through her apartment, so I don't expect him back before morning.

Hendrix pads barefoot across the living room until he hovers over us. He drags his eyes up the length of Syn's body and settles where my hand rests lightly on her ass.

"I can carry her upstairs and put her in his bed."

"I've got her tonight."

The sofa isn't the most ideal, and my arm is likely to fall asleep and go numb where her head is resting.

He leaves and returns minutes later carrying two blankets. One he spreads over us, the other he lays flat on the floor next to the couch, then lies down on it and falls asleep.

CHAPTER 33

Hidden in the shadows is where I'm most comfortable. Darkness is my friend.

But so is death.

"Fuck you," the guy from the alley wheezes, blood and air bubbles gurgling in his throat. I only left him with one functioning lung after I pierced his other with a knife. Had to make sure he wouldn't scream or try to call for help.

Duct-taped to one of Syn's small dining chairs which I placed in her shower, he can't do much other than curse me or topple over backward. Fucker already did that and knocked himself out for a few minutes when his head smashed against the tile shower wall.

As water rains down on him from the showerhead, he looks sideways at me through one slitted eye, the other too swollen to open. Pools of red wash down the drain and disappear without a trace. The shower will make clean-up easy. I'll bleed him dry, then dispose of the body. Shower curtains make great body wraps.

I tap the point of the knife to my cheek. "Just tell me

who hired you, and I'll end your suffering." It hurts like hell to talk. I've overused my voice too much the last few days.

"*Fuck... you.*"

"So you've said."

I'm getting impatient and need to have this done soon before morning comes.

"Tristan said you were at the Bierkeller. You're not very smart, are you?"

He must have followed Tristan and Hendrix to Syn's apartment. He was inside when I arrived, cleaning up the place and erasing any evidence that it had been tossed. Tristan is wrong about him. He's not after Syn in the way Tristan thinks. Which means there's another unknown out there. And since this guy isn't going to tell me, I'll have to find out another way.

Squatting on my haunches until we're at eye level, I grab his wet, slippery face and roughly twist it. I need to see the last flicker of life die in his eyes. Water drenches my forearm as I push the knife into the side of his neck, nicking the carotid artery in the same place Tristan said he did with a piece of bottle glass. It's not severe enough so that he'll bleed out immediately, but death will come in a matter of minutes.

His teeth are coated in a thin sheen of blood when he smiles, and it drips down his chin like a crimson waterfall. "She's going... to kill... all of you."

My blood heats at the thought. Sweet Syn. You never should've said the goddamn words in your sleep.

"No, she's not."

I snap his neck.

CHAPTER 34

I wake to light snoring and am plastered to a furnace of body heat. It doesn't take long for my eyes to acclimate once I open them because the room is dark. Not Constantine's room, but the living room. I'm still on the sofa with Tristan, my head at an odd angle and staring at his chin. That explains the cramp in my neck.

I take the quiet moment to study his slumbering face. Why do men look so damn sexy when they're sleeping? The frown lines I usually see aren't there. He's peaceful. Completely relaxed. I doubt Tristan often gets to exist much in that kind of serenity. I understand why a little better after we talked last night. Something I hope I don't come to regret. I'm not used to exposing myself like that. Letting others see my vulnerabilities. I may be naïve about a lot of things, but I'm smart enough to understand that vulnerabilities can be used against you.

I stare at the mouth that kissed me last night. Tristan's full lips have a slight curve to them, the upper lip more top-heavy than the bottom. The imperceptible bump on his nose where it was broken intrigues me, and there has to be a story behind the scar that slashes through one eyebrow. I want to imagine he got it as a boy playing something silly like knights and dragons or even a high school fight with the class bully, but I've seen the lash marks on his back and the burn on his hand left by his father.

"Tristan."

I need to use the restroom, but I've got to figure out how to get myself out from the tangram puzzle our bodies are twisted into.

He's dead to the world and doesn't move when I lift his arm off me. It takes a huge amount of flexibility, but I'm able to finally untangle my legs from between his and from under the blanket that's twisted around my foot.

With as much grace as a boulder tumbling down a steep cliffside, I do a turtle roll on my back, only to unceremoniously fall off the front of the couch—and land on something that is definitely not the floor.

Hendrix's eyes fly open just as mine widen in alarm when I crash on top of him, our noses bumping.

"What are you doing on the floor?"

He's on top of a blanket and using my pillow.

He swats my hair out of his face. "I *was* sleeping," he surly replies.

Still doesn't explain why he's sleeping in here and not his room. A lot of what Hendrix does doesn't make sense.

"Can you please remove your hand from my butt and let me up?"

That wicked grin I love to hate comes to life.

"You're the one who jumped me."

"Not on purpose."

"Doesn't matter."

In one lithe move, he rolls us over until he's the one on top.

"Get. Off."

He grinds a very impressive morning erection against my stomach. "Now *there's* an idea."

Dammit, I keep walking right into those.

"I need to pee and will happily do it on you if you don't move."

He pushes up on his arms in a plank position, and I get a side view of his biceps. Hendrix is tall, his muscles leaner and not as thickly compact as Constantine's.

He gives me enough wiggle room to slither out from underneath him, and because I'm feeling petty, I kick out one of his arms as soon as I'm upright. He faceplants into the pillow, and I dart away before he has a chance to retaliate.

A cell phone chimes from the living room right before the front door opens, and Constantine fills the doorway. He presses a code into the panel near the door to disengage the alarm. He's dressed in the clothes he was wearing last night. I can only presume what that means, and I don't like the instant jealousy it brings.

"Have you been out all night?"

Rationally, I know it's none of my business, but it would bother the hell out of me if he spent the night with another woman.

He drags his haggard body over to me and, like he can read my mind, he takes me in his arms and kisses the top of my head.

"Had work to do. Were you able to sleep okay?"

"Yes," I reply, wondering what kind of work involved

him being gone overnight. Another one of those secrets Tristan said they'd never be able to tell me?

I prop my chin on his chest and peer up at him. There are purple half-moons of fatigue under his eyes.

"Do you want me to make you some coffee or breakfast?"

"I've got it," Hendrix says as he walks past. The hard smack he delivers to my ass echoes between the walls of the foyer. "Payback," he quips and whistles a silly tune as he heads into the kitchen. He's so damn territorial about cooking.

"Why didn't you wake me?"

Tristan comes to my back, and I'm sandwiched between both of them. It feels like the most natural thing in the world to lean into him, which is why I don't.

"Didn't know I was supposed to."

His first class isn't until later in the morning, which means he can sleep in.

Tristan's soft, morning-husky voice is tantalizingly at my ear. "Never leave my bed without waking me first."

"We weren't in a bed."

He playfully pulls my hair, making my neck arch until my eyes meet Constantine's. Sexual desire thrums between us. Urges I shouldn't act on taunt me to take this further, see what it would be like.

Constantine spins me around and guides me up the stairs.

"Con, wait," Tristan says.

"Need to crash for a few hours."

"Anything I need to know?"

"Later," Constantine briskly reiterates.

Great. More secrets.

As soon as we enter his bedroom, he falls onto his bed, acting utterly exhausted. I motion for him to sit up and tap each arm for him to raise them so I can take his shirt off. He toes off his sneakers and socks but leaves his jeans on. Against his black sheets, the red pigment used in various tattoos is more distinct, making each image somewhat macabre because it looks too much like blood.

I pound his pillows to fluff them, then pick up his shoes and put them at the foot of the bed, so they aren't a trip hazard.

"I like this."

"What?"

"You taking care of me."

"Just paying it forward," I reply because Constantine is always doing things for me. Endearing things that show he cares.

He reaches a hand out, and I take it. The connection is immediate. Physically. Emotionally. Mentally.

Don't you dare fall for him, Syn. Don't fucking do it.

But it's too late.

"Get some sleep." I fumble my way to the door, wanting to leave but also wanting to stay. "I'll see you later," I tell him and close his door with a silent *snick*.

When I get to my room, I lock the door, grab my phone, then go into the bathroom and close and lock that door, too. I run water from the sink faucet to create a buffer of white noise to mask my voice, and I call home.

Alana answers on the first ring.

"Morning, sweetie. I wasn't expecting to hear from you until later. Did work go better last night?"

I take a seat on the closed toilet lid.

"No spilled beer."

I leave out the pervy guy who kept copping a feel. When I went back to his table, he and his friends were gone but they left a two-hundred-dollar cash tip. I'll funnel half of it in increments to Shelby over the next week. If she noticed an extra hundred in her tips for the night, she'd know something was up. Keith wouldn't lie to her if she asked, and she'd find out that I'd been surreptitiously giving her part of my tip money.

The distinctive loud crow of a rooster bellows over the line. Alana must be outside on the back patio, enjoying her first cup of coffee of the morning.

"Right on time," she says.

Cocky Bastard's circadian clock has him greeting the sunrise every morning. A sunrise I'm currently missing because I've sequestered myself in the bathroom.

"Who were my parents?"

That didn't come out the way I'd rehearsed it a million times in my head. It's Tristan's fault for planting the seed. Alana hasn't told me much, but I've also never really asked. After Tristan brought it up, I began to question why I never have. Wouldn't I want to know who they were? Where they're buried? Something? There has to be a record of it somewhere. An investigation or news article. Wouldn't I have had grandparents, a sibling, relatives, friends or someone who would have reached out to find out if I was okay? So, why in the hell have I never asked? It's bothering me—a lot. But I think what's bothering me the most is that maybe my inability to remember my past isn't stemmed from trauma like the doctors said. Maybe it's me. Maybe *I'm* the reason. Are their deaths my fault? Did I do something to cause it? The other thought that comes to mind is way worse.

Who in the hell am I?

Alana is quiet. The only noise coming over the line is from Cocky Bastard. The longer the silence stretches, the guiltier I feel. Alana saved me. She's my mother in every way that counts. She has loved and protected me for years. Given my life meaning when all I wanted to do was curl up and die. I owe her everything.

"Syn, sweetheart, why are you—"

"Do you know their names?"

More uncomfortable silence.

"I don't think this is a discussion to have over the phone. Why don't you come home this weekend? We can talk then."

This is where I lie to my mother for the second time in my life.

"I can't this weekend. Me and the girl from my calc class already made plans."

I can't tell her about New York.

"I hope it's something fun."

I don't want to add a third lie to the other two. "I'll come home next weekend."

Because I chose to leave my used two-door truck at the farm in case Alana needed it, I'll have to rent a car. Booking a last-minute flight now would be too expensive.

Alana solves my dilemma. "I'll come get you. That way we can talk on the drive back."

"Okay."

"Alright. Well, I love you, sweet girl. Have a good day."

She hangs up before I can say I love her, too. I didn't mean to upset her.

"Damn you, Tristan, for making me doubt

everything," I tell my mirror image, but the girl looking back at me is a stranger.

Instead of pretending that stranger doesn't exist, I'm going to find out who she is. Who *I* am. I've lived an ignorant existence that has been shattered in a matter of hours. There's no going back.

I turn off the faucet and type a message to Raquelle. I think she said she doesn't have any classes until the afternoon.

Me: Can you text me when you get up?

Her reply is immediate.

Raquelle: Hey! Been painting since four. What's up?

Me: I need a jailbreak.

Raquelle: Jailbreak? Literal or figurative? I can totally bake a cake with a nail file in it, but it'll take a couple of hours.

I chuckle at her joke.

Me: Figurative. I have three overbearing male roommates that act like overprotective big brothers. I need a break.

And an excuse for the guys not to tag along. Especially since I plan to walk into the den of the devil. I've got to start somewhere.

Raquelle: Text me your address. I'll pick you up in thirty.

I love this girl.

CHAPTER 35

Adjusting the strap of my shoulder bag laden with heavy books, I breeze into the kitchen to find Tristan and Hendrix eating bacon, egg, and cheese breakfast bagels at the counter island. There's one plated and a glass of orange juice beside it, which I assume are for me.

"Do you never eat at the table?"

Every time I come into the kitchen, they're eating while standing.

Tristan shrugs. "What's the point?"

Conversation. Camaraderie. Family. Alana and I would cook a nice dinner together and have it at the dining room table every night. We'd talk, bust out some board games, laugh. Things that helped bring normalcy to my life.

I take a sip of the orange juice and marvel that it's freshly squeezed and not from a bottle. Hendrix may be an ass, but he knows what he's doing in the kitchen. I grab the bagel and eagerly take a bite. It's freaking delicious like everything else he's made.

"See you later."

Tristan snags the strap of my bag. "It's not time for us to leave yet."

No avoiding the fight that's sure to come, so I woman up and hope I can remain resolute and not give in when Tristan goes apeshit.

"Raquelle is picking me up" —I check my crappy plastic watch— "in five minutes."

Tristan and Hendrix look at one another.

"The fuck she is," Tristan barks.

"Well, she is, so…" I indicate with my eyes for him to let go of my bag.

"You know the rules, Red."

I smack exasperated hands to my hips. "The rules suck and need to change. Raquelle is the first real friend I've ever made on my own, which sounds really fucking sad hearing it said out loud."

"We're your friends."

I aim an exaggerated eyebrow raise at Hendrix.

"Okay, maybe not him."

"Fuck you," Hendrix replies at being called out, but he doesn't disagree.

I focus my argument on Tristan, knowing he's the one I must convince.

"I need girl time with another female. I need to be a normal college student with normal social interactions outside of this house. I need some freedom."

Those sentiments are all true, except for the ulterior motive I leave out. Tristan would barricade me in a room and throw away the key if he discovered what I was really planning to do.

He double-downs with his obstinance. "One of us has to go with you. The twins can't be trusted."

The twins. His father. The entire goddamn world. Is there anyone other than Hendrix and Constantine that he does trust?

Losing my temper won't help and will only make things worse, so I try to think of a compromise.

"We're only going to hang out at her dorm room. It's in Danby. I'll be surrounded by people. I'll even share my location with you on my phone so you know exactly where I am. You can pick me up there before my class."

Hope kindles when he sighs loudly. I add a little emotional blackmail by making my eyes glass over with fake tears.

"Please, Tristan."

"Let her go."

I'm stunned that Hendrix would come to my defense.

"I haven't spoken with Con yet."

"He'd agree with me if he were here. Let her have some breathing room. Or have you forgotten what it's like?"

They're having a conversation I don't follow, and I'm not sure I want to.

"Give me your phone," Tristan insists.

I fish it out of my bag and hand it over. He does something and gives it back.

"Hendrix will come get you at ten thirty."

I can't believe it worked.

"Thank you," I overly enthuse and place a perfunctory kiss on his cheek.

"I agreed with you. Don't I get a thank you kiss?"

Since I'm feeling gracious, I skip over to Hendrix and pop on tiptoe to peck his cheek. His morning stubble is soft and not as prickly as Tristan's.

"Don't make me regret this," Tristan says when his

phone goes off, telling me Raquelle has arrived.

I wish there was a way for me to disable those alerts… and the cameras.

I'm already rushing to open the front door, afraid he'll change his mind. "I won't!"

I don't give Raquelle a chance to get out of her silver Mercedes. Opening the passenger side door, I drop my bag onto the floorboard and hurry into the seat.

"This is a very nice car."

A very expensive car. Another reminder that I'm the scholarship kid at a prestigious ivy league university.

"Sweet sixteen from Dad. Speaking of nice, that's a gorgeous house. Legacy, right?"

I have no idea what legacy means.

"It's just temporary until I can move back into my apartment."

"I've passed by here a few times. I actually thought about painting it. On canvas, not in real life."

I never took the time to look at the house from afar. It's regal with elegant lines and old-time charm. The brick is a deep red where the sun hits it but looks dark brown where it's in the shadows. Black shutters frame every window. An old filigree forged railing wraps around the porch and Doric columns. The only thing that's missing is a bright pop of color that could easily be fixed with flower beds or potted plants.

"What were you working on?" I ask, noticing that she's wearing a similar set of overalls like the ones from Tuesday, only this time they're lime green. Her hair is up in the cutest pair of Princess Leia side buns.

"An abstract minimalist using various shades of blue."

"I'll need you to translate that for a non-artist."

"I'll do one better and show you. I lucked out and don't have a dormmate this semester because she apparently decided at the last second to attend Harvard." She says the name of the other university in disgust, as if choosing Harvard over Darlington Founders is repulsive. "Upside is that I get the place to myself for the entire semester, so I set up a mini art studio on her empty side of the room."

I miss my little apartment. I was thinking of stopping off there after class to get some extra clothes for the trip tomorrow but remembered that I didn't bring any dresses with me from home. There's a small boutique store that sells women's clothing near the Bierkeller that I window-shopped a few times when walking to work. They should sell dresses. I hope. If I'm being forced to meet and mingle with the Knight family, I'm damn sure not wearing a T-shirt and yoga leggings to do so. The Knights are one of America's wealthiest, most renowned families. I'm a recipient of their academic scholarship that gives me a full ride to Darlington. And I'm going to look like a hobo meeting them if I don't find something more appropriate to wear. Oh, god. I'm going to embarrass myself.

Swallowing down the lump of queasiness I'm suddenly feeling, I reply, "I'd love to see what you're working on. And thank you again for coming to get me."

Putting the gearshift in reverse, Raquelle taps her fingers on the steering wheel.

"My pleasure. I was going to call you anyway to see if you wanted to grab breakfast, but it looks like you're already eating it."

I shove the rest of the bagel in my mouth to free up my hands so I can buckle in. She passes me a sealed bottle of water she takes out of the cup holder, and I gratefully accept it.

"If you see a dark-haired guy come outside, floor it."

"You mean the tall, dark yummy one or the other one who came to your rescue and is standing on the porch right now?"

Tristan leans against the railing, arms outstretched, his face set in stone, staring a hole through the windshield. I do a finger wave and smile.

"That's the one."

She slowly backs out of the short driveway using the rear camera. "Holy shit, girl. Who's the blond Adonis?"

Hendrix comes out and says something to Tristan, but I can't read lips.

"The devil."

Raquelle laughs. "Guys who look like that usually are."

Once we're driving down the road, I start to relax. I hadn't noticed how tense I'd gotten. Subterfuge is not my forte.

Raquelle has the windows rolled down, and I breathe in the fresh morning air as it whips through the interior. This is freedom.

"How do you do it?"

Sticking my hand out of the open window, I play with the wind with wiggling fingers. "Do what?"

Raquelle slows at the roundabout and merges into the circle on the outside lane. "You're living with three guys."

"Temporarily."

"Uh-huh." She flicks her blinker to indicate she's getting off the circle. "I know you said that you and Constantine were just friends, but how are you not sleeping with any of them? Because I'd be all over that."

No, she wouldn't. She's in love with Drake, and I don't get the impression that Raquelle is the kind of girl who would cheat.

"Depends on your definition of sleeping," I answer. Because I kind of am, but not in the way she's implying.

In no time, we're on campus, and she pulls into a parking lot filled with various Porsches, Mercedes, and Land Rovers, the only differences being their paint color. It's like the Stepford wives of cars. The light-colored limestone brick dormitory of Danby sits in a U-shape at the other end and rises four stories high, like a smaller replica of the palace of Versailles.

"What's *your* definition of sleeping?" she asks as she parks in an empty spot next to a G-Wagon.

"The Merriam-Webster version," I reply.

She laughs. "I have a feeling that won't last much longer based on how porch-hottie was looking at you."

With what happened last night with Tristan in the kitchen, she may be right.

When I blush, her face lights up. "You look guilty as hell. Spill."

Hoping to avoid the topic altogether, I open the car door, pick up my bag, and get out.

"Nothing to tell."

"Yet. But you want it to," she supplies, getting out as well and clicking the key fob to lock the doors.

It's only seven thirty, and the campus is already bustling with activity. Students stream out of the dorm in pairs or groups, and there are a few joggers out for their morning run.

As with every other time I'm on campus, my heart skips a beat, and my breath catches in awe and disbelief that I'm actually a student here. I have so many dreams of what I want for my future, and Darlington Founders is my first step to achieving that.

I follow Raquelle up the wide sidewalk that leads to the front entrance.

"I'm on the second floor, corner room," she says, pointing it out. "I'll need to sign you in at the registration desk since you don't live here. They'll scan your student ID."

She pulls one of the heavy double-glass doors open and waits for me to walk through. The lobby is airy and expansive with marble floors and wood panel details. Sunlight spills in from an extended pyramid skylight above. It casts a prismatic rectangular spotlight on the floor below.

"This looks like a hotel lobby."

"It basically is," she replies and leads me to the dark wood reception desk ten feet in front of us.

No one would be able to enter the building through the front without being noticed by whoever mans reception. I take a cursory glance around and locate the security cameras I can't seem to escape from no matter what part of Darlington I'm in. The house. Campus. Work. Come to think of it, I've noticed cameras around town as well during my walks. Some on buildings, others attached to power poles or streetlights. The city of London in the United Kingdom has a similar set up. Your every move can be tracked from start to finish. Big Brother is always watching.

When we approach, the guy behind the counter looks up from the book he's reading. Dark hair, glasses, Clark Kent looks. It's the TA from my biology lab.

"Morning," he greets us.

"Signing a visitor in," Raquelle announces.

He swivels a touchpad tablet mounted to the reception desk around. "You know the drill."

"Give me your ID," she tells me, and I unfasten it from the zipper pull of my bag where I keep it on a carabiner clip.

While she's signing me in, I make small talk.

"Evan, right?"

He grins and folds over the top corner of the paperback he was reading to mark his place. It's a collection of short stories by Ernest Hemingway.

"That's me."

"You work here, too?" How many jobs does this guy have?

Raquelle swipes my ID card in a thing that looks like a credit card reader and hands it back to me.

"Four to eight in the morning on Wednesdays and Thursdays. I'm Professor Carlyle's TA for his Monday and Tuesday labs. I'm a sophomore on financial aid, so need to supplement it where I can."

A sense of solidarity grows through our shared circumstances. It's nice to know someone else like me who's in a similar monetary situation.

"I'm on scholarship. I work part-time at the Bierkeller a few evenings a week."

"Which days?"

"Wednesday, Friday, Saturday."

He leans forward and props his elbows on top of the desk, hands loosely clasped together. There's a small Celtic cross tattoo on the underside of his wrist.

"It's been forever since I had one of their bacon burgers. Maybe I'll drop in sometime."

"Alright, done," Raquelle says, hooking her arm

through mine. “Thanks, Evan.”

He picks his book back up and opens it. “Have a lovely morning, ladies.”

The elevator doors open right when we get to them, and Raquelle ushers me through after everyone inside gets off.

“He’s such a nice guy. Cute, too.”

I have a feeling I know what she’s about to suggest with that setup.

“He saved me from my professor’s wrath on Tuesday,” I reply.

The doors open and we step off. A few doors are open that I peek into as we walk past. Laughter, music, the whir of hair dryers, and the slamming of doors make for a discordant cacophony. The noise levels alone would drive me insane, and it makes me grateful that I don’t live in a dorm.

“If you’re not interested in the guys you’re bunking with, Evan would be a good choice to consider,” she suggests.

And there it is.

“We’ll see,” I vaguely reply, because I’m definitely interested, just not in Evan.

When we get to the end of the corridor, she unlocks the door for room two-two-six. “This is me.”

I cough as soon as I walk inside and am surrounded by paint fumes and turpentine.

“Shit, sorry. I forgot to open the window and run the fan before I left.”

She rushes to do those things while I take a look around. The room is an explosion of color from the bright yellow bedspread to the sage green shag rug to the cerulean throw pillows piled against the headboard of the bed. Art deco framed photographs of her and Drake sit on the scuffed wood student desk next to a laptop covered in Hello Kitty stickers. Blank canvases of various sizes are stacked against one wall. She has a large tripod easel set up near the window displaying the painting she said she'd been working on. Even though it's a bunch of blue swirls, it's lovely and evokes thoughts of the deep blue sky on a summer's day… or Hendrix's turbulent blue eyes.

"This is beautiful."

"Thanks!" she chirps. "I'm in a blue phase right now."

Fresh air rolls in as soon as she shoves the window wide, and the rotating fan does the trick of quickly dissipating the fumes that had lingered like a thick smog.

I take a seat on the floor rug near the window and enjoy how the breeze caresses the fine hairs of my neck.

"Female question. I'm going to New York this weekend with a friend, and I'll be meeting the patrons who sponsored my scholarship. What should I wear because clearly this" —I gesture at myself— "is not going to cut it."

"Do you have a simple cocktail dress?"

"No."

"Skirt?"

"No."

"Sundress?"

"Nope. I grew up on a farm. The only dress I own was one my mother bought for me to wear to my high school graduation ceremony. It's currently hanging in my closet back home."

Clapping her hands, she spins around. "I've got ya covered. You look like my size with longer legs. You've got a great body, by the way. Curvy and tall. And your hair is amazing."

"It comes from a bottle."

I'm a natural blonde but started dying my hair a few years ago. I've had it pink, purple, blue, and even striped in rainbow colors. I did it as a form of camouflage. But unlike a chameleon that changes colors to blend in with its environment and becomes invisible, I always chose loud colors to draw people's attention away from my scars. Alana convinced me to go red and chose the color herself.

"Have you ever thought about modeling?"

I fall over, laughing so hard. I'm not even close to being model material. Raquelle, on the other hand, is absolutely gorgeous.

"When I first saw you, I thought you looked like Kerry Washington."

"Oh, I love her! We'll need to binge *Scandal* sometime."

Rifling through her small closet, she takes two dresses off their hangers and holds them up. I point to the royal blue one that looks like it's made of airy silk panels. It has gossamer long sleeves that would help hide the scars on my arm. The other one is a scrap of material that I doubt would cover much, so is an automatic no.

She places them flat on the bed. "Nope. You're taking both."

"You're so sweet, but I can't."

"Yes, you can," she insists and sits cross-legged in front of me. "Now that's done, are you going to tell me why you needed a jailbreak this morning?"

It's so hard to trust anyone new, but if I'm going to

find out the secrets of my past, I need help, and I have a strong intuition that Raquelle is worth the risk.

"I need to find someone."

"Who?"

"Me."

CHAPTER 36

Tristan is going to kill me.

"Are you sure you want to do this?" Raquelle asks, her shoulder touching mine as we stand outside the building that houses the bell tower and gaze upon it with equal shares of presentiments.

Not really.

My cheeks poof out when I exhale, "I'm sure."

The fucktwins apparently live here. Information Raquelle was able to procure for me after I spent an hour spilling my guts to her about everything. What happened to me. What I know of my past. What I don't know. The guys. My scars. She took everything I threw at her with aplomb and gentle understanding. I still feel like I want to throw up, but at least I didn't cry, no matter how badly I wanted to.

"Now's your chance to run," I offer for the hundredth time.

I wouldn't blame her. I'd run if I were in her shoes.

She takes my hand. It looks pallid next to her lustrous mocha brown complexion.

"Not on your life. Ride or die, girl. You're stuck with me."

Hearing her say that means more than she'll ever know.

I've got a little over an hour before Tristan picks me up for my ten-thirty class. I left my phone in Raquelle's room just in case he uses the location function to check up on me. If he does, he'll see that I'm where I said I would be. The only problem I foresee is if he tries to text me. When I don't reply, he'll come looking. I can use the excuse that Raquelle and I went to grab coffee, and I forgot my phone. It's a gamble, but one I'm willing to make.

"If he tries anything, I still have that video and will happily post it on every social media known to man."

"Wrong twin," I inform her. Aleksander is the person I want to speak with, not Aleksei.

She gives a dismissive wave of her hand. "They're twins. In the eyes of an everyday viewer, they're interchangeable."

We step out of the way when the entrance door to the building opens, and a brunette walks out, or more accurately, trips out. She's barefoot and has high-heeled sandals dangling from one hand while the other hand is holding her phone in front of her as she talks to someone over speaker.

"Asshole just kicked me out right after I went down on him. Didn't even get me off first," she complains to the person on the other end, even though Raquelle and I are right there to hear every word. "Hold on." She stops when she sees us. "Which one of you is Synthia?"

Caught off guard, I raise my hand like a complete imbecile.

She offers me the same derisory perusal Serena did the other morning. At least this girl is fully clothed.

"He's waiting for you. Take the elevator, third floor," she tells me before sashaying on her merry way.

Raquelle rotates around to watch the girl leave. "That was weird and mildly disturbing. How did he know you were here if he was... *you know...* getting busy with her?"

I'd be paranoid out of my mind if I wasn't already used to cameras watching my every move at the house. Sure enough, there's a dome camera mounted above the door. I point it out to her.

"We have eyes watching."

"Well, that just ups the creepy factor by a thousand." She raises her middle finger to the camera and smiles. "I don't want you going in there by yourself," she whispers through her teeth.

I've already asked too much of Raquelle, and I won't abuse that generosity or our new friendship. I also think that Aleksander will be more forthcoming if it's just me.

"Twenty minutes, tops. Promise." Because I have an uncharacteristic impulse to do it, I give her a quick hug. "Thank you. For everything. I owe you big time."

"No, you don't. There's no tit for tat between friends. And just an FYI, if you're not back in twenty, I'm pulling the fire alarm."

That's actually really smart. Both the campus and the Darlington police as well as the fire department would respond immediately.

With my heart lodged in my throat, I pull open the door. Cold air created by the pressure difference between inside and outside blasts my face and makes me jump.

Calm the hell down. Easier said than done. I'm literally walking into the lion's den, and I'm second guessing why I thought this was a good idea.

Once inside, I look around. It's an odd place to live, inside a bell tower. The building must have undergone extensive renovations to retrofit the top two floors into apartment units. The bell tower isn't really a tower at all. It's a square-shaped appendage sticking out from the rooftop of a normal-looking brick building. The first floor is empty. There's absolutely nothing. No sign of life. Bare walls. Sterile.

The girl said take the elevator to the third floor. My favorite pair of Keds that have a small hole where my big toe wore through the canvas are silent on the polished tile floor as I walk to the elevator on the far side of the room. The doors are open.

There's a short story by H.G. Wells. "A Door in the Wall." There are several interpretations of the meaning behind a man who keeps encountering a green door. I liked the opinion that the green door represented two worlds. Reality as you stood outside the door, and insanity once you opened it.

Today, I'm choosing insanity.

I get on and feel claustrophobic as soon as I'm shut inside. It's a small space, good for about two people to stand comfortably without knocking elbows. There are only three buttons. I press the top one, then tap my middle finger against my thigh and count from one to ten and back again. It's a sensory thing my therapist had me do to center myself and clear my mind.

Just as I reach the number ten, a single ding chimes. The doors pry wide, and I'm suddenly face to face with a shirtless Aleksander. Good god. He has more ink than Constantine. It covers him from collarbone to waist and makes his skin appear almost midnight black. It's hard to tell what the pictures are.

"I have to say, I was very surprised to see you standing outside."

Every time I hear him speak, it's surreal. For a man who looks like him—dangerous, imposing, lethal—he has a soft, cultured voice. But there's a cunning behind his gray eyes, like those of a cat that likes to play with and taunt its prey before it finally eats it. I know which animal I am in that scenario.

"Not as surprised as I am," I reply.

He turns to the side and sweeps an arm out, welcoming me into his residence. The refitted apartment is quite lovely. A large leather couch and matching armchairs take up a good amount of the open space that I assume is the living room. The cream-colored walls help make the room feel bigger than it is, and there are a few framed paintings Raquelle would find interesting. Dark wood beams cross the ceiling and add a touch of rustic to the simple aesthetic. Sunlight streams in through the large floor-to-ceiling window and gives the apartment a warmth that's lacking in the house the guys live in. From three stories up, the view of the campus and its grounds is amazing.

Aleksander watches me closely, his gunmetal gaze unnerving. "Does Amato know you're here?"

I keep close to the elevator. I didn't see a stairwell access downstairs, but there'd have to be one somewhere.

"I'm not here to talk about Tristan."

"I'll take that as a no." His smile is downright arctic.

"Would you like something to drink? Sparkling water? I was just about to make breakfast. You can join me."

He's being hospitable which only drives my anxiety higher.

"No, thank you. I don't plan to stay long." I remove the note from the tiny zipper pocket of my leggings. "Why did you put this in my bag? If you're trying to scare me, you're doing a shit job of it."

He takes the crumpled paper from my hand, his touch gentle as he extricates it from the death grip I have on it.

Giving it a cursory glance, he says, "I didn't write this."

"You took my bag on the elevator."

"Doesn't mean I wrote it or put it in there."

I snatch it away from him and mangle the paper when I shove it back into my pocket.

"Forgive me if I don't believe you."

I retreat when he comes forward, and the wall behind me prevents me from moving any farther. Aleksander brackets both hands on either side of my head, dwarfing me with his substantial size. It's a power move meant to be threatening, but I'm not scared. I'm determined. When you want something badly enough, you'll walk through hellfire to get it. And I want answers.

"I don't lie, little *pevchaya ptitsa,* unlike the men you're keeping company with."

I meet his hard stare with one of my own. "I don't care about whatever grievance you and Tristan have with one another. I'm not a part of that."

He *tsks* me. "You are very much a part of everything now, Synthia."

I really hate when he says my name. He draws out the

first syllable until the 's' sounds like the hiss of a snake.

"Why? I'm new here. I don't know anybody. Am I not allowed to make friends?"

"Not with us."

Why he would group himself in with the guys is ridiculous.

"*I* am *not* your friend."

Aleksander's arms bend at the elbows, bringing his face closer. There's a tiny star tattooed in the corner of his left eye that I'd mistaken for a mole.

"Not what I meant. You really don't know, do you?"

I roll my eyes for good measure. "Since I clearly don't, would you like to fill me in?"

Thinking about it, he eventually says, "I don't think I will. It'll be more fun to watch you find out on your own." He lightly grazes a blunt nail from under my eye down the apple of my cheek. "You have very unusual eyes. You're also very pretty. I can see why they're intrigued."

It's not a compliment.

"If you think you can use me as a way to hurt Tristan, Constantine, or Hendrix, then you're way off the mark. I'm nothing to them."

His smirk curls into an amused grin. "Who's lying now?"

I've wasted almost ten minutes with this posturing bullshit. I shove at his chest to get him to step back and am relieved when he does. I came here to confront him about the note and to find out what it meant. And as much as I don't want to, I believe him when he said he didn't write it. So, who the hell did?

Before I leave, I ask one last question. "Why do you and Tristan hate each other so much?"

The mirth on Aleksander's face disappears and is replaced with cold fury.

"His family stole my birthright."

My reply is drenched in incredulity when I say, "Tristan is not responsible for what his father or his family does."

Aleksander scoffs. "You couldn't be more wrong, *pevchaya ptitsa*."

I don't know whether he's calling me a bad word or not because I don't speak Russian.

"Thank you for your time." I need to get back to Raquelle before she really does pull the fire alarm. "It would be nice if you and your brother stopped following me around. If it happens again, I'll file a restraining order."

When I try to leave, he gets in my way.

"Please move."

The voice I often hear right before I come out of a nightmare wakes up.

"You seem like a nice girl, so I'm going to give you a word of advice."

My fingernails cut into my palms when my hands close into fists.

Aoife.

"And what would that be?"

Wake up. Wake up. Wake up.

"Run."

CHAPTER 37

Tristan, Con, and I are enjoying a beer out on the back patio while steaks sizzle on the gas grill. Syn said she wanted to pack for the trip tomorrow and hasn't come downstairs since she and Tristan got home. He's been looking up at her window every five seconds. It's getting annoying.

"Does Syn seem off to you tonight?"

I want to beat the shit out of him for being so damn stupid.

I fucking knew she was up to something this morning. The girl is a shit liar. It was written all over her face. Something Tristan should have picked up on, but he can't see clearly when Syn's involved.

I told him to let her go with her friend just so I could follow her. I'm glad I did.

My father once told me, *"Sometimes, the most beautiful thing is the one you have to fear."* He said this right before he killed his mistress in front of me. I had caught her that day snooping through his private office files.

"Seemed fine when I picked her up from Danby," I reply.

I need to know exactly why Syn went to see the fucktwins before I bring it to the guys. Tristan will start a war with Aleksander we're not ready for. Not yet. Nine more months before graduation. Nine months before we take our places within the Council.

And then the fun starts.

Death. Chaos. Blood.

It's going to be fucking fantastic.

"We need to find out everything we can on the girl, Raquelle. All her socials are just pictures of art or her and some guy."

"Stop being so paranoid."

A bit hypocritical, yes, given what Syn did today, but Tristan can't look at every fucking person who talks to her as a threat. The entire population of Darlington would be culpable. And if Raquelle knew the twins, she doesn't like them much based on the middle finger she held high right before Syn walked inside the bell tower.

"You going to tell us what you found at her apartment?" he asks Con.

Tristan's impatience is showing. Con's running on two hours of sleep and a shit-ton of coffee. If Tristan doesn't stop bugging the hell out of him, he's going to find himself knocked out when Con decks him.

When he doesn't answer, Tristan kicks at his foot to get his attention. Focused on his phone, Con somehow sees it coming and steps out of the way.

"Didn't find anything," he mumbles.

"You made me wait all fucking day to tell me that?"

Immersed in whatever he's looking at on his phone, Con shrugs a shoulder. One day, I'm going to hide his laptop and phone just to see what happens.

"At least going to New York will get her out of town for a couple of days."

I know Tristan is waiting for Tessa to get back to him. He still hasn't told Con yet that he contacted her. I don't like all the secrets we've been keeping from each other. Secrets imply mistrust, which is ironic because the only two people I do trust are them. I will never lie to Con or Tristan, but sometimes it's best to hold things close to the chest until all the pieces are put into place.

Taking the tongs off the metal hook, I flip the steaks over to sear a crosshatch pattern on the other side. "Hope she likes medium rare."

"Well-done," Con replies.

"How do you know?" Tristan asks.

Con finally puts his phone down, and he stares at Tristan for a long while before saying, "She mentioned it the other day. My fucking throat hurts, so stop asking me questions."

"Is that why you've been a surly git all evening?"

Con isn't the easiest person to be around on a good day, but this evening he's been more distant than usual.

"Take them off in three minutes but leave Syn's on until I come back out."

Well-done, my ass. She's getting medium-done at most. It's sacrilegious to burn good meat.

I hand Tristan the tongs and head inside to make Con some chamomile tea with honey. Filling the kettle with water from the sink faucet, I put it on one of the gas burners to heat.

"Are we eating outside?" Syn walks into the kitchen and immediately detours to the pantry when she sees what I'm doing. "Mint, Earl Grey, or chamomile?" her disembodied voice asks.

"Chamomile. Grab the honey, too."

She returns holding the jar of locally sourced clover honey and four Tazo tea packets.

"Con needs a break. Only sign to him tonight, so he doesn't talk."

She hops up onto the counter, and I get an eyeful of her toned, creamy thighs. Thighs I want to mark just like I did her chest. There are so many depraved things I would do to her body.

"What happened to him?" she asks softly, and I tear my thoughts away of her tied up and covered in my cum.

When Con was twelve, his father choked him out. Almost killed him. It fucked up his vocal cords, and Con never spoke again. Not until this week. Not until her.

"It's his story to tell if he wants you to know."

She bites her bottom lip, a habit I've noticed her do often.

"Full disclosure. I'm really nervous about meeting your family tomorrow. I want to impress them and show them how grateful I am for the scholarship. Your family's generosity is giving me my dream. There aren't enough thank yous for that."

This is actually the first year the Knights have awarded the scholarship. It's something my mother suggested last year while we were attending the annual Knight Foundation Christmas gala in London. I didn't really pay much attention. Mom is forever coming up with new philanthropic causes to support. Her way of hiding all the bad shit my family does. It's meaningless and only serves to make her feel self-important. Eva Knight is the most narcissistic woman on the planet.

"Just be yourself," I advise, but it holds a double meaning.

The kettle shrieks its high-pitched whistle, and I turn the burner off.

Syn jumps down from the counter and grabs four mugs from the cabinet, but I only fill two. One for Con, and one for her.

She adds the honey and plunks in the tea bags to steep. "Aren't you having some?"

I put the other two mugs back inside the cabinet. "Tristan doesn't drink it, and I like my tea made with a French press, not the instant shit."

She laughs, something I've come to enjoy hearing. It's slightly husky and raspy. Sexy.

"You are so stuck up."

"I just know what tastes good," I reply, my voice dropping when I zero in on her mouth.

It's fucking with my head how I don't trust her but want to fuck her all the same.

"You promised."

I bounce my gaze from her blush-colored lips to her blue bonnet eyes. "What?"

Picking up the mugs, she slides past me and hip-bumps the patio screen door open. "You said you'd give me my first lesson on Thursday. It's Thursday."

The lewd images of other kinds of *lessons* that have nothing to do with teaching her how to fight run rampant in my head.

Taking the Caesar salad I made earlier from the fridge, I follow her out. Tristan has the steaks plated and put on the patio table. Syn sidles up to Con and hands him the tea. Like it's the most natural thing to do, he wraps his arm around her shoulders, and she leans into him, a look of serene comfort on her face. Like he's her home. And I fucking hate how easy he is with her, and she with him.

What would it be like to have that kind of simple intimacy with someone? Feel those emotions for another human. I had once, a long time ago. I've been chasing the illusion of it for the past decade. Fucking every woman I meet to find even a semblance of it.

Tristan pulls out a chair for Syn to sit like a fucking gentleman, and I almost roll my damn eyes like a teenage girl.

"Is that mine?" she asks. Her nose wrinkles as she looks at the steak.

"Yes."

"It's not cooked."

Jesus. And she said I was stuck up.

"It's cooked just fine. Sit down and eat."

The sour look on her face grows more severe. "I'll just zap it in the microwave."

"The hell you will."

Microwaved food is as bad as well-done steak.

Syn picks her plate up, but I reach over and slam it back down on the table.

"Eat the fucking steak."

If looks could kill, I'd be stabbed a million times with the daggers she's glaring at me.

"I'll just have salad, thank you." She plops her pert ass down in the chair.

"What?" I snap when she looks at the salad and makes the same dour look.

"I don't like anchovies."

Fucking hell. "You can't even taste the bloody stuff in the Caesar dressing. Stop being a brat."

Con leaves and goes inside. I swear to god, if he makes her anything to eat, I'm going to lose my shit.

"Stop getting offended if someone doesn't like the food you cook. Not everyone wants raw meat and fish salad."

Tristan takes the seat next to her. "The two of you are giving me a fucking migraine."

He's saying it facetiously, but Syn takes it otherwise. Lifting his hand, she cradles it between hers and starts doing that pressure point shit she did last time.

My irritation increases along with my envy as I watch them together. Jealousy is a pernicious beast. It builds rapidly until it consumes everything. It also makes you do and say really stupid shit.

"You and Aleksander have a good time today?"

And fuck me for opening my damn mouth. I didn't want to say anything until I had more to go on.

Syn's head jerks up with guilty, wide blue eyes. "How did you—" Those wide eyes narrow with angry realization. "You *followed* me?"

CHAPTER 38

Unbelievable asshole.

Hendrix swayed Tristan into letting me go with Raquelle just so he could follow me. I should have known. Hendrix doesn't do anything with kindness. Everything he does is manipulative and self-serving.

And it hurts—more than it should because I know better. Hendrix Knight really is the devil.

The hand I was just massaging turns into a harsh grip around my wrist. "What is he talking about?" Tristan asks, or more like accuses.

"She went to see Aleksander this morning," Hendrix unhelpfully replies.

"Shut. Up!"

I'm livid and embarrassed and angrier than I've ever felt in my life. I'm shaking from the severity of it. Betrayal burns my skin and cuts me deep until all I want to do is double over and cry—or jab the steak knife in front of me into Hendrix's deceiving face.

I try to pull out of Tristan's punishing hold.

"Her location would have changed if she left Danby.

Unless…" he says like I'm not there, then jerks me closer until the metal arm of the patio chair cuts into my side. I don't like the way his eyes change as he looks at me with suspicion. "… you left your phone in the dorm room."

I didn't expect him to actually use the location tracking app, but who the hell am I kidding. I've been a prisoner to these men since the moment I walked out into the alley.

Tristan's fingers cleave into my circulation until my hand goes numb.

"Care to explain?"

"Let go."

Venom slips off his honeyed tongue when he says, "Oh, Red. You don't get to make demands. What you're going to do is open that pretty mouth and tell me everything."

The harsh tone of his voice sends chills down my spine. I've never been afraid of Tristan until now. The man who said sweet things to me and asked permission to touch me is no longer here. In his place is a stranger.

In a desperate move I don't think twice about making, I grab Tristan at the elbow and press down hard on a pressure point four fingers up on his arm. His hand spasms, and I'm able to slip free. I'm out of my chair in an instant, needing to get some distance away from him and Hendrix.

"How did you do that?"

My back is to the house, and I warily inch my way toward it.

"I learned it on YouTube," I sarcastically snipe because I don't recall where I learned to do that. "I didn't lie to you. I just didn't tell you what I was going to do. You'd never let me talk to him, so I took the initiative."

"Fucking straight, I'd never let you talk to that motherfucker!" Tristan bellows, rising from his chair.

In the corner of my periphery, I catch Hendrix move nearer. This is not going to end well for me. Like a trapped animal, I weigh my options. Fight or flight, stand my ground or run.

Aoife, the voice in my head screams. I squeeze my eyes closed, fighting to block it out.

"I asked him if he wrote the note."

The screen door cracks like a gunshot when it slams, and Constantine puts himself between me and Hendrix. He must have heard everything because he protectively tucks me behind him, shielding me from Tristan. I move to his side but stay close.

"Back the fuck up," Con tells Hendrix. "You okay?" he asks me, but I don't take my eyes off a furious Tristan.

"And what did he say?" Tristan's query oozes condescension, and my hackles rise.

"He said that he didn't."

"And you believed him?"

"Yes."

There's a pregnant pause. I can hear the insult coming before he even opens his mouth.

"You really are stupid."

"What the fuck, Tristan? Apologize," Constantine barks.

He needs to rest his voice before he does more damage. However, the damage Tristan's insult causes burrows inside my brain and finds a permanent home. Damn the tears that spill over. They make me feel weak and pathetic. His opinion of me shouldn't matter. But it does. *I* want to matter to *him*. And that really does make me the stupidest woman on the planet.

I wipe my cheek with the back of my hand.

"You're right."

Tristan's remorseful expression speaks louder than his apology. "Shit, Red. I'm sorry."

Constantine tries to help dry my tears, but I back away. The pained look he gives at my dismissal crushes me.

Can't they see how lost I feel? My life wasn't perfect before, but I was content to live it in denial. They forced their way in, sucked me into their crazy-ass lives of secrets and intrigue, and fucked everything up. They dragged me out of the complacency I had been perfectly happy to wallow in, and there's no going back to the way things used to be.

It's their fault that I'm now questioning who I am, who I can trust, and what really happened to me. And I'm terrified that the answers I may find will point right back at me. But I need to know. No more hiding.

"You want to know what Aleksander said? He told me to run. Get away from you as fast as I can. You make him out to be the big bad wolf, and maybe he is. But I have a feeling that what he said was the god's honest truth. Something you've failed to do. I've opened up to you. Told you things about myself that I've never told anyone else, but every time I ask you anything, you shut down or say you can't tell me."

He slams his fists down on the table and the entire patio shakes.

"Because I fucking can't!"

I'm not listening anymore, too lost in my misery and heartbreak.

"Well, here's a truth for you, Tristan Amato. You ready for it?"

I rip my shirt over my head and shed my shorts until I'm in nothing but my white cotton bra and pale pink panties. Under a half moon and starlit sky, I let the three of them get a good long look at the horrific parts of me that I try to hide. The parts that separate me from everyone else. Ugly. Damaged. Unworthy. Freakish.

"Fuck me," Hendrix breathes out.

"You want to know who I am?" I raise my arms over my head and turn to show the large, Frankensteined area of my side and hip that doesn't look any better, even after three skin grafts. "This is me." I touch each line where the knife slid in. "I'm the girl with no past because she doesn't want to remember it. I'm the girl no one wants. The broken, pathetic, *stupid* girl who looks like a monster."

All the air gets knocked out of me when Constantine pushes me up against the side of the house, cutting off my emotional tirade and anything else I was going to say.

He slams his body into mine, his hands holding my face. "You're so fucking wrong. You're the most beautiful fucking thing I have ever seen."

Before I know what's happening, he kisses me in front of his two best friends. Two best friends who I have also kissed. So many lines get blurred in that moment. I had daydreamed more times than I can count about being kissed by Constantine, but nothing could have prepared me for this. This isn't just a kiss. This is life-altering.

His tongue strokes between my lips, demanding entrance, and a low moan breaks free when he slips inside, tasting, taking, devouring me. Desire mainlines into my bloodstream, sending me on a high I never want to come down from.

The brick of the house radiates the sun's heat it soaked in during the day and abrades the skin along my back. I hardly notice, too consumed by Constantine to care. Whatever has been building between us breaks free from its cage, snarling, rabid, and ravenous.

He takes and takes, and I'm left clinging to him as my entire world flies apart.

Something soft brushes against my side, like a phantom tingle. Nerve endings that shouldn't work, spark to life, intense and overpowering.

"I'm sorry," I hear Tristan whisper, but I'm not quite sure what he's apologizing for: what he said or what was done to me.

I feel the sensation again.

And again. The same tingle, this time stronger. I breathlessly look down. Tristan kneels next to us, his lips on my mutilated skin.

"I'm so sorry," he says.

He presses plush kisses over the scars melted into my curves. With each touch of his mouth, he whispers how beautiful I am. My wounds. My body.

My emotions skitter all over the place. Where there was anger and hurt from minutes ago is replaced with need. So much fucking need. I *need* this. Their praise and their hands on my body. I'm starving for it after being denied it my whole life.

Tristan's hand runs up the length of my leg. "Our girl is so beautiful, isn't she, Con?"

Our girl.

Holy shit.

Constantine growls deep in his throat, turning my face to claim my lips once again, possessing me completely with every thrust of his tongue.

Is this really happening? Do I want this to happen?

I'm being kissed by two men. Touched by two men. The tiny voice inside my head that tells me this is so wrong gets shoved out of the way when Constantine shifts his stance and spins me in his arms. Tristan cradles my hips in his hands. His lips paint brushstrokes around the diamond stud at my belly button, and my abdominals quiver.

"I'm scared." My fear is spoken as just a trembled whisper in the breeze.

My two sexual experiences have been with Tristan and Hendrix, and that's not saying much since we didn't really do anything. I'm practically naked, standing out on their back patio. Exposed and vulnerable. Terrified out of my mind that I'm not emotionally ready for what my heart wants more than anything.

"I never got to kiss you here last night."

His hot breath fans over my mons, and those mischievous whiskey eyes smirk his intent.

"*Tristan.*"

He's not really going to— "*Oh my god.*"

Tristan's tongue flattens over the thin cotton of my panties, and he hums. The vibrations stimulate my clit, and I can feel my underwear soak through. Pleasure pulses a drumbeat that matches the pounding of my heart.

"So wet for us. Aren't you, Red?"

He licks me, and I moan. Loudly.

My head drops onto Constantine's shoulder, and I fall into the fathomless black of his heated gaze. He teases his hand down my chest to the front clasp of my bra, giving me time to say no, to stop. When I say nothing, he flicks the clasp. My bra falls open, and cool night air beads my nipples into hard peaks. Goose bumps scatter like falling stars across my chest and up my arms to my neck.

The rough calluses of his fingers scrape along the exposed swell of my breasts, and he traces the outline of where Hendrix marked me. His eyes raise and lock with mine, a silent question being asked. We have an entire conversation without speaking a word. If I say yes, it will change everything. It will fundamentally change *me*.

Hendrix appears in front of us. I had been so caught up in the moment that I forgot he was there, quietly watching. He doesn't try to touch me or join his friends in what's about to clearly happen. I may loathe him, but I'm not entirely sure I'd stop him if he tried. I really am screwed up.

"You ready for this, firefly?"

I take his question like a challenge. Hendrix thinks I'm naïve. Too innocent. I want to prove him wrong.

"Yes."

Constantine swipes his thumb over my aching nipple, and my legs buckle. I'd fall to the ground if he wasn't holding me up. Reaching behind me over my shoulders, I scrape my fingers through his short hair at the back and hold on.

Hendrix's pitch drops an octave. "You want this?"

"*Yes.*" No hesitation this time.

I'm rewarded with a gorgeous smile that makes my belly swoop. The longer he looks at me, the more turned on I get.

Hendrix erases the feet of distance between us. With Constantine behind me, Tristan in front, and Hendrix to my right, I'm surrounded and completely at their mercy.

I suck in a sharp gasp when he purrs in my ear, "You're going to beg so prettily for us to do the filthiest things to you." He moves away, and anticipation thickens the air. "Make her come."

It's as if we were all waiting for him to say that.

Constantine takes my mouth in a delicious kiss just as Tristan tears my underwear off my body like tissue paper. My entire being lights up like a thundercloud discharging bolts of lightning. Every nerve synapse fires, delivering jolts of need straight to my pussy.

Tristan gathers the wetness that drips down the inside of my thigh with a finger and coats my clit with it. I'm so close to coming, it's embarrassing.

He kisses my most intimate place and breathes in the scent of my heat. "So pretty," he says and focuses on rubbing small circles over my swollen nub that makes my toes curl and my eyes roll back.

My back arches when Constantine cups my breasts and pinches my sensitive nipples. Pleasure and pain. Complete opposites that send me soaring.

Tristan impales my slick, tight channel with one finger, then adds another. My pussy clamps down, and he groans his approval.

"That's it, baby. We're going to make you feel so fucking good. Don't fight it."

Constantine swallows every obscene moan I make as Tristan finger-fucks me slowly, keeping me right on the edge but not letting me tip over. It's beautiful torture.

"Syn."

My eyes fly open when Hendrix says my name. He's standing so close, looking heart-stoppingly handsome.

The devil with the face of an angel.

There's no lead-up or warning, just pure ecstasy when Tristan's soft lips and warm, wet tongue latch onto my clit.

"Come."

One word from Hendrix's wicked mouth, and I obey without thought. My muscles seize and pull my body tight, then split me wide open. I come violently, convulsing as I orgasm. Wave after wave. It's never-ending. It's too much and not enough and leaves me utterly shattered in the most splendid way.

When the aftershocks subside, I wilt in a repleted mess against Constantine, still gripping the back of his head because my fingers won't work. I think they broke me.

Tristan kisses his way up my body, stopping at each breast to lave them with tender affection, then kisses me lightly on the lips.

"You are magnificent."

I'm overcome with gratitude that I got to experience what it felt like to be wanted and desired, even if it's just this one time. And how pathetic is that?

Hendrix rubs the backs of his knuckles across my blushed, sweaty face. "Take her upstairs for aftercare."

I want to ask what that is but don't get the chance. Constantine sweeps me up in his arms, and I curl into him, burying my face in his neck as he carries me to his room. He nuzzles my cheek, whispering sweet words in a language I don't understand. Spanish? No, Portuguese.

Lulled by the sound of his hushed voice, I fall asleep in his arms before we even get to the top of the stairs.

CHAPTER 39

I'm a bastard.

I should have stopped things from getting out of hand. We shouldn't have touched her. Aleksander was right to tell her to run.

But it's too late for regrets.

I look down at Syn spread gloriously naked on my bed. Every inch of her is perfect from her kiss-swollen lips I got to taste for the first time, to her gorgeous pert tits, pink nipples, and hourglass curves my hands had the pleasure of touching. I ache to touch her again, and the impulse is too strong to resist. I lightly dust fingertips over her breasts and down her pale skin to her dark blonde pubic hair, a detail Tristan should have noticed.

A tidal wave of guilt consumes me. Not for what just happened on the patio, but for what I have to do.

Standing over her, I memorize every detail of the horrors that were done to her. Her scars are those of nightmares, but they attest to how fucking strong she is. How in the hell did she survive it, and where has she been all this time?

My search for answers hasn't brought any clarity, and I'm out of time because… *we shouldn't have fucking touched her.*

I lean over and kiss her sweet lips. Lips I have no right to kiss because she will never belong to me.

"Please forgive me. *Você é meu coração.*"

She rips my fucking heart out when she sighs in her sleep, "*Gheobhaidh mo chroí do chroí.*"

When she said it the first time, that's when I knew.

I fucking *knew.*

I'm ashamed that I didn't put the pieces together sooner. She looks completely different from the young girl I remember, but her eyes should have clued me in. The unique cornflower blue. The undeniable, magnetic pull we felt toward her. The things she knew how to do but didn't know *how* she knew.

I have to make myself leave, even though all I want to do is crawl in next to her and hold her forever.

She's not yours.

I quietly sneak out of the bedroom and into hers. I know exactly where to find her journal because I discovered it when I searched her room. When I saw what was in it—the drawings and disjointed phrases—fucking Christ. It broke me.

If there is one grace, at least she doesn't remember, and I pray to god that she never does, even if it means she never remembers us.

I still have so many questions, though. How is she still alive and how did we not know? That troubles me more than anything. And how in the hell is she here at Darlington Founders? It can't be a coincidence. Someone knows who she really is and is fucking with us, using her to do it.

What did the guy from the alley say before I snapped his neck? *She's going to kill all of you.* Was he talking about Syn or someone else?

I shouldn't have killed him so quickly. Given enough time, I could have broken him. They always break when the torture becomes too much, and they beg for a death I won't give them until they tell me exactly what I want to know.

Taking the journal out of her bag, I open it to the front where she keeps the pressed clover similar to the one I gave her, and am curious to see a familiar pressed flower as well. *Tristan.*

He's not going to understand. However, it's Hendrix I'm most worried about. He's going to hate himself for how he's treated her.

Like a man heading to the gallows, I go downstairs to find them.

"Any news from Tessa?" Hendrix asks from his reclined position on the couch just as I walk into the living room. He doesn't notice me because his attention is glued to a Formula 1 race on television.

"Hen, shut up," Tristan snaps when he sees me.

The only Tessa I know is Tessa Goodwyn from school. I connect the dots. Fucker went behind my back. Impatient jackass. I dragged my feet for a reason, and his impatience may have just placed a bigger target on Syn's back.

"Sit." My voice cracks like audio feedback from a speaker. I can barely talk above a whisper at this point.

Hendrix grabs the remote and mutes the sound. "Told you he was going to be pissed."

Propping a hip to the back of the couch, Tristan has

the foresight to look contrite. “She can access stuff we can’t. I was trying to help.”

Bullshit. He probably sensed I was stalling and decided to take matters into his own hands.

“Syn still upstairs?”

“Asleep.”

“Want to go wake her up?”

Hendrix takes the throw pillow from under his head and chucks it at him. “Her cunt can’t be that good.”

“Watch your fucking mouth,” I warn him.

He turns the volume on the television back up. “You’re moody as shit.”

I shove the journal at Tristan and back the hell up to the other side of the room. I could take him and Hen both if it came to it, but I’d rather avoid a fight if possible.

“Open it.”

Tristan turns the journal over to look at the back cover. “What is it?”

Pandora’s box.

“Answers.”

“About what?”

“Syn.”

He chuckles. “She’s going to have a fit if she finds out you went through her stuff. I’ll look at it later.”

“Look at it now.”

A million emotions churn like acid in my gut when he unties the leather cord and opens it. His brow furrows when he sees the clover. He flips to the first page.

Hendrix scoots over so he can see as well. “Like a diary? Oh, this should be good.” His cocky smirk falls as soon as he processes what he’s reading.

As Tristan flips the pages, his body language changes

—shock, disbelief, hope.

Hendrix snatches the journal away. "What the fuck is this?"

He and Tristan look at me, waiting for me to say it out loud. The silence is deafening. The calm before the storm.

"Aoife." I can barely utter her name. We haven't spoken it in over ten years. "Syn is Aoife."

CHAPTER 40

Ten and a half years ago

My bare feet scrape across cold rock, and darkness shrouds my head as I'm led like a sheep to the slaughterhouse. Low murmurs echo in a cavernous room, growing in excitement upon seeing me, even though I can't see them.

Damp air that smells of must and mold filters through the black satin that covers my head. My ears feel like they're filled with cotton, the only true sound I hear is the strong, even, steady thump of my heart and the hush of my breath as I breathe in through my nose and out my mouth.

Even though I've never been inside this room before, I know exactly what it is.

Tonight is the night my father has been preparing me for since I was three years old. Initiation night. My twelfth birthday when I am no longer considered a boy. My first test as a man to prove myself worthy. Of them.

Of him. Of the Council. If I fail, I know the fate that awaits me. Which is why I will *not* fail.

The cloth encasing my head is roughly ripped away, and within seconds, my sight adjusts to the dimness of the room, illuminated only by tall, ornate candelabras spaced within carved-out niches in the coal-black rock.

I'm standing in the center of an underground cavern, one decorated ostentatiously in regal accoutrements. Red velvet tapestries hang from the ceiling. Gold trinkets and fine sculptures sit atop Doric columns made of black obsidian.

I do not avert my gaze. I do not seek out the one person I hope isn't there to witness my capitulation into hell. I do not look at the men dressed in red and black cowls and matching horned masks surrounding me like a pack of savage hyenas.

And I do not lay eyes on the men sitting like kings on their godly thrones. The aristocratic men who dress in refined clothes and pretend to be respected pillars of their community, but they are not. They are the men whose only aspirations in life are power, wealth, and control through any means necessary.

My father comes around to my right side. I show no apprehension or fear. I keep my face blank and unemotive, even though my heart rate kicks up when he offers me the ruby-encrusted hilt of a medieval dagger.

Muffled grunts and cries reach my ears just as a man is shoved to his knees right in front of me. Again, I don't dare look at him. I can't. I can't meet his pleading eyes and make that connection. Give my conscience a reason to feel pity for him.

I accept the knife. It feels heavy in my grip, laden with the hundreds of souls whose lives it took. I wonder if the jewels embedded in its handle were once diamonds, clear and pristine, but were stained red over time with the blood of its victims.

I can feel my father's frigid stare weighing heavily on me.

"Constantine Ferreira," he announces for the benefit of the others in the room, the inflection of his deep voice cultured and refined. "Prove your worth."

Each family serves a purpose, a duty to uphold to the Society. I am the only son of Gabriel Ferreira, and like my father, I now serve them. I become Death.

The door to the room I was told to wait in cracks open, and a thin stream of light breaks the darkness before disappearing again. The padding of several silent footfalls creeps closer, but I know it's them.

"Con," Aoife whispers, her voice more beautiful than the bells that ring in the cathedral every Christmas Day.

"I can't see shit," Hendrix says and is immediately hushed by Tristan.

With effort, I force my abused body to sit up. After the ceremony, Father beat me. Apparently, I hesitated before slicing the man's neck open with the knife.

Aoife drops down in front of me and immediately clambers onto my lap. With our noses almost touching, I can see her angelic face as clearly as if the room was flooded with sunlight.

She reaches up and trails a soft touch from forehead to chin, then settles her fingertips against my lips. Her pale-blue eyes trace my features one by one like she's memorizing me.

"Did he do this?" she angrily asks, concern knitting her delicate brows together when she sees the gash on my cheek.

A lighter clicks on, and a small flame dances near my face. Tristan's scowl comes into view.

"Jesus, Con," he says when he sees the bruises and swollen cheek.

Hendrix opens the curtains to allow the moonlight to come in and sits down beside me. He and Aoife share a look. They've always been close even though she's three years younger than us. We won't see her much anymore after next month, when me and the guys are shipped off to a boarding school in Switzerland.

My mouth moves but no sound comes out. It hurts too much to talk. The last time Father beat me a few months ago, he went too far. Choked me until I passed out. I haven't been able to talk properly since.

Use your hands, Aoife signs.

Aoife has been learning ASL and has been teaching me, but we don't know enough words yet, so it's hard to communicate. I try to tell her that they shouldn't be here, but the only words I can remember to sign are *You. Not. Here.*

She shakes her head, not understanding.

"Get in trouble." I hate the broken, cracked sound of my voice. It's like glass crunching inside a blender.

Father left me in here a little while ago and told me to stay until he returned. They can't be here when he comes back. If he finds them here—

I can't take another beating.

"Fuck him," Tristan says. "You were there for me."

Tristan had his initiation last week. Hendrix's will come in a few months, and then Aoife when she comes of age.

"Ow! Shit."

The flame from the lighter extinguishes, but there's enough backdrop lighting coming in from the window to see. Tristan sucks on his thumb that got burned.

Big, fat tears leak from Aoife's beautiful eyes. Aoife never cries. We're conditioned not to. Tears imply weakness.

"I'm leaving," she says out of the blue, taking us all by surprise.

Hendrix nudges her arm to make her look at him. "What are you talking about?"

"Papa told me after the ceremony. He made me swear not to tell anyone, that it was a secret."

We sit in stunned silence. It has always been the four of us for as long as I can remember.

"When?" Tristan asks.

"He said we had to leave tonight, and we weren't coming back. Please don't tell anyone. Papa said something bad would happen if I told." More tears.

"We won't say anything. Promise." Tristan holds up his pinky, and she loops hers around it. A pinky promise.

I run my hand down her heart-shaped face and tuck the strands of her silky blonde hair behind her ears. "Promise."

"No," Hendrix says, being stubborn as usual. "You can't leave. We won't let you."

Aoife's smile is sad. "You'd be leaving me next month anyway."

"But not for forever! You just said you're never coming back."

"I will always come back to you," she tells him with

conviction and places her small hand over his heart. Then she does the same to me and Tristan. "*Gheobhaidh mo chroí do chroí*. My heart will find yours."

CHAPTER 41

Present Day

"You're out of your goddamned mind!"

My heart will find yours. She said it in her sleep. Twice. It's her, Con signs with aggravated hand gestures.

I can't believe it. I won't. There's no fucking way the girl upstairs is Aoife.

The alluring redhead with the haunting blue eyes. Familiar eyes.

No. Just no.

The things I've done to her. The terrible things I said to her.

Her scars. Her fucking scars. Someone doused her in acid. They stabbed her. They *set her on fire*.

I'm off the couch and make it to the small trash bin near the bookcase before I vomit. Nothing comes up but dry heave. I've endured some horrible shit in my life, but knowing someone hurt Aoife like that is the one thing that breaks me.

Tristan bends at the waist, as if he's physically in

pain. "How is this possible?"

I don't know, Con replies.

"We saw where they buried her and her parents. We saw her goddamn gravestone! This doesn't make any sense!" I shout, and Con motions for me to be quiet, pointing upstairs.

Syn.

But not Syn.

Aoife. Our tough little Aoife who loved to braid her curly blonde hair in pigtails and could kick any boy's ass who messed with her. Physically, she's changed. A lot. She's unrecognizable to the little girl who was my fucking sunshine. A little girl who's now a beautiful, infuriating woman. Mentally, she's still tough and feisty. A survivor. I can't wrap my head around it.

"Just because there's a grave marker doesn't mean anything. Anyone or no one could be buried under it." Tristan decides to be the voice of calm reason, while I'm fucking falling apart.

We found out Aoife was dead a few months after we got to Switzerland. Freak car accident caused by a drunk driver is what we were told killed her and her parents. Tristan's sister Dierdre committed suicide around the same time. Everything that month kind of blurred together. Dierdre's funeral was in Boston, but Aoife was buried in Ireland. We never knew that was where her father had taken her, but it made sense since he was from Cork. That entire period was a fucked-up mess of depression and grief. A decade later and we're still suffering their loss.

But Aoife's not dead. She's upstairs, sleeping. In Con's bed.

I strike out and clip Tristan's chin with my fist. His

head whips around, and he touches the small cut on his lip that starts to bleed.

"What the fuck, Hen?"

"You put your mouth on her," I seethe with barely controlled rage.

We defiled the only girl we've ever cared about on the back patio where any peeping Tom with a cheap pair of binoculars could see. Treated her like a whore.

Tristan spits a glob of blood at my feet, not caring that it might stain the rug, then wipes his chin. "You weren't complaining when you were standing there dictating when she could come."

When we lost Aoife, it was like a light had been extinguished, leaving us in total darkness. We were so fucking young, Aoife being the youngest of our unlikely group, but our childhood friendships were forged in steel. We needed each other. We needed *her*. She was the tiny angel in our world filled with evil. Nothing made sense after she was gone. Then we found out she died, and that's when we truly lost whatever frayed strands of our souls were left.

I'm not a good man. I've done and still do some really messed up shit. I kill when I'm told to. Torture people when I'm told to. I'm nothing but a trained beast at the heel of the Society, savage and deadly, doing my master's bidding.

"Fuck you."

I take another swing, but he's ready this time. He catches my fist and torques it, but it puts him off balance and I sweep his leg. He falls sideways onto the couch still gripping my hand and almost wrenches my arm out of its socket.

"You're the degenerate who bit her like a fucking

dog."

If he only knew about the other degrading shit I've done to her. She got turned on when I choked her. We came close to hate-fucking against the wall of the bedroom. She watched me jerk off and *liked it*. Aoife was my girl, but Syn hates my guts.

The fight suddenly drains out of me. I plummet to the sofa next to Tristan and rake my hands over my face and into my hair.

"Why doesn't she remember us?"

She doesn't seem to remember anything. Not even James or Caroline, her parents. They were the only decent adults I knew and actually loved their daughter, something me and the guys never had from our parents.

Con sits on the coffee table and cuffs my knee.

"Whatever the hell happened to her, she doesn't want to remember. But somewhere, deep down, she remembers us. She's here. She found us like she promised," Tristan says.

"There's another player," Con rasps. "Someone knows. They're using her."

"For what?"

I don't know, he signs.

If he says that one more time, he's the next person I'm going to punch. But what he said makes me uneasy. We were lied to about Aoife. Someone knows what happened. I get first dibs on whoever that is.

"We'll keep Tessa on it. Get access to the adoption records. Syn's social security number has to be a fake. Fake identity. Fake name. Which means the woman, Alana, knows something. When we get back, one of us needs to pay her a visit."

"What do we do about Aoife in the meantime?"

"We keep doing what we've been doing. Nothing changes. We treat her like Syn, not Aoife."

I don't know if I'll be able to do that. How can I continue to treat Aoife the way I've been treating Syn?

I pull at my hair in frustration. "We can't take her to New York. No one can know she's alive." In an afterthought, I add, "We need to keep her as far away from Aleksander as possible."

That fucker comes near her again, I'll kill him.

"Agreed. But she's the Fitzpatrick heir. It's her birthright to take her place at the Council when she graduates," Tristan argues.

He is so conditioned by his father about heirs and lineage and empires, he can't see the forest through the trees. Syn isn't Aoife. She's been away from this life for over ten years living on a fucking farm, of all places, in ho-bunk Dilliwyll. Why would he even want to bring her back in?

Instead of trying to appeal to his common sense, I go after his conscience. "You saw what was done to her. Whoever did it may still be out there. You want her dead, for real this time?"

"First of all, fuck you. You know I would die for that girl. Second, we can't ignore a summons. Your father expects her there. It would cause more questions and problems if we don't go. We'll keep her close. We can protect her."

We've done a piss-poor job of it. "You're an idiot."

I pick up her journal where it got tossed on the floor.

Wait, Con signs. "I need to…" He clears his throat. "… tell you what happened at her apartment."

Tristan comes forward, getting in Con's face. "You said you didn't find anything."

I can't handle another revelation tonight, so I walk out and head upstairs. When I get to Con's room, I stand at the side of the bed. I can't take my eyes off her. All that red hair. Her face, her breasts, her pussy. I try to see the Aoife I used to know, but she looks so different now.

I get to the marbled, patchwork of skin on her left side.

"I swear to you, I'll find who did this."

I'm going to set the world on fire and watch it burn.

Just like they tried to do to her.

CHAPTER 42

Someone's watching.

I bolt upright from a deep sleep and throw up my arm when I get hit in the face with blinding sunlight.

Shit. Class. We have a calc quiz today, and I didn't get any studying done because…

Why am I naked?

And then I remember. One incredible orgasm, and I passed right out. *Oh, god.* I cover my face with my hands. I can't believe I did that.

I take a minute to process the ache between my legs and touch my abraded, kiss-swollen lips. Last night really happened. I should feel guilty as hell about what I did—what I let them do—but I don't. How could I regret something that felt so good?

A coy smile spreads across my face, and I bite my bottom lip as I replay every amazing second.

When I look next to me, I'm disappointed when I find Constantine's side of the bed empty. It's the first time since I started coming to his room that I've woken up alone.

All the good feelings I'd just been having leach out as self-doubt creeps in. I may not regret what happened, but do they? Was last night out of pity?

"Constantine?" I groggily call out.

I figure out where he is when I see the closed bathroom door and hear the shower running. My internal body clock is so ingrained to waking at six every morning that it feels almost self-indulgent to have slept past sunrise.

I gather the sheet to wrap around myself when the A/C kicks on, blowing cold air from an overhead ceiling vent and chilling me to the point of shivers.

"Morning, firefly."

The scream I let out is worthy of a slasher film. Something crashes downstairs, and Tristan lets out a loud "motherfucker."

"Everyone needs to stop scaring the crap out of me!"

Hendrix is sitting in the chair tucked in the corner of the room, looking pleased with himself. No wonder I thought I felt eyes on me. How long has he been there?

I cinch the sheet tightly to my chin, practically strangling myself with it.

This is awkward.

"What are you doing?"

"Looking at you."

I've got nothing. No snarky comeback or chastising quip.

When he keeps staring, I try to knot the sheet in place so I can get up and go to my room but it's not cooperating.

"Do you mind?"

"Not at all."

"I meant, could you please leave?"

He smoothly transitions from the chair to the bed. I try to scramble away, but he puts his weight on the sheet and traps me. I'm contemplating whether to just walk out of here buck naked. It's not like he didn't see every exposed inch of me last night.

Keeping the bed covers pinned under his knees, he crawls over me until I'm pressed as far as I can go into the mattress.

"What are you doing?" I sound like a parrot.

"I'm looking at you," he says again, slowly, but the way he says it sends my heart rate rocketing.

I'm suspended in time, not able to move, as he devours me with his blue gaze. Everywhere his eyes stop on their journey across my face feels like the sweetest of kisses.

Air solidifies to concrete in my lungs when he lowers down to tenderly press his lips to my cheek.

"Good morning, Syn."

Syn, not firefly.

His simple morning greeting elicits a full body shudder. What the hell is going on?

The bathroom door opens and sandalwood fragrant steam billows out along with a gorgeously wet Constantine, towel tied loosely around his waist. I have a deer in headlights moment because Hendrix is basically on top of me, but Constantine doesn't seem to notice. He grabs a shirt from the chest of drawers, and I can't help but eye-fuck the heck out of him as he raises his arms, muscles flexing, and pulls the shirt over his head.

Sleep well?

What? Oh.

"Very."

Coffee?

"Okay."

This is so weird.

"I've got it," Hendrix says.

The mattress jostles as he climbs off, but then Tristan saunters into the bedroom, all handsome smiles and looking impeccably dressed as always in his blue-tailored shirt and dark trousers.

"Hey, beautiful."

Every time I hear that, it takes me by surprise. If we weren't the only people in the room, I'd look behind me to make sure he wasn't talking to somebody else.

Some innate force tugs at my heart when they line up together, shoulder to shoulder, a wall of three insanely hot men that addles my not-yet-fully-awake brain. They just stand there, looking *happy*... and... expectant, like they're waiting for something.

I snowplow my hair away from my face. "Am I being punked?"

Hendrix grins and props an elbow to Tristan's shoulder. "She's cute."

I'm cute?

What I am is confused as fuck.

"Could I please have some privacy?"

Hendrix is the first to leave, but he asks, "Chocolate chip pancakes good for you?"

Seeing as they're my favorite, I eagerly reply, "Yes."

"Everything packed?"

I turn my attention from the promise of pancakes to Tristan.

"Yep."

He tilts my chin up and kisses me affectionately on my nose. "Stop freaking out and don't overthink things.

Last night was just the beginning." He puts his lips right up to my ear. "I plan to put my mouth on you again. *Every-fucking-where.*"

I'm instantly wet, and he knows it based on his cocky chuckle as he leaves the room.

"I'll pick you up after class," he calls out.

Constantine pulls on a pair of frayed-at-the-knee jeans under his towel, then takes it off and dumps it in the hamper.

"How are you?" I ask him, touching my throat so he knows what I'm referring to.

Good.

He sits down on the bed next to me.

You?

"Good."

He takes a section of my hair and lets it sift through his fingers, then signs, *How are you really?*

Constantine has an uncanny ability to see past the bullshit. It's one of the things I like about him. He's quiet and reserved but that doesn't mean he's not aware of everything around him. And when he gives you his complete attention, nothing else exists. This man makes me feel so safe with just his presence alone.

I lean to the side so I can rest my head on his shoulder. "I don't know," I reply honestly.

I'm not a sexual person. At least, I didn't think I was. Then again, I was never given an opportunity to find out. I guess now is my chance. College is supposed to be about experimenting and discovering yourself, right? Constantine and Tristan have made their interests clear. So why the hell not? Nothing lasts forever. If I don't grab hold of whatever this is between us, I know I'll regret it for the rest of my life.

Twisting in the sheet, I turn toward him. "Are *you* okay with... this?" I circle my hand around.

If he said no and made me choose, I'd do it—no matter how attracted I am to Tristan and, god help me, Hendrix. The mere thought of causing Constantine pain makes me nauseous.

He captures my hand and threads our fingers together, then places our joined hands to his heart and holds it there. I count the beats as I feel them.

"You belong with us."

The swell of emotion is enormous. *I belong*.

"May I kiss you?"

Constantine's full smile takes my breath away. "Always."

Even though I'm the one who asked, he's the first to move. Hooking a finger at the knot in the sheet, he gives it a small tug and pulls me toward him. I relish the scrape of his stubble, the tiny pricks contrast with the softness of his lips when they finally meet mine.

"Get dressed and come downstairs for breakfast," he says and kisses me one last time before sliding out of bed.

Keeping the sheet wrapped around me, I happily hum as I go to my bathroom where I do a quick wash and plait my hair in a French braid. Before we leave this afternoon, I'll take a proper shower and dress in something more appropriate to meet Hendrix's family. Because every other decent piece of clothing I own is packed in my rolling suitcase for the trip to New York, I slip on my "*Just a Girl Who Likes Peckers*" tee with the big rooster on it and the shorts I wore yesterday.

Checking my phone, I don't see anything from Alana, which is odd.

My guilty fingers type out a reminder of the lie I told her.

Me: I'll be at my friend's dorm tonight.

No dots start bouncing. Maybe she's outside feeding the animals. I wait a minute to see if she replies.

I shouldn't have ambushed her with questions about my real parents. It was insensitive, and if I were in her shoes, I'd be hurt, too. She's given me everything. Loved me unconditionally. I could have broached the subject in a much better way.

Me: Please don't be mad.

Me: I love you.

Me: Mom.

CHAPTER 43

The pop quiz took Raquelle and me twenty minutes to complete, so we decided to sit outside near the quad's fountain while I wait for Hendrix. The guys' dumb rule about escorting me everywhere was still in effect, no matter how vehemently I protested. My visit to see Aleksander didn't help my case.

"That spot looks good." Raquelle points to a shady spot in the grass to sit.

The campus buzzes with Friday morning energy as excitement builds about the upcoming weekend and which party to go to, whereas I'm a bundle of nerves about meeting Hendrix's parents.

"Did you talk to Drake about—" I let the rest hang in the air like a cloud of suffocating smog.

When I was with her the other morning, we talked about ways I could go about finding out what happened to my biological parents. And to me. Raquelle said if anyone could help me find information about my past, it was her boyfriend-slash-stepbrother. When I asked her how, she told me I was better off not knowing.

Apparently, Drake used to run with one of the gangs in LA when he was a teen. Even though he's out of that life now, he still keeps those connections open. Finding that out didn't bother me. I'd be a hypocrite if it did, considering the men I was currently living with.

"We talked last night. Drake said he knew a guy who was good at finding… *stuff*."

A patch of clover catches my eye, and I look for any that have four leaves.

"Alana wants me to come home next weekend, so we can talk. I ambushed her about what happened to my real parents, and I think I upset her. Do you mind telling him to hold off on things for now?"

Raquelle gives my hand a friendly pat. "We'll do whatever you're comfortable with or do nothing at all. Oh, hey, I brought you something." Shuffling through her oversize tote bag, she pulls out a pair of strappy, gold high heels. "Size eight and a half, right?"

I covet the expensive stilettos dangling in front of me and am horrified that she was carrying them around loose in her bag. I know a pair of Monolo Blahniks when I see them. I saw them splashed inside enough magazines that I read while in the hospital.

"You can't be serious."

She jingles them like a set of keys. "These would look great with the blue dress."

"My feet are not worthy of a thousand-dollar shoes."

She places them in my lap. "Eight hundred, and you're wearing them, end of story. They'll make your ass look fantastic." She gives the air a chef's kiss.

I gawk at the shoes, then at her, feeling a little bit like Cinderella and she's my fairy godmother.

My spoken "thank you" doesn't even come close to the

gratitude I'm feeling.

Chewing on the paper straw of her drink, she sucks down the dregs of her iced latte that's mostly water and microscopic espresso grounds by this point.

"No problem. You can borrow any of my stuff whenever you want."

I'm not used to this easy kind of friendship, probably because I didn't have any close friends back home.

I sit dumbly as I try to figure out where to store the shoes. Placing them in my backpack seems disrespectful.

Raquelle adjusts her glasses. The photochromic lenses are now a dark brown. "Hey, isn't that Evan?"

I shield my eyes from the intense sun and catch sight of him walking past the library. A place I won't be too eager to walk inside anytime soon.

"Yeah."

Evan takes off his Beats headphones and stops to talk to a guy.

"You need to ask him out." She waves to get his attention, and I drag her arm down.

"No, I don't."

"And why is that?"

My eyes narrow when she can't hide the mischievous grin.

"You saw, didn't you?"

I thought Constantine and I were being discreet when he kissed me goodbye after dropping me off. Guess not.

Her grin spreads. "Do you know how badly I've been wanting to say something? I've waited a whole" —she checks her phone— "forty minutes!"

I laugh at her exuberance.

She pokes me with a pastel blue-tipped fingernail.

"So? Kissing definitely implies more than friends. But the hot way Constantine kissed *you* implies something else entirely."

"It's complicated."

It's not like I haven't already told her a lot of deep, personal stuff, but telling someone that you're fooling around with two men at the same time is a whole other level of personal. However, I can't talk to Alana about it, and I really need another woman to talk to about this stuff, so I take another leap of faith. If there's anyone who wouldn't judge me, it's Raquelle.

She gently bumps my shoulder. "I'm sleeping with my older stepbrother, so I'm basically shock-proof. Lay it on me."

Bending in half, I collapse forward to hide my red face between my knees. "I may have done something last night with all three of them."

"Except that," she says. "All three?"

I peek up at her. "Hendrix kind of watched."

"Kind of?" Raquelle bowls over and falls onto her back in the grass.

Catching her breath, she taps the ground beside her, indicating for me to join her. I lower myself to lie down, slip off my sandals, and dig my toes into the recently shorn blades of petal-soft Kentucky bluegrass. Being supine gives me great views of the white puffy clouds that meander overhead in the blue sky. One looks like a turtle. I raise my arm and trace the cloud's outline as it slowly moves along the invisible current of upper-level winds.

"When you and Drake got together, did it feel weird and taboo because he was older and your stepbrother, or did it feel right?"

Raquelle replies wistfully, "Seeing as I had been in love with the guy since the day we met, it felt like the most perfect thing in the world. It just took him a little longer to see it." She turns her head to look at me. "Men can be very obtuse and downright stupid when it comes to matters of the heart."

Wanting her advice, I cup my hand over my mouth and whisper, "Should I stop it? Does it make me a… slut that I liked it?"

I stripped my clothes off and let Tristan go down on me. In public. I'm treading deep waters I'm not sure I know how to swim.

"You enjoy that shit. Why do guys get to have all the fun without the derogatory labels?"

"What about manwhore?"

She laughs. "Men wear that moniker like a badge of honor."

A shadow moves over us, followed by an upside-down Hendrix. "Doing a little pareidolia?"

"Do you even know what that means?"

The blue of the sky perfectly matches the blue of his eyes.

"Finding random patterns or shapes in objects."

"Can you spell it?"

"Hell no."

We grin at each other before I come to my senses with a sobering thought. Hendrix is being nice. He's been acting nice all morning, and it's freaking me out a little.

Raquelle sits up. "Guess I should be making my way over to art."

Hendrix offers me a hand, which I scrutinize before accepting. His shirtsleeve rolls up when his bicep bulges as he helps me into an upright position.

Having nowhere to put the shoes Raquelle gave to me, I carefully place them in the front pocket where my journal lives, except it's not there. I briefly panic before I remember that I didn't check my bag before I left the house. My journal is more than likely sitting on the window bench where I like to write.

Raquelle hugs me, and I hug her back without any hesitation. Progress, I tell myself.

"Thank you so much for the shoes and dresses."

"Have fun in New York. Text me at least once. Proof of life. And don't be afraid to try new things," she says quietly, not being subtle in the least as to what she means.

Hendrix looks questioningly at the shoes sticking out of the front of my bag when he picks it up. "You have the next hour free, right?"

"I do."

"Good. I owe you a lesson."

The university fitness center buzzes with activity, the rhythmic clanging of weights and the grunts of masculine exertion creating a symphony of physical determination.

I hit the floor—again—and a jolt of impact courses through me as I land on my ass. At least the mat beneath me is forgiving and cushions my fall.

"I suck at this," I complain, dragging my tired body up from the floor.

My attire isn't helping either. I'm regretting not wearing my usual yoga leggings, but I'd already packed them to wear as pajama bottoms in New York.

When I regain my footing, cheers erupt from a group of three guys by the free weights who have been thoroughly entertained watching Hendrix toss me around like a ragdoll for the last half hour. Annoyed, I defiantly raise my middle finger, drawing raucous chuckles from the male spectators.

When Hendrix brought me to the student fitness center and I saw the hanging bags used for punching, I'd expected that he'd teach me how to throw punches or land kicks. However, that's not how things played out. According to Hendrix, the most important lesson of fighting is knowing how to fall down and get back up —a lesson I've been excelling at spectacularly.

"You're distracted. Focus."

I use my forearm to wipe away the sweat glistening on my forehead. I'm going to need to call it soon, so I don't show up to my last class sweaty and gross.

"Then put your shirt back on."

That devil-may-care grin appears. Hendrix doesn't need any more ego stroking; his ego is already inflated beyond measure.

"It's your tattoos, not you," I retort, not able to stop from stealing another glance at his impressive ink.

I've been trying to study them in between being thrown around. He has a similar angel to Constantine's on his back, but Hendrix's angel looks like she's ready to take flight, eager to ascend into the heavens. Another stunning design adorns the left side of his chest—a timepiece with the words "*counting down the minutes until I see you again*" circling the ornate clock face.

"Whatever you want to tell yourself, firefly. Get into a fight stance," he says with amusement.

I plant my feet and cock my fists.

Circling me, he gently nudges my left foot to reposition it.

"Good," he comments, his tone laced with approval.

Hendrix approaches from behind, his hands finding my waist. His touch feels possessive, his long fingers conforming to my curves. A gasp strangles in my throat when his warm breath cascades over my neck.

"The night I took you out to the lake, what did you feel right when you thought I was going to lock you in the trunk?" His whisper is laden with an underlying intensity.

That night is not something I want to rehash.

"I don't remember a lot of what happened after we got there."

I tremble when his teeth graze my skin.

"Try. How did you feel?"

"I don't know. Afraid, at first. Then, angry." I try to twist around, but the way he's bracing my hips denies me the opportunity. "I told you I don't remember."

"In the quad when I showed up late, what went through your mind before you grabbed me by the neck?"

My heart begins to pound. Why is he asking me these questions?

"I felt overwhelmed when you wouldn't leave me alone. And angry. I was so angry with you. The next thing I knew, Tristan and Constantine were there."

Like an anvil being lifted off my chest, I can breathe normally when his hands fall away.

"The common factor I heard was that you were angry. Maybe rage is something that triggers your PTSD."

I pirouette to face him. "How do you know I have

PTSD?"

I hadn't disclosed that or any of the myriad of other things I was diagnosed with.

His head quirks to the side, and a lock of blond hair falls across his brow.

"I know the signs," he replies cryptically, his response hinting at something more personal.

Hendrix doesn't wear his scars like me, Tristan, or Constantine, but I know they're there, lurking beneath his turbulent surface. He sleeps on the floor near the window in an empty bedroom. It took me over a year before I was able to sleep in a bed. After the first time I 'woke up' in the hospital, the staff had to either sedate me or strap me down every night because I kept getting up to crawl under the hospital bed. According to the psychologist who treated me, an instinctual response to severe trauma is seeking a position of less vulnerability.

"You do?" I ask, hoping that he'll open up to me a little.

Instead of answering me, he responds with an unexpected shove. Stumbling, I pitch backward before I can regain my balance.

"What was that for?"

"We're not talking about me. Pay attention and get into position."

When I recenter, he sweeps my legs, but I see it coming and am able to jump out of the way.

"Why can't we talk about you?" I ask, not giving up.

I dodge a slow forward jab, and swiftly block the next one, but my momentum is interrupted when he grabs my arm, momentarily arresting my movement.

I shift, instinctively aiming for the pressure points under his arm where his ulnar and median nerves are closest to the surface of the skin. When I strike the area with my knuckles, his hand immediately relaxes, and I slip free. Hendrix regards me with admiration as he shakes out his arm.

"I didn't hit you that hard. The numbness and tingling will go away soon."

"Where'd you learn how to do that pressure point shit?"

"Books."

"I thought you said YouTube."

Catching my gaff, I reply, "That, too."

"You don't remember, do you?"

Hendrix hooks his foot around my back leg, and I'm suddenly flat on my back, staring up at him. His muscular legs straddle my thighs, and his hands bracket my wrists, pinning me to the mat like an insect on a mounting board.

With him this close, I'm able to see more clearly one of the tattoos that had intrigued me. Directly above the right v-groove of his Apollo belt, there's a knight's shield, which I assume represents his surname. Adorning the crest is a geometric pattern that looks like a firebird. It reminds me of the phoenixes I draw in my journal. On impulse, I touch it. His abdominal muscles tighten, and I retract my hand.

"Sorry," I stammer.

"You can touch me anytime. Just know that I'll touch back."

Not used to Hendrix flirting with me, and not sure how to respond to it, I squirm underneath him, hoping he takes the hint to get off me. He doesn't.

"Let me up, please."

"I like where I am just fine. Car, motorcycle, or

helicopter?"

The change of subject is disconcerting.

"Huh?"

"Which mode of transportation would you like to take to New York? We can drive there or fly there in the family helicopter."

Of course the Knights own a helicopter. They probably have one of those luxury yachts and a private jet as well.

"What kind of motorcycle?"

"Ducati."

The temptation of riding on the back of a Ducati is enticing, and as much as I'd love to experience flying inside a helicopter, I choose the option that's more familiar.

"Car."

Hopefully, I can catch up on my studying on the way there.

He lowers down until our lips almost touch. "One day soon, I'll get you on the back of my bike and give you the ride of your life."

I burst out laughing.

"You and Tristan really do suck at suggestive innuendos."

Hands move from my wrists to my face, and the longing on his face steals the laughter right out of me.

"I've fucking missed you, Trouble."

A low buzzing fills my ears, intensifying with each passing second. Hendrix's face momentarily blurs before snapping back into focus.

"Why would you say that?"

His demeanor shifts from playful to guilt-ridden when he sees my disconcertment.

We both look over when the alarm he set on his phone beeps, alerting us that I have fifteen minutes to get to class.

"Looks like our time's up. Get your stuff."

He helps me off the floor, and I hurriedly collect my sandals where I'd left them and slide my feet in, then grab my bag and head to the front entrance doors where he's waiting for me.

CHAPTER 44

Tristan grabs the headrest and leans forward. "I need to piss."

My fingers stop mid-sentence on the Lit paper I'm working on, and I look away from the bright screen of the laptop resting precariously on my knees. Spots of color dance as my eyes adjust to the darkness inside the SUV.

From the seat in front of me, Hendrix tells Tristan, "We're ten minutes away. Just hold it."

"Con, seriously. Pull the fuck over."

Constantine's thumb taps out a beat on the steering wheel to the rock music playing through the speakers as he drives. "You can wait."

Shutting my laptop, I slide it inside my bag on the floorboard at my feet.

"Where are we?"

Unfamiliar scenery blurs past the back passenger side window, but it's too dark to discern details other than trees. Lots and lots of trees.

"Catskills," Hendrix replies.

Twisting the cap off my bottled water, I take a few swallows. We've been on the road for about four hours, only stopping once to gas up and grab drinks from a convenience store. The guys' Lexus LX may be luxurious, but I'll be glad for the trip to be over.

Hendrix mutes the radio and twists around in his seat.

"After we get there, do not go anywhere by yourself."

Not this nonsense again. "Does that include when I need to pee, too?" I reply sardonically, but he talks right over me.

"Don't talk to Con in front of anyone. This includes using ASL. Behind closed doors only when it's just us. If my father tries to draw you into conversation or asks you a question, say the bare minimum. Do not tell him anything too personal. And never, under any circumstances, be alone in a room with him. One of us is with you at all times."

I'm about to laugh off the last warning, but something stops me. He's worried. I glance around the car and feel the tension radiating off them. They all are.

"Okay," I acquiesce without argument, wondering what I'm about to walk into when we arrive.

Tristan stretches across me and unbuckles my seat belt, and I'm suddenly dragged into his lap.

"This isn't very safe," I admonish when his hands go to the tie of my wrap blouse.

"Don't fucking care."

My shirt opens and my head falls back on a moan when he cups my breasts, rubbing my nipples through my bra.

Last night unlocked a door I didn't know existed, but once I walked through it, things have been different between us. Tristan and Constantine haven't been shy about kissing or touching me whenever the hell they feel like it, which is often. I know this new dynamic between us is temporary and carries an expiration date, and I'm heeding Raquelle's advice and enjoying it before it does.

Taking the initiative, I brush my lips across his full mouth. Tristan has the softest lips.

There's a tug on my hair, and my back arches to meet Hendrix's baby blues. Tristan's hands move to support my weight, so I don't fall off his lap.

"We don't have time for this. We're here," Hendrix says as the car slows and makes a right turn onto a private drive.

With no help from Tristan, who's more of a hindrance because he keeps trying to feel me up, I quickly retie my shirt, smooth down the flyways that escaped the intricate topknot bun—which took me forty-five minutes and a dozen bobby pins to create—and get back in my seat.

All playfulness gone, Tristan takes my hand and rests it on top of his thigh. "We won't let anything happen to you."

When they keep alluding that something might, it only makes the anxiety of meeting the Knights worse. I still don't fully understand why Hendrix's father insisted that I come. Because he wants to meet the woman Hendrix is currently *supposedly* fucking? Because Tristan's dad said something? Neither seem plausible.

I look through the front windshield as we approach a foreboding, massive iron gate. There's a small gatehouse off to the left where a uniformed guard stands right outside, the gun in his side holster catching the headlights when he steps out to greet us.

Constantine lowers the driver's side window.

"Mr. Ferreira. Mr. Knight." He shines a flashlight into the back and gives me a dismissive glance before greeting Tristan. "Mr. Amato. Have a good evening."

He touches an earpiece and says something. The gates soundlessly swing inward, allowing us through. Constantine pulls forward, and I remain silent in my awe, too immersed in the scene of grandeur before me. Old-fashioned lamps line the cobblestone drive up to a mansion that stands like a beacon amid the landscape lights. Ivy creeps up the sides of the stone façade, something you don't often see adorning mansions. I liken the Knight estate to a modern-day Anglo-Saxon castle dropped amid the Catskills.

As we get closer, my first impressions change. The place is gorgeous, but there's something menacing about it. If houses had souls, its would be hollow.

"Stay close," Tristan says just as two men come to either side of the car and open the doors for Constantine and Hendrix to get out, then me and Tristan.

"Don't touch her," Hendrix clips when one of the men gets too close.

The man bows his head as if he's being spoken to by royalty. "Your father would like for you to join him in the parlor."

Placing his hand at the small of my back, Hendrix urges me forward.

"Tell him I'll be there after I get Synthia settled in."

I'm Synthia now. The formality is strange to hear.

The guys surround me as we walk up the wide mosaic tile steps laid out in a cream Wedgwood Renaissance pattern. I feel like such an impostor. The amount of wealth this place must be worth is incomprehensible to a small-town farm girl like me. I feel like I have a huge neon sign flashing above my head that says, *Doesn't Belong*.

Tall dark-wood double doors open.

"What's the square footage?" I ask, my head on a swivel as I try to take everything in. Sculptures. Vases. Paintings. The gigantic chandelier above our heads. The rug we're treading on that looks like it was spun from twenty-four carat gold thread.

"Thirty-four thousand, give or take."

"Thirty-four... *thousand*?"

The house I live in with Alana is a smidge under two thousand. Seventeen of them could easily fit inside here.

I hold tightly to Hendrix's arm to make sure I don't touch anything. I wouldn't be able to afford to replace even one of the small flower vases.

"Good evening, Mr. Knight," a man who looks like an elderly butler says.

He's dressed in what I would assume is butler attire: crisp suit with a black linen vest underneath and a starched white dress shirt.

He doesn't make eye contact with Hendrix or any of us. Like the guy outside, he keeps his head bowed.

"Please have Miss Carmichael's suitcase brought to my room."

That's news to me and not acceptable. I may be playing along because Hendrix asked me to, but that's as far as our arrangement goes.

I open my mouth to refuse and ask for my own room when Hendrix pinches me, warning me to stay quiet.

"Mr. Amato and Mr. Ferreira's rooms have been prepared in the west wing," the man states.

"They'll be staying in the rooms across from mine."

The man looks aghast. "But those are already taken, sir, for the other guests that will be arriving tomorrow."

Sir? Seriously? The man is old enough to be Hendrix's grandfather. It should be Hendrix calling him sir.

Hendrix snaps a glacial blue scowl at him. "What other guests?"

"For the dinner party tomorrow night," the man stammers. "Everyone will be attending."

He emphasizes *everyone*. I don't know who everyone entails, but from the guys' rigid stances and severely furrowed brows, they're not happy about it.

Hendrix tucks my hand at his elbow. "I don't care who's supposed to be in those rooms. Just get it done."

"Yes, sir. I'll tend to it immediately."

When the man hurriedly rushes off, I turn and pinch Hendrix's arm in retaliation.

"That hurt, asshole."

Tristan runs a hand over the back of his neck and hisses, "*Fuck*."

"What?" I ask when I'm unceremoniously dragged across the foyer and up a curved flight of stairs. "Dammit, Hendrix. Cut it out."

"Stop talking," he says, jerking me sideways as we round a corner.

Jackass Hendrix is back. I knew he wouldn't be able to sustain any type of amicability for long.

The labyrinth of halls and rooms I'm taken through will make it impossible for me to remember how to find anything. I'll more than likely get lost trying to get back downstairs without a map to guide my way.

With Hendrix leading me by the arm, I'm not able to enjoy the ostentatious décor. This place is more a museum than it is a home. A bronze sculpture of hands that sits atop a columned pedestal snares my full attention.

"Is that a Rodin?"

"Probably."

My confusticated irritation morphs into excitement when I see more pieces of artwork and sculptures from famous artists. I'm going to beg for a full tour of the house later.

When we get to the end of another hallway, Hendrix opens a door and ushers me inside. My mouth hangs as I take in the large room that looks like it was transplanted straight from Buckingham Palace.

"This is your bedroom?"

"Unfortunately."

Not letting his monosyllabic replies get to me, I walk over to the large glass French doors that open to an expansive balcony. The view looking down onto the back garden is spectacular. I really am Alice stepping into Wonderland.

Tristan closes the door. "Thanks for the fucking forewarning."

"I didn't fucking know!"

I glance at Constantine. The unemotive, blank look is back.

"Then go fucking find out!" Tristan shouts, angrily rubbing his temples.

Like a kid having a temper tantrum, Hendrix storms out, slamming the door behind him.

Tristan flinches, and I grow concerned when he looks at me and I see that his left pupil is blown.

"Where's your medication?"

I shut the curtains, trying to get the room as dark as possible.

"In my bag."

"I'll get it," Constantine says.

Climbing onto the raised four-poster bed, I pile pillows in front of me and point for Tristan to lie down.

"I'm fine. Just give me a minute."

"Don't be an obstinate ass. Come here."

Thankful he does what I say, I wait for him to get comfortable, then start massaging his head.

"Why are you and Hendrix going at each other over a dinner party?"

He blows out a pained sigh when I drag my thumbs along the bridge of his forehead.

"Because my father—"

There's a light knock on the bedroom door before it opens. Expecting to see Constantine, the person who walks in is not him.

Champagne-blonde hair cut into a sleek bob. Aquamarine blue eyes. An older, feminine version of Hendrix takes in the scene before her of Tristan lying on the bed with his head between my legs.

She raises a perfectly penciled eyebrow. "I'm sorry if I'm interrupting. I was looking for my son," Hendrix's mother says in a British accent I know all too well.

For fuck's sake. I can't catch a break.

CHAPTER 45

Entering the parlor, I find my father standing at the window, drink in hand and lost in thought. Physically, I resemble him—tall frame and breadth of shoulders. The one good grace of birth I was handed is that I don't look like him. My facial features, blond hair, and blue eyes are from my mother's Scandinavian heritage.

Without turning around, he knows I'm there.

"Derek Langstrom killed himself this morning. The man was always weak."

Langstrom was the guy Con and I were sent to Boston to set up. I guess he didn't take too well with being the focus of an FBI investigation. It was never explained to Con or me what the guy had done, only that he had asked the wrong questions, whatever the fuck that means.

"Care to share what he did to tick off the Council?"

My father looks over his shoulder, his cold hazel eyes finally acknowledging me.

"You don't get that privilege. Yet."

Nine months before graduation. Nine more months

before I'll no longer be stuck doing the Council's dirty work.

Dad holds his glass up, indicating for me to pour myself a drink. I know better than to refuse. Saying no to Patrick Knight is not an option. His kingdom. His rules. We're all just his servants who pander to his every whim.

"You look well," I prevaricate.

He has lost a lot of weight since the last time I saw him. The drastic change makes him appear gaunt and much older than fifty-three.

I take my time making a gin and tonic at the wet bar before taking a seat in one of the leather high back armchairs that looks pretty but is uncomfortable as hell. Every piece of furniture and décor in the house was chosen to showcase the Knight family wealth. It wasn't a home for a rambunctious child with wild energy who liked to play and run. I've lost count on how many times I was punished for touching something I shouldn't have or for running down the hallways. Those beatings pale in comparison to what I was forced to do as a teenager.

"How are your studies?"

I roll the tumbler between my hands. "Good."

Learning has always been easy for me. I tend to pick up concepts quickly and don't need to study much. I get someone else to write my papers because I can't be bothered doing it. It bores the hell out of me.

"Why is the girl living in the house?"

Patrick was never one for small talk, or my company, for that matter, which is fine by me because I can't stand being in the same room with him.

I sip my drink and envision slitting his throat.

"She needed a place to stay while her apartment is

being updated, and seeing as she's the recipient of the Knight scholarship fund, I thought it would be a nice gesture," I reply. "Besides, she's a good fuck, so it benefits me as well."

The gin and tonic tastes like bile on my tongue when I say that, but I have to keep up the pretense that she means nothing to me. If he or anyone else discovers who Syn really is, it would start a civil war among the Society members. It would also put her in our fathers' crosshairs even more than she already is. Right now, Syn is a nobody and of no concern. Aoife, however, is a whole other matter. James Fitzpatrick was the head of the Council before Francesco, making Aoife the next in line before Tristan.

"Interesting," he replies, and his libidinous grin makes me want to stab his eyes out with the ice pick on the wet bar. My father's sexual proclivities outrival mine. Then again, it's his fault I am the way I am. I was programmed to only derive pleasure from pain.

Needing to steer the conversation away from Syn, I state, "Heard we're having a dinner party tomorrow."

The leather of his chair creaks when he relaxes back and drains the rest of his bourbon. "Your mother insisted. She thought it would be good PR to parade the girl around. You know how she is about appearances."

At least now I know his insistence on me bringing Syn was at Mother's bequest to assuage her vanity. Syn is the first recipient of the scholarship fund she created. Mother would want to capitalize on that.

"Who's attending?" I casually ask and get up from the chair because it's making my ass fall asleep.

"The usual," he replies.

Fuck. Tristan was right to blow up. The usual entails

the entire Council, meaning Francesco and Con's father, Gabriel. The wolves are descending, and Syn will be the lone rabbit in the group.

"Where's Mum?"

He takes out a thin, mangled cigarette from his pocket and runs it under his nose. He gave up smoking years ago but enjoys the smell of tobacco. It's weird as hell to watch.

"Probably fucking the valet."

I'm not going to get into an argument with him about his wayward dick that's slept with half the state of New York. My father is also a horrible husband and a cold prick of a man. I don't blame my mother for looking elsewhere for companionship.

Placing my glass on the tray for the maid to gather later, I glide my finger across the edge of the table that displays the chess board no one is allowed to play. My father had one commissioned to look like the Pearl Royale set, since he was not able to get his hands on one of the three that were made.

"If that's all," I say, wanting to leave.

Father's biting glare tells me that it isn't. He hasn't laid a hand on me in eight years. Not since I fought back and told him if he ever touched me again, I'd cut off his dick and feed it to him.

"I'm giving my vote to the Stepanoffs."

When the fuck did he decide that? The Stepanoffs now have two of the three votes needed before they're granted a seat in the Council, and I know for damn sure that Francesco won't offer his up. He knows the bad blood between his son and Aleksander, and he wouldn't jeopardize Tristan's position. Francesco thinks that once he steps down, he'll still be in power, using his son as the puppet.

I hold in my anger and disguise it with a thick layer of ambivalence.

"Not that I care, but what changed your mind?"

Father goes back to the window and looks out over the darkness. "I don't have to justify myself to you. Please bring the girl to me. I'd like to meet her."

The day can't come soon enough when I can stand over my father's prone body and put him down like a dog.

"She's asleep," I quickly reply. "If there's nothing else, I'd like to do the same. The car journey was long."

He dismisses me with a flick of his hand. "Close the door on your way out."

With a locked jaw so I don't tell him where he can shove it, I shut the double doors behind me and take out my phone.

Me: Heading to the kitchen. Let me know what everyone wants.

I'll get dinner brought up to our rooms since we didn't stop for anything on the way.

Con: Your mom showed up.

I stop in the alcove where I can see the screen better. I knew I wouldn't be able to avoid her this weekend, but I'd hoped to put off seeing her until tomorrow.

Me: And?

Con texts like he talks, meaning he hardly says anything at all.

Con: T has a headache. I got his meds and made him stay in the room to rest. I'm with Syn and Eva in the conservatory.

Goddammit. This weekend has gone from already bad to fucking hell.

Me: On my way.

CHAPTER 46

Eva Knight is gorgeous. I can see where Hendrix gets his good looks. She's also the polar opposite of her son. So far, she's been nothing but warm, inviting, and kind, despite my disheveled appearance or the innocent but compromised position she found me in with Tristan.

"How are you liking Darlington?"

As nice as she's being, she acts like Constantine isn't standing right beside me. Do people always treat him that way because he doesn't talk? Like, by not contributing to the conversation, it makes him less worthy of notice.

When Mrs. Knight isn't looking, I skim my fingers against Constantine's hand, stealing a moment of intimacy that only the two of us understand. He and I don't need words to communicate—a glance, a touch, a smile is enough.

"The campus and classes are fantastic. I still can't believe that I'm actually a student there. Thank you so much for your generosity. I will never be able to say that enough for the scholarship or for the amazing opportunity you've given me. You've made my dream come true."

Constantine's mouth twitches. I know I'm gushing, but every word I said is how I really feel. Without that scholarship, Darlington wouldn't have been an option for me. Not even close.

Mrs. Knight's heels *click-clack* on the travertine floor as she strolls alongside me while I explore the conservatory. I don't know where to look since the entire room is made of glass, including the ceiling. Stars above me, a fantastic view of the gardens in front of me, an infinity pool to my right that looks like you'd swim right off the side of it, and what I think may be tennis courts to my left, and maybe a helipad.

"Your grades and test scores were exceptional. I was quite surprised that MIT, Harvard, or one of the other universities didn't snatch you up. Their loss is Darlington's gain."

Her compliments are humbling. Because I was a year behind, I worked my ass off to excel at school. Perfect grade-point average. A near-perfect score on the SATs.

"Thank you."

She draws my attention to a large trellis pot of climbing wisteria. Pale purple flower clusters hang down like grapes on the vine, their fragrance incredible.

"You're studying to become a doctor, correct?"

I'm surprised she knew that.

"Yes." I don't want to delve into the reason why I chose that field, and I pray she doesn't ask.

"Your mother must be proud of everything you've accomplished."

Mother, not parents. It seems she knows a lot about me, but it's stuff she could've gotten off my application… if I had filled one out or sent it in. My guidance counselor at school said I had been handpicked for the scholarship based on my test scores. No interview. Nothing. It just landed in my lap out of the blue.

"She is."

I haven't heard back from Alana, and I'm starting to worry. Although we've had our fair share of heated disagreements, she's never ghosted me before. I reached out to our neighbor, Mike, before I left the house with the guys. Mike comes by the farm every morning to pick up eggs laid by our chickens to sell at the farmers' market. He said Alana was fine this morning when he saw her.

The energy in the room suddenly changes, and I know it's Hendrix before I even see him. My senses are conditioned to his presence. The air carries a static charge when he's in a room that makes my skin spark.

Stopping several feet from her, Hendrix says, "Mother."

He sounds so distant. There isn't a fleck of warmth in the way he greets her.

She approaches him for a hug, and I frown when he sidesteps closer to me and out of her reach. My protective instincts kick in, and I slide myself in front of him, not knowing why but feeling the urge to create a barrier between him and his mother.

Her mauve-painted mouth purses slightly when Hendrix hooks his arm around me and holds me tightly to his body. I can see Constantine in the corner of my eye, his black gaze centered on Mrs. Knight. I'm not great with reading body language, but I've gotten somewhat adept at reading Constantine and know he does not like her. I thought I'd imagined it earlier.

Mrs. Knight smooths down her hair and fiddles with the diamond necklace draped around her neck. "Have you spoken with your father?"

Backing me up with him, Hendrix says, "Just left him in the parlor. If you don't mind, we're all tired and need to get something to eat before we turn in."

"I can get Clara to make something. We can eat in the dining room," she replies eagerly.

"No, thank you."

"Hendrix—"

"Have a good night," he says and shoves me out of the conservatory.

We don't pass a soul in sight as he guides me through the kitchen to a side staircase hidden around the corner of the butler's pantry. It must be for staff to use, like a dumb waiter but for people.

My empty stomach protests when I smell freshly baked bread and see the pyramid of pastries under the glass dome of a cloche on the counter island.

Hendrix not so nicely barrels me up the stairs. "I told you not to leave the fucking room."

"No, you didn't."

"You didn't," Constantine reiterates, catching me when I trip.

"Stay out of it."

When we get to a landing, Hendrix throws open the door. We're at the end of the hallway where his room is located. If I didn't recognize the artwork hanging on the wall, I'd be completely lost.

"Why are you so upset? She asked me to join her. I couldn't say no."

"Yes, you could." He smacks open the door to his

room.

Tristan startles from his place on Hendrix's bed. He's sitting in the dark, back against the headboard.

"Thanks for that, asshole."

"Now you know how I feel." I climb onto the bed and get close so I can see his eyes. His pupils look normal. "How are you feeling?"

"Fine. The meds kicked it quickly before it could get bad."

Tristan tries to pull me into his lap, but I swivel to confront an agitated Hendrix.

"Constantine was with me the entire time."

"That's not the bloody point," he snaps.

Frustrated he doesn't get the dilemma I'm in, I reply, "I'm not going to be purposely rude to the people who are basically paying for my entire four years of college."

Hendrix tosses his wallet, phone, and keys on the chaise lounge near the window. "I don't want you anywhere near Eva or my father."

This roundabout argument is going nowhere but in circles.

"Then why did you insist I come? Why didn't *you* say *no* to your father? A bit hypocritical, don't you think? Not to mention, I'm missing work to be here. Money I need because the scholarship only pays for the tuition."

Arms stretched overhead, he grabs the top rail of the canopy that spans between the two footboard posts and looms over me, a picture of angry masculine beauty.

"We can't say no when summoned."

"Hen," Tristan says with a slight shake of his head.

The things they allude to but never come right out and say is driving me nuts. They are so closed off, and I'm tired of beating my head against a brick wall, hoping they'll let me in.

I go up on my knees, and it puts me eye level with Hendrix's broad chest. "Why not?"

"Because we can't," the obdurate ass replies.

I give up.

"When you're ready to be more forthcoming, let me know." I hop down from the massive bed which is a good three feet up from the floor. "Can I sleep in your room?" I ask Constantine.

"No, you cannot. You're staying with me tonight." Hendrix rounds the bed, and I have the urge to cower or hide behind Constantine. I do neither and choose to stand my ground.

"You're delusional if you think that's going to happen."

"Let her stay in his room."

Hendrix sears Tristan with a scathing, "Easy for you to say since you'll be sleeping in the same bed with them."

Is that what this is all about? He wants to fuck me?

"I'm not a replacement for Serena who seems more than happy to ride your dick whenever you crook your finger. You want to fuck something?" I point to the attached en suite. "You have two hands. Pick one and have fun."

With an arrogant tilt to his chin, he grins, and I know I made a mistake.

His voice drops seductively, like a purr. "You'd like that, wouldn't you, firefly? I saw how badly you wanted to touch yourself when you watched me. I heard the moan you made when I came all over my hand."

"The fuck?" Tristan says.

My face boils red with mortification, and I can't

look at Tristan or Constantine to see their reactions to finding out that I had blatantly spied on Hendrix masturbating. How I was so turned on by it, I spent the next hour using the shower head to get myself off, and it still didn't help ease the ache between my legs.

"It wasn't like that! God, you make it so damn difficult to be your friend."

He scores a direct hit to my fragile self-esteem when he shouts, "I don't want to be your fucking friend!"

The room goes silent. Not even Tristan says anything.

At least Hendrix finally said it, no matter how much it hurts to hear. No one likes to be rejected, but it's the story of my life. I don't know why I care so much. Hendrix and I can barely stand to be in the same room with each other without it turning into a fight.

"If that's what you want, fine."

Hendrix takes me by the throat and crashes me back into Constantine. "I don't think you're understanding me, Syn. I don't want to be your friend. I want *so... much... more*."

Any protest I would make withers to a moan when he tightens his grip.

His blue eyes change, the deep sapphire turning to a light cyan, and he stares deeply at me, searching for something.

"You like it when I touch you this way?" he asks, sounding almost confused.

There's no place in this room for lies. Not now when I'm so close to getting what I desperately want.

"Yes."

He glances over in Tristan's direction when he asks, "Did you like it when I marked you?"

"I..."

I was furious with him at the time, but when that rage abated, I couldn't deny that I enjoyed feeling the bruise he left.

"Answer him, Red."

"I did. It made me feel..." My eyes flutter close as I push past the anger that had erupted between us to relive that moment when he lifted me in his arms and slammed me against the wall.

"What?" he asks tenderly.

"Alive."

Hendrix leans in and scrapes his teeth over my bottom lip, drawing blood, and my chest vibrates with satisfaction.

"There's my dirty girl."

His praise should be offensive, but I love it. I want to be claimed. I want to belong to them. I want to feel all the amazing, debauched things they did to me last night over and over again. Constantine, Tristan, and Hendrix unknowingly unlocked the cage I'd been imprisoned in since the day I woke up in the hospital; a damaged girl whose mind won't allow her to remember her past. In a profound way, I am but I'm also not that girl anymore. They changed me. Last night changed me. Because of them, I'm now a woman who wants to experience everything and take what she wants.

"Who says I'm *your* dirty girl?" I inflect.

I'm scared to death, absolutely terrified, at what I'm about to initiate. I'm inexperienced and have nothing to go on but the desire pulsating through my blood. But the want overrides the fear. I fucking *want* this.

Hendrix has no other choice but to let go when I turn to face Constantine and drop to my knees.

"Syn, what are you doing?" Tristan asks, but my eyes

are solely on the devastatingly handsome, dark-haired man looking down at me with unconcealed emotion and lust.

"Do you want me?"

"God, yes," Constantine replies, a deep need in the husk of his voice.

My hands shake as they reach for his zipper. "Tell me what to do."

"Are you sure?"

I find Tristan to my left, sitting on the side of the bed. The pulse point in his neck thrums rapidly, his whiskey eyes wild. He's excited. He wants this as much as I do.

"Yes. Do you want me?" I ask him.

Tristan erases any doubt when he says, "You know I do, Red. I've wanted you from the first moment I saw you. You're mine, baby. You're ours."

I breathe that in like pure oxygen. I'm theirs.

Hendrix lowers to his haunches behind me and strokes my hair. The soothing machinations and his voice in my ear put me in a trance.

"Be a good girl and take his cock out."

This is really happening. I peer up at Constantine, our gazes colliding once more. How can I tell this man who says so little but sees so much, how much I appreciate that he sees *me*? I place a kiss to the side of his hand when he cups my face and smiles. Actions really do speak louder than words, and I'm going to try my best to show him how much he means to me with the only gift I can give. My innocence.

"Look at what you do to him, firefly. See how much he wants you?" Hendrix's hands roam up and down my back, across my neck, over my shoulders and down my arms, leaving forests of goose bumps everywhere he touches.

Constantine's cock is already hard and pushing against the zipper of his jeans. I lick my lips, and my core clenches with anticipation. Eagerness builds as I tug on the small metal pull, the teeth slowly clicking apart one by one until his length unexpectedly springs free. He's not wearing underwear. I help push his jeans the rest of the way down his legs until he's able to step out of them.

Curls of dark pubic hair frame his thick shaft. Like Hendrix, Constantine has a piercing. Two, in fact. One above the tip, and one underneath.

Fascinated, I touch each silver ball, then trail a finger over the head where pearls of liquid bead. I look up at Constantine's jagged inhalation and suck his precum off my finger. The salt and musk of him explodes over my tongue. Getting braver, I wrap my hand around him. My fingers can barely circle his girth. I run my closed fist up, then down, reveling in how his cock can be both hard as steel and smooth like satin. A rush of arousal floods my panties, and like ambrosia in the air, Hendrix can scent it.

"You smell delicious, Syn. Let's see if you taste just as sweet."

"She tastes like heaven," Tristan comments, his voice closer, and heat suffuses from my core to my cheeks.

Hendrix's clever fingers sneak inside my pants and slide down to tease the folds of my pussy.

"Widen your legs and push back."

I do as he instructs until he can spoon me and take my weight. The new position opens me up for him, and he pushes one finger inside me, groaning when my walls clamp down.

"So fucking tight," he says and removes his hand.

"Open."

I curl my tongue around his finger, soaked with my desire, and suck it into my mouth, liking how my essence blends with Constantine's.

"So good, firefly. You won't be able to take the three of us tonight. We'll have to work up to that. But for now, suck Con's dick like the dirty girl you are, and I'll make you come so hard you'll scream my name."

His filthy promise makes me whimper, but something's missing.

"Tristan."

Lips kiss my bare shoulder. "I'm right here, baby."

I hadn't heard him get off the bed. I turn my head to meet his lips, the kiss we share possessive and carnal.

"Off," Hendrix says, already pulling my top up.

I let go of Constantine to raise my arms, so Hendrix can slip my shirt over my head. My bra is next, and this time I'm not ashamed to expose my body to them. These men, despite their secrets and their flaws, and despite the way we met, don't treat me like I'm damaged.

"You're so beautiful," Constantine says, and a shiver races down my spine when Hendrix takes my breasts in each hand and lightly twists the nipples. The jolt of pleasure that connects straight to my core is like a massive electric shock.

"Wait," I rush out when Constantine grabs his shirt from behind and yanks it over his head.

I salivate at seeing his naked body for the first time. All that magnificent ink, sun-kissed olive skin, and hard, defined muscle.

"I want… I…"

They wait for me to finish, but a lump of emotion

suddenly lodges in my throat, swelling it shut. God, I'm ruining this.

"You have the power here, Syn. You control what happens. You want to stop, we will." Tristan kisses me with such tenderness, I want to cry.

Constantine always takes care of me in little ways that mean so much, but Tristan does, too, in his own way. The power of choice and the power to say no are two very potent and life-changing things for a woman, especially when she's never had them.

I take a deep breath. "I don't want that. I just..." *Just fucking say it, Syn. Tell them what you want.* Another breath. "I want Constantine to be my first."

CHAPTER 47

The room pulsates with charged silence, but the scorching desire smoldering behind Constantine's ebony stare is what sends my heart into a frenzied state of exhilaration. I can feel it burning through me, so strong and powerful that it becomes tangible.

"You're such a good girl for telling us what you want."

The words 'good girl' roll off Hendrix's tongue like honey, awakening a deep longing inside me, and a satisfied shudder rakes over my skin. I drink in the sound of it, desperate to hear those two words again and again.

Hoping they understand, I say, "I want all of you. It's just… I've never…" Why is it so hard to say? They already know I'm a virgin. "I want it to be good for you, too. Will you teach me?"

Hendrix's chest judders with a low, content hum, and I gasp with pleasure when his tongue moves up the side of my neck and his hands squeeze my breasts.

"You're so goddamn perfect."

Good girl. Perfect. Beautiful.

Every spoken plaudit makes my pussy contract and release a rush of arousal that pools between my legs.

Tristan pushes on my sternum until I lean all the way back into Hendrix's embrace. "Look how much Con wants you," he says, dipping his head to take the nipple Hendrix offers him. Every pull of his hot, wet mouth stokes the fire that burns low in my belly.

With eyes shuttered at half-mast, I look up at Constantine and moan when he fists his cock, stroking it slowly. His eyelids droop, and he pulls his bottom lip between his teeth every time his fingers graze the piercing on the underside of his shaft. I can't wait to take him inside my mouth and let my tongue play over the tiny silver balls.

"Your heart is pounding, firefly. You like to watch us pleasure ourselves, don't you?"

Oh, god. My clit throbs at the image of him masturbating, remembering the moment he climaxed, how his face twisted in euphoric agony and he said my name.

I whimper in answer.

"Con's cock is going to feel so good inside you. Tell him how badly you want him to fuck you."

The dirty things Hendrix whispers in my ear are as seductive as his touch.

My eyes never leave Constantine when I tell him, "I want you to fuck me. I ache for you."

His eyes go impossibly black, and his chest expands with a deep groan.

"Keep watching him, Syn. Let him see how beautiful you are when you come."

While Tristan tortures my breasts with his mouth, Hendrix tangles our fingers together and slides our joined hands down my stomach to my pussy. The denim of my shorts restricts our movements and traps our hands. The friction causes a flurry of tingles that coalesce into a ball of pressure that starts to expand as Hendrix guides my finger over the tight bundle of nerves.

"That's it, Syn. Take your pleasure."

I rub tighter and tighter circles on my clit, chasing the orgasm as it hurtles toward me like a bolt of lightning.

"Boston," I call to Tristan and twist his shirt in my grip, needing him with me when I jump off the edge.

His sinful lips release my nipple, and he smiles at hearing the nickname. Pressure coils and churns in my stomach. Tighter and tighter. *So close. So close.* My hips punch forward, muscles locking as I reach for the peak and jump.

I pant out, "Kiss. Me."

Tristan's mouth crashes on mine just as Hendrix digs his teeth into the tendon of my shoulder, and I explode. The orgasm shreds me open like the chrysalis of a butterfly and hurls me out on gossamer wings of unrelenting bliss.

Twitching with aftershocks, my body slumps and all the tension drains as I come back to earth.

Hendrix sucks my juices off each finger, then bends down to kiss me. I lick myself off his lips, and he grins.

"See, you are my dirty girl."

I don't see how pleasure can be considered dirty. Not when it feels so fucking good. I'm ready to dive into whatever sexual adventure these men want to take me on.

I reach for Constantine, and he lifts me in his arms,

holding me intimately against his bare skin. I trace the contours of his face with soft kisses and caress my cheek against the roughened texture of his stubble. Being held in his arms feels like home.

I stare deeply into eyes that see every part of me. "Make me yours."

Our mouths hungrily come together without further words. The connection we share, the one I've felt since the day after I met him, says more than any conversation ever could.

He lays me on the bed and stands over me, and I gaze up at him, memorizing every detail about this moment. About him.

Because of our soft curves and delicate femininity, women's bodies are lauded as being the most attractive of the sexes. I disagree. Men are equally as beautiful. Masculine grace, I think it's called. I look at Constantine, standing magnificently naked in front of me, and don't think I've ever seen anything more beautiful. Intricate lines in red and black paint stunning images over his skin. A solid, broad chest tapers to a lean waist that frame rock-hard abs. His arms and thighs are ruggedly muscled, evidence of how powerful he is. Long, dark lashes that are every girl's envy surround dark brown, almost coal-black eyes that are set in one of the most alluring faces I have ever seen.

"I want you."

Constantine runs his hands up my legs from ankles to thighs, and tingles travel up my body, popping along my skin like champagne bubbles. When he gets to my shorts, he deftly unzips them and eases them down my legs.

Tristan and Hendrix settle on the massive bed on

either side of me. A tiny tremor runs through me when I lie there, my scars fully exposed for them to see. Tristan is the first to graze his fingertips over the pitted, discolored patches of skin.

"Do you remember what I said?" he asks, gliding his finger down my scarred arm.

Tiny sparks of sensation prick to life as he tickles a path from my shoulder to my forearm and on to my hip. I had thought the nerves long dead, but I swear I feel him.

"You said I was beautiful chaos."

Hendrix rolls my nipple into a tight peak. "Are you on the pill, firefly?"

I started taking birth control to help with the severe cramps I used to get with my periods.

"Y... yes." It's almost impossible to think clearly when three sets of hands are touching me.

"Can Con take you bare?" He switches to the other nipple, pinching with more pressure until a pleasant sting radiates.

Tristan slips off the bed and comes back holding a condom packet, making sure I know I have a choice.

Constantine lifts one leg, nibbling open-mouthed kisses up my inner thigh, then hooks my knee over his shoulder. He does the same with the other leg until I'm spread wide open.

I'm steeped in sensation and don't know who to focus on. The messages being carried to my brain go haywire, and I raise my arms above my head and reach for Tristan and Hendrix, needing them to be with me and Constantine. Just because I chose him to be my first doesn't lessen how much I want them, too.

"I want to feel Constantine inside me. No barrier," I'm

finally able to reply.

"Good girl."

Constantine's warm breath puffs against my pussy, and I'm given only the span of a blink before he buries his head and absolutely destroys me. I didn't think I would be able to come again so quickly after the first time, but his mouth proves otherwise. He stretches my tight channel, relentlessly fucking me with his tongue. I can feel the tidal wave coming and tighten my grip on Hendrix and Tristan's hand as the wave rises up and smashes into me. Constantine's name screams out of me on a sob as I climax hard.

"Goddamn, you're gorgeous when you come."

Constantine lifts his head and licks his lips, and the smile he gives me is pure sin.

"Please. Now," I beg, needing him to fill me.

He takes his time to crawl up my body, driving me to madness as he nips kisses up my torso. He suckles each breast until I'm writhing underneath him. When my hands are set free, I immediately wrap them around him and lift up to seal our mouths together. Our tongues tangle in their own sybaritic dance as Constantine guides his cock to my pussy. Everything around me falls away until there is only him.

The bulbous head breaches my entrance, but he stops. His eyes cinch close and his face pinches, like he's in pain.

"Constantine?" My voice sounds tiny and unsure. Does he want to stop?

He raises on one arm and presses the palm of his other hand to my chest. I do the same to him and feel the strong thump of his heart and the hard muscle of his pectoral.

With some intangible, intense emotion shining in his eyes, he says, "You are my heartbeat," and thrusts forward, taking my virginity.

I know I'm supposed to feel some kind of pain, but I don't. I only feel him. And then, when he starts to move, I only feel the beautiful way he fucks me.

"Constantine."

He pulls a hedonistic moan from me when he scrapes the metal piercings across my sensitive walls, hitting places inside me that curl my damn toes. Each jagged stroke brings another animalistic moan from my throat, and his name spills from my lips like a benediction. His thrusts become more urgent, and I wrap my ankles around his waist and lift my hips eagerly to meet him, our rhythm maintaining the exquisite pressure that drives us both higher and higher toward sweet oblivion. Our kiss becomes ravenous as he pounds into me, rocking the bed and making my tits bounce with every snap of his hips, the time to be gentle long gone.

Strangled noises sound above me, and my lust-glossed eyes find Tristan and Hendrix again. They're both naked, kneeling on the bed, eyes locked on me as they masturbate to Constantine and me fucking. I haven't seen Tristan's cock before, but dear god, he's huge. His hand barely circles its girth as he pumps it with angry strokes.

Liquid fire mainlines my veins at the sight. Constantine grunts when my pussy clamps down hard at the pornographic sight.

"Fuck, you're tight."

He lowers to suck my nipple, and my nails score into his back. It's all too much—the sights and sounds and the smell of sex that permeates the air.

I never knew my life could be this. That *I* could be this. Happy and free from the shackles of the scars that have defined me for most of my life. To have three gorgeous men who see me as beautiful and want me just the way that I am.

"Together," Constantine pants against my lips.

"Together."

I feel him thicken and swell, and then the most wondrous feeling of him coming inside me, filling me with pulses of warmth. His release triggers my own, and with a blinding intensity, I climax on a scream.

Constantine nuzzles my neck, whispering words in Portuguese that I wish I could understand but love hearing them just the same. His cum leaks out of me when he rolls to my side, and I tip my head back to watch Hendrix and Tristan.

"Open," Hendrix commands, and I part my lips just as he and Tristan paint me with their cum.

It's perverted and filthy and I fucking love it.

With sated groans, they collapse down onto the bed with me and Constantine.

Tristan gathers my hair and fans it out all around me, then twines my red tresses around his fingers and lets them slide between the gaps like sand in an hourglass.

"You were made for us, Red. We're never letting you go."

I don't mean to cry, but I can't stop the silent tears that stream down my cheeks. They're not tears of sadness but ones of happiness.

Rolling over onto my stomach, I cup Constantine's cheek. "Thank you." I kiss him, then Tristan and Hendrix.

Hendrix draws swirls on my neck. "Firefly, fucking you every chance we get will be our absolute pleasure."

When I realize what he's doing, I ask, "Are you fingerpainting on me with your cum?"

The boyish grin he gives me is full of mischievousness. I'm not used to seeing that playful, softer side of him. I don't know what changed between us, but something has. We still bicker, and he still irritates the hell out of me, but underneath all that, there's something… else.

Tristan plays with my tits. I'm coming to learn that he's very tactile, which is why he's always touching me in some way.

"Would you like a shower?"

I shake my head and snuggle into Constantine's side. He throws my leg over him and palms my ass to hold me close.

"I'll have food brought up," Hendrix says, climbing off the bed.

Food sounds really good. "Ice cream with hot fudge and whipped cream?"

Hendrix sends me a disparaging look. "Real food, woman."

Teasing him, I reply, "I'll let you cover me in whipped cream and fudge sauce and eat it off me."

CHAPTER 48

I lie still, listening for the noise that woke me, but only hear Tristan's light snoring and the drumbeat of three hearts.

Three. Not four.

Tristan sleeps flush to my back with his arm draped heavily over my side, his hand possessively cupping my left tit. I'm half spread out over Constantine, who's on my other side. My head rests atop his chest, and it feels like I'm bobbing along gentle swells of the ocean with each slow breath he takes.

The muffled grunt that pulled me from sleep comes again, and I know whose heartbeat is missing.

My naked body protests when I rise on elbow. Tristan's hand falls away from my breast, and I wince. I'm sore everywhere. Muscles I never knew existed make themselves known for the first time. My lips sting and feel puffy, my breasts are so sensitive that a slight breeze against my nipples makes them ache, and my pussy throbs from the punishment it took from being fucked for the first time. But it's a good pain. One I want to wake up to every morning.

When my eyes finally adjust, I search the room and find Hendrix asleep on the floor near the doors that open to the balcony. With another grunt, his body jerks in his sleep. Nightmares. I know them all too well.

Wedged between two large men, it's difficult to move, so I choose the easiest option and slither over Constantine. His chest hair grazes my abraded skin littered with hickeys and bites. Sweet reminders that what happened last night was real. I'm glad I packed Rochelle's royal blue, long-sleeved silk-panel dress to wear later instead of the other one she insisted I have. The blue dress will help cover most of the marks. The ones I'm sure are on my neck can be concealed with makeup, and I can leave my hair down instead of putting it up like I usually do.

A palm settles on my backside when I'm directly on top of Constantine.

"Shh. Go back to sleep. Everything's okay," I tell him when his eyes open.

His other hand cuffs my neck, and he pulls me down. I melt into him like warmed wax when his tongue licks inside my mouth, and he kisses me slowly, savoringly.

"You okay?" he asks, switching from my mouth to behind my ear.

Better than okay. I feel whole. Complete. Fundamentally changed in a wonderfully profound way. Like a piece of my heart that had been missing has finally been found.

I smile with the effulgent happiness I'm feeling. "More than okay."

He struggles to say something, but when he does, it

rocks my world to its foundation.

"I love you, you know."

The frantically beating organ inside my chest slams against my ribcage, wanting to burst free and sacrifice itself to him. The tumult of sentiment that overtakes me is painful, as are the tears prised from my eyes. I'm not a believer in love at first sight. Love takes time to build. It grows as each day passes and with every shared word and touch and smile. But when I search the deepest part of my soul, I can't deny that I love him, too. In a way I'm not able to explain, it's like I've loved him forever.

I press myself to him as close as I can get and feel him harden against my stomach. Taking his face, I crush my mouth to his, telling him with my kiss that I love him back.

Our private moment is broken when Hendrix twitches and lets out another small groan.

"Go. He needs you."

It's going to take some time for me to get used to the dynamics of being involved with more than one man. Constantine just said he loves me, yet he wants to share me with his two best friends. When this weekend is over and we're back in Darlington, the four of us will need to sit down and talk. Define what this is and what our expectations are.

"Are you sure?"

He nods and helps me ease off the side of the bed, then rolls over to his side, the intensity of his gaze following me as I walk over to the tortured man whose demons, like mine, stalk him in his sleep.

Easing down to the floor, I brush Hendrix's hair from his face. Asleep, he looks younger… familiar… the phantom image fades before it fully forms.

"Hendrix."

My forearm is suddenly caught in a viselike grip. Pacific blue eyes pop open in the same instant I'm rolled over to my back and hemmed in. When he registers it's me, the tension in his body eases, and he collapses down on top of me.

"Don't ever sneak up on me when I'm asleep."

His brow dips, then raises when he swivels his hips, and I gasp when his cock grazes my clit. That signature cocky smirk comes out.

"I changed my mind. You can wake me up naked anytime."

He grinds down on me, and even though I'm sore as hell and don't know how I could have another orgasm after the four they've already given me, my pussy slicks with arousal, wanting to be fucked again.

"You were having a nightmare."

He pretends not to hear me and tongues over the bites he put on my chest. "You taste like my cum," he says, sounding very pleased about it.

He knows what his cum tastes like?

"That's because I'm covered in it. I need a shower."

I probably should have thought about a shower before I fell asleep, but I was too warm and too sated and didn't give a damn that I was covered in two men's cum.

"I'm down with that."

I'm tumbled over and lifted up, then tossed over his shoulder before I can get a word out.

"Hendrix," I hiss, trying to keep my voice down so I don't wake up Tristan.

He smacks me on the back of my thigh.

I push up on his back, and Constantine grins at me

from the bed as Hendrix carries me into the bathroom.

He taps a panel on the wall, and the lights turn on.

"No lights." I don't like looking at my naked body in the mirror.

With a slide of his finger, the lights dim to a faint glow, like candlelight. Hendrix sets me on the wide vanity, the stone of countertop cold on my bare ass.

He presses a button and water begins to fill the enormous garden tub. Wisps of steam curl up and disappear. I was expecting a quick shower, but he's making me a bath.

"I think we can forgo modesty at this point," he says, unscrewing a jar of what looks like bath salts. He sniffs it before pouring some in.

It's not about him seeing me. It's that *I* don't want to see me. Mirrors and I are not friends.

I use the quiet lapse of time as the tub fills to look at him. There's something about a man's muscular back that is so sexy in the way broad shoulders taper to narrow hips. And goddamn that tight ass. There is not a millimeter of fat on him. He's all lean, corded muscle and delicious body art.

"What changed?" I ask and hop down when he turns around and reaches for me.

His cock bobs at half-mast, and I stare at the barbell piercing. I want to feel that inside me. Constantine's felt incredible when they razed my inner walls, so I know Hendrix's will feel just as good.

He takes my hand and helps me into the tub, then steps in after me. It looks more than large enough for two people, but Hendrix is a big guy.

"What do you mean?" he asks as we ease down into the almost scalding water.

Once seated, Hendrix bends his long legs and situates me between them. The soothing effects of the hot water and the lavender-scented bath salts on my sore muscles are instantaneous.

"Your sudden interest. You being... *nice*. I thought you hated me."

He gathers my hair and fans it over his shoulder so I can recline back into him without it getting pulled.

"I never hated you."

My quiet snort of skepticism calls bullshit.

Smiling, he nuzzles my temple. "I'm just an asshole."

"A major asshole."

He lifts my arms to rest on his knees, then grabs a rolled washcloth from the tray that sits on the lip of the tub, along with a bottle of liquid soap labeled Hermes. When he pours some out onto the cloth, a sharp explosion of citrus hits my nose. With a gentleness I wouldn't have expected from him, Hendrix starts to wash me.

"There was this girl," he begins, and I literally hold my breath waiting for him to continue.

I've wanted them to let me in. To be real and not so closed off and secretive. I don't need to know everything. I'd be happy with just a few scraps of honesty tossed my way. Getting involved with dangerous men with mysterious pasts is the epitome of stupid, but I'm already in too deep. Too many feelings are now involved. I care about them. I'm falling for them. I feel alive with them. I wouldn't be able to walk away now if I tried.

Hendrix takes his time, gently lathering suds over my breasts then down my stomach. I jerk and slosh water over the side when the soft cotton probes between my legs.

"Tender?"

Air whooshes out with a breathy, "Yeah."

He lets the washcloth go and cups my pussy. The heat of his hand feels even better than the bath water.

His lips dip to kiss the side of my neck. "Relax, firefly."

"Kind of difficult to do with your hand..."

My fingers score the tops of his knees as my back arches, and I trail off with a pleasured moan when he rubs circles on my clit.

"There was this girl. It didn't matter that we were just kids. I loved her as much as a young heart could."

He increases the pressure on my clit, and my knees shake from the exertion of holding back the orgasm he's so effortlessly driving me to.

"She was my sunshine. My little golden-haired angel. My soulmate."

His fingers scissor and jerk the tiny nub, jacking me off like he would his own dick, and I can't hold the tidal wave of my climax back any longer.

"I'm going to co—"

He grabs my face and forces my head back to capture my scream of release with his kiss. I'm no longer in control of my body as it convulses with wave after wave of unrelenting ecstasy.

"Everything in me died the day she was taken. The only light I had to guide me was extinguished, and I've been living in the dark ever since." He eases a slippery finger inside me as I ride out the aftershocks.

What a depressing conversation to have while he's making me come.

"What happened to her?" I pant.

He shakes his head, apparently not able to talk about

it.

Reaching behind me, I cup his morning-stubbled face and peer up at him upside down. "I'm so sorry." Such a useless platitude for the loss of someone you love.

His blue eyes hold me captive. "But then you came along, all fiery red hair, sass, and full of trouble. I don't hate you, Syn. You're the first person since her who has made me *feel*. I didn't know how to handle it. It's not an excuse."

It sort of is. It explains a lot.

A sleepy Tristan stumbles in, looking sexier than anyone has a right to first thing in the morning. "Room for one more?"

Hendrix points to the bathroom armoire next to the glass-enclosed shower. "Get me the medical kit, top shelf, so I can take out her stitches."

I had forgotten all about it since it hasn't bothered me at all. I try to twist around to see over my shoulder.

"How does it look?"

"You look thoroughly and gorgeously fucked," Tristan replies.

"Not what I was referring to."

He comes back with a black plastic case and sits on the floor next to the tub. After a quick rummage, he hands Hendrix a pair of tweezers and a small set of scissors. I feel a tiny tug, but nothing else.

Hendrix touches around the area on my shoulder. "I did a damn good job, if I say so myself."

"There's only one doctor in our house, and Syn has dibs," Tristan yawns out, scratching his chest, and it's ridiculous how much joy hearing him say *our house* brings me.

"Is Constantine still awake?" I ask him.

"Don't move," Hendrix says. I feel the stitches tug and slide out when he snips and pulls, but the sting isn't bad.

"He was messing on his phone when I woke up. Surprised he wasn't in here with you two." Tristan drops his gaze to my chest. "Goddamn, Hen. Did you have to leave so many?"

"I don't hear her complaining… *and* done." Hendrix drops the scissors, tweezers, and cut pieces of dental floss that he used to stitch me up with onto the side bath tray.

"You have spectacular tits." Tristan flicks a nipple and grins when my boob jiggles and creates ripples on the surface of the water.

"You are so juvenile."

"She's really sore, so lay off," Hendrix warns him.

Tristan pouts. "Didn't stop you from finger fucking her."

Before they get into an argument, I stand up. Water cascades down my legs and my skin turns to gooseflesh being exposed to the open air.

"I have a solution," I offer when Tristan takes my hips and kisses my navel ring.

"Does it involve fucking you?" he asks hopefully.

I run my hand through his thick, sleep-mussed hair. "No. My vagina is off limits for the next twenty-four hours. But my solution does involve blow jobs in the shower."

I shriek and dissolve into a fit of laughter when he lifts me bodily out of the tub, spilling water everywhere, and almost drops me when I start to slide right out of his arms.

"Fuck, yeah. Con! Get your ass in here!"

CHAPTER 49

Taking a little more time to look presentable, I dab my favorite Ulta berry-tinted gloss stick on my cheeks and rub it in, then sweep the color across my lips. I had no choice but to choose my powder-blue high-collared long-sleeved blouse to hide the evidence of last night. I doubt Hendrix's parents would be pleased to see their son's handiwork on my skin over the breakfast table. I finished the ensemble with my best pair of dark-washed jeans and paired the outfit with the high heels Raquelle gave me, hoping it would add a little sexy to the casual look. Because I plan to style my long hair tonight, I do a fast fishtail braid and let it hang over one shoulder.

Taking a selfie, I send it to Raquelle.

Me: Proof of life.

"When do I get a tour of the house?" I ask as I walk out of Hendrix's bathroom with more confidence than I feel while teetering in these deathtraps for shoes.

You know a man invented high heels because no woman in her right mind would think uncomfortable sticks worn on your feet were a good idea, no matter how good Raquelle says they make your ass look.

Hendrix whistles low and long, and I duck my head to hide my blush. I normally wear a T-shirt and leggings around them, so being able to look a little nicer, even if it's just a blouse and denim, feels good.

You look beautiful, Con signs, and my heart flutters. He could say it a million times, and I would still have the same reaction.

Tristan sits up on the bed where he'd been sprawled out and hooks a finger at me. He stands when I walk over, and in the heels, I'm almost as tall as he is.

"I want to fuck you in only these heels tonight."

The clean pair of panties I put on are instantly wet.

My phone vibrates in my hand, pulling us out of our sexually charged stare-off.

Raquelle: YOU HAD SEX!

"Excuse me for a sec," I tell the guys and slip outside onto the balcony for some privacy.

Three dots bounce under her text as she types a new message. As I wait, I look down at the grounds and notice several men loitering around. Matching dark suits and dark glasses, like secret service agents.

When Raquelle's next message comes in, it's a jumble of chili peppers, eggplants, peaches, and what looks like sideways spit emojis.

Me: How can you tell?

Raquelle: My special witchy magic. You also have that glow that only great sex can put on a woman's face. I want full details when you get back. Just tell me one thing. 1, 2, or 3?

Huh? *Oh.*

Me: I don't kiss and tell.

She sends me a bunch of animated GIFs that make me

chuckle.

Raquelle: Serious this time. You good? Do I need to get Drake to come beat some asses?

Me: I'm happy.

It's silly to feel happy about losing your virginity, but I doubt many women's first time was as wonderful as mine. The stories I overheard the girls at school tell each other were filled with sweaty, grabby hands, slobbering kisses, and the guy coming two seconds after he awkwardly stumbled his dick inside you.

Raquelle: Oh, hon. I'm happy for you. Go have fun and call me when you get back.

Me: Will do. <kiss emoji>

Before I go back inside, I try Mom for the third time this morning, but it goes straight to voice mail.

"Hey, it's me. Again. Why haven't you called me back? Mike said he saw you yesterday, but I'm really getting freaked out now. Please call or text me and let me know that you're okay."

When I hang up and turn around, Constantine is standing just outside the French doors.

Your mom?

Pocketing my phone, I reply, "I haven't been able to reach her. Our neighbor said she was fine, but..." I shrug. "I know I'm probably overreacting."

He holds out his hand, and I take it. His strong arms engulf me in a hug, and I breathe in the familiar sandalwood of his cologne. Of him.

"Cuddle later. I'm hungry," Hendrix says from the doorway.

"Can we eat outside?" I optimistically ask. I'm dying to see the gardens after getting a bird's-eye view of them from the balcony.

"Don't see why not."

Hendrix twines our fingers together when we leave the room, reminding me of the roles we have to play for the benefit of his father and everyone else. However, that farce doesn't seem so fake anymore.

"Is that real?" I ask when we pass the hand sculpture as we head down the long hallway.

"All the crap in this house is just another way for my father to stroke his ego. Elevator or stairs?"

"Your house has an elevator?"

He presses a button next to what I think is a bedroom door until I notice there's no doorknob. I watch it slide open to reveal the inside of a small elevator car with bevel-edged, recessed wood panel walls.

"That is really cool."

Hendrix chuckles and pulls me inside. With the four of us, it's a tight fit.

"What's this button for? The basement?"

The house is two stories but there are three buttons, all unmarked.

"Family crypt. Off limits and only accessible with a biometric key code," he says, pointing to what looks like a thumbprint scanner.

The thought of living in a house that sits on top of a cemetery is *Poltergeist*-level creepy.

Within seconds, the door opens to another hallway lined with massive framed portraits of constipated-looking men who look like they are bored to death to be forced to stand while someone paints them. The majority of the men captured on canvas have blue eyes and sandy blond hair.

"Are these—"

"Yes," Hendrix answers, knowing what I was about to

ask.

The portraits are all men. Where are the women, the mothers and grandmothers of his family?

I do a double take when I'm hurried past a room that has a Steinway grand piano surrounded by an ethereal spotlight created by an overhead dome made of stained glass. I taught myself how to play using a free online app and a cheap portable piano that I could set in front of me on the hospital bed.

There's a dissonance of overlapping noises when we turn another corner and walk into a kitchen bustling with frantic activity. Everyone and everything go pin-drop silent, and the sudden loss of sound weirdly makes my ears ring. All heads lower in clear subservience. It was bizarre to witness it last night when we arrived, and even more so now because the guys act like it's normal for people to turn into subjugated statues in their presence.

"Have coffee brought out to the courtyard immediately and prepare both a continental and an American breakfast for four," Hendrix barks at one of the women, who stares at the floor as she rushes off to do his bidding.

As soon as I'm escorted out a side door, the noise levels from the kitchen rise.

I hold my tongue until I'm positive we're out of earshot before saying, "You know it's uncomfortable as hell to see grown adults act like your servants."

"Because they are servants," Hendrix replies.

"They're people who deserve to be treated with respect no matter what job they do."

Sunlight beams in through a large set of French doors that, when pulled open, lead to a paver stone courtyard and the gardens beyond. It's like walking out into an oasis tucked into a pocket of the Catskill Mountains. Flowers of every color of the rainbow tip their faces up to the morning rays of the sun, happy for the new day.

"It's demeaning."

"It's how things are," Tristan retorts.

Getting annoyed, I reply, "Then things need to change." I slip off my heels and leave them on the steps that lead down into the grass, not willing to break my neck by trying to walk on spongy sod. "Let me know when breakfast arrives."

I perform a mock curtsy in the most sarcastic way I can, but its effects are the opposite of the point I was making because the handsome jackasses smile.

CHAPTER 50

Standing under an arbor of climbing roses, I watch Con and Syn as they stroll through the garden, stopping every once in a while for Syn to look closer at a flower. Every so often, their hands gravitate together for brief touches as they walk. Con tucks a flower in her hair, and whatever he says has her throwing her head back and laughing.

"That's a damn beautiful sight."

"It is," Hendrix agrees, not able to keep his eyes off her. "Even if she's pissed at us."

I pick a rosebud from its thorny vine and tear the petals off one at a time. As a child, Aoife fought against the status quo of our world in her own way. She greeted every lower member and servant by their name and treated them as equals. She would bring them gifts, little things like a flower garland she'd make herself out of wild clover or honeysuckle, or cupcakes she would bake with the help of her governess.

"How are you feeling about last night? That she chose him to be her first and not us."

I suck in a jagged breath and let it out slowly. Aoife loved all three of us, but her connection with Con was different. Deeper. But I get what he's saying. For Syn, Con will always hold a unique space in her heart because he took her virginity.

"We need to tell her who she really is."

Hendrix hits me with icy, glacial eyes. "Will you fucking get over that already? You know we can't. At least not until we clean house."

Such a simple euphemism for what we have planned.

We both look over when two men in dark suits walk by. Armed guards. The house and grounds will be teaming with them in an hour. Extra security since the highest-ranking members of the Society will be here.

"I don't like this. Syn's going to notice and ask questions."

"I'm pretty sure she already has noticed." Hendrix follows my line of sight. "Dad was more vague than usual last night when we spoke. Fuck. I forgot to tell you. He's giving his vote to the Stepanoffs."

The brief calm of serenity I was having watching Syn and Con together gets blown all to hell. I back him up until we're hidden from view under the arbor.

"You better have a fucking good explanation why you didn't tell me immediately last night." I tighten a leash on my anger to counter the insurmountable urge to punch him.

He swipes my hand off his upper arm. "Because I knew you'd lose your shit, and there isn't a damn thing we can do about it."

"There you are," a voice calls out from nearby.

I smooth out my features when Eva materializes on the courtyard. As soon as she steps off the stone patio and into the grass, her ridiculously high heels sink into the ground as she walks, making her canter like that of a newborn giraffe. Syn was smart when she took hers off to walk barefoot in the grass.

Eva hasn't had the same amount of plastic surgery as my mother, but she's just as fake. And hidden behind her expensive nose job, polished, glossy veneers, and diamonds is a woman just as ruthless and power-hungry as her husband.

Her oversized designer sunglasses hide half her face, making it hard to tell who she's looking at.

"Your father would like to speak with you."

Hendrix waves her off. "He can wait."

"Not yours. Tristan's."

Knots twist in my gut. I hadn't expected him for another hour.

"He's here?"

"He and your mother just arrived. They—"

There's a hollow *pop* just as blood and brain matter explode sideways out of Eva's head, and she crumples to the grass like a rag doll that's lost its stuffing.

"Mum!"

Hendrix and I have no time to react before several men come out of nowhere, guns trained on us with lethal accuracy. Two of them I recognize as the armed guards who'd been patrolling the grounds. They'd been here the entire time in plain sight.

But my murderous fury is locked on the gray-eyed Russian who comes forward, a malicious smile spread across his face.

"I did warn you that you had no idea what was coming for you."

CHAPTER 51

Constantine follows me as I meander from one blooming shrub to another. The morning sunshine lights the gardens in crisp detail, making the colors seem more vibrant and the smells stronger.

"What's this one called?" I ask, touching the bright indigo pinwheel made of flowers.

I must be driving him crazy with all the questions. The man has the patience of a saint.

"Scaevola."

"That sounds made up. How in the heck do you and Tristan know all the names to things?"

He plucks one of the small flowers from the bush and adds it to the five others he's tucked into my braid. The romance of it isn't lost on me.

I do a quick reconnaissance to see if anyone is looking. We lost sight of Tristan and Hendrix standing under an archway a while ago.

Snipping a flower off its stem with my nails, I push it behind the helix of his ear and laugh when his eyebrows shoot up with amusement.

This moment right here—this is happiness. It's simple and silly. This is what I always hoped falling in love would feel like. Effortless.

"You're so pretty." I giggle, and he grins. I live for his smile because they are so rare. Often when he's near, I find myself longing for his eyes to seek me out, hoping to be graced with one of his beautiful smiles.

Constantine looks around, then snags the belt loop on my jeans and hauls me toward him. He drops his mouth on mine, and my arms tighten around him, my fingers digging into his back. His hands go to my ass, lifting me until my feet barely touch the ground. And when our tongues touch, glide, stroke, savor, all other thoughts dissolve from my mind.

"I love the way you kiss me," I sigh when we break apart.

Tristan's kisses are all power and possession. Hendrix's are filled with wicked seduction. But Constantine kisses me slowly, like I'm the air he needs to breathe.

He presses our foreheads together, then loops his pinky finger around mine and continues walking.

When we get to the center of the garden, there's an old-fashioned maze made from hedgerows of dark-green boxwoods.

With child-like enthusiasm, I grin up at Constantine. "Hey, do you want to—"

Pop.

I freeze at the familiar sound I remember all too well from the alley. So does Constantine.

With a quickness that defies logic, he has me flattened to the ground with his body over mine. Tiny, jagged pieces of rock cut into my palms, cheek, and stomach.

"Don't make a sound," he whispers, and I nod to let him know that I heard him.

With his heavy weight on top of me, I can only take shallow breaths, and the lack of oxygen with my heart beating so rapidly makes me woozy.

He lifts on his arms, his black gaze darting all around.

Snick.

"Hello, Constantine."

Aleksei's cold words stab through the air like a steel blade as two other men appear on either side of us.

"One wrong move and Miss Carmichael will get a bullet through her pretty little head." Aleksei none too gently digs the nozzle of his gun into my skull, leaving no doubt that he wouldn't hesitate to pull the trigger if Constantine didn't comply. "On your feet," he tells Constantine.

Fear shakes me to the core when Constantine does what he says and slowly lifts off me. I watch in horror as the two men grab him by the arms and cruelly kick out his legs, forcing him to his knees in front of Aleksei.

Aoife. Wake up.

"Do you know how much I'm going to enjoy killing you?" Even though he says it to Constantine, he points his gun straight at me.

"Fuck. You," Constantine growls.

In a flash of movement, one of the men lashes out with a brutal heel-kick that slams Constantine face first to the ground.

Aleksei cocks his shaved head and laughs. "Death can speak! It's been a while. Honestly, I prefer you mute."

I try to think of a way to distract him. Give Constantine time to figure out how to get us out of this situation. Tristan and Hendrix will come for us. Unless...

"Where's Aleksander?"

Aleksander seems to be the more rational twin. He may be an asshole, but he treated me with a semblance of respect when I went to the bell tower. He could have done anything to me while I was there, but he didn't. Maybe I can convince him—

"Busy with your other boyfriends."

Aleksei squats down and forces my head up with his gun under my chin. The acrid stench of cordite crawls into my nostrils, and the heat radiating from the metal barrel singes my skin, indicating that it was recently fired.

"Aleksander wants you alive, but he never said in what condition."

A white-hot searing pain shoots through my skull when he slams the butt of his gun into my temple. My vision wavers, but Constantine's angry, raspy shouts promising death snap me back into focus. My ears fill with the sickening thuds of boots on flesh and bone as the two men kick him with sadistic fury in the side, the legs, the back, the head.

"Stop!" My fingernails break as I claw at the ground, scrambling to crawl to Constantine.

Time slows to a flicker, each second stretching into eternity. Aleksei aims his gun, the metal glinting malevolently in the stark sunlight. My mind races with terror as I watch him take aim at Constantine, his finger curling around the trigger.

"Please! No! Aleksei, please! Please, don't do this!" I sob. I beg. My cries of desperation reach up to the heavens where even God himself would hear them.

Don't take him from me. We just found each other. "Constantine!"

A sickening trickle of crimson liquid drips from Constantine's mouth to the ground from the gashes littering his face. His pained eyes meet mine, sheer agony pouring out of them like an open wound.

No.

No.

"*Você é meu coração,*" he chokes out.

My feral scream shatters my voice and echoes across miles. "*Gheobhaidh mo chroí do chroí! Gheobhaidh mo chroí do chroí!*"

AOIFE! WAKE THE FUCK UP!

...

...

Bang!

Their story continues in Beautiful Sinners (Beautiful Sin Series Book 2).

Keep reading for an exclusive sneak peek at Beautiful Sinners.

EXCLUSIVE SNEAK PEEK AT BEAUTIFUL SINNERS

Prologue
Ten Years Ago

"I hate you!" I scream at my father when he rips the letter I'd been writing and tosses the pieces into the fireplace. The flames turn them to smoldering black ash in seconds.

I don't hate him. I'm just angry at him and Mama for taking me away. They won't let me talk to Con, Hendrix, and Tristan. No phone call, no email, no text message. Not even a letter—which I had been in the middle of writing before Papa discovered me. Every attempt I make to contact the boys fails. I miss them so much.

"Aoife, apologize to your father," my mother scolds, hands on her hips and her mouth pursed in a disapproving line. She's fed up with my belligerent behavior and daily temper tantrums.

We've been in Ireland for months now. I'm not allowed to go outside or go to school or do anything.

They won't tell me why. Only that it's too dangerous.

I glare at my mother, refusing to back down. She throws her hands up in the air in infuriated exasperation, then hits me with a hard truth that stops me in my tracks just as I start to storm off.

"You are so bloody ungrateful! Everything we've done has been for you! To protect you and keep you safe. Do you think your father and I want *this*?" she shouts, arms spread wide in gesticulation of the new house we're currently living in. A house in the middle of nowhere that is much smaller and less opulent than the one back home.

I actually like it better than our old house. I love the verdant pastural land that stretches as far as my eye can see. The thatched roof, pot-marked wood floors, wood-burning fireplace that fills the air with the pleasing smell of crisp cedar, and thick window glass that makes the world outside look wavy and distorted.

"Caroline," Papa harshly clips, sending her an admonishing shake of the head.

She whirls on him, all anger and righteous fury. "No, James. I'm sick and tired of her pouty, obdurate attitude. We gave up everything for her!"

Papa's face contorts into something horrible. It's a look I can't describe in words, but one that sends ominous shivers down my spine. He takes a menacing step toward her, hands curled into tight fists at his sides. Mama stumbles backward at his approach, her usually rosy-tinted cheeks pallid with fear.

"Are you willing to trade our daughter's life for—"

Her eyes dart from him to me in censure as she cuts him off. "That's not fair! You can't expect me to choose between—"

I jump when Papa's arm strikes out like the biting attack of a fanged snake, his punishing grip around her neck preventing her from speaking further. With a brutal jerk, he pulls her to him.

"Even after I discovered your betrayal, I stayed. I loved you. So don't you fucking dare—"

"*James*," she hisses.

I don't understand what they're talking about, and the way they keep interrupting each other makes it clear that they don't want me to know.

"Papa?" I query, coming closer. I've never seen him so angry with Mama before. I don't like it.

As if coming out of a trance, he shoves her away and drops to his haunches, opening his arms wide for me to walk into his embrace.

"I'm sorry, *a stór*," he says, his beard snagging strands of my hair as he nuzzles his cheek against my face. "Everything's okay. I didn't mean to—"

I cry out when window glass shatters into a million, knife-edged pieces, slicing across my back, neck, and arms. Papa protectively curls his big body over me just as shouts and screams intermix in a confusing cacophony that I can't understand. The air clogs with tiny particulate matter as loud pops of gunfire puncture holes through the wall, leaving behind perfectly circular peepholes.

"Caroline!" Papa's bellow makes my ears ring.

When Mama doesn't answer, I twist around to see her dragging her body across the floor toward us, a line of thick crimson trailing behind her. She's hurt.

I claw at my father's arms, wanting to get to Mama.

With a deafening roar, the front door crashes inward and splinters as two men storm into the house, their guns drawn.

"Aoife! Run!"

But my feet won't budge. My legs have become stone pillars, refusing to bend. I struggle to hear anything over the thunderous beat of my heart. I see one of the men's mouths move as his cold green eyes find us, but no sound carries to my ears. And then a wave of fury, unlike any I've ever experienced, consumes me, scorches through my blood until my veins sizzle.

"Aoife, no!" Papa calls out.

But it's too late.

Rage burns my vision as I launch myself at the green-eyed man. Everything becomes pure instinct when my training takes over as primal energy crackles through me with unstoppable force. Muscle memory flares to life and manifests into a wild, deranged violence that I unleash upon the intruder. My only coherent thought is to protect my parents. It pulses like a siren in my brain, blocking out everything else.

Kill them all.

"Fuck!" the guy shouts just as I wrest his arm to the side when his finger pulls the trigger. I don't react to the loud bang when it discharges near my ear or the heat that burns my left hand when I grab the barrel.

With an animalistic savagery, my fist punches into the underside of his arm, and he releases the gun completely when his hand goes numb. There is no mercy in my gaze as I turn the gun in my hand, point it at his chest, and fire. Point-blank range to the sweet spot straight through his heart. Thick bloody droplets shower down on me, decorating my pale skin with its sticky warmth.

"Aoife, move!"

I drop and roll just as a blur flies by me when Papa barrels into the second man. They crash over the small coffee table and tumble to the floor with a jolting thud. Mama whimpers as she pulls herself into a sitting position with her back against the wall. There's so much blood, her clothes are drenched in it.

I don't have time to go and help Papa because another man runs into the room. He must have come in through the back door. He hears Mama's raspy cry and turns toward her, a sick smile spreading across his face.

Kill them all.

Thigh and calf muscles bunch like spring-loaded coils, then release as I run at the man. Falling to the floor, I elongate my thin body and slide between his legs, grabbing at his right ankle. My momentum pulls him off his feet, and he timbers like a tree to the floor. There's a satisfying crunch of bone when he slams face-first onto the hard wood. My body collides with the baseboard, and I use my legs to kick off it and scramble up. I grapple onto the man's back in an instant.

His head explodes like a gory piñata when I pull the trigger, and his legs and arms twitch violently for a few seconds as phantom electrical signals from what remains of his mind fight to communicate with his corpse.

Holding the large, heavy pistol with a steady, white-knuckled grip, I take merciless strides toward my father and his assailant. Papa lets the man pin him to the floor, which gives me a clear and unobstructed line of sight to unload the rest of the magazine into his skull. The man becomes dead weight and collapses forward on top of Papa.

Our gazes meet across the carnage and pride fills

my father's eyes. That pride quickly transforms into a warning that comes too late.

My father's enraged shout disintegrates in my ears as pain detonates across the back of my head and dark oblivion quickly follows.

Their story continues in Beautiful Sinners (Beautiful Sin Series Book 2).

LETTER TO READERS

Dear Reader,

To say this year has been insane would be an understatement. There has been a lot of bad mixed in with the good; for example, lightning struck our house on July 4th and damaged a lot of stuff. Not the type of fireworks we were wanting to celebrate that holiday. But I'm a glass half full kind of person and will focus on the happy things. So far this year, three of my book babies have been up for awards. ***Savage Princess, Wanderlost, and The Boyfriend List*** were all HOLT Medallion Award Finalists in erotic romance, contemporary romance, and young adult fiction, respectively. ***The Boyfriend List*** actually won the HOLT Medallion Award, and ***Wanderlost*** won the Contemporary Romance Writers Reader's Choice Award! ***Wanderlost*** was also a Carolyn Reader's Choice Award Finalist and a Contemporary Romance Writers Stiletto Finalist. I'm honored and humbled and absolutely grateful that my stories have touched so many people's hearts. Thank you so very much from the bottom of my heart!

Now, back to ***Beautiful Sin***. I hope you enjoyed the beginning of Syn, Tristan, Hendrix, and Constantine's story as much as I enjoyed writing it. There is still so much more to come because you know how I love to throw those unexpected twists at you. Oh! Did you find all those Easter eggs I planted? I already told you about the journal (***Savage Series*** and ***About That Night***) and the knife (***Savage Series***). Did you spot any others?

I hinted about Andie, Keane, and Jax in ***Beautiful Sin***. The Savage crew will definitely make an appearance in book 2, ***Beautiful Sinners***, so if you haven't read that series and don't want any spoilers, you can grab them on Amazon, read for free with Kindle Unlimited, or listen to the audiobooks narrated by the very talented Keira Grace.

Now for my thank yous.

Thank you to my beta readers: Caroline, Jordan, and Rita. Your extra eyes helped make sure I was crossing all those T's and dotting all those I's.

Thank you to Ellie, my awesome copy editor at My Brother's Editor, for your support and love for my stories, and for the hard work you put in.

Thank you to my readers who have given me daily doses of excitement about getting this series done and published.

Thank you to all the book bloggers who support me, and the supportive author community on Instagram.

Thank you, Nala, for our weekly author meetings where I can hash out ideas, get inspiration, and meet my goals. Your organizing skills are truly inspirational!

Thank you to my PA, Bree, for all your hype posts and reels.

Thank you to Jennifer and Wordsmith Publicity for letting me sign on as one of your authors and for all the hard work you have done to promote my books (and a special thank you to Jennifer for letting me text you with thousands of questions).

A huge shout out to my awesome ARC and Hype teams! You ladies and gents are the absolute best!

Thank you to my husband and family who support me one hundred percent every day. Love you so much!

And thank you, reader, for coming along this crazy journey with me and supporting independent authors like myself.

If you haven't read my other books, check them out. I have a reputation for drinking the tears of my readers and have been called the queen of WTF twists. My Fallen Brook Series (***All Our Next Times, Paper Stars Rewritten, Broken Butterfly***) is an angsty, twisty-turny emotional roller coaster that involves a love quadrangle between childhood friends. You'll definitely want some tissues for *Broken Butterfly*. The Montgomerys series of stand-alones takes place right after *Broken Butt*erfly and each book focuses on one of the half siblings of Fallon Montgomery. ***That Girl*** is Aurora + JD's story; ***Wanderlost*** is Harper + Bennett's; ***About That Night*** is Jordan + Douglass's; and Sebastian's story will be up next. If you want something darker, check out my Savage Kingdom reverse harem/why choose series (***Savage Princess, Savage Kings, Savage Kingdom***). Each of my books is packed with my signature WTF moments, strong women, and swoon-worthy book boyfriends. All my books are on Amazon and Kindle Unlimited. You can also visit https://www.jennilynnwyer.com/ for a complete list.

Until next time,
Love and happy reading,

ALSO BY THE AUTHOR

Under Jennilynn Wyer (New Adult & College, Contemporary romance)

The Fallen Brook Series

#1 **All Our Next Times**

#2 **Paper Stars Rewritten**

#3 **Broken Butterfly**

The Fallen Brook Boxed Set with bonus novella, Fallen Brook Forever

4 **Reflections of You** (Coming 2024)

The Montgomerys: Fallen Brook Stand-alone Novels

That Girl [Aurora + JD]
* *Winner of the Rudy Award for Romantic Suspense*
* *A Contemporary Romance Writers Stiletto Finalist*

Wanderlost [Harper + Bennett]
* *Contemporary Romance Writers Reader's Choice Award Winner*
* *Contemporary Romance Writers Stiletto Finalist*
* *HOLT Medallion Finalist*

** Carolyn Reader's Choice Award Finalist*

About That Night [Jordan + Douglass]

The Fallen Brook Romance Series: The Montgomerys + bonus novella, Second Chance Hearts (Mason's story)

Savage Kingdom Series: A dark, enemies to lovers, mafia, why choose romance

#1 **Savage Princess**
** HOLT Medallion Finalist*

#2 **Savage Kings**

#3 **Savage Kingdom**

The Savage Kingdom Series is now available as audiobooks (Narrated by Keira Grace)

Forever M/M Romance Series (A Fallen Brook Spin-off)

#1 **Forever His** (Julien's POV)
** A Contemporary Romance Writers Stiletto Finalist*

#2 **Forever Yours** (Elijah's POV)

#3 **Forever Mine** (Dual POV)

Beautiful Sin Series: A dark, enemies to lovers, reverse harem/why choose

#1 **Beautiful Sin**

#2 **Beautiful Sinners**

#3 **Beautiful Chaos**

Anthologies

Blue Collar Babes (Releases October 1, 2023. Pre-order your copy today and help support the charity Jobs for Justice.)

*My novella in the anthology is titled ***Tate*** and takes place in my Fallen Brook world.

Under J.L. Wyer (High School & Young Adult)

The Fallen Brook High School Young Adult Romance Series: a reimagining of the adult Fallen Brook Series for a YA audience

#1 **Jayson**

#2 **Ryder**

#3 **Fallon**

#4 **Elizabeth**

The Fallen Brook High School YA Romance Series Boxed Set (Books 1-4) with bonus alternate endings

YA Standalones

The Boyfriend List

** HOLT Medallion Award Winner*

** A Contemporary Romance Writers 2022 Stiletto Finalist*

ABOUT THE AUTHOR

Jennilynn Wyer is multi-award-winning romance author (Rudy Award winner for Romantic Suspense, HOLT Medallion Award winner, Contemporary Romance Writers Reader's Choice Award winner, four-time Contemporary Romance Writers Stiletto Finalist, three-time HOLT Medallion Award Finalist, Carolyn Reader's Choice Award Finalist) and an international Amazon best-selling author of romantic fiction. She writes steamy, New Adult romances as well as dark reverse harem romances. She also pens YA romance under the pen name JL Wyer.

Jennilynn is a sassy Southern belle who lives a real-life friends-to-lovers trope with her blue-eyed British husband. When not writing, she's nestled in her favorite reading spot, e-reader in one hand and a cup of coffee in the other, enjoying the latest romance novel.

Connect with the Author

Website: https://www.jennilynnwyer.com

Linktree: https://linktr.ee/jennilynnwyer

Email: jennilynnwyerauthor@gmail.com

Facebook: https://www.facebook.com/JennilynnWyerRomanceAuthor/

Twitter: https://www.twitter.com/JennilynnWyer

Instagram: https://www.instagram.com/jennilynnwyer

TikTok: https://www.tiktok.com/@jennilynnwyer

Threads: https://www.threads.net/@jennilynnwyer

Verve Romance: https://ververomance.com/app/JennilynnWyer

Goodreads: https://www.goodreads.com/author/show/20502667.Jennilynn_Wyer

BookBub: https://www.bookbub.com/authors/jennilynn-wyer

BingeBooks: https://bingebooks.com/author/jennilynn-wyer

Books2Read: https://books2read.com/ap/nAAgBb/Jennilynn-Wyer

Amazon Author Page: https://www.amazon.com/author/jennilynnwyer

Newsletter: https://forms.gle/vYX64JHJVBX7iQvy8

SUBSCRIBE TO MY NEWSLETTER for news on upcoming releases, cover reveals, sneak peeks, author giveaways, and other fun stuff!

JOIN THE J-CREW: A JENNILYNN WYER ROMANCE READER GROUP

Join link https://www.facebook.com/groups/190212596147435